Nancy Pickard
Presents

MALICE DOMESTIC 13: MYSTERY MOST GEOGRAPHICAL

MALICE DOMESTIC ANTHOLOGY SERIES

Elizabeth Peters Presents *Malice Domestic 1*

Mary Higgins Clark Presents *Malice Domestic 2*

Nancy Pickard Presents *Malice Domestic 3*

Carolyn G. Hart Presents *Malice Domestic 4*

Phyllis A. Whitney Presents *Malice Domestic 5*

Anne Perry Presents *Malice Domestic 6*

Sharyn McCrumb Presents *Malice Domestic 7*

Margaret Maron Presents *Malice Domestic 8*

Joan Hess Presents *Malice Domestic 9*

Nevada Barr Presents *Malice Domestic 10*

Katherine Hall Page Presents *Malice Domestic 11: Murder Most Conventional*

Charlaine Harris Presents *Malice Domestic 12: Mystery Most Historical*

Nancy Pickard Presents *Malice Domestic 13: Mystery Most Geographical*

Nancy Pickard Presents

MALICE DOMESTIC 13: MYSTERY MOST GEOGRAPHICAL

An Anthology

Edited by
Verena Rose, Shawn Reilly Simmons
and Rita Owen

Published by Wildside Press LLC
www.wildsidepress.com

Dedicated to the late

Joan Hess,

whose stories and humor were mainstays of

Malice Domestic for 29 years.

ACKNOWLEDGEMENTS

The editors would like to thank John Betancourt and Carla Coupe at Wildside Press for their constant and unwavering support to Malice Domestic and these editors.

Nancy Gordon in New Jersey has been generous in her unfailing dedication to the excellence of proofreading of this Anthology and Malice Domestic's annual convention materials.

The editors would also like to express their special thanks to the selection committee—Aaron Elkins, G. M. Malliet, and Gigi Pandian. As a result of their hard work and dedication to excellence, we present for your reading enjoyment *Malice Domestic 13: Mystery Most Geographical.*

TABLE OF CONTENTS

All stories are original to this Anthology

PREFACE

NANCY PICKARD PRESENTS

The authors of these 30 original short stories were given a challenge to whet anyone's travel lust: "Write a mystery that takes readers into an intriguing setting anywhere in this wide world."

And, boy, have they ever met that challenge!

Have you ever longed to see Tahiti?

How about northwest Canada, by train?

Or the coast of Maine, by schooner?

And London, of course. London has to be stamped on any passport to mystery. (A side trip to Stepney, England, included.)

How about Burkina Faso, and a ski lodge in France?

And the Maryland seashore, Nicaragua, an island in the Gulf of Mexico? And speaking of islands: Easter Island, Hawaii . . .

Pack your all-weather, all-terrain gear, because you're about to hop from mystery to mystery, from the Scottish Highlands to the European lowlands, from a tiny town in the Blue Ridge Mountains to the border of the desert Southwest, from England's spectacular Jurassic coast to a cruise ship on the Caribbean Sea.

You'd better pack your time machine, too, because some of these stories will not only take you to fascinating places but back in time, as well. You'll have a real scream at the Chicago Exposition of 1893. You'll drop in on Washington City in 1860, Prague in 1968, Russia in 1911, Alaska in 1964, Pennsylvania in 1899. Hold onto your antique hats; it can get windy in time tunnels.

But wait. Before you fly off to sunny or snowy climes, let me tell you about your "travel agency." You wouldn't hop on just any bus, would you? You'd probably like to know that it has an established and sterling reputation for unearthing the most mysterious places on the globe.

Fear not. Or, well, maybe you will feel a teensy bit afraid during the suspenseful moments of some of these trips. But really, you'll be fine because you're traveling under the auspices of "Malice Domestic," a famous convention of mystery writers and readers, held annually since 1989 in the Washington, D.C., area. It started as a small gathering devoted to mysteries of the Agatha Christie variety, but now welcomes readers from all over the mystery universe. Like this anthology, it embraces writers who bring the two words of its own title to life: malice and domestic. In this collection, you'll find stories for "cozy" mystery lovers, and for detective fans, for readers of psychological suspense, and even a story with a hint of horror for readers who love to shiver. In many cases, the detective will be none other than . . . you. Can you beat the writer to the solution of what really happened in that house? And why that skier told his spooky story? Can the pastor solve the biggest mysteries of all? What will that mother do to save her n'er-do-well son? How will the daughter escape the infamy of her father?

You have a lot of mysteries to figure out, so off you go . . .

Bon voyage and happy reading, dear armchair traveler.

Nancy Pickard

MYSTERY MOST GEOGRAPHICAL

THE BARRISTER'S CLERK

by Michael Robertson

Destination: London, England
What do the Royal Mail, a mysterious busker, a barrister's clerk, and a hostile takeover have in common? Visit Baker Street to unravel the case of the Special Delivery letter.

The commuters flowing out of Baker Street Station and onto Marylebone Road were bunching up like debris in a rocky stream, because right at the foot of the larger-than-life-sized bronze statue of Sherlock Holmes was a motionless human figure.

But not motionless for long. He was a letter carrier for the Royal Mail. He had only managed to walk into the statue because he had skipped lunch and was momentarily distracted by a commuter with a fresh paper box of fish and chips. Fortunately he had a hard head; he recovered quickly and got straightaway onto his hands and knees to gather the spilled contents of his mailbag.

Helpful, honest Londoners surrounded him, handing back missives that had fallen from his delivery bag.

"You all right, guv?"

"Oh yes. Quite. Bloody idiot that I am."

He stood finally, with his wits and his bag of mail fully gathered about him. Or at least he hoped he had all of it.

"Thank you all very much."

"Careful next time, lad."

The letter carrier nodded appreciatively and continued on his mission.

Some moments later, a tall man with a violin case came up the stairs. He gave a passing glance to the base of the statue where the letter carrier had fallen, then walked across the street and turned immediately to his right, onto the two hundred block of Baker Street.

He walked about a quarter way up the block and stopped. He had a special delivery envelope in his hand. He looked at the envelope, and then at the building in front of him.

From the corner to where he was standing now, the two hundred block of Baker Street comprised just one structure—a modern limestone building, polished in appearance, with wide glass doors at the main entrance and an engraved copper placard above them that read Baker Street House.

The tall man knew this was the right place, but he was delayed when he got to the doors, because several tourists of various nationalities were milling about in front of him with puzzled expressions and mobile phone cameras at the ready, walking back and forth between the main doors and the door of the next establishment up the block.

One of the American tourists turned toward the tall man as he opened the heavy glass door.

"Is this where—?"

"No."

"But the next door up is the Beatles store at 231 Baker Street, and there are no other address numbers between here and the beginning of the block. So this must be where—"

"It isn't, he doesn't, and he'd be long since dead if he ever did. Excuse me, please."

"But—"

"Please, get a life," said the tall man, as he pushed through the door and into the wide marble-floored lobby.

He walked quickly toward the lift, shaking his head slightly, annoyed with himself. He should not have been rude. He especially, because he, more than most people, fully understood.

But there were more important matters at hand.

The lobby directory listed three offices for the main level. One was for Dorset National Corporate Headquarters, which the tall man knew was the company that owned the building. The other two offices were for a consumer banking branch and an insurance service.

But for the second floor, the directory listed only one name, a sublet tenant—something calling itself Baker Street Chambers.

The tall man got in the lift and pressed a button.

On the second floor, a fiftyish woman, short in height and comfortably plump in the English way, dressed in pleasant shades of business gray and pastel apricot, pondered a stack of letters on her desk. The Royal Mail letter carrier—a young man who looked like he might have recently bumped his head and who was her only visitor so far that morning—had delivered them some ten minutes earlier.

There were simply so many of the letters—today's delivery on top of the ones still unanswered from the week before—that she didn't quite know what to do.

They weren't addressed to her, of course. But also they weren't addressed generally to Baker Street Chambers, or personally to either the senior or junior barrister (there were only the two of them, the Heath brothers) that she worked for.

No, the letters were addressed to someone else entirely. And that made them a problem.

There were times when she wished simply that the man himself were real, that the person to whom the letters were addressed actually existed to receive them.

But of course he wasn't real, he was fictional. Only the letters were real, and they were on Lois's desk, and so Lois had a real problem. She sighed and closed her eyes, wishing the bloody things would just go away.

But her wish was interrupted. She couldn't even have the satisfaction of imagining it, because now a little bell chimed, alerting her that the lift had brought someone up.

The doors opened. A tall man carrying a violin case stepped out of the lift onto the hardwood floor and paused to get his office bearings.

He was rather unkempt. And he did not have the look of the chamber's usual visitors, who were typically solicitors in somber brown suits, looking for a barrister to represent their clients. If anything, this man must be one of the clients.

But Lois was no snob, and was disinclined to act on presuppositions, so she smiled pleasantly as he stepped up to her desk.

"How can I help you?" said Lois.

"I gather business is not exactly humming," said the man. "At least, not the paying kind."

"Why do you say that?"

"It's obvious. A law chambers that has only one person—you—as receptionist, barrister's clerk, and secretary—cannot be doing terribly well."

"I didn't ask how you came to the conclusion," said Lois. "I asked why you said it. I mean, it's an odd way of requesting a barrister's assistance."

"I'm not requesting a barrister's assistance," said the tall man. "At least, not in a barrister's capacity."

Lois puzzled over that for a moment. She studied the man closely.

"You look familiar," said Lois.

"Yes," said the tall man. "I suppose I do."

"I've seen you in the Underground. You're a busker. You play the violin for tips."

"Yes," he said. "I believe you tossed in a tenner once. I appreciated it."

"It was rather an accident," said Lois. "I was searching for something smaller, and when I realized it was all I had, I was too embarrassed to toss in nothing at all."

"I appreciated it, either way."

She studied him a moment longer.

"Do you . . . make much of a living doing that?"

"Not as bad as you might think. Not enough to keep a flat in London, of course, but the city is where the tips are. I take the very first morning train in from out of town."

"From where, exactly?"

"That's not important."

"Do you have a name?"

"My friends call me Sig."

"Unusual. Short for Sigmund?"

"What else would it be short for?"

"Oh, I don't know. It's difficult to think of names that begin with —"

"Sig, or Sigerson, either one is acceptable," said the man quickly, as if he wanted to dismiss the subject. "In any case, I can see that your employer is not here, and you are no longer certain of when he will return. He is on his honeymoon, I surmise, and has rather irresponsibly decided to extend it."

"What makes you say that?"

"Are you asking how I reached the conclusion this time, or why I bothered pointing it out?"

"This time I'm asking about both."

"Very well. You have a dozen barrister's briefs, all nicely tied up in the traditional purple ribbons, on the shelf behind you. Briefs are typically brought in only a few days before the barrister is needed for the court appearance, but the ones on your shelf have gathered dust. Which tells me they've been there at least a week. And your barrister must be out longer than expected, or you would not have accepted them at all.

"And then there's the wedding photo card that you have unfolded on your desk. The edges are sharp and the image quite glossy; clearly you received it recently. You are in the photo, part of the wedding party, but not a relative, because if you were you would have received a photo in a size more suitable for framing. So it's most likely a work relationship, albeit a close one. The groom—that tall fellow with the self-satisfied smirk—is clearly a barrister. He must be the head of this chambers. I suppose one could attribute his expression just to his incredible luck at snagging that red-headed beauty standing next to him, but the confidence of his expression indicates that he's had this smugness for some time—therefore he is a QC. The fellow on the other side of him is clearly the younger brother—the family resemblance is strong—so he is the junior barrister here. And there you are, one of two bridesmaids, but your dress was clearly altered at the last minute. My guess would be . . ."

The tall man hesitated.

"Go ahead," said Lois. "I don't get my feelings hurt."

"You were added at the last minute, because the earlier candidate suddenly canceled. It happens sometimes at weddings—I would guess that she was the girlfriend of the best man. The upcoming wedding started him thinking about making it official between them, and started her thinking about keeping her freedom—and she chose the latter."

"Fair enough," said Lois. "I confirm or deny nothing, because it's none of your business. But I'll allow you to believe what you like."

"You are very kind," said the tall man, "and I mean that sincerely. But I care not a whit about your employer's family issues, and only indirectly about the success of his chambers. What I care about is that he appears to be neglecting his duty regarding these—"

The tall man slapped his hand on the stack of letters on Lois's desk.

"When you say these—what, exactly, is it that you think—"

The man shook his head dismissively and picked up a handful of the unopened envelopes. He read their addresses in rapid succession:

"'To Mr. Sherlock Holmes, at 221B Baker Street.' And 'To Mr. Sherlock Holmes, Consulting Detective, at 221B Baker Street.' And 'To Mr. Sherlock Holmes and Dr. John Watson, at 221B Baker Street.' Shall I go on?"

"Um . . . what, exactly, is your point?"

The tall man sighed.

"It is common knowledge, you know. Prior to the 1930s, there was no two hundred block of Baker Street. But then the street was extended, a banking establishment put up this building for its headquarters—right where 221B Baker Street would have been all along—and from that moment on, whenever someone wrote a letter to Sherlock Holmes, this is where the Royal Mail would deliver it. The occupants of this address have always faithfully fulfilled their duties in caring for the letters. Your employer—the QC for whom you clerk—only began to receive them just recently, when he took the sublet of this floor. That made him, and his chambers, responsible for responding to the letters."

"Yes, yes, that is all true. But you don't understand. Or rather, you observe, but you don't get it, if you don't mind my saying so. Reggie Heath QC and his brother are both away. There is only me right now. I am only the clerk, and I cannot take on such a responsibility. They are both lawyers. I never even went to university!"

The tall man smiled kindly, looked her in the eye, and sat down in the guest chair by her desk.

"Forgive me, dear woman, but it is you who does not understand. The qualifications are not at all what you think they are. Here. I will show you."

He picked up one of the letters. Lois gasped in apprehension as he opened it.

He proceeded to read it aloud.

"Dear Mr. Sherlock Holmes. Can you find my cat? He's orange and white. I'm seven years old. My cat is three. Thank you, Melissa. Los Angeles, California."

He handed the letter to Lois to see for herself.

"This one is really too easy, of course," he continued. "All it requires is to send a letter back saying that Sherlock Holmes is a work of fiction and does not exist, and Bob's your uncle. Or, given the Los Angeles postmark, I suppose one might also say something about cats versus cars and coyotes."

"Oh, I couldn't do that!" said Lois. "It would just be mean. She's only seven!"

"What would you suggest then?"

"I'd tell her that he is retired and keeping bees in Sussex. And it being springtime, her cat is probably out doing—well, you know, springtime things—and will be home soon enough, and not to worry about it in any event, because cats are such independent creatures, and are always fine."

"Hmm," said the tall man. "Fair enough. Your answer is much kinder than mine, I must say. Here, read the next one yourself."

Lois did so, and then summarized.

"This one is a marriage proposal," she said, "from a 90-year-old woman in Argentina. But she wants Mr. Sherlock Holmes to first confirm for her whether he is still alive, and if so, which century he was born in."

"And?"

"I suppose the response could be that he doesn't date younger women."

"Excellent!" said the tall man. He sat back in his chair, seeming quite pleased. "You have a knack!"

Lois considered that for a moment, and then she said, "Oh, no.

No, no, no."

"What's wrong?"

"Not me. I cannot do the letters."

"It seems to me you do just fine."

"These were not a fair test! The letters can be much more complicated. And more serious. I can't just send a form letter in response. The clerks of the bank that occupied these premises for seventy years before us are said to have always sent individual replies. And some of the letters are so touching and genuine. How will I know when something more needs to be said? How am I to know when to just send a standard response, or when to send a very specific, personalized one, or when to call the local authorities?"

"You'll know," said the tall man. "And now I must be going."

"But—"

The tall man stood, looked at Lois's concerned face—and then began to open his violin case.

Lois hoped he wasn't going to play a tune. She hadn't anything to offer as a tip. All she had in her purse was another tenner.

But the tall man didn't lift the violin from its case. Instead he brought out a large envelope.

"What is that?" said Lois.

"Something I meant to show you. Perhaps it will help explain."

"That's a special delivery letter."

"Yes. I found it in the Underground less than an hour ago. The draught from a passing train pulled it right into my case as I was playing."

"Really? Does that happen often?"

"More often than you might think, but it's not always letters. Discarded ice cream wrappers and thrice-read scraps of newspaper are what I usually get. The ice cream wrappers are sticky and a bother, but I do read the news when it arrives."

"I see," said Lois, reaching for the envelope. "Well, thank you very much for bringing it."

But the tall man held it back.

"Oh no," he said. "It is not addressed to you. Not to Baker Street Chambers at all. Nor to Sherlock Holmes. It is addressed to the Dorset National Headquarters downstairs."

"Oh. Then why did you bring it up here?"

"Perhaps I thought someone here might like to know what is inside."

"Sir," said Lois with due alarm, "it is against the law to open and read other people's mail!"

"Oh, I have no intention of seeing it opened, I assure you. But I do know what's in it."

"You mean you held it up to a candle or something?"

The tall man smiled patiently. "Hardly. That doesn't work with paper such as this. But I know what the contents are."

"How?"

"From the Financial Times, primarily. When it blows up against my violin case in the Underground, I read it. And I've been closely following a proposed bank merger and takeover of Dorset National—the company that currently owns this building and grants your employer his lease."

"Oh," said Lois.

"The negotiations have reached a tipping point. I don't think it is an entirely friendly takeover. If a white knight were to come along—and one might, given a bit more time—my personal opinion is that Dorset would be able to decline the offer. But an ultimatum has been issued, and a final take-it-or-leave-it offer was prepared, with an acceptance deadline of five o'clock today. The final offer was sent by special delivery under care of the Royal Mail—and this is that offer."

"You seem very certain of yourself in your analysis."

"Yes, I have been accused of that."

"The document needs to be delivered to the Dorset corporate headquarters downstairs then," said Lois. "I still don't see why you brought it up here."

The tall man considered that for a moment, and then he put the special delivery envelope back in his violin case.

"No reason," he said. "Except that I wanted to see whether the letters, at this moment, are in good hands." He paused, looking Lois in the eye before he continued. "Now I see that they are. It is important to me that they continue to be."

Lois took a moment to absorb that, and then, when she had done so and realized that he was about to leave, she spoke quickly. "Wait. There are so many different letters. I will face a new question with each, and the circumstances will never be the same. How am I to always know what to do?"

"Good point," said the tall man, nodding. "It is not always easy to know what to do."

He turned toward the lift, then paused and looked back at Lois.

"I must make a decision as well," he said. "It is an offense against the crown to interfere with delivery of the Royal Mail. But I am under no affirmative obligation to perform the duties of the Royal Mail letter carriers for them. So what shall I do? Shall I return this to the place where I found it—amidst the debris on the lowest floor of the Baker Street Tube Station? Or shall I go down to the lobby before they close and seek out the receiving officer for

Dorset National and place this document in his hands before the deadline expires—knowing that if I do, circumstances will compel Dorset to accept an offer that they might very well refuse if given another day to consider it—and by so doing, place the future of the letters at great risk?"

Lois's eyes were wide, but she did not hesitate in her response. "You should do what your conscience tells you is the decent thing."

The tall man nodded and smiled at her. As the lift doors began to close, he blocked them with his violin case—just for a moment—just long enough to take one step back toward Lois's desk, and stretch out his long arm to touch the stack of letters on her desk.

"As will you," he said.

THE BELLE HOPE

by Peter DiChellis

Destination: Coastal Maine
A Boston P.I. is hired to find two missing divers who were seeking WWII treasure lost off the coast of Maine's Unorganized Territories.

"How much do you know about sunken treasure lost at sea in shipwrecks?"

The young lady asking me the question occupied the solitary visitor's chair in my cramped walk-up office. She leaned forward, her brown eyes enthusiastic and impossibly large. Before I could say "Not much. I get seasick just holding a glass of water," I decided, as she was probably on the verge of unleashing a whopping tall tale, I'd launch a small fib of my own.

"I know a little bit," I said. After all, a good Boston private eye is supposed to know a little bit about everything. And in fairness, like most locals, I knew that storms, shoals, legendary buccaneers, and even World War II Nazi torpedoes had claimed countless ships off New England's coast.

My visitor, who'd introduced herself as Ms. Aliza Marie Evangeline, lowered her voice and leaned forward a tad more. "The story you're about to hear is confidential, completely secret. Only a few people ever knew what actually happened. And most of them died horrifying deaths. Just horrifying! I'm willing to tell you as much as I'm allowed—I have business partners, you understand—but only if you promise you won't reveal anything I say to another soul, not a soul."

I guessed she was all of nineteen or twenty years old. Short brown hair, no makeup. Jeans and a gray T-shirt under a black blazer. A modest diamond engagement ring but no other jewelry. Except for the excitement about storytelling that danced in her eyes, some people might describe her as forgettable.

"I promise," I told her. "Not a soul." I settled in, keen to hear whatever wild account came next.

"OK," she said. "This is the story, at least as much as I can tell you. In 1939 my great-grandfather hopped a steamship to Europe to help a Frenchman he knew from the First World War. The

Frenchman, who cured my great-grandfather's trench foot when the two men served on the Western Front, was working as a bookkeeper for three shady but prosperous shop owners. The shop owners were concerned that another great war might erupt in Europe. So they decided to convert their savings into the then-popular Saint-Gaudens twenty dollar U.S. gold coins that were circulating in Europe and transport them to America for safekeeping. They feared only an American citizen would be able to leave France and enter America with the coins."

"And how exactly do you know all this?" I asked, trying hard to keep my voice free of both skepticism and amusement.

Her hand and wrist made a quick motion through the air, as if writing. "My great-grandmother kept the Frenchman's handwritten letters to my great-grandfather, as well as a letter from my great-grandfather himself, sent to her before he left Europe. I discovered the letters in a blue hatbox in her closet after she passed away. I found her diary and some old newspaper clippings in there, too."

I'm a sucker for a weird yarn and I wanted to see how far she'd push her story, so I nodded encouragement for her to continue.

"By the time my great-grandfather arrived in Europe, the Frenchman and the three shop owners were in complete panic over the impending war. They'd bought one thousand twenty dollar Saint-Gaudens coins, a small fortune at the time. Normal travel arrangements had become impossible, so my great-grandfather hid the coins, over sixty pounds of gold, in the bottom of a steamer trunk filled with cotton towels, ginger tea, and toothpaste—from the shop owners, you see. And then he bribed a sympathetic Moroccan stevedore to let him stow away on a tramp freighter, the S.S. *Belle Hope*, bound from Marseilles to Boston. I swear! It's all in his letters."

"Quite a tale," I said.

She turned as serious as a bank robber. "Wait till you hear the next part."

I nodded again, surprised that I hadn't burst.

"The story ends in supreme tragedy. According to the newspaper clippings I found in the hatbox, as the *Belle Hope* made for Boston she encountered a brutal hurricane-force storm. The captain, trying to stay away from the highest waves and strongest winds, steered for the clean side of the storm. But the hurricane shifted direction and the ship sailed far off course. On the second day, the exhausted captain lost steering-way and the *Belle Hope* was struck by a monster wave. She drifted, foundered, and sank off the Gulf of Maine. The ship then broke apart and her hull and cargo scattered across miles of seabed. Every life was lost." Aliza Marie

Evangeline paused to give a sad shake of her head. "And as far as anyone knows, the Frenchman and the three shop owners all died in the Second World War."

"A supreme tragedy," I agreed. "And so many years ago."

Her impossibly large brown eyes somehow grew even larger. "Exactly the point. Today, those thousand long-lost Saint-Gaudens coins are worth over a thousand dollars each!"

I tried to test her. "Except the coins have been immersed in salt water for nearly eight decades."

"You're confusing gold with silver or copper," she said. "Seawater doesn't damage gold. Undersea treasure hunters have recovered gold in perfect condition after centuries. I've studied this carefully, everything about it. I'm no daydreamer. I'm an ambitious, self-motivated entrepreneur. I've taken three accounting classes and three oceanography courses. I started a high-potential business with two partners who are expert divers. We've invested in software for charting and mapping and we use special diving equipment. Trust me, we know what we're doing."

I couldn't resist a smile.

"Just imagine," she continued, her eyes practically sparkling now, "over a million dollars in rare gold coins, lost in a hurricane because my great-grandfather, a man I never knew, was a loyal friend to a sly Frenchman and a wily smuggler who tragically perished on the high seas!"

"And you want me, as a private investigator, to help you find this million dollars worth of gold coins, lost somewhere at the bottom of the ocean amid a miles-long trail of hurricane-strewn debris from a nearly eighty-year-old shipwreck?"

Her face turned serious again. "Don't be ridiculous," she said. "We already found the coins."

***

"Rum Bomb!" the wiry man teetering at the bar thundered. "Another Rum Bomb!"

As the tavern door closed behind me, the bartender carried a bottle of dark rum and a mug of draft beer toward his lone customer. He poured a hit of the rum into the wiry man's empty shot glass and replaced his dead draft with the fresh mug.

And what the hell was I doing here, in a rundown bar on the coast of Hancock County, Maine? I wasn't searching for sunken treasure. At least not exactly.

It turned out my new client's declaration that she'd "already found" the gold coins was based on a text message from one of her business partners, who also happened to be her younger brother, Donnie. The text read *wet 4 souveneers 2day!* which she interpreted to mean her partners had successfully made the dive (gotten "wet") in order to ("4") recover the coins ("souveneers") the same morning she'd received the text ("2day"). She also confided to me the text's exclamation point might be especially meaningful.

But she'd gotten the text two days ago and hadn't heard from her brother since, or from her other "business partner," her twenty-something fiancé, Jason Kinnert, who'd recently finished a hitch as a Navy diver. No word from either, despite her texting them and even calling their phones. She'd also called the Hancock County Sheriff's Office and the county hospital, but learned nothing. Although she wouldn't admit it, I knew Aliza Marie Evangeline was worried. She hired me to find Donnie and Jason and help them in any way I could. So I traced their path, driving my battered but reliable decade-old Jeep Cherokee up I-95 North to Route 1 to arrive "Down East" among the craggy inlets and remote lighthouses of coastal Maine.

The wiry man drinking Rum Bombs, who on closer inspection looked like something a discerning sea monster found inedible and spit onto the shore a hundred years ago, eyed me as I approached.

"You're from away," he said. "Not from Maine."

I tried to ignore him and signaled the bartender for a draft. When the barkeep set my brew in front of me, I gave him a good tip and said I hoped he could help me locate some friends visiting the area. I hadn't found any place open in the tiny seaside village except the tavern, so decided I'd start making my inquiries here. And the underwater photos and diving memorabilia decorating the walls told me it was a fine a place to start.

"My friends are two young guys who drove up from Boston to dive near Blood Rock Island," I said to the bartender. "I'm not sure where they are now."

"Blood Rock!" the Rum Bomb man hollered in my ear. "Nobody dives Blood Rock!" He downed his rum, followed it with a gulp of draft, and his voice fell to a hoarse whisper. "The current that churns Blood Rock Island is a killing machine. Blood Rock's ruby-red water will drag you to the bottom of the sea and murder you cold and dead!"

I looked at the bartender.

"Blood Rock is a dangerous dive area," he said. "There's a nasty down current that can pull divers way too deep to survive with ordinary compressed air tanks. And Blood Rock's water is toxic from the same algae that turns the island shore red."

"The water is red from the blood of lost sailors," the Rum Bomb man shrieked. "Dead from a murdering sea!"

The bartender heaved a sigh and leaned toward me over the bar. "I hate to tell you this, but I heard that a boat cruising past Blood Rock pulled two divers' dead bodies from the water late this afternoon. Maybe your friends changed their minds about where to dive. I hope so."

Donnie and Jason wouldn't have changed the dive site, of course. They were convinced they'd find a million dollars in gold coins there. But something else stuck in my mind. I excused myself to the far end of the bar and called my client.

"You mentioned Donnie and Jason use special diving equipment," I said "What kind of air tanks?"

"They're breathing a specialty gas called trimix," Aliza Marie said. "The dive's too deep for ordinary compressed air or nitrox, especially considering the strong down current. People think we're just kids, but we know our business. Did you find out something?"

"I'm still working on it," I said. I couldn't bring myself to tell her what the bartender had just told me.

I returned to my draft beer, got a motel recommendation from the bartender, and left him with the Rum Bomb man. But before heading back to Route 1 and the motel, I confirmed that just a single boat-rental shop in the area could have accommodated Donnie and Jason for a deep-water salvage dive. Aliza Marie's business records identified the same shop on Donnie and Jason's itinerary, so of course I planned to visit it. I also learned that Blood Rock Island, like many small islands off the Maine coast, was not part of Hancock County but fell instead within Maine's so-called Unorganized Territories, with no municipal government and no police department. That not only explained why my client's phone calls to the county sheriff and hospital had proved unproductive, it also meant the boat-rental shop, a local divers' hub, might be the best place to begin scoping out who'd recovered the two bodies today and whether anyone knew the victims' identities.

Could the dead divers be Donnie and Jason? I ran through some possibilities. If, as the bartender speculated, these were accidental deaths from diving too deep using compressed air tanks, the bodies probably were not Donnie and Jason, two experienced divers using special air tanks because they knew about Blood Rock's dangerous depths and currents. Then again, since the locals seemed to avoid Blood Rock, even warned outsiders away from it, how many two-person diving teams would have been in those waters at the same time?

Of course, if the dead bodies were Donnie and Jason, treasure hunters on the trail of a million-dollar score, everything I'd learned suggested their deaths probably weren't diving accidents. Probably not accidents at all.

***

The next morning I gulped take-out coffee on an hour-long ferry ride that left Hancock County's rocky coastline miles behind. It was just the first leg of my trip to the boat-rental shop, which wasn't located on secluded Blood Rock but on the larger but still remote Snowen Island, known to locals as Snow and Ice Land for its harsh conditions during Maine winters. I felt grateful for the balmy summer day and supposed diving would be impossible here during weather-bound winter months. From the Snowen Island ferry landing, a dawdling half-hour taxi ride deposited me at last on the boat rental shop's rickety wooden pier.

"How the hell would I know who drowned off Blood Rock Island?" the boat shop owner shot back at me. "Nobody from here dives Blood Rock."

"Can you tell me if you rented a dive boat to a couple of younger guys from Boston, Donnie Evangeline and Jason Kinnert?" I asked.

"That boat. Right there." He pointed to a moored aluminum-hull cruiser that looked about thirty feet long. A ladder attached to the side reached down to the water and a contraption I assumed was a winch hovered above the deck. I noticed a nasty spatter of brownish-maroon stains on the boat's hull next to the ladder just above the waterline. Corrosion? Algae? Blood?

I nodded toward the boat. "When did Donnie and Jason return it to you?" I asked the shop owner.

"They didn't," he said. "They never showed up to take it out on the water."

***

The boat shop owner referred me to the two-person Snowen Island Police Department, part of the patchwork of local government agencies that provided services in various parts of the Unorganized Territories.

The burly Snowen cop on desk duty turned my inquiries back to me as questions. "You say you're here about the two divers? You family?"

"I represent a family member," I said.

"But you say you're a private eye, not a lawyer?"

"Yes."

"If you're not family and not a lawyer, I can't help you."

"Can you at least tell me whether you identified the victims as Donnie Evangeline and Jason Kinnert?"

"Back here! Back here!" Two voices down a hallway sounded in unison.

"Oh, those two divers," the cop said. "I thought you were here about the dead two. For the two back there, bail is two hundred dollars each. Cash only."

I handed him four hundred, which left my wallet empty.

***

It turned out Donnie and Jason hadn't arrived at the boat rental shop because, after they'd ferried to Snowen Island, they'd rented a car, driven it full speed past a local cop's radar gun, and hadn't been able to pay the fine. The cops confiscated their phones and other belongings at the police station's jailhouse, but let them use the landline there. Jason called his bank to check whether his balance would cover the fines. It wouldn't. Donnie called in a pizza order because "All they had here was baloney sandwiches." ("Here" meaning jail.) The cops then announced the bad news that Donnie and Jason were allowed only one phone call each, and jailed them until a bail bondsman, a brother-in-law to one of the cops, could ferry over in a few days. When I asked Donnie about his "souveneers" text to Aliza Marie, he said it was "just a way to psych up the enthusiasm" for the dive they'd planned later that day.

I also learned the two dead divers were out-of-state boaters, briefly jailed in the adjoining cell on drunk and disorderly charges. They must have overheard Donnie and Jason talking about the treasure dive. But the boaters had no business diving Blood Rock and paid with their lives.

***

Two days later Ms. Aliza Marie Evangeline was back in the visitor's chair in my Boston office. "I want to thank you for everything," she said. "And I swear you'll get reimbursed for the bail money. I swear it."

"And the balance of my retainer is due," I reminded her.

"Not a problem," she said. "My business partners are going back to Maine to retrieve the coins, so I can pay you in gold as soon as they return. Or I can write you a check now, but you can't cash it for a couple of weeks. Whichever way works for you."

"What would work for me is—"

"I bet I know exactly what you're going to say and I already took the liberty of discussing it with my business partners. We didn't budget for two trips to Maine, of course, so we need additional funding. And, yes, we are open to having you as an investor."

"An investor?"

"Absolutely. We're willing to accept the four hundred dollars and the rest of your retainer as an investment in our business. You wouldn't be a partner, you understand. But as an investor you'll be paid back with interest and dividends. Or you can keep your money invested with us for future treasure dives."

"Keep my money invested for future treasure dives?"

She leaned forward. "How much do you know about The Dread Pirate of New England, Dixie Bull?"

I could only shake my head.

She leaned forward a tad more, her brown eyes shining. "The story you're about to hear is completely confidential . . ."

***

NOTE: This story is an original work of creative fiction. The people and events described or depicted are entirely fictional. Any resemblance to actual individuals or events is unintended and coincidental. Additionally, although Maine does indeed have Unorganized Territories (including a number of small islands) that operate much as described in the story, Blood Rock Island and Snowen Island are fictional names and places. Jeep Cherokee is a registered trademark of FCA US LLC.

ARROYO

by Michael Bracken

Destination: Southwest Texas
Two churches. Temptation. Godliness. The town of Redemption and an arroyo called Sinners Creek await the arrival of two robbers fleeing into a thirsty land.

Early Sunday morning, when night had not yet been washed from the sky, Pastor John Peterson, spiritual leader of Redemption Revival Church, slowed his aging Dodge Dakota to a stop, grabbed two one-gallon jugs of water and a plastic trash bag, and stepped down to the caliche. An ankle-level cloud of white dust accompanied him as he walked to one of several unofficial water stations he maintained along a twenty-mile stretch of Sinners Creek, an arroyo that passed nine miles east of Redemption in southwest Texas.

Migrants coming north from Mexico used the arroyo as a highway to a better future, the walking far easier in the caliche of the dry creek bed than on the uneven ground to either side of it. But it wasn't always safe. A heavy rain on the mesas could send run-off thundering down the arroyo, creating a wall of water pushing heavy debris until finally dissipating in an alluvial fan a great many miles removed from the water's source. These flash floods could surprise even the most seasoned desert-dweller, but in all the years he had served Redemption Revival Church, Pastor John had only ever seen Sinners Creek bone dry. That's why he had established the water stations. Too many migrants had succumbed to heat and dehydration while traveling north through the inhospitable terrain, including an adolescent girl whose body he had stumbled upon seven years earlier.

Beneath a knee-high metal sign displaying the international drinking water symbol—a stylized faucet and glass of water against a green background—he found two empty water jugs in the plastic milk crate fastened to the metal pole holding the sign. He put the two empty jugs in his trash bag and replaced them with the two new water jugs. Then he looked around until he found the caps and plastic rings that had sealed the empties and dropped them into the trash bag.

Pastor John made nine more stops that morning before returning home to the one-bedroom parsonage behind Redemption Revival Church. He was removing the trash bag filled with empty water jugs from the bed of his truck when Deacon Calvin Miller caught his attention.

"You were out there again, weren't you?" he challenged.

"Every morning," Pastor John said as he carried the trash bag to the dumpster behind the church. Calvin followed two steps behind him. "Water is life."

"Well, all that water's killing us," Calvin said. "The board's asked you to stop."

"I can't turn my back on those who may be suffering."

"But you're spending hundreds of dollars a month on bottled water."

"And saving countless lives."

"That's right," the deacon said. "You can't count them. You have no idea if what you're doing is helping anyone, but we can't repair the roof or replace the air conditioning—"

"Now, Calvin," Pastor John said as he placed one hand on the other man's shoulder, "all you're doing is turning water into whine."

***

More than 2,500 people attended service each Sunday morning to hear the Right Reverend Will B. Dunne preach the gospel of giving at Heavenly Manna Bible Church in Ft. Worth, Texas, and the cash tithings encouraged by the reverend often piled several feet deep around the pulpit during the offertory. Though tithings via automatic bank transfers and regularly scheduled credit card charges provided a significant portion of the church's revenue, there was nothing like the sight of a heaping mound of cash to fire up the reverend's motivational messages.

For almost two years, Roy Lynn Reese had worked in Heavenly Manna Bible Church's counting room, separating bills by denomination, and running them through currency counting machines. Though Christmas or Easter brought in the greatest single-day revenue in any given year, the tens of thousands of dollars that flowed through Roy Lynn's fingers on a typical Sunday were more than enough temptation to make her question her commitment to at least one of the Ten Commandments.

Then she spotted a flaw in the church's security system, and late one night explained it to Merle Hanzlik, the ex-con with whom she fornicated on a semi-regular basis. At the end of each service, three church employees using hand-held vacuums that resembled leaf blowers sucked the loose currency into attached bags, which were emptied into larger plastic trash bags before being transported in a high-sided wagon to the counting room downstairs.

Though an armed security guard was stationed outside the counting room, there were no armed guards in the worship auditorium or in the hallway leading from the auditorium to the elevator. Halfway between the worship auditorium's rear door and the elevator was a single exit that led directly to the employee parking lot behind the church. The following Sunday, when it was her turn again to help suck up the money, Roy Lynn jammed the door's lock.

Wearing a black knit ski mask that was soaked with sweat by the time he opened the door from outside, Merle waved a Dirty Harry-sized Smith & Wesson .44 Magnum at Roy Lynn and the two other church employees accompanying the money wagon.

"Make one sound," he threatened, "and y'all are dead."

He tossed zip ties and silver duct tape to Roy Lynn, waving the revolver at her as he commanded her to secure her co-workers.

She protested. "But, I can't—"

"Which one you want me to shoot first?"

Roy Lynn acquiesced and soon had her co-workers trussed up like feral hogs on a spit, duct tape covering their eyes and sealing their mouths. Then, with Roy Lynn protesting every one of Merle's cursed commands as if she were not cooperating with him, they shoved the money wagon through the door to where an older model white SUV—stolen that morning when Merle saw the keys dangling from the ignition as he was scoping out cars in an H-E-B parking lot—waited with its rear hatch open.

After tossing all the currency-filled trash bags into the back and slamming the hatch, Roy Lynn grabbed her purse from the bottom shelf of the money cart and they climbed in. Merle pulled off the ski mask and keyed the ignition. The SUV's engine groaned before turning over, and they sped away through the employee parking lot to the street beyond.

"Where did you get the gun?" Roy Lynn asked.

"Impressive, ain't it?" Merle said as he drove with one hand and waved the revolver at her with the other. "Del Rio sold it to me for fifty."

Her eyes narrowed. "What's wrong with it?"

"Ain't nothing wrong with it."

She pried it from his hand. "Something's wrong with it or Del Rio wouldn't have let you have it so cheap."

Merle remained silent.

"Well?"

Merle shot a glance at Roy Lynn before answering. "Del Rio

said the last guy what had it shot a cop. He didn't want it in his inventory no more."

Roy Lynn smacked Merle on the side of his head with the flat of her hand. "What did I tell you about Del Rio? He'd cheat his mama out of a—"

"But it done what needed done," Merle said. "Did you see the look on they's faces when I pulled it out?"

Roy Lynn smiled at the memory. "Dickie Webster almost gave birth."

Then they both laughed as Merle caught the on-ramp for Interstate 820 and headed southwest around the city, unaware of a heavy storm brewing northeast of the Dallas-Ft. Worth Metroplex and headed in the same general direction they were. The white SUV Merle had stolen that morning looked just like dozens of others on the highway that Sunday afternoon and he stuck to the center lane, pacing traffic and doing nothing to draw attention to their vehicle.

Roy Lynn leaned forward and toyed with the radio, settling on a news radio station, listening to news from around the world and regular updates about the storm brewing north of the Metroplex. As they exited the Interstate at U.S. Route 377, they heard the first mention of the daring daylight robbery of Ft. Worth's largest megachurch and learned that the armed-and-dangerous robber had taken a female church employee hostage.

"He helps those what help themselves," Merle said, "and we done sure helped ourselves."

"You realize we're going to Hell for this."

"You ain't never been in prison," Merle said as he glanced at Roy Lynn. "Hell cain't be no worse."

"We won't go to jail because we won't get caught," Roy Lynn said. "Not if you do what I tell you."

They were headed southwest, toward her uncle Calvin's home, where her unexpected visit was likely to surprise the old man. She planned to hole up for the night, count the money and stack it neatly for easier transportation, exchange vehicles, and then continue the next day alone, having left Merle somewhere in the desert before she reached Interstate 10.

***

"There's a storm coming, Calvin," Pastor John said after the service. "Perhaps you could help me put out the buckets."

The deacon had remained behind to count the money in the collection plates, a task that had not strained his mathematical skills and never had. He tucked eighty-three dollars and seventeen cents into an envelope, added a deposit slip, and slipped it into his jacket pocket to drop into the bank's night deposit box on his way home. He said, "Be better if we just fixed the roof, but we don't have the money because—"

Pastor John placed his hand on Calvin's shoulder and said, "God will provide."

"Look around, John," the deacon said. "What has God ever provided us? Nothing but heartache and misery."

"He brought us here for a reason."

"Maybe he brought you here, but I was born in Redemption and, unlike my little sister who went off to the big city nearly forty years ago, I'm likely to die here. You could leave, get reassigned to one of those fancy city churches with a big budget and—"

"My work is here, Calvin." He stared into the other man's eyes for a moment before adding, "Now, let's set out the buckets."

***

Soon Roy Lynn and Merle lost the news radio signal, and the megachurch robbery did not rate a mention during the every-hour-on-the-hour news reports of the country music station they tuned in. The storm, however, rated mentions every twenty minutes or so, but they remained well ahead of it.

Around dinnertime, they stopped in Quarryville for chopped brisket, potato salad, and cold cans of Dr Pepper—one for Roy Lynn and two for Merle. The SUV was reluctant to start after dinner and again after filling the gas tank at the town's full-service Texaco station, but once it did, they blew through Chicken Junction and Mertz without stopping.

More than an hour after they left Quarryville, Roy Lynn had Merle turn off the state highway onto a Ranch to Market Road.

"There ain't nothing out here," Merle said. "You sure you got me driving on the right road?"

A city girl who had never traveled much outside the Dallas-Ft. Worth Metroplex—not even to visit her uncle—Roy Lynn was relying on directions provided by her smartphone's navigation app. "You turned where the phone said to turn, didn't you?"

"I done what you said."

"Then just drive," she said. "Everything's fine."

But Roy Lynn began to wonder about the directions her phone provided when they turned onto an unpaved road that stretched into the distance. She knew nothing about the desert or about how many roads were little more than hard-packed dirt without bridges to cross the eternally dry streambeds.

Shortly after passing a sign that informed them Redemption was ten miles ahead, Merle pulled to the side of the road and shifted the SUV into *Park*, not realizing he had stopped in an arroyo.

Roy Lynn said, "What are you doing?"

"I have to take a leak."

"Well, don't turn off the—"

Merle silenced the engine, pulled the key from the ignition, and stuffed the key ring into his pocket as he slid out of the SUV. When he returned a few minutes later and opened the door, Roy Lynn had the .44 Magnum pointed at him. Merle hesitated.

She said, "Hand me the keys."

"You ain't thinking of leaving me out here, are you?" Merle said. "You wouldn't do that, not after all I done for you."

"You're lucky I don't shoot you where you stand. Hand me the keys."

Merle fished them from his pocket and tossed them on the seat.

"Now get back."

Once Merle stood well away from the SUV, Roy Lynn retrieved the keys, walked around the SUV, and slid into the driver's seat. She keyed the ignition. The engine ground for a moment and then stopped making any sound at all. Roy Lynn tried again and again, but the engine would not respond.

She climbed out of the SUV and motioned with the barrel of the .44 Magnum. "Get the money."

"What are we going to do?"

"Redemption's less than ten miles. We can walk that far."

Merle retrieved the tithe-filled trash bags from the back, tied knots in the open ends to give him something to grip, and hefted them. All told, the trash bags contained nearly forty pounds of currency, and he did his best to balance the weight in each hand.

They had barely gone a dozen steps from the SUV when Merle asked, "What's that sound?"

Though the night sky remained cloud-free above them, the rainstorm they had outraced had found another way to catch them. A black wall of debris pushed from behind by water from a heavy rainstorm fifty miles north and six hours earlier bore down on them. The water rushed down the arroyo so fast the hard-packed caliche could not absorb it. The leading edge of the flood had become clogged with debris accumulated in the arroyo since the last flood many years earlier—trees, bushes, rocks, animal remains, human discards of all kinds—that slowed the leading edge while the water behind continued to rush forward, pushing, pushing, pushing.

When he saw the wall of debris rushing toward them, Merle shouted, "Run!"

He stumbled over the trash bags swinging from his arms, and he fell. He abandoned them, scrambled to his feet, and resumed running.

"Don't leave me, Merle!" Roy Lynn shouted. She had never fired a gun in her life, but she raised the Smith & Wesson .44 Magnum and squeezed the trigger.

The bullet tore through Merle's left knee, sending him sprawling face-first into the caliche. The revolver's kick knocked Roy Lynn backward onto one of the money-filled trash bags. She wrapped her arms around it just as the wall of debris washed over her.

Hell wasn't sulfur and brimstone. Hell was a wall of water rushing through the desert that knocked them unconscious, drowned them in a churning blender of debris, and burst open all but one of their tithe-filled trash bags.

For a moment, Roy Lynn's body caught on one of the knee-high metal signs that lined the arroyo every two miles.

***

First thing Monday morning, Pastor John collected all the buckets he and Deacon Calvin put out the afternoon before, none of which contained water because the anticipated storm never reached Redemption. Then he loaded twenty one-gallon jugs of water into his Dodge Dakota and drove to Sinners Creek.

He didn't recognize it. The previous evening's flash flood had passed in the dark of night, depositing debris along the creek banks before the water dissipated in an alluvial fan forty miles downstream. A few small pools of water remained, and a thin skin of rapidly drying mud clung to the caliche, bits of paper poking up from the mud.

Pastor John parked his truck alongside the first knee-high metal sign displaying the international drinking water symbol, the pole bent half over from the force of rushing water, and untangled a plastic trash bag clinging to it. The bag's contents rustled. Curious, he untied the knot holding the bag closed and looked inside.

While Pastor John stared into the currency-filled trash bag, desert scavengers found Merle and Roy Lynn's getaway vehicle eleven miles downstream where the flash flood had deposited it upside down. They disappeared the stolen SUV into a junkyard and days later stripped it for usable parts and scrap metal.

But right then, overwhelmed by his discovery, Pastor John held the tithe-filled trash bag and stared downstream. Several minutes passed before he realized the wet bits of paper littering the drying creek bed were currency. If Heaven could have streets paved with gold, then Heaven on Earth could have a migrant highway littered with cash. Pastor John had no idea how far the money trail stretched downstream, but he knew it went well beyond what he could see.

He also knew he needed help collecting all the loose currency, so he took out his cellphone and called Calvin Miller. When the deacon answered, Pastor John said, "You need to come out to the creek to see what I see."

***

News of the megachurch robbery in Ft. Worth never reached Redemption, and by the time Merle and Roy Lynn's bodies were discovered a year later, their unidentifiable remains were presumed to be those of unlucky migrants. No one cared but Pastor John and, when the county released them, he buried Merle and Roy Lynn in pauper's graves next to the adolescent girl whose body had prompted him to aid those traveling north through the inhospitable terrain of southwest Texas. In the meantime, Redemption Revival Church replaced its roof, updated its HVAC system, and repaired the fresh-water stations along the arroyo known as Sinners Creek.

And every morning Calvin Miller joined Pastor John to replenish those stations.

MUSKEG MAN

by Keenan Powell

Destination: Alaska
An earthquake can disturb more than just your nerves. When the 1964 quake unearths a mystery, Ernestine Brady has a fight on her hands if she wants to save her homestead.

Friday, March 27, 1964
Anchorage, Alaska

The shed door swung open. Ernestine stomped snow off her boots, making the doorstep, an old shipping pallet, wobble like a teeter-totter underfoot.

She set her backpack on the spongy plywood floor, softened by years of rain and snow leaking in. She pulled off her boots, dropped them on the ground, held onto the doorframe, and hauled herself up into the shed. Once inside, Ernestine left the door open to air out the smells of old lady, canned foods, and burnt coffee. She hung Douglas' down parka on a nail by the door.

A framed wedding photo on the back wall caught her eye. Young Ernestine, flaming red hair, sturdy, pretty (everyone said so), tending the campfire while Douglas and his fishermen friends drank beer. Floating across the glass was a ghostly reflection of old Ernestine: gray straggly hair, face all pouches and jowls, still sturdy but not so pretty. Funny, it should be reversed. Young Ernestine was the ghost.

She pulled the backpack onto the little TV table she'd found along the roadside—it was amazing what good stuff people threw away—and unpacked her hoard. In a dumpster, she had found a window screen with just one small tear. With a bit of wire, she could patch it up. She could nail the screen over the one window which was nothing more than a square hole in the wall. In the winter, she covered the window with plywood to keep out the cold. But in the summer, she left it open so she could hear the loons call. The problem was, mosquitoes got in. The screen would fix that.

There was no better way to start the day than with loon song. Every summer morning, just before the sun crested the Chugach mountains, they called to each other. Ernestine would lie still on her back, a soft cool breeze washing over her face, the sky lightening to streaks of pink and pale blue, lavender birch trees taking form against black-green leaves, as the loons cooed and chortled.

She'd named them George and Gracie. She wondered if this George and Gracie were the same pair who had come back year after year since she first homesteaded almost twenty years ago. Could be. Loons live a long time if no one's shooting at them.

George and Gracie nested in the reeds where they raised a little family of fluffy loon babies every year. About mid-summer, a parent would lead them around the lake, the babies paddling in single file. So serious were those babies, it was funny. Then fall would come and one morning, there would be no call from George to Gracie and no answer from Gracie to George. Ernestine would know the loon family was gone for the winter, but they would be back.

Not yet, though, it was only March.

George and Gracie weren't the only creatures Ernestine shared her home with. Most nights, a mama moose ambled down the trail with a yearling in tow. Mama moose would stop right in front of the shed and teach her baby how to peel the bark off the birch trees and which tender shoots were good for nibbling.

In the fall, the yearling would disappear, off to find his own trail, but mama moose kept coming back. As the winter wore on, her belly would get bigger and bigger with the new calf she was carrying. Come spring, she'd disappear into the woods for a while and when she came back, a tiny baby would be following her.

Once Ernestine had watched the calf get born just a few yards from her shed. Mama moose must have felt safe near the shed after all these years, knowing Ernestine wouldn't hurt her. When the nasty old grizzly came around looking for mama and baby, Ernestine would go out and bang an old trash can lid with a spoon to drive him away. If that didn't work, Ernestine shot at him. She didn't mean to kill him, just scare him off—she didn't need a nasty old bear carcass stinking up her woods. He'd amble away with snorts and filthy looks over his shoulder and mama moose and baby would be safe again.

Douglas always said moose were good eating and how silly it was Ernestine wouldn't let him shoot mama when she practically delivered herself up for dinner. "Two-fer," he said. "Mama and baby." You never, ever shoot a mama moose, Ernestine told him, and you especially never, ever shoot a baby moose. It ain't right. There were plenty of trout in the lake and salmon in the river come summer. Plenty of ptarmigan, geese, and duck. Mama moose trusted Ernestine and Ernestine wasn't going to let anyone hurt her.

She sat on the cot and picked through her findings. During her scouting expedition, she had also found a broken pack of cigarettes just lying in a parking lot. Not good enough for whoever threw them away, but there was nothing wrong with the tobacco. Ernestine split open a couple of the cigarettes, poured the leaf into a paper and rolled back and forth, tighter and tighter. Once it was solid enough to burn, she licked the paper and glued it closed. She put it in her mouth and looked around for a match.

Then she heard a low growl, sounded like that old grizzly. She hadn't seen any paw prints yet this spring. But it was unusually warm, maybe he woke up early. She sure didn't need some just-woke-up hungry bear busting in her house.

As she stood to pull the door closed, the building shuddered. The grizz must've nudged the back wall, seeing how easy it was to get in. The shed was built on top of cinder blocks to keep it off freezing and thawing ground so it didn't take much to move. Then the growl got louder and the plywood walls creaked.

Ernestine was reaching out for the door's rope handle when the shed shifted a couple of inches. She braced herself. The shed stopped moving and it was quiet. Eerily quiet.

That wasn't no grizzly bear.

The rumble started again and got louder and louder. The earth rolled. Ernestine held onto the doorframe with all her might as her body swung back inside, her feet slewing out from under her. The tin coffee pot on the camp stove lifted into the air then crashed on the ground. The cot skittered across the floor, knocking over the TV tray and the camp stove. The propane tank banged around the shed, gas hissing from a leak. The shed's frame shrieked and groaned as it swayed side to side like a hula dancer.

Ernestine rode the next wave, arms stretched out for balance. As the shaking slowed, she pulled herself to a stand. Was it over or was it just the beginning? Then with a crash so loud only God could have made the sound, the shed flew away and she tumbled into the light.

***

When she woke, she was face down in frozen leaf litter. The insides of her head ached. The right side of her face burned from sliding to a stop. Grit in her eyes made them water so much she couldn't see. Her lips were peeled back, leaves and dirt packed into her mouth. When she pushed herself up and spit out the muck, pain stabbed the base of her skull. She rolled to hands and knees, as wobbly as that newborn baby moose and sick to her stomach. She didn't know how long she'd been out but she could tell by the fading light that it had been a while.

There was silence all around. The busy city noise just a few miles away was gone. At first, she wondered if she had hit her head and gone deaf. Then a squirrel scuttled up a tree. When she heard his nails scratch in the otherwise deathly quiet, she remembered what had happened.

Earthquake.

She pulled herself up to sit. Her jeans, sweatshirt, and the ground were wet from the lake a few yards away splashing up and soaking everything. The dirt was churned into chunks of mud.

"Mrs. Brady, you alright?" a young man's voice came to her from the direction of the road. She was still dizzy but she tried to pull herself to a stand, focusing on a rock in front of her. She heard him run up. He placed a hand on her shoulder, holding her down. "Whoa, now. Take it easy. We'll get you out of here in no time."

She squinted at him, eyesight still bleary, taking in his jeans, sneakers, and T-shirt, "Who are you?"

"Kenny. You know me, Mrs. Brady. From the Campbell homestead down the road. My mom sent me to check on you."

She struggled to get out from under his grip. "I don't need no one checking on me. I've been doing just fine all by myself."

"Ma'am, you can't stay here. Your house got flattened."

She slapped at his hand.

The earth rolled again. They froze. Was a bigger one coming or was it just an aftershock? You never knew.

The tree tops swayed, sunlight glittering through their waving limbs for a few seconds and then it was over.

The kid let her go and stood upright. "What the hell?"

Something strange, something unnatural, was sticking up from the churned earth. It looked like a rotten old tree stump, maybe a sapling mama moose had eaten and killed. But Ernestine knew every leaf on her homestead and that dead tree hadn't been there before. That orange color was all wrong. Then she made out the shape.

That ain't no tree. That was a man's arm.

***

Not long after that kid found her, and she saw that arm she didn't want to think about, more men came tromping through the woods. They stood around the arm for a while, talking to themselves in that important way men do when they want women to think they know what they're doing. Then they practically carried her to the road.

She told them she wanted to stay but they said it wasn't safe.

They wouldn't even crawl into the shed to get her coat. They stuck her in the front seat of an old Jeep with some other people they had picked up crowded in back. Probably thought they were rescuing folks, but it was kidnapping if you asked Ernestine.

The buckled roads made driving across town slow. Chunks of asphalt stuck up at weird angles. Long gashes in the road looked deep enough to go straight to Hell. After a while, the road was so torn up the driver had to pull off and drive real slow through mud and snow. They drove east toward the mountains, toward solid ground. If anything was left standing, it'd be at the foot of the Chugach range.

Anchorage was starkly peaceful after so much violence. Patches of snow were draped against the slate blue mountains. The sky was pearly gray. And it was all so quiet, without cars zooming up and down the roads, without airplanes buzzing overhead.

The driver turned on the truck's radio from time to time but only got static. For all they knew, they were the only survivors, but later, they saw a line of headlights in the distance snaking toward the mountains.

When they got to shelter, a church rectory, there was no heat, no water, and no food. She might as well be home, so she took off walking. Another truck of young men hunted her down and brought her back.

Ernestine Brady had come to Alaska to homestead when WWII was over and returning soldiers put her out of her factory job. She knew she could build a house, hunt, fish, and grow her own vegetables. Hell, she'd done a man's job all through the war. Wasn't anything special about being a man. They might be bigger and stronger but she was smart and she could work just as hard. All she wanted was to be free of people's interference and here in this church shelter they treated her like an escaped prisoner.

She'd homesteaded the property before she met Douglas. She'd been working in a bar when he came in, all young and healthy with great big muscles and a great big roguish smile. By that time, she had her little shack built and was living in it, just like now. As the long winter nights wore on, she told him about her property and her plans to build a real log cabin and live off the land. He said that was his dream, too.

Pretty soon, he was living in the shed with her, gone commercial fishing most of the summer and helping her to build when he was home. She had to admit, even though she could live without a man, living with one was nice sometimes. A warm bed was nice. Talking to another human being was nice. It took a few years, but they got the log cabin built. When it was finished, he complained that it was her property and her cabin and he had nothing to show for his contribution, would she marry him.

It wasn't the proposal she'd hoped for but she wasn't getting any younger. So, they invited all his fishing buddies, had a big party, and got married.

***

"Sure enough, that's an arm," the little man on his knees said. He rocked back on his heels, carefully slipped a tiny pick into a pocket protector, and crossed his arms. "And, no, before you ask, I can't tell you how long he's been here. It could have been ten years or ten thousand years. I'll know more once the body is removed."

"Were there people in Alaska ten thousand years ago?" Adam Hollister asked. Hollister was wearing the uniform of a state mid-level bureaucrat: black suit, white shirt, thin black tie, black brogues, impractical for tramping through bog. Bits of leaf and twigs had slipped into his shoes and were stabbing his feet. He yearned for his neat, orderly office cubicle with the in-boxes and out-boxes and a map on the wall.

"It's a figure of speech." When the little man stood, he barely came to Hollister's chin. The thick lenses on his glasses made his eyes look huge, like a bug's. He had a small button nose and flat face. "Generally, it's thought the Athabaskans, people who lived in this area before whites came, walked across a land bridge from Asia thousands of years ago. But then we're always finding new evidence, so these theories are subject to change. In fact,"—the little man turned to consider the arm again—"this could well be a major find."

After the earthquake, Adam Hollister's department had been tasked with evaluating the damage, determining what could be repaired, what had to be torn down, and what lands could be built upon given what they knew now about earthquakes. This bog certainly was not habitable. The old lady's plywood shack had been destroyed. You wouldn't know it'd been a home if it weren't for the corrugated tin roof on top of the pile of rubble.

She'd never be allowed back. The state would take her land and append it to the airport expansion. Meanwhile she was still in a hospital recovering from her injuries, reportedly senile. Or maybe she'd always been crazy. You never knew with those old sourdoughs, hermits by another name.

Hollister had heard about the arm but he didn't believe it any more than he believed in Big Foot. When Hollister came to the bog to examine the house, he saw it for himself—just sticking out of the ground. Not a whole arm, only the elbow. But it sure looked like those mummies he'd seen in *National Geographic*. When he reported his find to his superiors, the next thing he knew they were on the phone to the Smithsonian. A week later, this little man, the professor, in his multi-pocketed vest, blue jeans, and Wellington boots, got off the plane.

Well, that was fine with Hollister. The professor could dig up the old body. And Anchorage could go back to rebuilding. It would be bigger and better than ever before with all the federal disaster money rolling in.

"Remind me. What's the Alaskan word for bog?" the professor asked.

"Muskeg?" Hollister answered.

"That's right, muskeg. We'll call him Muskeg Man."

***

"We're calling him Muskeg Man," the little gent said, looking like a teddy bear dressed for some sort of expedition. He pushed the horn-rimmed glasses back up his short nose. "'Muskeg' means 'bog,' Mrs. Brady."

Standing behind the little gent was another man, a suit from the government, looking both bored with the visit and amused by the big talk of the little gent. They'd introduced themselves when they came into the sunroom but Ernestine had already forgotten their names.

She looked up at the gent like he was crazy. He seemed to get the hint.

He talked faster. "We suspect your homestead is on top of a pre-contact Athabaskan village. The secrets lie down there, buried in the bog."

Ernestine fidgeted in her chair.

"Do you understand what I'm saying, Mrs. Brady?"

"You want to dig up my land."

"The Smithsonian wants to excavate your land. We'll have photographers there and it'll all go into *National Geographic* magazine. Won't that be exciting?" he said, like he was bribing a little kid with a lollipop.

"That's my home."

"Not for long," the suit said.

Weeks had passed since the Good Friday earthquake. By now, George and Gracie would be back on the lake with their fluffy little babies paddling behind them and mama moose would be leading her baby around. If the grizzly didn't get them. Or some idiot with a gun.

Back in the emergency housing, someone decided she must have gotten hit in the head or maybe she was just dingy, being an old lady hermit all alone in the middle of the woods and needed to be taken care of. They said they were moving her some place where she could recover but she knew what this place really was. An asylum. She could tell because all the other patients ran around screaming or snored in their chairs all day long after getting doped up.

Ernestine Brady wasn't nuts.

Since the quake, as more Outsiders came up to rescue them and the radio station was up and running again, they found out just how bad the damage was. Fifteen people had died in the quake and another one hundred and twenty-four died in tidal waves. Some folks would never go home again, their houses in ruins. But Ernestine's home was just a shack. She'd built it all by herself and she could build another one, so she didn't understand why they had locked her up.

"If you get me back to my place in time, I could have something up before the snow flies."

"That's not in my power, Mrs. Brady," the suit said. "But you're in luck. The state is interested in your land. We're prepared to make a generous offer."

Ernestine remembered the little gent had just said something about a Muskeg Man.

"What Muskeg Man?"

"It's a mummy that was found after the Good Friday earthquake. They've been turning up all over the world, where conditions are right for preserving bodies. Places like Ireland, Norway, Alaska. It's a terrific find for us." His voice was hushed as if he was telling her a secret. "A pre-contact Athabaskan settlement has never been discovered. The Smithsonian sent me. We'd like to look for the civilization that existed long before Anchorage was settled. When we're done, the government is going to build a great, big modern airport right there."

"Absolutely not." Ernestine shook her head violently. "No, no, no, no."

The two men stepped back when Ernestine began pounding her fists in her lap. She was working the crazy thing for all it was worth. "You're not digging up my home. No, no, no, no, no!"

"Nurse!" the suit called.

The nurse came and gave her a shot. She nodded off and when she woke up the little gent and the suit were staring at her.

"Do you have any family, ma'am?" the suit asked.

"No one but Douglas."

"Who is Douglas?"

"My husband. Or ex-husband. I don't know what you'd call him. Haven't seen him in years." Not since that night he got drunk.

He was lying in bed, guzzling from a vodka bottle when he heard mama moose brushing through the shrubs. He jumped up, grabbed his gun, ran out of the cabin stark naked, and leveled at mama moose.

Wasn't no one, bear nor man, going to hurt mama moose on Ernestine's watch. After it was all over, she had burned down the cabin with all his stuff in it and moved back into the drafty shed, her home, the one she'd built all by herself with her own two hands. Now that was gone, too.

Maybe she'd take that offer and go live somewhere warm. Where no one could find her.

"How much money are we talking about?"

***

In August, the professor and his students were knee-deep in bog, slapping at mosquitoes as big as B-52s, when Muskeg Man was finally uncovered, naked and curled on his side in the fetal position.

The professor stepped out of the trench to direct a young woman with a camera on how to photograph the body *in situ*.

"What's that?" the young woman asked.

"What's what?" the professor said.

"Down there near the hand," she pointed. "Something glittery."

"Take five," the professor said and watched as the girl went back to the tent to flirt with her boyfriend.

The professor stepped back into the hole, leaned over the body and saw, barely visible in the mud, something gold. Most unexpected. In his grant proposal, the professor had theorized that the body was a pre-contact Athabaskan and that this was a site of an Athabaskan burial, or home, or village even. This find would be his ticket to fame. He would write a glossy magazine article. He would put together a traveling exhibition. He would give speeches at universities.

But pre-contact Athabaskans didn't have gold.

The professor tapped the gold thing with his tiny pick, pushed it around this way and that. The muck fell away and then he saw what it was. A gold wedding ring. He picked it up, looked around to make sure no one was watching and read the inscription: D & E.

Then he slipped the ring into a vest pocket. No one needed to know.

THE END OF THE WORLD

by Susan Breen

Destination: Tahiti
There are many kinds of sharks in the paradise that is called Tahiti, but not all of them are denizens of the ocean.

Toward the close of her father's trial for murder, Cosima Bell happened to see an advertisement for Tahiti. The colors transfixed her. Violet skies and aquamarine lagoons and flaming orange sunsets. Sometimes Cosima saw colors in her mind when she played the piano, but never like these. She decided in that moment that when the trial was over and her father condemned—because there was never any doubt about the verdict—she would go to Tahiti and disappear.

Get away from all the horrors. The lurid crime scene photos, weeping families, voyeuristic spectators, her father in manacles. Horrible reporters. They kept taking her picture and shouting questions:

"Cosima, how did you not hear what was taking place in the basement of your house?"

"Cosima, how can you still be loyal to your father after what he's done?"

"Cosima, how can you say you still love him?"

Cosima didn't even try to explain because the fact was, unless you'd grown up with her father, there was no way to understand him.

Leonard Bell was a great pianist, possibly the greatest of his generation. He retired from the concert stage when he was a young man so that he could focus on the music of the eccentric 19th-century composer Franz Liszt. That was his passion, his obsession. To dominate Liszt. Over and over and over her father worked on Liszt's difficult pieces, pounding the Steinway so hard that sometimes the piano wires would spring right out of their pins and slash the walls of their conservatory. Cosima's job was to sit at his side. That was her life. Her father'd named her after Liszt's daughter, and from the moment she was born, he groomed her to be his attendant. Cosima's mother left when she was just a girl; her father homeschooled her. She grew into her job. Took care of his correspondence, handled his money, listened to him, tuned the piano. Critiqued him. She was the only one in the world whose criticism he trusted.

So their life might have continued forever, except for a fluke. One night her father went out on one of his rambles, as he liked to call them. A police officer pulled him over because the car's right tail light was out. While he was writing up the ticket, the police officer noticed a finger hanging out of the trunk.

"You had no idea? You suspected nothing?

Cosima was twenty-four years old. She'd spent her life in thrall to her father. He was her world, her life, even her vocabulary. No, she had no idea.

***

To get to Tahiti, Cosima had to fly from New York to Los Angeles and then on to Papeete's Fa'a'ä International Airport. From there she took a high-speed ferry across the Sea of the Moon and at the dock, she was met by the hotel driver.

He was a slight man dressed in the hotel uniform of red shirt and white shorts. In his hands was a splendid lei made out of orchids, and he smiled as he walked toward Cosima, preparing to drape the necklace over her head. She smiled back at him. Impossible not to, he seemed so warm and friendly. The whole place smelled of vanilla and coconut. Even the birdsong was welcoming, fluting melodies from colorful birds that darted overhead.

Yet, when he began to put the lei over her head, Cosima flinched with terror. Her mind flashed back to the crime scene photos, to the six men whose necks had been garroted with piano wire. She saw their gaping mouths, their bulging eyes, pictured the scuffle as they grabbed for the wire tightening around their necks. She couldn't help herself. She smacked away his hands, the lei fluttering to the ground, a puddle of red at her feet.

The guide never stopped smiling. He just leaned over, picked up the flowers, and handed them to her, gesturing that she should put it on herself.

"Sorry," she said, but he'd moved on, not concerned, not interested, which was in itself remarkable. Cosima'd become used to being the center of attention. Her face had been plastered all over the newspaper and internet. Even *People* magazine had run an article on her, "Satan's Daughter." But this man didn't know her, didn't desire her, didn't care about her.

Cosima felt something inside her relax. She remembered what the travel agent had said when she'd booked her reservation.

"You're going to The End of the World," she'd said. "That's what the missionaries called it, you know. When they settled there. They thought Tahiti was as far from civilization as you could be." And then the travel agent had blushed. Perhaps, Cosima thought, wondering what civilization meant to a woman whose father had just been sentenced to six life sentences, one for every man he'd killed.

Now Cosima's guide led her to a minivan, put her luggage in the back, and drove off. She was surprised no one else got in; the plane had been crowded enough.

"Where is everyone?" she asked.

"No," he said, roaring forward onto a surprisingly busy highway. "Moa."

Cosima surveyed the empty van. It seemed cavernous, smelled as though it had been freshly washed. She noticed a small shell tucked into the seat's crease. She pictured a child hiding it there. As a warning? She could see the frightened child trying to save herself. She heard the prosecutor's voice. Her father had lured men into his car and taken them back to the basement. No one knew why, or from where this murderous rage came. Cosima began plucking at her sleeve. She felt so vulnerable, so alone. She was at the mercy of this guide. She wanted to scream. Where is everyone?

And then they turned onto a driveway and the hotel loomed in front of her: a modern reception building surrounded by blooming shrubs, and, in the background, a huge shark's tooth seeming to be molded out of the earth. A staggering vista, and beyond that the infinity of the gentle ocean. Waves broke far away from this shelter, and nestled into the lagoon were a string of small thatched villas, one of them her own.

"Beautiful," she whispered. It truly was the end of the world. She'd escaped.

***

That night Cosima sat on her private deck and watched the stars glitter. She'd ordered her dinner to be delivered, and a waiter had canoed over to bring the food: papaya, mahi-mahi roasted in bread fruit, a carafe of white wine. She felt satiated. She looked forward to sleeping in the huge bed that dominated the villa. There was a gauzy curtain around it and on the blankets a heart made out of orchids had been tenderly placed. In the center of the floor was a window, so that she could look down at the reef and watch the fish swim by. But it was here, outside, on her little deck, that she felt happiest. Surrounded by soft waves, listening to music from some far-off party, she felt at peace. She could stay here forever, she thought. She had money. Residuals from her father's recordings.

She'd sold off the house, given the proceeds to the families of the six victims, but the royalties from her father's recordings would be enough to keep her here.

That was when she heard the couple arguing.

"You're not going to screw this up," a woman said. "This is our one chance."

Her voice crackled like lightning across the night sky.

"But we have so much," a man growled, his voice tight with anger. "We can do whatever we want now. There are no limits."

"Don't be a fool, Jack. There are always limits."

"Ten million dollars!" he cried out.

"And it's mine," she snapped. "It's my name on the check. How does that feel, lover?"

Cosima noticed one of the other villas had a light on. The argument must be coming from there. About fifty feet away from where she sat. Should she intervene? Knock on the door? She remembered the sound of a reporter's voice: *You heard nothing, Cosima. You expect us to believe that?*

"You're my wife. The money's mine, too."

"We'll see," the woman said. She began to giggle then. "We'll see if you can earn it, lover."

A hard wave slapped against the dock. A door slammed shut, and in the quiet of the night, Cosima heard a woman moaning. She blushed and went inside her villa, laid down in bed and then got up again and put a chair against her door.

***

Cosima dreamed that night of her namesake, Cosima Liszt, who had gone on to marry Hans von Bulow, one of her father's students and a well-known conductor. On their honeymoon, they paid a visit to the great composer, Richard Wagner, and at the sight of him, Cosima fell down before him and covered his hands with tears and kisses. Eventually she left her husband for Wagner, and her passion for him sustained her for the rest of her life. Even von Bulow acknowledged Wagner to be the better man. That sort of ruthless passion had always disturbed Cosima. To make such a sharp break with the past, to throw away normal life, to commit yourself so fully to another.

She felt sodden when she woke up the next morning. The sky was gray, the shark tooth mountain loomed like a warning. Off in the distance she could see waves crashing at the end of the lagoon. Cosima peered through the window in her floor and saw schools of brightly colored fish dash by, all of them in a hurry. Being chased perhaps?

Someone knocked on her door and she jumped, but it was only

the guide, holding a tray of breakfast foods.

"For you," he said, setting it down on the table outside.

She nodded, and then he looked out at the sea and gestured. "Moa," he said. "Be careful."

Suddenly the sun burst out, scattering away all the clouds, and as quickly as that Tahiti was vivid again, the blues and the yellows and the orange-colored fish. Cosima was hungry. She quickly put on some pants and a shirt, then settled herself on the deck and began to eat. And that was when she heard someone calling to her.

"Hey. Hey. Hello."

Startled, Cosima turned toward the sound. She recognized the voice from the argument the previous night. There was a woman standing three villas away, waving at her. She was a blousy sort of woman, as her father would have put it. Lank hair, overweight, with a surprisingly large pearl necklace around her neck.

"Hey there," the woman called out again. "You're another brave one."

"What do you mean, brave?" Cosima asked, tilting toward her, minding the staircase.

"Haven't you heard?"

"No," Cosima said.

"About the shark attack?"

"No."

The woman leaned toward her and shouted a sort of whisper. "A little kid. Right here at this hotel. In these villas. Fell off the pier and was eaten by a shark. All that was left of him was a foot. Terrible, right? Everyone canceled. That's why no one's here. You should go talk to the people at the front desk. Renegotiate your price. They'll give you a discount. Everyone canceled. Tourism's down here anyway. They say people aren't coming to Tahiti anymore. It's too expensive. I got them to take twenty-five percent off our price."

A man came out and stood alongside the woman. He looked strong, Cosima thought. Like a person who worked with his hands. He scowled in her direction, but perhaps that was his normal expression. Cosima's father had a natural scowl. The only time she'd ever seen him smile was at the end of his farewell concert at Carnegie Hall, and after the verdict was read. Then he'd smiled sadly and bowed to her.

"This is Jack," the woman said. "And I'm Jill. I know, I know. Everyone makes the same joke."

"What joke?" Cosima asked.

That made Jill laugh, though in fact Cosima had no idea what she was talking about. When your father is a musical genius, you miss out on a lot of the normal cues.

"Hey, you must have heard us arguing last night," Jill cried out. "You must have thought we were crazy people. Never could keep my mouth shut. Oh Jack, look at her face. You really do think we're crazy, don't you? And here you are, all by yourself. A beautiful girl like you. You have a story. I can feel it, I always do. No one like you would wind up here without a story. Right Jack? I want to hear it. Come over for drinks tonight, OK? Tell us your story, and I'll order one of those seared red tunas with creamy vanilla sauce and I'll show you my new black pearl necklace. What do you think, Jack?" she said, though Jack had added absolutely nothing to this torrent of words.

Playfully she punched his shoulder. "Don't mind him," she said. "He's harmless. Please, you will come to dinner, won't you?"

***

There was no way to refuse the invitation. Beyond the fact that they seemed to be the only people at the resort, Jill struck Cosima as being one of those people who would come pound on your door to get you to do what she wanted. But Cosima was curious about this couple, and intrigued to meet them. She knew so few people outside of the world of music, and the courthouse. She wanted to go, but what to wear?

She'd not been able to bring herself to go vacation shopping after her father's trial. It was hardly appropriate, and so she'd arrived in Tahiti with one black bathing suit, a green dress, a few pairs of pants, and a silk blouse. None of those things seemed suitable for a casual Tahitian dinner. So Cosima asked at the reception desk and they directed her to a local store.

The proprietor was delighted to help her. She showed Cosima an array of floral dresses and sarongs, but one particular fabric compelled her. It was a black sheath with vibrant purple blossoms. Cosima knew it would look striking against her fair skin and blonde hair. She bought some sandals as well. That night, she brushed out her hair and tucked a hibiscus bloom behind her ear. She was satisfied when she looked at herself in the mirror.

***

Jill screamed at the sight of her. "Well, look at you, you super model you. Why do I even try?" She gestured at her own sarong that seemed to bulge out in all directions. "You're so beautiful. You must tell me who you are. It's driving me crazy. You're a movie star, aren't you?"

She was so warm, so friendly. Cosima'd never known anyone like her.

"Come on in," Jill cried out. She didn't seem able to speak softly.

"Jack," she yelled, as though he were a mile away. "Jack. C'mon. Now what's your name? Forgot to ask."

Cosima had considered that very question. Her own name was too unique. "Connie," she said.

"Connie. You don't look like a Connie, but OK. Hope you're hungry."

Cosima was stunned to see a whole array of food spread out in front of her. The villa was the same as hers, and yet it felt larger. Brighter. Maybe it was all the aromas from the food, or all the colors, or Jill's voice which seemed to reverberate all around her as though they were in a canyon. She handed Cosima a beer. A kneeling woman was pictured on the can. "Hinano," she said. "They brew it here. It's the only stuff worth drinking. Don't drink any of that pineapple shit, you'll be throwing up for days."

"Jack," she yelled, and finally he emerged. He must have been taking a shower. He gleamed. His brown hair was slicked back, his shoulders slightly hunched. Automatically Cosima looked at his hands, which were large. She suspected he could cover two octaves.

"There he is," Jill said. "Finally. Prettying yourself up, are you?"

Cosima cringed, but Jack didn't seem offended. He looked bemused, as though it were all a joke, but when Jill went up to him and kissed him, Cosima was surprised at how strongly he kissed her back. Jill rocked back on her heels for a moment, and ran her tongue across her lips. A spot of blood was on her chin. He leaned toward her and wiped it away.

Jill shook her head and resumed. "Isn't Connie like a movie star? You must have men throwing themselves at you all the time. Or maybe you're a princess?"

"No," Cosima said. "Nothing like that."

"I don't believe you," Jill said. "I'll get it out of you."

She picked up an empty plate and handed to Cosima. "Take," she said. "Whatever you want. We might as well finish it all up." She began piling food on her own plate, mounds of it, while Jack picked up one piece of grilled fish.

"No appetite?" Jill asked him.

"I'll eat when I'm ready."

"Oh, I see." She looked like she wanted to say more, to fight over it, but decided better of it because she turned once again to Cosima.

"Oh, don't mind him," Jill said. "He doesn't want to be here.

He's sulking. Tahiti's not his dream vacation. He doesn't want to be all alone on an island. He wanted to go helicopter skiing, but I said forget it. No one's dropping me off a mountain. Knowing this one, he'd drop me onto a tree. Murderous tendencies." She winked.

"Why didn't you want to come to Tahiti?" Cosima asked him.

"He doesn't like to leave the United States," Jill said. "He feels there's enough to see there."

"It's the truth," Jack said, warming to the subject. "Why do I want to go anywhere else when we have so much in America?"

"You see," Jill said. "That's how he is. Stick in the mud. But not me. I want to see everything. Japan and China and Russia and Antarctica and Chile."

Cosima laughed. "You must have a big budget."

"Oh, we do," Jill said. "We have ten million dollars."

"My goodness."

"I know. What happened was this. We were coming home from visiting Jack's aunt in Indiana. Driving on the highway and I had to make a pit stop. Jack doesn't like to stop. Matter of principle with him, but I had to go. I mean really bad. Begging and begging, but he wouldn't stop. Finally, we hit some traffic and I slam open the door and start to run for the gas station. He's mad. Of course. So I figure, what the heck, I'll take my time. Go to the little store and buy a lottery ticket. Scratch off the numbers and damned if I didn't win ten million dollars."

She poked Jack then. "All because I had to pee."

Jill threw back her head and laughed. Guffawed. There was something frightening about seeing her neck exposed like that. Cosima caught Jack's eye in that moment and she felt sure that had he been holding a piano wire he would have tugged it around his wife's neck. She felt the hatred coming off of him in sharp waves. She knew then that he planned to kill his wife. That was why they were here, in this isolated location.

Cosima's heart began to beat wildly. She closed her eyes, hearing Liszt's "Mephisto Waltz." Just so had her heart hammered when her father played it. Faster and faster and faster. Calling up the demons of hell.

"But you must admire my black pearl necklace," Jill said.

She took off the necklace and handed it to Cosima. "Isn't it gorgeous? The best one on the island. I paid a fortune for it, but it's worth every penny. From now on, it's only top quality for me."

She glared at Jack. "So you better watch out, mister."

He was going to kill her. Cosima could feel it. She could see it in his eyes. She had to stop him. She hadn't been able to prevent the murders that took place in her own house. But she could prevent this one.

***

That night Cosima watched and waited. She could hear Jill's voice. She heard them arguing. It went on for a long time, and then the lights in their villa went out. She found herself thinking of a story her father used to tell about Cosima Wagner. As a birthday present for her, Richard Wagner arranged one year to have an orchestra assemble on her staircase and perform a melody he'd written just for her. What would it be like, Cosima had always wondered, to have someone love you like that? She'd dreamed that someday she would find such love. She thought then of Jack's eyes and the way he'd looked at her. The night was so quiet. A fish bumped against the floor window and she imagined a shark hunting her. And then she fell asleep.

***

Cosima woke to the sound of someone knocking on her door. She assumed it was the waiter delivering breakfast by canoe, but when she opened the door, she found Jack standing there, holding Jill's black pearl necklace.

"Jill said to give this to you."

"I can't take that," Cosima said. "Please thank her, but it's too valuable."

"She left," he said. He was standing in the doorway, then he took a step toward her.

"Left. How? When?"

"Last night. We had an argument and she left me. Had enough."

"In the middle of the night?"

He shrugged. "When you have ten million dollars, you can hire a plane to pick you up whenever you want."

"I didn't hear a plane."

He stepped in further. Closed the door behind him. Up close he was much larger than he'd seemed when Jill was alongside him. His face was tanned, weathered. Tiny grooves marked his skin.

He surveyed her room. "It's nice here. Clean."

Then he looked down at her. "I recognized you," he said. "The murderer's daughter. Knew that right off. Saw you in *People* magazine. The picture didn't do you justice."

He stood in front of her, unmoving. She felt so vulnerable in her thin pants and shirt. She put her hand in her pocket. She needed some part of her to be hidden.

"I admired you for staying with your father," Jack said. "Most people wouldn't. Most people aren't loyal like that."

He moved away, toward the kitchen, sat down at one of the bar stools.

"Jill couldn't understand that the money wasn't important to me. Never was. I never cared about it. Money just screws things up. I wanted love and loyalty. A woman like you."

"Is that why she left?" Cosima asked, edging herself against the wall.

He shrugged. "She didn't think I was serious, but I was. I've always been much more serious than she gave me credit for being. You're serious. You don't think life's a joke. I can see that."

He began speaking more urgently. "You want the same thing I do. You want to live life on your own terms, right? You don't care about the rules."

She crossed her arms.

"You did know, didn't you?" he said. "You knew what he was doing. You had to know."

"No," she said.

"I saw the pictures of the house and how thin the walls were. You can tell me the truth. I don't care. I'm not going to report you. I just want to know. I want to know you. You must really love your father."

His eyes bored into her. He reminded her of her father. Always so certain. She remembered then an afternoon when her father decided she would learn to play one of the Liszt pieces. Her hands were small, she wasn't as talented as he, but he was determined. He put his hands over hers and said "Now." For hours, he pressed his hands on top of hers, taking possession of her, forcing her hands to play. She was a child, she cried. He continued through the night. He was merciless. "You must," he said. "You must."

She clenched her hands together. She would not be forced. She would not be owned. She put her hand back in her pocket and felt for the little packet she always kept there, as she had done since she was a child. A packet of piano wire. So that no matter when her father needed it, she would have it. So that no matter when she needed it, she would have it.

"Would you open that bottle of wine?" she asked.

"So early," Jack said. "Sure, why not."

It was so easy. He turned his back to her. She was so fast, so strong.

He didn't hear her coming. None of them had. She thought of what the prosecutor had said, how no great strength was needed to garrote someone with a piano wire. Just the element of surprise.

***

The body would be easy to dispose of, she thought afterwards.

She could throw him into the sea. Probably no one would miss him. The hotel would assume he left with Jill, and Jill wouldn't be looking for him. If in fact she had left the island.

Cosima sat back down on her bed. Out the window she could see the volcanic mountain rising into the sky. The sun was out, everything was pristine.

Her father had asked to talk to her after the verdict, before they led him off to jail. She knew the police officer didn't want to allow it, but she smiled at him. She'd discovered that her smile often got her what she wanted. "Please," she'd whispered and he nodded.

"Just for a minute ma'am. Miss."

They couldn't go into a separate room, but she stood close to her father, so that he could whisper. The manacles were heavy on his hands. She could see how they weighed on him.

"This I do for you willingly," her father said to her. "I blame this aberration on myself. On my demands on you and my punishments. I should not have exposed you to Liszt at such an early age. It was no sort of life for you.

"But Cosima," he went on, "you must promise me this. Promise me you will go far away. You will remove yourself from temptation. Promise me this."

"Yes, father," she said now, in her villa at the end of the world.

TO PROTECT THE GUILTY

by Kerry Hammond

Destination: Megève, France
An isolated ski lodge and a blizzard. Four men share drinks and stories. One begins, "I have known a murderer."

If I hadn't been stranded at a remote ski lodge with no way to get down the mountain, it might have been a picturesque setting. Instead, it felt a bit like captivity. Not that anyone was waiting for me at the bottom, since I'd traveled to France alone and on a whim. I wasn't alone at the lodge, though. There were four of us, five if you included the bartender, but he wasn't paying much attention to us now that we had our drinks. He dried glasses and wandered in and out of his stockroom, looking unconcerned about the weather, which was somewhat comforting.

The four of us sipped our drinks in silence. We had yet to introduce ourselves, but had identified our countries of origin when we first sat down by comparing the skiing in our respective countries to that of Megève. We sat in front of the fire, relaxing after a full day on the slopes, listening to the howling wind. Each of us had made the unfortunate decision to stop at the mid-mountain lodge for a drink before finishing our final run. Almost as soon as we'd taken off our boots, the weather had gotten so bad that it would have been dangerous to continue down. It was now snowing so hard that we couldn't see a thing out of the large picture window next to the door. I found myself glancing over every few minutes to see if there was any sign of it letting up. There wasn't. It was like we were caught in a snow globe and someone had just given it a good shake.

We might not be able to make it back down the mountain, but at least we were comfortable. I sipped my Scotch and sat in an armchair across from a massive fireplace, feeling warm both inside and out. I had already decided that the worst case scenario would be to spend the night in the cozy lodge with a bunch of strangers. At least I'd have another story to tell my friends back home.

I looked around at my fellow skiers and wondered what had brought them to Megève. It was one of the fanciest resorts in France, and you had to have money to be able to come here. I wasn't about to share that my vacation had been paid for from a generous divorce settlement. My cheating ex-wife had practically handed over the money for the privilege of being with her new boyfriend, a younger version of me. Or so I liked to think.

Our small group consisted of a tall Swede with stereotypical blonde hair; I pegged him for an IT guy; his geeky glasses were probably quite stylish in Stockholm. The Finn was short, he couldn't have been more than 5' 4". I couldn't really get a read on him, but for some reason, I thought military. Maybe it was the haircut. The last was an older Austrian guy that I guessed to be about fifty-five. He had a salt-and-pepper beard and my wife, ex-wife, would have called him distinguished. My money was on him being a professor or a writer. He had spoken very little since we sat down.

It was no surprise that the conversation revolved around the weather and how fast the storm had rolled in. The Swede and the Finn were discussing whether or not the forecasters should have warned us about the storm. No skier worth his salt would fail to check the weather report before setting out, but the morning's forecast hadn't predicted the blizzard that now trapped us.

Our skis were outside in the racks, braving the wind and snow. There was no one working the valet room to check our boots, so they were lined up against the wall by the door, underneath the window with no view. The bartender had gotten us each a pair of fur-lined slippers from the valet room and the drinks were on the house. The Austrian and I each had a backpack that sat at our feet. I noticed that his had a luggage tag hanging from the side, a nice plastic one attached with a small carabiner. I made a mental note to get myself one like it: you never knew when you might leave your bag behind. I was getting back into the sport after a ten-year hiatus, and all of the equipment was new and improved. I was still compiling the gear I needed.

A loud thwump resonated through the lodge as a large piece of ice and snow dislodged and came crashing down against the window. It looked much darker outside, but I couldn't tell if it was the storm or the time of day. It was only four in the afternoon, but the sun set early in January. The sky looked ominous and the silence between the gusts of wind was eerie.

I was a bit taken aback when I tuned into the conversation once again and heard the Swede asking the Finn if he had ever known a murderer. With his accent, it sounded like moor-dur. I had no idea where this conversation had come from, but I vaguely recalled hearing the Finn say something about his wife murdering him if he didn't make it back to the hotel tonight. That might have been the catalyst.

I looked at each person in turn. The Swede was looking proud of himself for thinking of the question, the Finn was giving it serious thought, and the Austrian was staring into the fire, oblivious to the conversation.

"You mean like an accident, like in a motor crash?" said the Finn.

"No, I mean on purpose. The kind of murder that is planned and maybe the guilty person is caught by the police and maybe he is not," said the Swede.

The Finn nodded in understanding and continued to ponder the question.

I wasn't sure if the question was meant for all of us, but I was about to weigh in and admit that I hadn't known a murderer when the lights flickered and went out. All conversation ceased until the lights came back on a few seconds later. They were dimmer than before and I wondered if a generator had kicked on. I realized I had been holding my breath and I let it out slowly.

The Finn gave a nervous little chuckle, and the Austrian took of sip of his cognac and cleared his throat. When the Austrian started talking I noticed how melodic his voice was. It had a cadence to it that could lull a baby to sleep. It had been a while since he'd uttered a word and the two Scandinavians looked over at him in surprise. The Swede's mouth hung slightly open.

"Have you ever heard the phrase 'sleep the sleep of the innocent person'?" He looked at us one by one. The Finn and the Swede seemed to be dumbstruck and continued to stare at him. I managed to nod my head to let him know I knew the phrase, or a version of it.

"I think that they have it wrong," he said. "I think that it should be 'to sleep the sleep of the guilty person.' A guilty person has no conscience and therefore he may sleep more soundly and without any amount of worry." He smiled slightly when he finished, more a smile of accomplishment than mirth. But it still put everyone at ease and I wasn't the only one who relaxed.

His next sentence came as a shock. "I have known a murderer," he said.

His tone of voice belied the gravity of his words and it took me a second to process what he had said. My companions clued in at the same time as I did and the three of us exchanged glances. Mine said is this guy for real?

When I glanced back at the Austrian, he sat, silent, as if he intended to let his sentence sink in before he continued. He was a stocky guy, and very fit, maybe a bit like Hemingway. I noticed he was wearing a wedding band on his left ring finger.

It was the Swede who finally spoke and filled the silence. "Are you pulling our legs?" he said.

The Austrian continued as if the Swede hadn't spoken.

"I say I have known a murderer, but perhaps it would be more accurate to say that I've met a murderer." He nodded his head at this, as if he were agreeing with himself.

His English was very precise and his accent was evident but slight. "It was at a ski resort like this one, which is why the story comes to my mind."

As he continued talking, the only other sounds were the crackling fire and the whistling wind. The three of us didn't so much as cough. The bartender was nowhere to be found, probably trying to figure out how to keep the lights on.

"As I said, it was at a ski lodge much like this one, in Austria," he continued. "I had stopped in for a cognac before I finished my final run and met a man at the bar. We started talking and he seemed to be troubled. I asked him if he had had a bad day of skiing and he sighed and shook his head. 'In a way,' he said. 'I'm mourning the loss of my friend. The last time I skied, we were together.'"

The Austrian paused and a melancholy look appeared on his face, like he was reliving the exchange and it had made him sad.

"I told him I was sorry to hear that; it is always hard to lose a friend. He thanked me but told me that it was worse than I thought. He didn't just lose a friend, he caused his friend's death."

I thought of the Finn's comment earlier about a car crash and wondered if that's where the story was going.

"I told him that sometimes we feel we are to blame when bad things happen," the Austrian said. "But he made a noise that told me that I did not understand his meaning. I decided that he was hoping to unburden himself, so I let him continue his tale. Perhaps I imagined it, but I thought I noticed his manner become lighter as he spoke."

The Austrian looked up from his drink and gazed at each of us in the eye, one at a time, perhaps making sure we were paying attention.

"He told me that he had caused the death of his best friend on that very same ski slope the year before," he said gravely. "It had been a year to the day. As we all know, this can be a dangerous sport and we all ski at our own risk. I assumed he and his friend were skiing in an area that was off limits and unsafe, but when he continued I understood that wasn't the case.

"He told me that he and his friend were skiing together on a very difficult run and they were the only two people in that area.

They decided to explore and came upon a cornice. When they looked over, they saw that it was not a cornice but the edge of a cliff, with ice and rocks many meters below."

Here he paused, perhaps for effect, and took a sip of his cognac. I decided that he must be a writer rather than a professor. He knew how to tell a story and keep his audience on the edge of their seats. I even wondered if he was spinning a fictional tale, but didn't mind because it was passing the time and had stopped my obsessive checking of the weather conditions.

I had almost convinced myself that it was just a sad story, but his next sentence made my blood turn cold.

"He told me he pushed his friend off the cliff to his death," he said.

We all slowly looked back and forth at each other, afraid to speak and interrupt the story. By silent agreement, we all remained quiet to see if he would continue. After about twenty seconds he did.

"I can see that I've shocked you," he said. He chuckled, but there was no humor in it. "I thought he must have been telling me a fiction."

I found it ironic that I had just had the same thought.

"The reason I thought this was a fiction was that before he told me he had committed murder, he had told me his name," he said with a smirk. "Sure, you are thinking that he could have invented a fake name, and I thought of that too. But the name he gave sounded familiar to me."

The Swede spoke and I jumped.

"What was his name?"

The Austrian smiled as if he'd expected that very question and was glad that it had been asked."

"He was called Walter Grüber."

He pronounced the W like the V in Volkswagen.

The Finn and I looked confused but the Swede wrinkled his brow like he might have heard the name before.

"You may not know the name Walter Grüber, but you are not Austrian," he said. "Grüber was a reclusive Austrian businessman who married his business partner's wife three months after the partner's death, a death on a ski slope that had been ruled an accident.

"I decided not to admit that I had heard of him. I have seen the American crime movies," he said.

He gave me a nod as if I must have seen them, too, since I was American. The truth was that I had seen them, and I knew what he meant. When the killer lets you see his face or worse, tells you his name, you are not going to live to tell the tale. I didn't blame him for not letting on that he knew.

The rest of the story came out in a steady stream, as if he were running out of time and wanted to get it all out. The snow didn't look like it was letting up, so I didn't quite see the urgency. But it was his story, so I kept my mouth shut.

"I decided it would be best to let him continue and pretend that I did not know the story," he said. "The story he told was very close to the newspaper account I remembered, everything but the fact that it wasn't an accident and instead he had committed murder. Grüber told me that when he pushed his friend off the cliff it was an act of impulse. It wasn't planned, but he had dreamed many times of his friend's death. You see, he had wanted something that his friend had. Not his money or his business, this they both shared. What he wanted was his wife. This was the only thing that he couldn't have, at least while his friend was alive.

"Each time they went rock climbing, hiking, or skiing, dangerous sports they both loved, Walter dreamed of his friend's accidental death. He hoped and hoped that it would happen naturally, but it never did. When he looked down over the cliff that day and saw the rocks below, the temptation was too powerful. He made the decision that he no longer wanted to wait for a natural death. He would help things along. It was the easiest and the hardest thing he had ever done.

"What followed was an investigation into the death. I had also read about this in the newspaper and his information was the same. Grüber told the authorities he and his friend found themselves off of the trail and lost. That his friend had skied up to the cliff thinking that it was just a small ridge and by the time he realized his mistake it was too late; his momentum took him over the edge.

"His ski tracks also went right up to the edge, but he explained that he had cautiously skied over to try and help his friend before he realized how far he had fallen. There was no way for him to reach his friend, and his only option was to ski down the mountain and find help. Of course, by the time he got to the bottom and the ski patrol found his friend's body, it was too late.

"When they asked him why he didn't ski to the mid-mountain station, Grüber told them that he didn't know it was there, but he admitted to me that he did know. He wanted more time to make sure his friend was dead. The police may have scratched their heads, but they didn't question this further.

"There was a funeral for his friend and he played his part like a perfect actor. He showed his grief, which was real grief in some ways. More important, he comforted the widow for the loss of her husband. It was only three months later that he married her."

"'I know you must think that I got what I wanted,' Grüber said to me. 'And I did, in a way.'"

"You see, he did get what he wanted, but he soon realized that the memory of his friend would always be between him and the woman he committed murder to marry. She could not get past the death of her husband. Yes, she married him, but only because she needed him, not because she wanted him. He was a poor substitute for his friend and he found he was more miserable than he had been when his friend was alive.

"Grief and regret began to eat a hole in his heart and he said he couldn't do it anymore. I wondered what he meant by that last comment, but I told myself that if you don't want to know the answer, don't ask the question. I wasn't sure if he intended to go to the police or end his life. So I stayed silent."

The Austrian stopped talking and took a sip of his drink. He readjusted himself in the chair and closed his eyes. Was he finished with his story? Was he going to nod off now, content that he had entertained us?

The Finn must have thought he had finished. "Was that really his name, Walter Grüber?" he said. "Or have you changed the name to protect the innocent."

He gave a nervous chuckle, perhaps unsure if the Austrian would appreciate his joke, and the reference to the previous conversation about guilt and innocence.

The Austrian opened his eyes and looked directly at the Finn.

"Perhaps I have changed the name to protect the guilty," he said.

When the Finn's eyes grew wide, the Austrian let out a loud laugh, like a man who has made a joke he hadn't intended to and was pleasantly surprised. The three of us joined him, but mine was a nervous laugh. I was still a bit on edge from the story.

With that, he got up and walked toward the large window. He stood in front of it, looking out, even though there was absolutely no visibility beyond the glass.

The Finn, the Swede, and I slid forward in our chairs and leaned our heads toward each other so that we could whisper and not be overheard. But when we got into our huddle, no one spoke. Instead, we just exchanged confused looks and shoulder shrugs indicating no one knew what to make of what had just happened.

We heard a loud snap and straightened back up, turning our heads toward the sound. The Austrian was standing at the door with his ski boots on. The snap had been the sound of a buckle as he snapped one into place. He secured the second buckle and stood up. Without looking back, he opened the door and went out into the swirling snow.

I looked at my companions and then turned to gaze at the door, half expecting the Austrian to come back in, stomping his feet and shaking off the snow. We all sat in silence for what seemed like an eternity.

I looked at the chair that the man had vacated. His backpack was still on the floor. I jumped up and grabbed it, preparing to head toward the door to call him back. But some part of me knew that I wouldn't find him in the blizzard.

I looked down at the bag in my hand and wondered if I should just hang on to it and mail it back to him when I got to town, or turn it in to lost and found. I touched the plastic tag I had admired earlier and read the name printed on the card inside. It read Walter Grüber.

***

Even with my minimal grasp of the French language, I could read the article in the newspaper the next day. It seemed that one year to the day after the death of his best friend and business partner on an Austrian ski slope, software developer Walter Grüber had met a similar fate. While skiing alone in France, he wandered off into a blizzard and was never seen again. His body had yet to be recovered and search teams had been forced to suspend the search due to treacherous conditions. Authorities speculate if they're unable to find Mr. Grüber, the summer thaw might provide closure for his widow and her two children from her previous marriage.

DYING IN DOKESVILLE

by Alan Orloff

Destination: Dokesville, South Carolina
Not everyone in Dokesville is concentrating on watching the total eclipse. For two locals, the rich out-of-towners might provide a means of escape, except that easy pickings don't always turn out to be easy, after all.

The annual Peach Festival was a big deal in Dokesville, South Carolina, but not this big.

Visitors descended on the tiny town in the shadow of the Blue Ridge Mountains like hungry locusts on a field of corn. They came in their blocky Winnebagos and shiny space-aged Airstreams, their sporty camper tops and suburban minivans, their sedans and motorcycles. They filled the campgrounds west and south of the city, and they stuffed the cheap motels clustered by the interstate.

The richer ones arrived by air and pulled up to Gracemanor Inn, the town's only posh resort, in hired Town Cars.

Some came for the spectacle.

Some came seeking a spiritual awakening.

Others came to be a part of history, for this was the Great American Eclipse 2017, and Dokesville stood squarely in the path of totality.

They came to get a glimpse of the sun completely disappearing from the sky for two minutes and eleven seconds.

And they all came with their silly paper glasses.

***

Cyrus Tinsley attacked his pecan waffle with gusto, but his girlfriend, LuAnn Haskins, just picked at her hamburger. They were grabbing a quick lunch at the Waffle House before they started their afternoon shifts at Gracemanor Inn. Cyrus was third-in-charge on the four-man maintenance crew, and LuAnn worked her butt off in housekeeping. Although the town was packed, the Waffle House was no busier than usual.

"Something wrong with your burger?" Cyrus asked.

"Never mind my eating. I got something I want to talk to you about."

"OK."

"You know that family renting the luxury suites?"

"Yeah. What about them?" Cyrus poured more syrup on his waffle and spread it around with the back of his fork.

"Well, you shoulda been there last night, Cy," LuAnn said. "You woulda died. I was bringing them some extra towels, but instead of just handing them over at the door, they wanted me to freshen up the bathroom—their words. So while I was tidying up, I heard them arguing. Everyone seemed to be bullying the old lady, who—I found out later from Izzy at the front desk—had gathered everyone together and was paying for the three luxury suites. Calling her names, telling her she was out-of-touch. One of them even called her a bitch."

"Don't sound very grateful," Cyrus said around a mouthful of waffle.

"Not hardly." She pulled a miniscule piece off her hamburger bun and popped it into her mouth. "Her name is Mary Margaret Sesco, and she's the widow of some rich banker-dude from New Jersey. Not just rich. Super rich."

"How'd you find that out?"

"Ever hear of Google? You know, on a computer?"

Cyrus just nodded. He didn't like when LuAnn got all sarcastic. Made him feel small.

"It got me to thinking. Rich people live different than us, and not always better. We could teach them a lesson and solve our problem at the same time."

"What problem?" Cyrus asked.

"Born here, live here, die here. Being stuck in this backward town. That problem." She raised an eyebrow at Cyrus like he was an idiot. He'd seen that look enough to know to keep his trap shut. LuAnn would get to her point without any prompting from him. "When I was leaving their room, I saw the biggest and sparkliest necklace ever. Must have been worth twenty, forty, hell, coulda been worth eighty thousand dollars."

"Whoa." Cyrus swiped his last piece of waffle through a puddle of syrup and forked it into his mouth. LuAnn hadn't taken more than two bites of her burger. Who orders a hamburger at Waffle House, anyway?

"Well, maybe these rich snobs shouldn't be the only ones getting some kind of enlightenment out of this eclipse. Maybe we should get enlightened, too."

"What do you mean?"

LuAnn pushed her plate aside. Leaned in close. "That necklace would buy us a lot of enlightenment."

"Not sure I'm getting your point." Cyrus had a pretty good idea, but he couldn't believe LuAnn really meant it.

"We take it. We sell it. We are free from this place."

"Stealing ain't right."

"These people are so rich they won't miss it. Besides, if we take it, then when old lady Sesco kicks—and let me tell you, she's pretty damn near death now—her bitchy family won't get it. After how they treated her, they sure don't deserve it. It'll teach them a lesson, all right."

"I'm not sure you're thinking straight, Lu."

"Oh, I am. In fact, I've thought this all the way through." She paused, locked eyes with Cyrus. "Listen up, OK? These people came here for one reason, to see the eclipse, right? That means everyone—every single person—will be out on the veranda or the back lawn, gaping up at the sun with those ridiculous glasses. That means the rooms will be empty. What could be easier than taking something from an empty room?"

Cyrus knew from an early age about things that sounded too good to be true. "I'm not sure—"

LuAnn barreled ahead. "I read up on this eclipse. The totality thing happens tomorrow at 2:38. Everyone'll be out back long before then, watching the moon slowly move in front of the sun. Should give you plenty of time to get into the suite, look around, find the stuff, and get out."

"Me?"

She glared at him. "Yes, you."

Cyrus thought about asking why LuAnn didn't just steal it herself, but she was the brains in this relationship, and he, well, wasn't. "I don't know. What if something goes wrong? What if someone sees me in their suite poking around?"

"Just tell them you're from maintenance and got a report their toilet was clogged up. I mean, you do work in maintenance, right? But don't worry, everyone's going to be outside. No one's going to be wandering the halls of the inn. It's why they came to our stupid little town. It's a freaking total eclipse, Cy!"

"Doesn't seem like the right thing to do."

LuAnn reached into her pocket, pulled out a key card and slapped it on the table. "Here's an extra master key from housekeeping. It's unassigned, which means there's no way to trace who's coming and going. Use it to get in. When you're done, just put on a pair of those glasses and go out and watch the sky like everyone else."

Cyrus swallowed, didn't say a thing.

"You want to die in this crappy town? I sure don't." She rose, eyes blazing. "I'm going to the ladies' room. When I get back you better have your mind made up. And let me be clear. This is a deal-breaker. If you want to stay together, you'll figure out the right answer." She stomped off toward the back of the restaurant.

LuAnn spoke the truth. Cyrus Tinsley had been born in Dokesville. Cyrus Tinsley grew up in Dokesville. And unless something drastic happened, Cyrus Tinsley would die in Dokesville.

And Dokesville was a dull place to live. Or die.

Even though it wasn't in his nature to take things that didn't belong to him, LuAnn made a good case. He didn't want to die fifty years from now in Dokesville. Poor. Alone.

He slid the master keycard into his pocket.

***

The next day, just after one o'clock, Cyrus strolled around the back corner of the inn for a smoke break. He lit up under a majestic magnolia tree, watching the crowd of eclipse-viewers. A sense of excitement filled the air as more and more people spilled out onto the veranda and the wide lawn beyond, everyone's head lifted upward, gazing at the sun through their protective glasses. Cyrus had his own pair in his pocket, but he was waiting until after he'd completed his task before putting them on. Sort of a reward for a job well done.

Excited voices floated on the breeze. On the veranda, he spotted a loud group of people who had taken over one end of the deck. At the center of it all, an ancient white-haired woman—Mary Margaret Sesco, no doubt—sat by herself. She seemed to be the only one, besides him, not wearing glasses and gawking at the eclipse.

Cyrus's phone buzzed with a text from his boss: Please check out the icemaker. Kitchen staff says it just cut off.

Can't run an inn without an icemaker. Cyrus dropped his cigarette butt and ground it out with his heel, then hurried off to fix the problem. Part of him worried he wouldn't be finished in time. The other part of him hoped he wouldn't.

***

It didn't take long for Cyrus to trace the problem with the icemaker to a tripped circuit breaker, and he fixed it without any trouble. When he was satisfied that the kitchen could once again serve cold drinks, he glanced at his watch. Show time.

He crept through the main part of the inn to the back stairs, then hustled up the four flights to the top level, which housed three luxury suites. He opened the fire door a smidge and peered out.

LuAnn was right; everyone seemed to be outside. The inn was deserted.

He exited the stairwell and stopped at the landing to look out the back window. He wasn't sure if things had gotten appreciably darker outside, but the quality of the light had changed. Kinda weird. Still fifteen minutes to go before totality.

He walked down the hall to Suite 501, then glanced around. No one in sight, so he removed the master passkey from his pocket. Held it up to the lock sensor. The light flashed green and he turned the knob, slowly pushing the door open. The hinges didn't squeak—he'd oiled them yesterday afternoon, right after LuAnn had outlined their plan.

He slipped in and gently closed the door behind him. Listened for signs that anyone was there.

All quiet.

LuAnn said she saw the jewelry in the bedroom, so Cyrus quickly crossed the large living area—the luxury suites really were quite luxurious—to the master bedroom. The door was ajar; he pushed it back and peeked inside.

An old lady—Mary Margaret—stared at him from her bed, propped up on three pillows.

Cyrus felt as if he'd just been in an elevator that dropped two stories without warning. "Uh, sorry, ma'am."

"Room service?"

"Room service? Yes, yes. Room service," Cyrus said. Maybe if he got her out of the suite, he could still get what he came for. "You know the eclipse is about to happen. The total part of it, anyway. There's still time to go see it."

"It's so hot outside, and I'm not feeling very well. I wanted to be comfortable. I don't need to see it." She tapped her head. "I've got a pretty good imagination. 'Sides, it gets dark pretty near every night." She laughed at her own joke, and that sent her sputtering into a series of coughs. Which in turn blossomed into a full-fledged hacking attack. She managed to squeak out, "Water, please?"

Cyrus just stood there, watching her cough.

"Water!"

He snapped out of it. "Yes, of course. Just a sec." He rushed out to the bar in the living room and fetched a glass of water.

When he'd brought it back to the bedroom, she had stopped coughing and seemed to be holding something beneath the covers.

"I'm OK now. Will you put the glass on the nightstand, in case it happens again?"

"Sure." Cyrus set the glass down, noticed the nightstand drawer cracked open. Had it been open before? He glanced at the clock: 2:28.

Mary Margaret cleared her throat, stared at him for a beat. "I didn't call room service."

He swallowed. "Uh, I must have gotten the rooms mixed up."

"I don't think so." Her hands shifted underneath the blanket. "I don't think so at all."

Cyrus pictured a gun, aimed right at him.

"I know why you're really here."

Cyrus didn't say anything. He figured if he lunged at her, he might get to the gun before she could pull the trigger. She was damn old, after all. Then he could take off with the goods. But he had a tough enough time stealing. How would murder sit with him?

Underneath the covers, the lady's hands wavered. Cyrus's heart raced. One flinch of her bony trigger finger and he was dead meat.

"You came to pray with me, didn't you? The Lord asked you to offer me comfort in my time of need. He sent you."

Cyrus thought about agreeing with her, but lying about what God did or did not do made him uncomfortable. "I don't think so, ma'am."

"Stop ma'am-ing me. My name is Mary Margaret."

"Yes, ma'am. Uh, Mary Margaret."

She fixed him with her cloudy gray eyes. "What's your name?"

"Cyrus," he blurted out, pure reflex, then cursed himself under his breath. Any competent crook would have used a fake name. Although, at this point, it didn't really matter. His main goal now was to get out of the room before she put a slug into his gut. Forget the necklace. Forget LuAnn. Dying in Dokesville looked pretty good, as long as it wasn't today.

"You may not realize it, but the Lord sent you, He most definitely did. He works in mysterious ways, you know." She exhaled, and Cyrus got a whiff of old lady breath. "Like today. Surely blotting out the sun is a sign only the Lord could pull off."

Cyrus shrugged one shoulder. "I suppose."

"I saw you yesterday, fixing the downspout. Thought to myself, what a fine, hard-working young man. This country needs more men like you."

"Thanks." Cyrus couldn't peel his gaze from the covers where Mary Margaret's hands seemed to be struggling to keep the gun pointed at him.

"My whole family can't wait for me to pass so they can get my fortune. You know that? Most of them are good people, just a little greedy, but my nephew Anthony is a real piece of work. Lazy. Wasteful. Mean. My brother didn't show him enough love when he was a boy. Made some poor choices. Broke the law. Broke my brother's heart, too. Long time ago." Her eyes glazed over, hands dipped. Then all of a sudden her head snapped up along with her hands, still working beneath the covers. "You're not like Anthony, are you?"

"I try not to be." He glanced at the clock—2:33—and then out the window. Getting darker. He focused again on Mary Margaret.

Mary Margaret closed her eyes and moved her lips without a sound. It seemed to Cyrus like she was doing a complicated arithmetic problem in her head. After a while, she opened her eyes and spoke in a softer tone. "You've got a good heart, I can tell. I want you to have something."

"Oh?"

"Open up the nightstand drawer."

"Sure." Cyrus took a step toward the nightstand and pulled open the drawer. Looked inside. LuAnn had been right. The biggest and shiniest necklace he'd ever seen sparkled at him. "You want me to have the necklace?"

"Pfft! Why would you want that? Just a fancy piece of glass, is all. My daughter-in-law won't let me wear the real stuff. Too valuable. It's in a safe deposit box back home." She gave a little snort, then started coughing again, wet and deep. After about thirty seconds, she calmed down and continued as if she hadn't stopped to hack up a lung. "Take the Bible."

Cyrus pulled out the good book, encased in a heavily-padded, blue-and-pink embroidered cover. "Uh, thanks and all, but I don't really need a Bible. I'm not very relig—"

"I've had that Bible since I was a child. I'm not giving it to you—I'm going to be buried with it." She nodded, once, emphatically. "Look inside the cover."

Cyrus opened the book. He took a moment to find where the cover stopped and the Bible started, then he worked his fingers inside a flap and wiggled out a stack of bills. Benjamins. Lots of them.

"I . . . I don't know what to say."

"There's more. In the back part, too."

Cyrus flipped the Bible over, repeated his excavation. When he finished, he had a healthy handful of crisp and clean one hundred-dollar bills.

"I want you to have it. The Lord wants you to have it. He's given me a sign. You coming to me in my time of need. To help ease my journey. I can tell you're a little lost, so this money—eight thousand dollars—will help you find your way on your own journey. You don't want to end up like Anthony or any of my other good-for-nothing relatives. They won't miss this money, either, if that's what you're thinking. It's my secret Praise the Lord fund."

Cyrus heard Mary Margaret's words, every last one, but he wasn't sure he understood their true meaning. "You're giving this money to me? All of it?"

"Why don't you leave me a hundred? I'd like to tip housekeeping. They did a fine job with the room, you know, cleaning up after my sloppy relatives."

Just then, the room darkened—a lot—and Cyrus noticed the clock had clicked over to 2:38. Totality time. He went to the window. From his angle, he couldn't see the sun itself, but he got a good view of all the inn's guests gazing up at the sky, most no longer wearing their eclipse glasses. He could hear them whooping and hollering, too, as if the home team had just scored the winning touchdown.

Mesmerized, he watched the crowd celebrate for about two minutes. When everyone put their glasses back on, Cyrus turned away from the window and stepped over to Mary Margaret on the bed.

Her eyes had closed. She wore a serene smile. Her chest no longer moved up and down. Mary Margaret had passed over to the other side, her journey in this world complete.

The covers had slipped down, revealing not a gun, but a rosary with a very large silver crucifix which she still clutched in her lifeless hands.

Maybe there was something to this eclipse thing.

Getting caught with a fistful of money in a dead guest's bedroom wouldn't be the easiest thing to explain to management—or the cops—so he quickly bowed his head to Mary Margaret in a moment of tribute.

Then he stuck a hundred-dollar bill inside an envelope, wrote Housekeeping on the front, and left it on the nightstand.

Eight grand might not be enough to get two people out of Dokesville, but it was enough to get one out.

He hightailed it from the suite and rushed down the stairs, pushed through the back door, put on his silly paper glasses, and watched the glorious sun fully reappear.

THE HOUSE IN GLAMAIG'S SHADOW

by William Burton McCormick

Destination: Isle of Skye, Scotland
A writer's retreat in the Scottish Hills might provide inspiration, but it can also instill fear when a decoded cipher threatens something worse than writer's block.

1989

The red conical summit of Glamaig lay ahead of Nigel Boorman, a path as treacherous as the man upon it. An abundance of slippery scree covered these slopes, the great Corbett a stimulating climb requiring balance, endurance and patience to conquer. One careless step and an unlucky hiker might betray his footing and find himself sliding down the coarse gradient with ever-growing speed, a terrible inertia carrying him along four hundred meters of rock-filled slope, depositing him very much worse for wear into a lonely Highland glen.

But the forty-six-year-old Englishman was determined to reach the apex, where he might gaze out over the other Red Hills south of Glamaig or at the Black Cuillin Mountains that form the backbone of this Isle of Skye. When visiting Sgurr Mhairi, as the Highlanders called Glamaig's summit, Nigel would look across the glittering sound to the rugged Isle of Raasay or seek a glimpse of the Scottish mainland beyond. Stirring vistas materialized with every dawn on Skye, inspiring imagery useful to a professional writer like Nigel.

Most of all he desired to see the spot where his benefactor, Lyle MacPhate, had died, to touch the jagged rocks at the summit where the greatest Highland writer of his generation collapsed after ascending Glamaig eighteen years earlier.

A tragedy for Scotland.

A loss for world literature.

A boon for Nigel Boorman. It made him rich. Or, more accurately, made him once rich, those monies long spent.

Surmounting the summit, Nigel followed a worn, winding path to the place of MacPhate's demise. Flowers, books, and notes left by the literary devout lay pinned beneath stones here, these remembrances weighted down securely to resist heavy Hebrides winds.

Nigel found this makeshift shrine amusing for reasons all his own, a mirth tempered when, after a few minutes rummaging through the mementos to MacPhate, his eyes fell on a black stone dedicated to someone else. On its surface, in wind-smeared chalk, was written "Nigel Boorman."

His pulse, just recovering from the climb, began to rise again.

He lifted the stone.

Beneath was a small, clear plastic bag. He picked up the package, wiped off the grime, and weighed it in his hand. The packet was little more than a sandwich baggie, the contents nothing but the jumbled pieces of a child's puzzle.

Odd.

Nigel felt a knotting dread. He disliked being associated with MacPhate, especially at some ramshackle remembrance on the late author's home island. People were ruthlessly protective of their heroes out here.

Nigel suspected conspiracy. What kind of prankster would climb treacherous Glamaig to play a game with him? And who even knew he'd planned to hike the Red Hills today?

The owners of his writers' retreat in the valley were the obvious answer. The pub-goers in Sconser another. He'd drunk too much the night before. Talked too much. Anyone on Skye could have dropped in at the public house, overhead his ambitious plans to reach Sgurr Mhairi.

He felt his face flush in anger. Well, he sure as hell wasn't going to assemble a puzzle on any windswept hilltop. Nigel slipped the baggie into his jacket pocket, zipped it tight. He was the sole occupant of Gill Hall for the next two months. Plenty of time to figure this out.

He walked away over loose, shifting scree to the edge of the downward slope. Nigel's gaze found his lodgings far below at the foot of the Corbett. Despite being known as a hall, the Gill Writers' Retreat was little more than a stone cottage. A river skirted the building on two sides, a grove of oaks cutting off the view of a small dirt road that connected Gill Hall to the world outside. Roe deer grazed on the golden autumn grasses that grew beside the hall's gate. A perfect scene. A perfect place to write.

In theory.

At this height, nothing looked real to Nigel. The hall, the road, river, trees, and deer were props on a museum panorama, accessories to a child's train set. The view from Glamaig made man's incursions on Skye feel inconsequential.

Nigel took a robust breath, made sure the baggie was secure in his pocket, and began his journey down the slopes of Glamaig.

***

Sitting near the Gill Hall study window, with the river waters rushing below, Nigel typed:

At work
I watch the clocks
At home
Alone
I listen to them

His fingers drummed on the desktop. You're a piss poor poet, Nigel Boorman, you know that? He tore the paper from the typewriter, slipped it into the bin, then caressed his tired brow. Three weeks. Three weeks and less than forty pages, half of those unusable . . .

He calculated the cost per day, the cost per page for staying here. He must be as mad as they said. Nigel glanced at the clock on the desk. Three a.m.

No more.

Nigel set the cover over the typewriter, sat in the study listening to the river outside. Beyond, if he concentrated, if he held his breath, he could hear the distant roar of the sea. Impossibly large, this Highland country.

Nigel breathed slowly. He should be inspired here. This landscape was magnificent, this house's study a miracle, a perfect muse to any writer who ever set foot in Gill Hall. The "Cascading Study" he sat in exceeded in fame the retreat itself. Mirrors positioned on walls and ceiling magnified the small waterfall outside, pulling river vistas in through wide curtainless windows. With the laws of physics reversed by clever reflection, waterfalls cascaded up walls and the river flowed backwards across the ceiling. Except for the desk, chair, and a single black door, the whole room appeared crafted out of surging, white water. London *Times* best sellers were written within this beautiful maelstrom, masterpieces drafted by authors who felt serenity with Nature or the touch of God himself.

Yet Nigel's talents remained inadequate to the wonders around him. All poetry and prose tonight binned.

He sighed. Whisky. He needed whisky.

Nigel exited through the black door, left his comfortable, modern upstairs, and descended a narrow stairway to the ground floor which the absent owners had decorated with stiff period furniture. The whole house in darkness, the only light came from the embers of the dying hearth fire, and above those, from the suspicious, yellow eyes of the Gill Hall cat, its black form lounging on the fireplace mantle.

He flipped on the electric light in the kitchen, found the Talisker Skye whisky and poured himself a glass. As he took a sip, Nigel's eyes strayed across the counter to the puzzle bag he'd left there. He took another drink. He told himself he wouldn't touch that riddle until five pages—publishable pages—were written. But even that magnificent study above couldn't keep him focused on writing or dampen his curiosity about what lay inside that packet affixed with his name.

An itch needed scratching . . .

To Hell with the five pages.

Nigel pulled up a stool, untied the baggie, and depositing the pieces onto the countertop, fended off the cat to assemble the puzzle. It quickly became evident this was a promotional puzzle for Blackadder the Third, Rowan Atkinson and Hugh Laurie dressed in flowery period costumes. Odder still was the handwriting made in marker over the puzzle's face. When assembled the writing said: *Picture the End of Gill Hall* followed by a sequence of numerals and letters:

U35 T41 O23 E12 M53 O39 O21 L21 N23 A24 G33 A21 Z05 R04 E14 O12 F53 S34 N27 N05 E38 A17 O18 O22 C11 D05 A13 T42 Q23 O48 A33 N23 A24 G33 A21 Z05 R04 E14 O12 F53 S34 N27 A05 E12 E28 L56 O23 Z06 X01 D02 A03 C04 U07 I08 Y09 E28 A13 M33 Q05 R04 R31 T43 S34 O33 V23 A15 A12 A21 K27 O42 G23 Z07 E12 A14 O33 A23 A05 P53 P21 D23 T11 O31 E23

A cipher! His favorite hobby at Oxford. Obviously, some old compatriot had come to Skye, discovered he was in residence at Gill Hall and decided to play a trick. After all, Nigel loved Blackadder. He'd even worked on a treatment of his second novel with Ben Elton before it all went sour.

"Picture the End of Gill Hall," he mumbled.

Picture . . .?

Could that be a reference to something other than a mental image? A literal picture? A physical photograph or painting? There was only one picture hung in all of Gill Hall, an observation he'd made while pacing the floors during nights of writer's block.

Nigel retreated to an alcove under the stairs where the picture hung crooked and dusty, half-eclipsed by a potted fern. He pulled the picture from the wall. It was a framed print comprised of ten portrait photographs arranged in two rows of five. He knew them well. They were the first ten authors to reside at the retreat.

Dougal Andrewson, October-December 1968
Fiona Quillan, February-April 1969
Crag MacDonald, September-November 1969
Elspeth Selkirk, LLD, January-March 1970
D. P. MacManus, February 1971
Lyle T. MacPhate, March-May 1971
John F. Reid, October-December 1971
Raymond Philpott, MBE, December 1972-January 1973
Alexina O'Cain, March 1973
William Boyd, April-May 1973

Gifted authors all, conservatively dressed in their portraits as befitting the Tartan Tory affiliations of the Hall's owners. Only grizzly, unshaven MacPhate wore casual clothes, a jumper with the words Townsend Brewery broadly across the breast, a jumper he'd famously been buried in after his heart attack atop Glamaig. Nigel was always surprised they'd included such an informal photograph among the studio portraits.

But who could omit MacPhate? The population would riot.

He took another swig of Talisker and set his mind to the cipher's challenge. "Townsend" was obviously connected to the "end" referenced in this puzzler's note. If one assumed Townsend as the starting point, he thought, then the digits may be offsets from MacPhate's position among the portraits.

This proved correct.

After a few minutes in the kitchen, Nigel moved to the desk in the mirrored study, pipe firmly in mouth, note and picture before him, working out the game. In the end, it was a rather simple cipher for a pro like him, taking too brief a time to be entertaining.

The first numeral indicated the offset from MacPhate, the letters determined the direction of counting. Consonants were counted backward, vowels forward. The last numeral showed the letter to be used within the selected author's name. So that U35 revealed an 'I' from Alexina O'Cain while T41 was an 'F' plucked from Fiona Quillan.

He continued transposing the code. The message when revealed sent a shot of cold adrenaline through Nigel's body:

IF YOU'RE SMART ENOUGH TO READ THIS, BE SMART ENOUGH TO PAY. LYLE MACPHATE COMES FOR HIS MONEY TUESDAY

Nigel leaned back in his chair, those spinning mirrored waters suddenly dizzying. A message from the past, one that stabbed at his heart, turned his skin cold and clammy. MacPhate's death brought fortune to Nigel. Now years later, someone wanted payment for that long-ago-spent wealth.

He thought back to uneasy days. Gulped his whisky.

Nigel had arrived at Gill Hall for the first time in 1975, four years after MacPhate's death. Nigel's own writing proceeded slowly during that first residency until he discovered a complete manuscript stuffed inside a wall crack behind a study mirror. Why the notoriously secretive MacPhate had hidden it remained a mystery, but after sending out feelers to the publishing world, Nigel concluded the work and its subject were completely unknown outside these walls.

MacPhate's loss became his gain.

Nigel published the manuscript under his own name eleven months later. An international best seller, *Remembered Tomorrows,* made his career, brought him fame, women, riches. A series starring Brian Blessed premiered on *BBC One*. A movie adaption in America sold for sixty thousand dollars.

However, Nigel was never able to match this success. Sales of follow-ups, crafted by his own pen, were lukewarm at best, the reviews torturous. He became a "one-hit-wonder." A joke. A hack who somehow produced one masterpiece, then fell out of public favor.

The affairs dwindled. Nigel married for money, a tolerable enough arrangement until Daphne grew tired of supporting him. Now, her alimony to him paid his Gill Hall fees.

Nigel clung to *Remembered Tomorrows*. It was all that sustained him.

And now someone knew his one success in life was a lie.

***

"Mornin', sir," said Gillies, the courier for Hebrides Custom Delivery. "Did you enjoy your hike?"

"I did." Nigel sat on an oaken stump outside the Hall's gate, smoking his pipe. The old deliveryman approached by bicycle, his basket loaded with Monday parcels. The courier resembled an aging hippy forced to conform, with a salty grey ponytail flapping from behind his delivery cap and astrological tattoos peeking out of the cuffs and collar of his drab uniform.

"I even made Sgurr Mhairi. See me up there, Gillies?"

"No, sir."

"Then how do you know I was hiking?"

Gillies slowed to a stop in front of him, dismounted. "Why, I delivered those mountain boots to you weeks ago. Figured you'd put some wear on them, with the great scenery we have around here."

"Fair enough."

Gillies plucked a large parcel from his basket, offered him a pen.

"Another package for you, sir. Sign here, here, and here. Lots of papers for this one."

"Should be. It's a family heirloom." Nigel stood, took the package, and scribbled his name across the documents. "Old dueling pistol from my grandfather. World War One variety. Grandpapa shot some Austrian over Grandma's hand in marriage. Good thing for me he did."

"Dueling pistol? No wonder the special forms. What are your plans for it, sir?"

He looked at the courier blankly.

"Defend the family honor."

"Sir?"

"Kill things, Gillies. Kill whoever creeps over the Gill Hall gate after dark."

***

Three hours later, Nigel fired the family heirloom at stones along the gate wall, pretending they were the faces of Lyle MacPhate's collectors, peeking over at night.

He was a damn good shot, had been since his army days. His string of bulls-eyes remained unbroken until somebody shouted:

"Stop!"

Nigel turned to face the road. A burly constable emerged from a police cruiser two sizes too small for him.

"Good afternoon, Officer."

"Constable MacAskill," he said gruffly, a stern expression above his red whiskers. "You have a license for that handgun, Mr. Boorman?"

"I have a collector's permit to own rare firearms."

"But not a license to fire them?"

"No. Not in Scotland. Not since they changed the bloody law last year."

This answer troubled MacAskill. "Look, Mr. Boorman, I don't want to bring you in. I agree. Why should lawyers in London tell us what to do with our guns up here?" A slight smile appeared within the beard. "My family adores *Remembered Tomorrows*, you know. You've a Scottish perspective rare for a John Bull. Impressive."

"I'm obliged."

That smile expanded. "We've a small jail cell. You wouldn't

like it. No writing desks. We even had Lyle MacPhate in for brawling back in his days. He had to dictate his work to an assistant through the bars. No room for two." He clasped Nigel on the shoulder. "So, stop shooting. All right? Mind that gun only as a collector."

"Certainly."

"Good. We'll chat soon. Sheep are blocking the A87 presently. Can't find anyone else to drive 'em. away."

The officer retreated to his car.

A curious thought came to Nigel.

"Constable MacAskill," he shouted, "how did you know I was firing a pistol?"

"Heard the shots from the road."

When the squad car was lost behind the oaks, Nigel took one last shot at a stone on the wall, listened to the thin pop of his antique gun.

And wondered how anyone could hear it from the road.

***

Tuesday passed. Then five weeks without incident.

Nigel began to tentatively hope nothing would come of the message, prayed he'd made erroneous assumptions about the meaning of the ciphered note. Yet he remained uneasy at Gill Hall and spent his days in the village, writing until closing time at the local pub. Fear became his muse. A plot mimicking life came rushing up from his subconscious. At last, the words began to flow.

Nigel intended to finish the first draft late one Friday night, had the portable typewriter out of his backpack, but was pulled into a conversation with the local pub-goers. He bought them drinks, told the young Scots he was an author researching a detective novel set in Skye. The girl with the perfect bum wanted her copy as soon as it was published. He kept enough sobriety not to take her home.

Sometime past midnight Nigel bicycled back towards Gill Hall. It was a cool night even for November, mist in the air, red Glamaig rising above all save the moon in the heavens. As he followed the edge of the Corbett around, the hills cut off the glow of the village behind. Ahead remained only the homestead lights of his nearest neighbor, Angus MacDonald—weren't they all MacDonalds out here?—and when that house was passed he found himself briefly peddling into darkness, navigating as much by the feel of the bicycle as by sight. He enjoyed sensing the changes of gravel, grass, and mud beneath his wheels, and it pleasantly startled him as it always did when he passed over the hard-stone bridge across the River Sligachan. Now and again he heard the bleating of sheep, and his eyes caught the shaggy shapes of Highland cattle grazing at the roadside.

At last the hills parted, and he saw the outline of distant Gill Hall, the porch lights turned on by his landlord's electric timer. Nigel expected this to be the only manmade illumination, but some hundred meters from the house, at the base of mighty Glamaig, the pinpoint light of a lantern shown. It rested in unsteady hands, or perhaps was buffeted by unfelt winds, for the light with its peculiarly red cast shook visibly.

As Nigel grew nearer the lantern went out.

He waited for it to relight as he rode up to the Gill Hall gate, but the lantern light did not return. Perhaps the owners were climbers attempting a nighttime ascent of Glamaig by moonlight alone. That seemed an ill-advised plan. He thought briefly of poor Alexina O'Cain, lying comatose for years in that hospital on the mainland. He briefly wondered what became of her manuscript here.

Nigel set the bike against the old stone wall, opened the gate and was soon at rest in the mirrored study, the moonlight waters of the river swirling around him. A soothing scene that put him at ease as he composed at the typewriter . . .

Until a coffin rose up the wall.

For a fleeting moment, Nigel believed he'd nodded off, dreaming of impossible things. Or that somebody at the pub slipped a slow-acting narcotic into his beer. But the phantom coffin did not dissipate. It remained inside the room, as visible as his own hand before him. After climbing the waterfall, the casket floated across his celling and down the other wall.

At last Nigel comprehended. The bizarre sight was a reflection up from the river below, twisted by the funhouse mirrors about him. Gazing through the window, he saw the same coffin bobbing among the waters, carried by the current toward a rocky bend at the mouth of the oaken grove.

Up on Glamaig, that unsteady lantern light was shining again.

By the time Nigel exited the house and reached the river, the current had driven the coffin into the edge-water stones, the worm-eaten wood shattered like egg shells.

A skeleton thrown over the rocks.

Nigel's electric torch hid nothing. He saw the empty eye sockets, the long switchblade fingernails, and the rotten fabric of a jumper on the body, "Townsend Brewery" clear as day on the front.

Lyle MacPhate had come for his money.

***

"Vandals, Mr. Boorman," said Constable MacAskill, sitting in a Gill Hall chair, gently stroking the retreat's cat. "Someone's idea of a ghoulish joke. Diggin' up poor Lyle and dumping him in the river. We get sick ones out here sometimes. The vastness of the wilderness can affect the mind . . ."

"I think I was meant to see that corpse, Constable," said Nigel tersely, standing behind MacAskill's chair. "I'm certain of it."

"Why do you think so, Mr. Boorman?"

Nigel balanced answers and omissions. "MacPhate was an alumnus of Gill Hall, I'm in residency now . . . It seems a local has an axe to grind with this retreat. Wishes to drive me away. Probably some sad Skye writer rejected for a place."

"That's a flimsy reason to dig up a coffin, Mr. Boorman. And to deface MacPhate's grave especially. We love Lyle MacPhate out here. He's family to us. If someone means to discredit him, they're from the mainland. Probably not even Scottish."

"Who would trek all the way out here for a prank?"

"With motivation, men will travel anywhere, Mr. Boorman. But I doubt the defiling has anything to do with you personally." He shrugged. "If it did concern you, as you claim, would this tickle your blood?"

MacAskill withdrew a paper from his jacket pocket, a familiar pattern of letters and numbers written across the page:

> *A48 A21 O42 T44 S54 E15 E42 M41 N05 A23 S05 R27 O37 M53 F23 I22 U35 I27 C24 A12 Q53 U26 U27 S23 U05 I12 C54 S01 I21 O24 G55 U35 P54 E38 R28 B28 B47 A24 U24 H42 J42 O05 J12 I31 I32 I37 A33 C06 B05 K04 A14 O22 C05 U14 E41 B34 M27 H05 E16 P28 U46 F26 T47 A21 Z11 E31 J02*

"I found it scrawled in chalk on MacPhate's gravestone near Achachork, Mr. Boorman. Can't make heads or tails of it. Any ideas?"

"Never seen anything like it."

"I read in your book bio, you were a cipher expert at university. Thought you might want first crack at it."

"It's gibberish from some juvenile hooligan."

"Looks like a code to me." The constable returned the page to his pocket, set the cat aside, and stood to leave. "I'll send it to Edinburgh next week. We'll keep you informed of any developments."

"Thanks."

"You leave that pistol in its case. Understand?"

"Of course."

"Where'd you get the gun, anyways?"

"I had it sent from home, had Gillies from the courier company bring it here."

"Gillies is a good man. But he reads his clients' mail. Lost his job at the Royal Mail for it. Spent a year in prison. Been working at different private delivery services since. If you need confidentiality, Mr. Boorman, don't have Gillies deliver anything."

"I'll remember."

"Good."

When Constable MacAskill was out the door, crossing the mossy stepping-stones toward his police car, Nigel shouted:

"Will that cipher be published in the papers?"

"No time soon, Mr. Boorman. We don't want copycat crimes."

"Then do me a favor. Leave a duplicate of the script."

The constable smiled, returned to the cottage, and handed Nigel the note. "You can keep this copy if you agree not to publish it."

Nigel didn't publish it. But as soon as MacAskill was gone he translated the script:

BRING FIFTY THOUSAND POUNDS TO GLAMAIG'S SUMMIT. ALONE. TEN AT NIGHT. SATURDAY.

***

Nigel Boorman's climb to Glamaig's summit was slow going that Saturday. Finding secure footing at night, with a creeping sea fog reducing visibility further, made the ascent tortuously slow. He arrived at Sgurr Mhairi late and found no one waiting. He loitered on the hilltop, more from fear of descent in such weather than any threat brought by his blackmailer.

Cold and tired, with despondent thoughts in his brain, Nigel sat on the rock pile that marked Lyle MacPhate's demise. A chance turn of his electric torch revealed a large stone chalked up with the Boorman name.

Girding his strength for whatever might come, he rose, approached the stone, and moved it aside. Beneath was a ram's horn, rimmed to serve as an alarm or musical instrument. Tape affixed to the horn said, "Blow."

At least it wasn't another bloody cipher.

Seeing no alternative, he blew the horn. It echoed throughout the endless Highland night.

Nothing. He blew again. In some distant vale, dogs barked in response.

The second set of echoes had barely died away when a red glow appeared over the summit's edge, the source somewhere on the south face of Glamaig.

Nigel discarded the horn and withdrew the dueling pistol from his jacket's pocket. Summoning his courage, he walked to the south edge of Sgurr Mhairi.

He was surprised as he looked down. The fog had thickened since his ascent, covering the lower section of the Corbett so that the hilltop Nigel stood upon seemed a perfect cone of red rock floating on an endless, grey-white ocean. The ridge that connected Glamaig with the other, lower Red Hills to the south was submerged below the fog level. Yet the figure of a man could be seen on that ridgetop, standing unmoving within the mists. He might have been invisible save for the red lantern shining brightly in his hands

"You're late, Boorman!" came a voice from below. "Did you bring the money?"

"I did."

"Throw it down."

Adrenaline in his veins and hyperaware, Nigel noticed the lantern light was not directly upon him. Instead, the blackmailer's steady beam remained focused on the Corbett slope five meters below. Atop this summit, he must be little more than a shadow in his opponent's eyes.

Now was his chance.

Nigel raised the pistol. Fired three shots.

The man's body shuddered. The lantern fell and went out. The silhouette sunk into the fog below.

All went silent.

Pulse drumming in his ears, fingers trembling, Nigel reloaded his gun. Then he stood on the summit, his electric torch beam searching the mists. Nothing.

What now?

He could not assume his nemesis dead. Despite all instincts, Nigel trudged down to the ridge, enveloped within the surrounding fog. The dread of blundering blind off some precipice quickly eclipsed the fear of any wounded man. The ridgetop was saddle shaped, deep slants on either side dropping away to sheer cliffs. Beneath his mountain boots the scree shifted and slid, like walking on marbles, threatening to topple his balance with every step.

Nigel crept unsteadily along the ridge's center to the spot where the man had stood, his perception confirmed by the broken lantern just within his torch's range.

Yet there was no body. Pivoting on the unsteady surface, he rotated the beam outward . . .

There!

Down the western slope of the ridge, a man lay unmoving on

the ground, the dark bulky form resting where the incline fell away to a cliff.

Family honor, he thought. Nigel took a few cautious steps down the slope to make certain his blackmailer was dead.

He heard another's boots scaping over loose stones nearby. Heavy breath shifted the fog.

He started to turn, but a brutal shove sent Nigel toppling forward, chest and stomach hard against the ground, pistol jarred from his hand, the torch lens shattered into darkness.

Shock and pain were quickly replaced with horror. He was accelerating forward, sliding faster and faster down the blind slope. Nigel grasped at stones too small to slow his descent. He dug his fingers into the earth, the effort scraping away skin, tearing off nails, but it was too late, the momentum had grown beyond his power to stop. He plummeted through fog and night, sliding toward his death.

Seconds before Nigel Boorman went over the fatal edge, he glimpsed the body, passing near enough in his slide that even darkness and mist could not obscure the figure—the decoy—he'd shot from Sgurr Mhairi's heights.

The man was a straw scarecrow stuffed into an old delivery courier uniform.

***

"If there is anything more we can bring you, Miss Brown," said Gillies, handing the parcel to the latest writer-in-residence at Gill Hall, "please don't hesitate to call. I work all hours."

"It's kind of you," replied the East Anglia poetess, a censure in her gratitude. "But it's Ms. Brown. And I can visit the post office myself."

The courier chuckled. "As you will. But take the roads. Stay off the Red Hills, especially after dark. The scree is deadly slippery when it rains."

She thought of poor Nigel Boorman, two years earlier. "I'm no hiker."

"Wise. If you need letters or manuscripts routed, just give us a ring. We've delivered for all the Gill House greats—MacPhate, O'Cain, Boorman—"

"Goodnight, Mr. Gillies."

"Inspiration, Ms. Brown. I look forward to reading your work."

When Gillies had bicycled out of sight and Sandra was certain the courier would not return, she left Mother's parcel in the kitchen and climbed the stairs to the "Cascading Study." Silently, tense for no real reason, she moved back the ancient looking glass and withdrew the rolled papers wedged into a crack in the wall. The

Gill Hall cat, its black form reflected in every mirror, watched Sandra unfurl the manuscript.

LESSONS OF SGURR MHAIRI
by
Nigel Boorman

It was a nearly complete manuscript. Easily the best thing Boorman had done in two decades. The publishing world, the revivalists needed to know . . .

Or should know. Sandra wondered if anyone else was aware of this novel-in-progress.

Dark possibilities hung on the edge of her consciousness. She could break into the prose fiction market at long last . . . No more academia . . . Who would know?

Sandra flipped toward the end to finish the epilogue interrupted by Gillies's arrival. Clipped to the last page was a scrap of paper, on it a bizarre series of characters:

U28 L53 A48 E44 O42 S23 I29 G45 G44 J51 R24 A33 I21 O42 M28 T27

The soon-to-be-infamous Sandra Brown did not solve the message's puzzle. Somehow, she never considered it a warning.

SUMMER SMUGGLERS

by Triss Stein

Destination: Upper New York State
Playing smugglers and lawmen turns frightening when reality intervenes on a moonlit night along the St. Lawrence River.

One whole summer, in the days when summer lasted forever, we played a game of smugglers and lawmen. "We" meant me and my little sister, Sandy; our cousins, Ricky and Jeff, whose family shared our cottage on the river; my best pal Jack, and whatever random children happened to be in the row of summer cottages any given week. We made the transient ones be the crew while we were the captains.

The surprising part of the smugglers game was not that we played it then but that we'd never thought of it before. Stories of smugglers abounded. How could they not? We were just steps from the cold water of the St. Lawrence River, the border between Canada and New York State. It was only about twelve miles across to Canada if you could avoid the numerous islands. The explorers weren't joking when they named it the Thousand Islands. Actually there were closer to 1,700 as we all learned in state social studies class. Some were big enough to hold small villages and grand mansions, some only had enough soil for a lone stunted tree.

There were winters the river froze right across. We had seen cars parked on the ice and horses racing with special shoes. A person could walk all the way to Canada, bring back anything in a knapsack or on a sled, if he had the right boots. North Country kids, we already knew about the need for good boots.

True, crossing the river in summer would be a substantial canoe paddle but with an outboard motor? Easy. And everyone had an outboard motor.

It was a location made for smuggling.

I was a grownup before I realized that, during Prohibition, silenced boats really did bring whiskey from Canada at night, and I probably knew both the people who had brought it and some who had tried to stop it. Back then, Prohibition was only a couple of generations earlier. In our time, that prosperous and safe American mid-century, it was all just legend.

For our summer-long game, we had teams, smugglers and treasury men or the border patrol. There were arguments about whether there could be treasury women. Believe me, we bossy little girls won that one. We played tricks on each other. We adopted tough names. I was usually Nelly the Knife, except when I changed sides and became Special Agent Strong Hand.

Sandy and sunburned, we messed around close to shore those long summer days and only went inside when we heard our mothers calling us to dinner. No one worried about us there, where everyone knew all the kids on that obscure road with the ramshackle board cottages. Even the post office didn't deliver mail. We picked it up from a forest of mailboxes on posts, where the dirt road met the highway. Did it even have a name then? We always called it Cottage Road.

The only worry was the river, and we'd all been brought up with strict rules about it. As Jack once said, "If I get drowned, my dad will kill me."

Some of those players are dead now and some disappeared from our lives in other ways. Those of us who remain are old, with aches and pains and fears. Now it's the grandchildren who stay at the cottages. Sometimes the great-grandchildren. And those rickety, handmade summer cottages have long since been modernized and winterized.

But when we get together, as we do some summers, we have a barbecue, bring corn just picked from the farm down the road and homemade pies, and sit at the splintery picnic tables watching the sun sink over the great river. The air smells of smoke and lighter fluid and singed meat. We laugh and tell stories and slap mosquitoes, just as we did those evenings all those years ago. We tell some ghost stories, too. And if we have become the ghosts, so what?

My best summer friend was a boy named Jack, middle brother from the big family in the farmhouse at the end of the road. We shared an interest in catching frogs and bugs. As soon as we arrived each summer, I was out of the house and down the road. My little sister Sandy often tagged along, no matter how mean we were to her. She would feed the chickens Jack's mother raised while Jack and I caught up and planned.

That summer when we were ten, his news was that he'd met a retired border patrol man.

We knew about the border patrol. They were the men who asked questions when you drove with your parents over the bridge to Canada and when you drove back. They waved and said, "Have a good time!" or "Welcome back," depending.

Who knew they could actually arrest bad guys? Just like on TV. Jack had just learned this. And that they pursued smugglers, who were practically pirates. He'd heard a lot of exciting stories. Some were even true. We looked at each other and instantly had the same idea.

We couldn't get the words out fast enough, the roles, the adventures, his dad's little rowboat, a signal system between our houses. Secret passwords. A secret oath. Better, a blood oath.

"I can handle the blood," I said with dishonest certainty, "but maybe Sandy would cry. And you know my mom will make us include her."

He nodded. "I'd be stuck with Charlie. And your cousins, too?"

"Ricky? Of course. Maybe even Jeff. And he's an awful little tattle-tale."

"Shucks. OK. No blood. We'll use ketchup."

***

We wrote out rules, and everyone had to sign them in ketchup. Ricky certainly wanted in and because he was almost our age, he mistakenly thought he had some say in things.

We didn't play it every day. Sometimes we just wanted to swim and dig in the sand and sometimes our parents had other plans for us, like chores. Sometimes we had a quarrel, once even with real fighting. We all lied to our parents about the bruises. But the next day or the day after, someone would be at someone else's door right after breakfast saying, "I have a plan for today."

Then Jack's little brother Charlie began to sleepwalk again.

Jack was deeply embarrassed by the baby gate across the stairs to his attic room doorway, but he shared it with Charlie, and Charlie might be found in the morning sleeping on the floor or in bed with Jack or curled up with their big dog. The baby gate was to keep him from falling down the stairs. Once the refrigerator door was open and cereal was all over the floor. Charlie got a scolding and insisted he had not done it.

He never remembered how he got there and the doctor said he would outgrow it. We older kids thought it was funny and weird—he was always "weird Charlie" to us—and we longed to see him some time wandering around, eyes wide open but fast asleep.

On a road where house doors were never locked and car keys were left in the cars, his parents locked the doors to keep him in. They didn't know he could already climb up on the side of the bathtub and reach the bathroom window, and open it to catch the river breeze in those pre-airconditioned days.

He woke up one morning in Jack's bed, babbling about his

nighttime adventure. Charlie insisted that in the night he was lying on the ground in the woods, face and hands scraped.

"I was scared, Jack. At first I was. I cried but then I thought I must be in a dream. And I was confused. I heard the river lapping the dock." He rubbed his tired eyes. "And voices."

Later, his parents insisted he was making it up. Or it really must have been a dream. But couldn't they see the skinned palms of his hands? And the big root in the path to the dock, with a scrap of cloth from his cowboy pajamas? Jack and I had not read Hardy Boys and Nancy Drew books for nothing. We didn't even need to discuss it. We headed to the beach, Charlie holding my hand, sniffling from the morning scolding he'd had.

He told us he heard men's voices and he went to look. In the moonlight reflecting off the water, he could see a boat, like a rowboat but bigger. And grownups, he said. They spoke softly, but every so often a clear word would come through.

We sat him down and demanded more.

"You tell us everything," Jack said, "or you'll be crying over more than Mom scolding you."

Charlie stuck out his chin. "I'm not afraid of you."

"I know you're not, big guy." Jack put his hands on Charlie's shoulders. "But you gotta tell us. 'Cause we're pals."

"I heard 'captain,' I think, and a name. Maybe Harry?" His voice shook a little. "It was dark. I don't want to remember the rest."

"Oh, yes, you do. Now!"

"Tomorrow?"

"No, dopey, right now."

He shook his head. "No, I mean someone said that. I think." He stood up. "I'm going home now. Mom said I shouldn't leave my room. I'm tired, too."

His compact little body trotted up the path. Of course he was tired. He'd been up walking around in the night.

We played and swam, but when we parted, all I had to say was, "What time tonight?"

And all he said was, "After they're all in bed. Stand under my window and signal with your flashlight."

We had done this before.

We didn't know what we would find but we were sure it would be something important. We were on the case. If Nancy could do it, and Joe and Frank, why couldn't we?

My fears that I would fall asleep accidentally were groundless. I was too excited. I'd gone to bed with clothes on under my seersucker nightie. When I heard the grownups say goodnight, and

I could not see a single glimmer of light in the house or a lit cigarette in the garden, I held my breath, carried my sandals and flashlight, and tiptoed downstairs from the attic room. Sandy was sound asleep, worn out by a day of sun and play. Good. We didn't need any little kids on this mission.

Nighttime made the familiar road unfamiliar and spine-tingling. There was a moon and I had my flashlight but I'd never been out this late for any reason. I was relieved when my flash into Jack's window was answered right back and he was on the chilly, damp yard with me in no time.

We pointed our lights down, so we would not trip like Charlie had, and walked the familiar path to the little beach. There was a tumble-down old shack where the trees met the beach, left over from the days when it was a working farm. A spring house, perhaps, with river–chilled sand keeping food cool in the pre-refrigerator days? It was weather-battered, dark and buggy. Our parents said it was dangerous and we had to stay away. Our desire to explore was never quite worth the risk of our being seen and punished.

It was convenient tonight though. We could hunker down behind it, hidden but still able to keep an eye on the dock. We did, too, for what seemed like hours, though the moon had not moved much across the sky. Jack had brought supplies, two candy bars, so that kept us awake for a little while. Just as we were reaching the point of admitting that this adventure was a bust, and it was either fall asleep right there or go home, the gentle rhythmic splashing of the river changed to the steady sound of oars slicing in and out of the water. We peeked around a corner. A large rowboat was edging up to the dock. Someone leaped out onto the dock with a thump and tied up.

The shadowy figures were dreamlike, but the twigs digging into our bare legs and the new mosquito bites told us we were wide awake. I shivered and whispered, "Just the breeze off the river. Chilly."

Jack never moved from his post at the corner of the shack. He motioned to me to put down my flashlight, but I had already done it. No accidental light was going to give us away.

We almost made some noise though when they started walking towards us. Jack and I clutched each other's arms, and muffled our own mouths with our free hands.

They went into the shack. We could not see what they did, but heard one of them curse when he banged into something and someone else say "Shut up" with words we were not supposed to use or even know. Sounds of dragging. Footsteps moving away from the front of the shack and a whispered, "Where you going?"

"Out back to take a leak."

By then we were too scared to giggle at his rude words. He was coming out to the back. Where we were.

He didn't come all the way around the shack. We heard watery pattering on the leaves and his footsteps going away from us. The dragging sounds moved toward the dock. We could tell they were loading something and were busy and now we could not resist taking a peek. We motioned to each other to move back, under the trees, where we could be hidden but still see the beach. We were safe, weren't we, under the trees? It was too dark to see us there.

So we stood up and looked. There was a bright moon reflecting off the water, just enough to see shapes and activity.

They were almost done loading cartons onto the boat. They would row away to wherever they were going, and we could go back to our warm beds, having had enough adventure for one night.

Then one of them pulled something shiny, reflecting the moonlight, from a carton. A bottle. In a flash the whispering became shouting and cursing. Neither of us thought of covering our ears as our mothers would have insisted!

"What the #$&*#? You're taking a bottle, you #$&*#?"

"Hey, just one. Look at all there is. It's the premium stuff. No one will give a #$&*#!"

"Are you crazy? Harry counts it all and it's all his! He'll skin you and all of us."

"Stop me!"

Wrong thing to say. We heard the crash of a bottle breaking. Even in the dark we could see two men jumping a third, throwing him onto the dock. We heard grunts and incoherent words and pounding. We saw it. They pounded and pounded. Then, suddenly, it all went quiet.

We were too scared to move or even to breathe. This was definitely not a game anymore.

We saw two bulky figures lean over, pick something up, grunt some more, and toss it into the water at the end of the dock. The splash sounded like someone diving. But not exactly. After, there were no kicking sounds.

Just when I didn't think I could stand still anymore, they got into the boat and pushed off the dock. Light splashing of oars and then the sound of a motor. We finally started breathing again.

We walked up the path as fast as we could. I could feel Jack next to me, shaking a little, and I'm sure he could feel me, too. We walked too fast to talk, but when we got to my house, he said fiercely, "Not a word, OK? Not to anyone!"

"Of course not. Meet up in the morning? Just us?"

"Uh-huh."

Easier to say than do. Sandy kept dragging on my blanket, whining, "Wake up, wake up. I want to go play!" I kept telling her to go away. When she finally did, it was to our mom who came to see if I was sick. Why else would a child on summer vacation sleep the morning away? When she brought the thermometer I gave up, got up, and pretended I was fine.

Ricky had heard it all though. The boys' room was right on the other side of the plywood wall that divided the attic. I settled Sandy with her pail and shovel under the willow and kept an eye out for Jack, but Ricky would not get lost no matter what I did or said. Not even when I told him I found a raspberry patch in the woods, way, way over there—I pointed dramatically—and said our moms would make pie if he picked some.

He just squinted at me and said, "I know you have a secret." When Jack came to get me, there he was, hanging around no matter how awful Jack was to him. We said we had a plan and he was too little. That didn't work well—he was only a year younger and already taller than me. I said I'd tell his mother about the forbidden comic books hidden under his bed. He said he'd tell my mother I was out after bedtime.

With that, we recognized defeat.

We made him promise never to tell. Jack whipped his Boy Scout pocket knife and said it had to be a blood oath. Ricky never flinched. It's only now, a lifetime later, that I wonder how he did not get tetanus from the knife. We told him about our adventure and he said we were lying. After we took him down to the dock and showed him the pieces of glass, he took his accusation back like a champ.

That was when we saw a white blob in the water, drifting in and out from under the dock. A fish we could try to catch? A fabled giant muskie? A lost toy? I leaned over the dock while the boys held my feet.

"Get me up! Get me up!" I panicked, fearing I would throw up.

It was a hand.

They said it wasn't. I said, "See for yourself." I was close to tears and in a second, so were they.

"What you heard," Ricky gasped. "Falling into the water."

"We have to go to town," I said. "We have to be good citizens and tell someone."

Ricky asked what he could do.

"Go back and tell the moms we're walking to town for ice cream."

"No, the library would be better," he said. "They'll say it's too early for ice cream and not let us go."

He had a point.

And so the three of us marched into the village center together and walked right into the little storefront village satellite office of the county sheriff and told our story. Jack knew the deputy on duty, so he led off. He wasn't afraid. I told myself I wasn't either.

"Playing cops and robbers, were you?"

The deputy's smile was an insult.

"No, sir. No, sir! We know what we saw."

"Now what did you really see? Middle of the night, you can't see much and the dark plays tricks." He smiled again. "Bet you saw ghosts too."

Ricky stepped up and, without a word, put his hand in his pocket and slapped something on the desk. It was a piece of glass with a bit of a label on it.

The deputy sheriff suddenly looked interested. "Where'd that come from?"

"I took it off the dock this morning. There's a lot more."

"Really? More?" He drummed his fingers on the desk, then came to a decision. "You kids just step out on the sidewalk for a minute. I have to make a phone call. Better yet,"—he handed Ricky a couple of dollars—"go across the street." He pointed to the nearest ice cream shop. A summer town, we had several. "Get yourselves ice cream cones and when you've eaten them, come back here. Got that?"

We took our time, got double scoops, walked up the little main street while we ate them, checking things out. A big tour boat, all windows and decks, was at the dock, playing music. Early as it was, a handful of tourists were already lining up at the docks waiting to take a boat tour of the islands. Sugary, chocolaty smells poured from the fudge shop. We debated using the change from the ice cream to buy candy and decided it was a mistake to mess with a lawman's money. We looked at fishing gear in the window of the shop near the boat rentals and waved to the man at the bait stand. We did stop at the library, but it would not open until later.

What we did not do was talk about what might happen next.

Finally, we turned back.

There was a new car in front of the office. It said Border Patrol in bright letters on the door. They took us home in the sheriff's car, with the other one right behind. How much trouble were we in? Could they arrest us for wandering at night without our parents knowing?

Finally Jack, the local kid, got up the courage to ask.

“Why, son, you are not in trouble. You kids told us something that just might be useful. We’re going to take a look. But you saw something you weren't meant to see, so we are just a little concerned about that. That’s why we’re going to talk to everyone's parents, me and my buddy from the border patrol.”

We looked at each other with relief and fear. What would our parents say about our completely against-the-rules adventure? That was a lot scarier than the men we’d seen. And we all knew we were too old to claim we didn’t know the rules.

“Sir. Officer. Uh . . .”

“Deputy will do.”

“Our parents will be so mad. At us. I mean, really mad.”

Jack and Ricky nodded emphatically.

“My dad,” Jack said, “he doesn't believe in excuses. He’s going to be . . . I don't know. Really mad. Smoke coming out of his head mad.”

“I know your dad.” Was that deputy grinning? “He doesn’t seem all that scary to me.”

“You don’t know him well enough then.”

“Leave them to us, OK? Maybe we can get you off with just a day in your room or something.”

They went to our cottage first but soon we saw Jack’s mom hustling down the road. His dad was at work but mine was there, since we were on vacation.

They all told us to sit on the porch and wait and not move even a step.

We didn’t move.

Then the two officers went down to the dock and when they came back, they looked very pale under their tans.

Our moms called us in. Ricky was sent off because he hadn't actually done anything, so we didn't speak to him for a week. Or a few days, anyway. Jack and me? We got read the Riot Act. Out at night after bedtime. The dock at night. Playing around the forbidden shack. Not telling them what happened. The list went on and on.

It ended with the worst. “What they just told us is scary. You could have gotten hurt! We trusted you both to obey the rules and have more sense.” So then we could feel guilty on top of the rest.

It was actually the second scariest thing. The worst was Jack’s mom’s last words. “Wait till your father gets home.” That phrase put fear into the bravest heart.

Funny thing was his father was not as mad as Jack steeled himself to expect. The deputy sheriff had reached him before he got home. We only learned that days later from one of Jack’s sisters.

A much longer time later, after we were home and school had started, Jack sent me a clipping from the weekly Thousand Islands paper. A prominent local boatyard operator nicknamed Captain Billy had been arrested for running a liquor smuggling operation. A connection was suspected to a body found in the river on the U.S. shore in August.

I read it about a hundred times. I put it in my treasure box with three Girl Scout pins, a signed photo from my favorite Mouseketeer, and some campaign buttons with JFK's picture.

We had a few more summers when the days rolled out ahead of us forever, but we never played smugglers and lawmen again. Never even talked about it. Then things changed. My aunt and uncle shockingly got a divorce and the cousins would only come for a week or so. To my surprise, we missed Ricky, and even his little brother.

And then there were summer jobs, driving lessons, summer school, and we would only be at the cottage on and off. Then college. I went off to study art. Jack's R.O.T.C. scholarship saw him through engineering school, and he owed some years to the military. When I was in grad school, protesting that pointless adventure in Vietnam, he was there fighting. He didn't come back. I was shocked and grieved but the truth was that it had been a long time since we were close.

That treasure box came to hold a dried-out prom corsage, a silly pajama party photo, a letter from a favorite author. My college acceptance letter. And in time, the box was lost as I moved around and my parents downsized.

Sandy bought out my share of the cottage after our parents died. I was welcome to come for a week or two and I did, teaching her kids and mine and, in due time, my grandkids to build sandcastles and cook hot dogs on a stick.

Sometimes Charlie joined us for a barbecue. His sisters scattered but he kept the old house for vacations and every few years we'd be there at the same time. As adults, we became close, professors whose paths occasionally crossed in real life. Who would have expected it when he was a weird little kid who tagged along in our games?

The other night, he mentioned a sleepwalking grandson, and memories I had somehow misplaced along the way came rushing back to me.

"Do you remember? The time you really saw something scary? And we made you tell us? Don't you remember?"

He didn't, though he started laughing about the cereal on the kitchen floor.

But I remembered every moment that I had mostly forgotten or thought we'd mixed up with our game.

The shack was long gone, the rough path to the dock grown over with maple shoots and a smooth new stone one laid down nearby. The wooden dock was destroyed in a winter storm and replaced with metal. But I saw that dark night so clearly, heard the threatening noises, felt the breeze off the river. It seemed as if I could turn and see Jack next to me, hear him whispering some plan for a game that would last the whole summer.

THE JAMAICAN ICE MYSTERY

by John Gregory Betancourt

Destination: Caribbean Cruise
When you're octogenarians and successful mystery writers, a little theft and murder is just the thing to spice up a cruise to Jamaica.

"I despair," said Martin Leroy, frowning. From his deck chair, he raised his glass to the brilliant Caribbean sun, now setting across the cruise ship's port side, and sighed. He studied the yellowish liquid through thick, horn-rimmed glasses. "Gimlets are a lost art."

"You're showing your age, old man," said his writing partner, King Danforth. Trim with short silver hair, at eighty-nine he still had a vitality that a sixty-year-old would have envied. "Time you switched to something modern. Nobody drinks gimlets anymore. Haven't since the sixties."

"I think the bartender used lemon juice instead of lime," Martin went on glumly. He sniffed the cocktail. "I definitely smell lemons!"

"And probably canned lemon juice at that," said his wife, Helen. "But when you have a body like that man's, you don't have to know how to mix a gimlet. He looks just like Tab Hunter!"

She settled her plump form on the deck chair next to Martin and fanned herself slowly with the brim of her pink straw hat. At eighty-six, she was the youngest of the party.

The Danforths and the Leroys were relaxing on the *Jamaica Queen*'s deck following an exquisite buffet dinner, enjoying a languid tropical evening. The temperature hovered around eighty, and a light salt-scented breeze swept across the deck. The ship's engines thrummed beneath their feet. Other passengers clustered at the tiki bars, splashed in the pool, or played shuffleboard. From the main salon came the sultry tones of a blues singer.

They seldom needed reasons for taking cruises—the four of them had managed at least one per year for most of the last sixty years—but ostensibly this time they were celebrating the Danforths' sixty-fifth wedding anniversary. King and Martin had been writing partners almost as long, penning the Leroy King mysteries, editing *Leroy King's Mystery Magazine*, and generally enjoying the fame and fortune brought by selling ninety million books worldwide—not to mention two television shows, a string of movies, and a Netflix miniseries (though the less said of that one, the better, everyone agreed).

Carol Danforth leaned on the railing and gazed out to sea. "Do you remember our first cruise?" she asked.

Helen snorted. "Like yesterday. Before we made it to our first port, we had a murder aboard ship!"

King turned, eyes sparkling. "Those were the days!" he said. "The unsettled '60s! A mystery in every port! We haven't had a decent murder to solve in decades."

"Thank goodness for that!" Helen said. "You two aren't detectives, you're writers. Count your blessings that everything is quiet and peaceful these days. And besides, you're much too old to solve crimes!"

Martin said, "You're only as old as you feel, m'love."

He took a sip of his gimlet, grimaced, and set it down on the little table between his deck chair and his wife's. "This drink is a crime," he said. "I don't think there's gin in it, either. It might be vermouth. I should have words with the captain about it."

"Don't you dare—" Helen began.

"Look!" said Carol, turning and gazing wide-eyed up the deck. "You spoke too soon, Helen. I think something has happened."

A white-uniformed porter was hurrying toward them. Blond, blue-eyed, maybe twenty-two or twenty-three years old, he had clearly spotted the Danforths and Leroys and was zeroing in on them.

King Danforth straightened. "Ten dollars says it's murder!"

"You're on," said Martin, grinning. "He's not panicked enough for murder. Clearly it's theft!"

Helen laughed. "You both need to clean your glasses. Can't you see he's carrying a note? Clearly your publisher is trying to get in touch. Did either of you remember your phones today?"

King and Martin began patting their pockets.

"I swear," Helen said, "if your heads weren't attached . . ."

"I have your phone, King." Carol swiftly pulled a cell phone from her purse, poked at it, and announced, "Nothing from your publisher, but you have an email from your foreign rights agent. She just sold Russian language rights to *Murder Strikes Out*. Doesn't look urgent." She tucked the phone away. "My ten bucks is on the captain."

"The captain?" Martin frowned. "I don't think the captain was murdered."

"I'm sure he wants to have dinner with the famous Leroy King.

Tomorrow, we'll all be seated at the captain's table!"

The porter drew up before them. Sure enough, he had an envelope in his right hand.

"Mr. Danforth?" he asked, looking from Martin to King and back again.

"Here," said King.

Silently, the young man handed him the envelope. King opened it, read the handwritten note, and nodded. He kept his face carefully neutral.

"Give us two minutes," he said.

"Thank you, sir." The porter turned and jogged back the way he'd come.

Martin grabbed his cane and levered himself to his feet. "Well?" he demanded, trying to see the note. "Who wins the big money?"

"It's a tie," said King. "There's been a murder." His lips pressed together. "And a theft. In the suite next to Carol's and mine, apparently. And the captain wants to see Carol and me. Unfortunately, I don't think it's a dinner invitation."

"Hmpf. Probably wants to ask if you heard any mysterious screams or the thumps of bodies hitting the floor," Martin said. "Well, let's go!"

"He doesn't want you, dear," said Helen, fanning herself with her hat again. "Just the Danforths."

"Stay here if you want, but I'm not getting left out," said Martin. "This could be our next big case!"

"You don't have cases," grumbled Helen. "You're writers. Not that that's ever stopped you."

Carol said, "Next door? It has to be that nice Mrs. Peabody. Do you remember her, King? She borrowed our ice bucket last night."

"I remember someone knocking . . . Was it about ten o'clock?"

"If you'd ever get your nose out of your laptop, you'd see more!"

"Clearly you have a vital clue to the time of death," Martin said. He pointed with his cane. "Tally ho! Off to the crime scene!"

"I see where this is heading." Helen sighed and climbed to her feet. "Lead on, Macduffs! And don't let the maguffins bite."

***

They found the captain standing in the doorway of the suite next to the Danforths'. He wore a white uniform with large gold buttons, gold braid at the shoulders, and a white cap with a shiny black brim. His hands were on his hips as he watched something inside.

Then he noticed them and turned, shifting his body to block

most of the doorway from their view. He couldn't be more than forty years old, King decided. Despite his command position, the man's face held none of the age lines he and Martin now sported.

"I'm King Danforth, from 305." King stuck out his hand. "You wanted to speak to my wife and me, Captain?"

The captain shook hands automatically. His grip was firm but not overpowering. King leaned forward slightly and peered around him into the foyer of Suite 307. Two men in white ship's uniforms were covering what appeared to be a body on the floor with a sheet.

"I'm Captain Ingalls," he said, not smiling. He reached back and pulled the door closed, then indicated the passageway to his left. "If you'll come with me? The authorities in Jamaica asked me to take statements before we reach port tomorrow."

"What sort of statements?" Martin demanded. He'd come up beside King. "Should we have our lawyers present?"

"This is my writing partner, Martin Leroy, and his wife Helen." King indicated the Leroys. "They're in the next suite down, 303. And this is my wife, Carol."

"Writing partner?" Captain Ingalls's brow furrowed. "I know who you are—you write those Leroy King Mysteries. Someone told me you had shipped out with us. My parents read your books all the time."

The captain shook hands with everyone. Then he lowered his voice, so only they could hear.

"Mrs. Peabody is dead, and it looks suspicious to me. I reported it to the authorities in Jamaica."

"Poisoning is always suspicious, I'd say," said Martin, leaning on his cane.

The captain did a double-take. "How—?"

"The color of her skin," explained King. "I only caught a glimpse, but that blue-gray hue isn't natural, even for a corpse."

"Has to be cyanide. Just like in our book, *Blue Death*, right, King?" Martin nodded sagely. "Clearly someone had it in for Mrs. Peabody."

"You knew her—Mrs. Peabody?" The captain looked at each of them.

Carol spoke up. "She borrowed our ice bucket last night to chill some champagne. We chatted for a minute or two."

"Champagne," said Martin. "That reminds me. I want to lodge a complaint about the bartender who made my gimlet this afternoon—"

"The captain doesn't want to hear about an incorrectly made drink," Helen said. "This is a murder investigation, dear."

Captain Ingalls said, "I need to get your statements in writing.

Is this a good time?"

King nodded. "Sure. We're all happy to help."

***

The four of them followed Captain Ingalls to a small, wood-paneled meeting room with a long rectangular table and a dozen tall-backed chairs. Not enough room to swing a dead cat, as Martin might have said. A red-headed kid dressed in white, no more than eighteen or twenty, already sat at the table with a laptop.

"This is Dennis, the assistant bursar," Ingalls said, giving a broad smile and nod to Dennis, who grinned and wiggled in his seat like a happy puppy. "He'll take notes while I go through the list of questions the police sent."

The captain started with Martin and Helen. Neither of the Leroys had heard anything suspicious the night before. Martin had turned in early, and Helen soon followed.

"Asleep by nine o'clock," Martin said. "One too many gimlets, I'm afraid. The bartender in the main salon, he knew how to make them."

"But not when to cut off customers who had too many," his wife added pointedly. "Martin was asleep and snoring by nine. I can attest to that. And I couldn't hear anything over the racket he makes." She lowered her voice conspiratorially. "Deviated septum, I think."

Martin snorted. "Now who's sharing too much?"

Captain Ingalls said to Dennis, "Put down that they did not see or hear anything unusual the night of the seventeenth."

"As for me," King said, "I vaguely recall someone knocking on the door, but I couldn't say exactly when. Sometime around ten o'clock, I think. I didn't see Mrs. Peabody at all. I was revising the final chapter of *Aloha, Murder!* in the bedroom."

"She knocked on the connecting door between our rooms," Carol said, "and I remember glancing at my watch. It was exactly 9:58."

"This could be important," the captain said. He nodded to Dennis. "Be sure to put that down: 9:58 exactly."

"Yes, sir," said the kid, typing.

Carol continued, "She introduced herself, we chatted for a minute about the trip, and then she asked to borrow our ice bucket to chill a bottle of champagne. She said she didn't have a bucket in her suite, but I think she really wanted to meet King. She asked me if he wrote the Leroy King books, and I told her he wrote them with Martin. She seemed like such a nice young lady. Very polite."

At that, the captain smiled. "I guess age is relative," he said. "I thought she was a nice older lady. She had to be nearly fifty."

"A mere child," said Martin with a dismissive wave of his hand.

Carol continued, "After that, I looked at Facebook on my iPad and answered fan emails. King stayed up till a little after midnight. When he's working on a book, he's in a world all his own. I don't think he would have heard a scream for help even if it came from next door."

"Of course I would have," said King. "But poison is a quiet killer. I didn't hear a sound."

"When he finished, we both went to bed. It was a little after midnight."

"Thanks," said the captain. "I think that's all we'll need for now. Of course, the authorities may want to interview you once we reach Jamaica. I trust you'll make yourselves available, if needed."

They all agreed.

Dennis sent the statements he had typed up to a wireless printer, then went to retrieve them. As they waited for his return, King asked the question that had been bothering him.

"Your note said there had been a theft. May I ask what was stolen?"

"One of those collar necklaces. Aren't they called chokers? It had a large diamond in the middle, with three lines of smaller diamonds on either side. Mrs. Peabody wore it to dinner last night, and when I went to her room, it seemed to have disappeared." He looked a little embarrassed. "I told her to keep it in the bursar's safe, but she just laughed."

"You had dinner with her?" Martin asked, eyebrows rising.

"The Peabodys own a significant amount of company stock. Several million shares, in fact. Dining at the captain's table is one of the perks."

King blinked. Several million shares of stock had to be worth twenty or thirty million dollars.

He said, "She's not—Amelia Peabody?"

Her nasty divorce from a real estate mogul had filled the tabloids for months. All that name-calling, back-stabbing, and never-ending accusations of everything from hiding assets offshore to infidelity on both sides . . .

The captain nodded. "Her divorce was just finalized, and she was going to meet some friends in Jamaica to celebrate."

Dennis returned at that moment. Once they reviewed and signed their statements, the captain collected the pages and left to find more potential witnesses.

"So much for dinner at the captain's table," King heard Carol mutter under her breath.

***

They returned to the Danforths' suite in a more subdued mood. Martin immediately rang the steward and ordered drinks: a mojito for Helen, a strawberry daiquiri for Carol, a vodka martini for King, and a gimlet for himself.

King shook his head. "You never learn!"

"Sometimes they get it right," Martin said defensively. He opened the sliders onto their tiny balcony, letting in a gust of salty air, then plopped down on the sofa. "Amelia Peabody, a fan of our work. Who would have guessed?"

"She had to be one of the richest women in America," King said, settling into an armchair. Helen sat next to her husband on the sofa, and Carol took the other armchair.

"I wonder . . ." Martin glanced at the closed door between the Danforths' suite and Amelia Peabody's.

"What?" said King.

"Did she really want to borrow your ice bucket, or was it an excuse to try to meet you?"

"She was holding a champagne bottle when she knocked," Carol said. "One of those skinny half-size ones." She slapped the arm of the chair. "Darn it! I forgot to mention that in my statement."

Helen laughed. "I don't think it matters."

"I was trying so hard to remember everything, too."

"Of course it matters," said Martin. "It proves she really wanted the ice bucket and wasn't visiting to gawp at King."

"Ten o'clock's a little late for champagne," said Helen. "Unless . . ."

"Unless she had a date!" said Carol.

"A romantic evening rendezvous." Helen giggled. "She did have quite a reputation, according to the *Tatler*. They called her the Nantucket Nympho!"

"You and those trashy tabloids," growled Martin.

"I don't think the thief will get away with it," said Carol. "A necklace that big is going to be hard to hide."

King said, "If I stole it, I'd pry out the stones and dispose of the setting. Loose diamonds are a lot harder to identify. And a lot easier to hide."

"But the gold in a choker would be worth thousands," Helen said.

"Chicken feed, if the diamonds are good quality," said Martin. "What's a few thousand in gold versus a quarter million in gems?"

"But the murderer would still have to dispose of it."

"Simple enough." Martin glanced pointedly at the balcony.

"Toss it overboard."

"Agreed," said King. "That's how we'd plot it for a book. But we still don't have a suspect."

"How about the captain?" said Helen. "He knew about the necklace. He saw it at dinner."

"He's gay," said King.

"What!" said Martin. "No!"

"No wedding ring, not that it means much in and of itself. But didn't you see how he looked at Dennis?"

"Oh . . .?" said Martin. Then, "Oh!"

"It's OK," said Helen, patting his knee. "You're always the last to know. I noticed, too, King. A little more than fatherly affection there, I'd say. Besides, the good captain wasn't Amelia's type. According to the *Tatler*, she liked her boy-toys young and hunky."

Martin snorted. "Sounds like the bartender who ruined my gimlet!"

"Why not?" said Carol, turning. "A bartender who can't mix drinks might not be a bartender at all."

"A fake!" said Helen, warming to the idea. "Why, I bet he took the bartending job under false pretenses, hoping to find a sugar-mama on the cruise!"

King said, "Amelia Peabody certainly qualifies."

"I hate to rain on your murder theory," said Martin, "but a gold-digging bartender wouldn't murder her. She's worth far more alive to a gigolo."

"Mmm." King chewed his lip. "The bartender wouldn't be our murderer, then. But the bartender can still be our thief. What if it's a crime of opportunity?"

Carol said, "You mean the bartender showed up, found Amelia dead or dying, and swiped the necklace?"

"Exactly. He'd spent days wooing her, finally got an invite to her cabin for champagne and la-de-da, showed up only to find she'd started the party without him . . . with poisoned champagne. With her out of the picture, he'd have to start over and find a new patron. He'd want to be compensated for lost time and effort. He might even think the necklace was his rightful due."

"It's too hard to poison champagne," said Martin. "It's sealed with foil, a cork, and a metal tie. Better to poison an accompaniment—say, Beluga caviar. Or crackers."

Helen said, "Ooh, Beluga caviar, that's good. It could have been sent by her sleazebag ex-husband in a gift basket. Amelia would never suspect a bon voyage present—especially if it came with a card signed with her best friend's name. And her ex would certainly know which name to sign."

Helen clapped her hands. "Brilliant! But where are the gems now?"

"The bartender wouldn't risk having them on his person," said King slowly. "He'd have to stash them somewhere safe."

Carol said, "Maybe . . . the ice bucket? Fill it with water and ice, and you'd never see loose diamonds at the bottom. He could leave it in her room and pick it up later."

"Almost a Purloined Letter solution," said King, beaming at his wife. "Ingenious."

"Still, the Jamaican police will search Amelia's room," said Helen. "There's a chance they'll find the diamonds."

Martin snorted. "Does Jamaica even have a forensics team? More likely a couple of cops will show up, photograph the body, remove the bottle and glasses for fingerprinting, and poke around for obvious clues. As long as the bartender beats the maid into the room, he can retrieve the ice bucket and get away clean. Who would suspect a bartender carrying an ice bucket of smuggling, if you'll pardon the pun, ice? Even if the Jamaicans do have a forensics team, they'll be looking for fingerprints on the outside of the ice bucket, not the inside."

They all stared at each other.

"Could be," said King. "Could just be." Then he laughed. "Or not. Maybe we can use it as the plot of our next novel."

At that moment, a knock came at the door. Carol rose and admitted a bartender—the hunky one who looked like a young Tab Hunter, dressed in his usual suave white jacket and black bow tie over too-tight white Bermuda shorts. He set the tray of drinks on the coffee table, accepted a five dollar tip from Carol, had her sign the check, and gave her a wink on the way out. Carol blushed.

After the man had gone, Martin sipped his gimlet and made a face. "Thief or not," he growled, "that man is no bartender."

***

They reached the Montego Bay port early the next morning. The four of them stood at the rail as the giant cruise ship eased up to a long wooden pier. It took surprisingly little time before it slowed to a stop. Crewmen flung giant ropes down to dock workers, who looped them around pylons.

While most of the passengers hurried to disembark for the two-day stopover, lured by the blue sea, the dazzling white beach dotted with palm trees, picture-postcard palm-thatched buildings, and all the tourist shops, the Danforths and Leroys found excuses to linger on deck, watching.

Twenty minutes after the other passengers had disembarked, a police squad arrived on foot, lugging cameras, crime scene tape, and cases of various shapes and sizes. There were six of them on the team, four dark-skinned men and two women, all in short-sleeved uniforms.

"Listen to this," said Carol, poking at King's phone with one finger. "Wikipedia says Jamaica does have a forensics team—the Institute of Forensic Science and Legal Medicine. They're headquartered in Kingston."

"I stand corrected," said Martin. "Probably had to scramble to get here as fast as they did. Kingston's a good bit away."

"Look!" Carol pointed to the pier. "I bet those people are waiting for Amelia."

A small group of men in Hawaiian shirts and shorts and women in bikinis and colorful hats stood on the dock looking up at the ship expectantly. One woman had a cell phone in her hand.

King and Martin exchanged a glance.

"Do you suppose we ought to . . ." Martin began.

But then Captain Ingalls appeared on the gangplank and approached the waiting group. After a moment several of the women began to cry. The men led them away.

King swallowed and, to his surprise, found a lump in his throat.

"Damn it," said Helen. "Amelia didn't deserve to die."

"Let's get off this tub," King said, his voice husky. "I think we all need a change of scenery."

***

By nightfall, the day's fun had begun to wind down: too much good food, too many tropical drinks (and the occasional gimlet), and a long but enjoyable day of touristing had taken its toll. Martin kept asking, "Why did the Jamaican chicken cross the road?" then broke up laughing because, for the life of him, he couldn't remember the punchline. King's yawns grew wider and his eyes drooped. Helen had nodded off at least once in the restaurant, and Carol looked ready to follow.

By unspoken mutual consent, they headed back to the *Jamaica Queen*. Martin's cane kept him from falling several times. They finally reached the gangplank, boarded, and made their way to their suites. Crime scene tape covered Amelia Peabody's door. No one was getting in there.

King pulled out his keycard and was just about to put it in the lock when Carol grabbed his arm.

"The door's ajar!" she whispered. "Someone's been in our room."

King stared down. Sure enough, the door hadn't quite closed.

Frantically, he motioned to Martin and Helen, and they teetered over to join them.

“What’s up—” Martin began, but King motioned for quiet and pointed at the door. Martin frowned and nodded. He raised his cane like a baseball bat.

The door to their suite suddenly opened and they came face to face with the Tab Hunter bartender. And he was holding an ice bucket. He smiled like nothing was wrong.

“I’ve left drinks on your coffee table, with the captain’s compliments,” he said smoothly. “He wanted to thank you for all your help.”

“That’s kind of him,” said Carol. She glanced at the ice bucket in his hands and reached for it. “Is that for us? We loaned ours to Mrs. Peabody next door.”

For a split second, he looked confused, then he said, “I’ll just get you some more ice.”

Stepping around her, he started down the hall. Martin leapt forward and hooked the man’s ankle with the handle of his cane.

The bartender went sprawling. The lid of the ice bucket popped off, and water sloshed across the carpet. As it seeped in, a glittering trail of sparkling diamonds was left behind.

On hands and knees, the bartender frantically began scooping them back into the bucket.

“Tab, honey!” said Helen as she plopped her two hundred pounds down on his back. The breath whooshed from his lungs. “Tell me you love me like you loved Amelia!”

Carol dropped onto one of his legs, and King sat on the other. The bartender flailed, but couldn’t get up.

“I better find the captain,” said Martin. “Damn it, I wish I had my phone. This calls for a picture!”

“Here, I have King’s,” said Carol. She pulled it from her handbag, thumbed it to the camera setting, and handed it to him. “It’ll look great on your Twitter feed.”

Martin circled and snapped a dozen quick photos. The bartender groaned. Carol smoothed her hair, and Helen grinned. King posed like Mickey Spillane. Somehow, he thought he came across more like Mickey Rooney.

***

By the time Martin returned with the captain and two burly crewmen, the bartender had stopped struggling. King told Captain Ingalls their theory—that it had been an impulse crime, not a murder—and, sobbing a little, the bartender confessed.

“She was dead when I got there,” he told them all. “I didn’t kill her! I didn’t!”

“Lock him up,” the captain said, and the two crewmen half led, half dragged him away. Then, looking at the four of them with new respect, he added, "I'll summon the police."

"But the murder isn't solved," said King. "Just the theft of the diamond choker."

"You haven't heard? The police solved the murder hours ago," said Captain Ingalls.

"Let me guess," said Helen. "Mrs. Peabody's husband?"

The captain nodded. "He sent a gift basket filled with her favorite foods, all stuffed with rat poison. He says he just wanted to make her sick. Never thought it would kill her."

"We suspected as much," King said.

Helen and Carol had been picking up the diamonds and dropping them into the ice bucket. They stood and offered the bucket to the captain, who took it by the handle.

"Tomorrow," he said, "I hope you'll all have dinner with me at the captain's table. I'd love to hear how you worked all this out."

"We'd be delighted!" said Carol. And, under her breath, King heard her add, "Finally!"

DEATH AT THE CONGRESSIONAL CEMETERY

by Verena Rose

Destination: Washington City
Is a man found dead the victim of retaliation for the beating of a Congressman? Or is the reason for his death a result of tensions growing between pro-slavery and abolitionist elements in the nation's capital? Constable Zeke Wallace investigates.

Washington City
1860

Since the mid-to-late 1850s, Washington City had become a hotbed of contention. Unfortunately, the capital of the United States was situated between Maryland and Virginia, both slave-holding states. In fact, each of these states had provided land for the creation of the capital city. This coupled with the passage of the Kansas/Nebraska Act of 1854, which caused the debates and violence to begin regarding the institution of slavery, meant Washington City was the center of both pro-slavery and abolitionist activities. And at the time of this event, slavery was still legal within Washington City.

***

It was exceptionally quiet on the streets surrounding the Congressional Cemetery this cold dark night in early January 1860. A light snow was falling, muffling the clip-clop of the horses' hooves. All the houses were closed up tight along E Street and there were no pedestrians to see the wagon stopping at the entrance to the cemetery. A lone man got down and walked through the gate, pushing a heavily laden wheelbarrow.

***

Constable Hezekiah Wallace, known as Zeke to most, arrived at headquarters early. It was snowing and he assumed there wouldn't be much going on in the way of crime. He sat down at his desk, intending to spend the day catching up on his paperwork. However, he couldn't have been more wrong.

"Ah, Zeke, you're in early. Good man," said Captain

Wentworth. "I got word a while ago that there's a body lying in the Congressional Cemetery. I need you to go over there now. Dr. Kingsley and his man will meet you there. Once you've examined the scene for evidence they will take the body back to the morgue."

Nodding to his captain, Zeke got up, put his coat and hat back on, and left the station.

***

"Horace. Noah. What have we got?" asked Zeke as he walked up to join his friends. They were examining a body draped over the top of one of the cenotaphs located along the main walkway of the cemetery.

"Zeke, it's good to see you and I'm glad you were assigned this case. On initial examination it looks like this man was beaten to death. In fact, there is a blood-splattered, gold-capped cane lying on the ground at the base of the cenotaph, close to the body. However, due to the lack of blood around the body I'm thinking that the murder probably took place elsewhere," answered Horace Kingsley, the coroner for Washington City and Zeke's longtime friend.

Zeke walked closer to get a better look at the body and the area around it. "Do we have any idea who the victim is?"

"We found a letter in his jacket pocket addressed to a Frank Mills. The letter contains instructions for creating discord within the abolitionist movement here in Washington City. From that I take it this man is a pro-slavery advocate and someone took exception to his beliefs," said Horace as he turned back to examining the body.

"Frank Mills, you say? I don't think I've heard that name in connection with the pro-slavery troublemakers. Now that the issue of slavery has come to the fore, we've started a list of those known to actively agitate on both sides, pro-slavery and abolitionist. Even though it's a worthy cause, if this is a case of retaliation, the abolitionist movement cannot break the law without suffering the consequences. Horace, a question—what is a cenotaph? That's what this is called, correct?"

"Yes, Zeke, it is. The federal government started erecting these in 1839 to honor Members of Congress who die in office and who are, most times, buried elsewhere. They are constructed of sandstone as are the President's House and the Capitol and painted white, with a square base and pointed top, forming a visual connection with these nearby symbols of Federal government, and a contrast to the surrounding gravestones. In this particular case the dedication is to Preston Smith Brooks who died in 1857," answered Horace.

"I appreciate the information and, not to rush you or anything, but when do you think you'll have the autopsy completed?"

Answering his friend with a shake of his head, Horace said, "Zeke, you never change, do you? Noah and I will be taking the body back to my surgery shortly, and I hope to conduct the postmortem this afternoon. That is, barring any unforeseen interruptions."

Relenting so as not to annoy his friend, Zeke turned to go and said over his shoulder, "OK, I'll check in with you later."

***

Zeke returned to the police station to report to his captain. After knocking on his superior's office door, he stuck his head in and said, "The deceased appears to be a man by the name of Frank Mills. Dr. Kingsley is taking the body back to the morgue for examination and hopes to have at least a preliminary report by later this afternoon."

Looking up, Captain Wentworth motioned his constable inside. "Do we know anything besides his name?"

"Not yet, but curiously the body was draped over a cenotaph dedicated to a congressman named Preston Smith Brooks."

"Cenotaph? What the blue blazes is a cenotaph?" asked the captain.

Zeke enjoyed telling his captain what he'd learned about cenotaphs from Horace at the cemetery.

Looking perplexed, the captain didn't say anything for several moments. Then all of the sudden he slapped his desk and shouted, "Ah ha! I knew the name Preston Smith Brooks sounded familiar. He's the man who beat Senator Charles Sumner with a cane on the Senate floor back in 1856. Sumner was lucky to survive and wasn't able to return to Washington until just last year."

Getting excited, Zeke said, "With a cane, you say? There was a gold-capped cane lying next to the cenotaph near the body. I think we may have found the motive for this murder. Retaliation!"

"I agree. That theory does have promise. I think you should look into who Frank Mills is associated with—is he part of one of the active pro-slavery groups? Also, track his movements over the last couple of days," the captain instructed.

***

After leaving his captain's office, Zeke Wallace checked the station files for any information on Frank Mills. He found that Mr. Mills had been arrested only a month before for his participation in an attack on a group of abolitionists who were peacefully demonstrating in front of the President's House.

***

Hearing a knock, Jelena Wallace wiped flour from her hands and went to answer the door. She opened it to find Horace Kingsley and his dog Gulliver standing on her doorstep.

"Good evening, Jelena. I hope I'm not interrupting you," he said, noticing some flour on her apron.

Opening the door wider, she said, "Of course not, Horace. Come in out of the cold. Zeke's not here but I do expect him shortly. You and Gulliver can warm yourselves by the stove while you wait."

"Oh, do forgive me. I'm interfering with your dinner preparations," he said, smelling a delicious aroma as he followed Jelena into the kitchen. "I sent word to Zeke earlier that I'd come round to give him the results of an examination I did this afternoon. By the way, will Lizzy object to Gulliver being here?"

"You're not interfering at all, Horace. And don't worry about the cat, she's upstairs in her favorite place, sleeping on my pillow. Have a seat and let me see if I can find a treat for Gulliver."

A few minutes later they heard the door open and close and a call from the hall. "Jelena, I'm home."

"In here, dear. In the kitchen," she called back.

Walking into the kitchen, Zeke found his friend Horace with Gulliver lying by his feet enjoying a bone. "I'm sorry I kept you waiting."

"It's not a problem at all, Zeke. I only arrived a few minutes ago and your lovely wife has allowed me to sit with her while she finishes preparing your dinner."

Smiling warmly at her husband, Jelena turned to Horace and said, "Since dinner is almost ready, why don't you join us? The children are away visiting their grandparents and we'd enjoy having you stay. I know you don't often get home cooked meals and I'm sure Gulliver would welcome a few morsels, too."

Taking up the cue from his wife, Zeke offered his agreement. "Yes, do stay. We don't often get the chance to visit away from work. I know you've come with your examination results but let's wait until after dinner to discuss them."

Feeling very blessed to have such good friends, Horace agreed to stay. The three settled in, talking about everyday things until the meal was ready.

***

When they'd finished their meal, Zeke and Horace retired to the Wallace's small drawing room to discuss business over brandies.

Taking a taste of the amber liquid, Horace smiled and complimented his friend on his hospitality. "This is a fine brandy,

Zeke. I know on your salary this must be very dear and not easily parted with."

"It was a gift from my father-in-law that I treasure and only partake in on rare occasions. Having you join us for dinner and an evening of good conversation seemed an appropriate time to enjoy a glass with a friend. Now, what are the results of your examination of Mr. Mills?" Zeke asked.

"It's a strange case, Zeke. Frank Mills did not die from a beating."

"What? How can that be? His head was bashed in and we found the cane covered in blood lying next to his body."

"Yes, that is true, however, my findings show that he was dead before he was beaten. He died because his heart stopped beating. There are signs that his heart has been diseased for some time and I suspect that it just gave out. That would also be the primary reason so little blood was found at the cemetery. Since his heart was not pumping, the blows to his head would bleed very little."

Shaking his head, Zeke said, "That sheds a whole new light on the case. Why would the abolitionists beat a man who was already dead and place him in the cemetery? It would serve no purpose at all and certainly draw undue attention to their cause. Everyone would come to the obvious conclusion that they killed Frank Mills in retaliation for the beating that Charles Sumner received at the hands of a pro-slaver."

"On the other hand, now that we know he was already dead, a whole different set of conclusions can be drawn," suggested Horace.

***

The next morning Zeke went to see his captain to give him the news he had received from Horace the night before. "Captain Wentworth, do you have a few minutes? I need to update you on the Frank Mills case."

Zeke updated his captain on the latest information and with his agreement and approval set out to spend the day tracking down known associates of Frank Mills. Zeke was convinced that advocates for the pro-slavery movement in the city were behind this murder, not the abolitionists.

After determining Mr. Mills' address, Zeke set out from the station to investigate further.

***

Arriving at a well-kept brick house not far from Capitol Hill, Zeke knocked on the door. It was opened quickly by a tall negro man dressed in butler's livery. "Yes, sir. How may I help you?"

"My name is Constable Hezekiah Wallace. I'm here to speak

with Mrs. Mills."

"Please wait here, sir, while I check to see if the missus is receiving visitors," the butler said, showing him inside.

The butler walked down the hallway and knocked first, then entered what appeared to be the parlor. He returned a few minutes later and directed Zeke to follow him back into the room. "Constable Wallace to see you missus."

"Thank you, Brutus, that will be all. If I need you, I'll ring," said an attractive woman with dark hair and piercing blue eyes. "Constable Wallace, won't you have a seat?"

"Thank you, ma'am. You are most kind."

"What can I do for you?" the woman said.

"I'm afraid I have some distressing news," Zeke said carefully. "First, though, can you tell me when you last saw your husband?"

Looking at him with concern, Aletha Mills answered, "Mr. Mills has been away on a business trip since Monday. Why do you ask?"

"I am very sorry to have to tell you this. Your husband was found dead yesterday morning."

Jumping to her feet she raised her voice. "Dead? It's not possible!"

Hearing his mistress' shout, Brutus rushed into the room. "Missus Mills, are you alright? What has happened?"

"Your mistress has just received some terrible news. I've had to inform her that her husband has been found dead. Does she have a maid that can come and tend to her?" asked Zeke.

"Fleur is her lady's maid. I'll send her in immediately. In the meantime, I'll send for the missus' doctor."

"Maybe a glass of whiskey will help to calm her until the doctor arrives," Zeke suggested.

Not happy at being talked around, Aletha Mills sat back down and glared at them both. In a calmer tone, she turned to Zeke and said, "Constable, will you please tell me what has happened to my husband?"

In as detailed but delicate a manner as possible, Zeke told Mrs. Mills about the discovery of her husband's body in the Congressional Cemetery and the subsequent results of the medical examination. He did not, however, tell her about the postmortem beating or its implications. Zeke stayed long enough to get some names of individuals Mr. Mills had business dealings with, then he took his leave after Mrs. Mills' maid arrived with a restorative drink.

***

After leaving the Mills residence, Zeke trudged through the

snow back to the station house. He'd decided to get some of the other constables to assist him. He wanted to question some of Frank Mills' associates but preferred to bring backup. The names Mrs. Mills had given him were of men known to be radical opponents of abolition. In fact, they were already suspects in several attacks on businesses owned by members of the abolitionist movement.

***

Entering the station house, Zeke called out, "Jake, are you and Charlie available to go out with me this afternoon?"

Coming out of a back room, Charlie answered, "Yes, sir. We'd welcome the chance to get out for a bit. Where are we going?"

"There are new developments in the Frank Mills case and I need you to back me up when I go to question some of his associates."

"Are you expecting trouble, sir?" asked Jake.

"I don't know what to expect, but I'd rather be prepared. These are dangerous men and based on evidence, I believe they staged the scene at the Congressional Cemetery to implicate the abolitionists."

Charlie nodded his head and said, "That's right. We saw the report Dr. Kingsley filed. It's hard to believe they'd beat their dead friend's body with a cane like that. But it does make sense. The word on the street is the abolitionists are looking to get revenge for that infamous beating. It looks like the pro-slavers have made the first move."

***

The three men made their way through the snow-covered streets of Washington City, and headed for Miller's Tavern. It was only a couple of blocks from the President's House and was often used to hold slave auctions. Zeke also knew it to be an important meeting place for radicals intent on keeping the institution of slavery alive.

As soon as the constables entered the tavern all conversation stopped and the room became deathly quiet. Zeke walked farther into the room and said, "I'm here to discuss the death of Frank Mills. I understand that he was one of your group and that you may be able to shed light on how he died."

A burly man stood up and approached Zeke. "Police aren't welcome here. Get out!"

Not backing down, Zeke said, "We'll leave after we've gotten the answers to our questions. I believe you know that your friend was found dead on Monday night, his head bashed in. I also believe you know who did it."

"This is my tavern and we have protection, which means we

don't have to answer your questions," a man said from behind the bar.

"So you're Adam Miller, the owner. I've heard of you and none of it good. You might have protection for now but things are changing here in Washington City. In the meantime I'll leave you to your plots, but be warned, I'll get the evidence I need. And when I do, I'll be back."

Zeke, Jake, and Charlie left the tavern. "Zeke, can't we take him and his partners in there down to the station for questioning?" asked Jake.

"Unfortunately, no. He has many friends in the current government who provide protection for those who are pro-slavery. That's why he's played the protection card and I can't risk our careers on bringing them in right now. Once we get the goods on him and the others then we can haul them in, but not before."

***

"There you are, Zeke. Someone's here waiting to see you," said the station clerk when he returned.

Looking puzzled, Zeke asked, "Who is it?"

"It's a well-spoken negro man. I think he said his name was Brutus. I put him in the interrogation room. He's been waiting about thirty minutes."

Quickly standing as Zeke entered the interrogation room, Brutus said, "Sir, if the missus finds out I've been here . . ."

"Sit down, Brutus, and tell me why you've taken the risk of coming to see me."

"I know what happened to the master. He didn't go on a business trip at all. He died at home. There was a meeting at the house Monday evening with some of the other men working to keep us in slavery. There was a heated argument and the master had an attack and died."

Zeke said, "Go on."

"The missus was called into the library where the men were meeting. Seeing that there was no help for her husband, she decided to use his death to advance the pro-slavery movement. You see, she is the powerful one. She instructed the other men to take her husband's body and make it look like he was murdered. Then she told them to put him where he would be easily found. It was supposed to look as though the abolitionists murdered him for revenge," said Brutus.

"And at first it did, Brutus. The initial evidence at the cemetery where your master's body was found suggested he'd been beaten to death with a cane. However, once the coroner did his examination, it became clear that the cause of death was something else. We then began suspecting the scene was staged to make us believe he'd been murdered by the abolitionists," Zeke said.

"I don't believe there is anything that can be done, at least not now. My mistress is very powerful and has many friends in the government who are working tirelessly to uphold slavery. I came to you so that you would know the truth of what happened. But I'm begging you not to confront her, else she'll know I talked to you. I was born free in Louisiana but was caught without my papers one night and sold into slavery. I want to be free again and I'm willing to take the necessary risks. There are many of us, both free and enslaved, here in Washington City, doing whatever we can to help the cause of emancipation. It's only a matter of time."

***

After Brutus left the station, Zeke gave Captain Wentworth the bad news.

"Captain, I've just received information that verifies what Horace and I believed about how Frank Mills died. I've also been informed that a group of pro-slavery advocates were responsible for the postmortem beating and staging the scene at the Congressional Cemetery at the direction of his wife, Aletha Mills."

"Aletha Mills. Her father was Benjamin Mills, a very powerful southern plantation owner. When he died, she inherited everything —money and slaves—making her one of the most influential and powerful women in Washington City. Who gave you the information?"

"Her butler, Brutus, came to see me. He is part of a group of free and enslaved Negroes doing what they can to work toward abolition. I also went to Miller's Tavern earlier and was informed by Adam Miller, the owner, that he had protection and didn't have to answer police inquiries. It looks like the pro-slavery advocates have the upper hand for now," answered Zeke.

"As always, you and Horace have done an outstanding job. Even though it turned out there was no murder, it's unfortunate that we can't bring those causing the discord in our city to task for their misdeeds."

Not happy that the case could not be resolved more satisfactorily, as he left the captain's office Zeke said, "At least not yet! As I was recently reminded, the storm is coming, and when it does, justice will be done."

CABIN IN THE WOODS

by Sylvia Maultash Warsh

Destination: Ontario, Canada
When her estranged mother dies, Franny has to deal with the cabin where she'd been happy as a young child. Will the sketch of the cabin her mother insisted she keep help her learn the truth about the father who deserted them years ago?

Franny eased her Civic down the scrubby drive. Branches tugged at the sides of the car in the half-light, the afternoon sun blocked by the canopy of trees. Finally, the clearing, the log cabin. Why was she here? She could easily have arranged everything by phone from Toronto. The house stood surprisingly free of vegetation, except for a few junipers held in check by judicious clipping. She couldn't picture her mother gardening. She was eighteen the last time she'd been here, a dozen years ago. Even then her mother had been on her case. Franny moved to Montreal to get away from her mother's soul-destroying criticism. She even stopped taking her phone calls, those attack sessions that sent her spiraling into depression.

Well, there would be no more phone calls. Her mother was dead.

She sat in the car in front of the cabin, going over the long-distance call from the lawyer yesterday. Was it just yesterday? *"I'm sorry, Miss Callum, but your mother has died of a heart attack."* It had been a shock, despite the animosity, the years of bitter arguments. There had been only the two of them. Her father had walked out when she was four. She was sure her mother had pushed him away just as she had done with Franny.

She'd left early that morning, driving the six hours from Montreal to Toronto in a haze, her body on automatic. The lawyer on the phone explained that her mother had appointed him executor of her estate. She hadn't wanted a funeral, a waste of money, she'd said, and had arranged to be cremated. In fact, she'd instructed him to go ahead with the cremation before informing Franny she was dead. Franny had just sat there, stunned, with the phone in her hand. The lawyer said her mother had wanted to spare her the morbid details. But Franny knew better. Her mother wanted the last word: *This is what you get for not speaking to me for three years.*

Franny picked up the pen and ink drawing of the cabin from the passenger seat. The lawyer said her mother had wanted her to have it. Why, she couldn't imagine. Nothing like her mother's usual style. Not artistic at all. More architectural. Just the log house with the flagstone walkway along the side of the yard. Except the walkway didn't extend that far. It stopped after five feet. And her mother had forgotten Franny's favorite spot, the bench on the flagstone patio in the back. Maybe she had gone senile.

In their brief meeting, the lawyer had announced that, in addition to a small amount of savings, her mother had left her the cabin. Franny assumed she'd leave it to charity, or make it an artists' retreat. Franny had loved the place as a child, enthralled when her mother described how the cabin stood in a moraine, a geological feature left behind by a retreating glacier during the last ice age. Franny couldn't fathom ice two kilometers thick, let alone how it carved out hills and valleys that turned into forests like the one that surrounded them. If only her combative relationship with her mother hadn't spoiled the more recent years.

Reluctantly, Franny climbed the rickety stairs to the veranda, waving flies away from her face. She held her breath as she unlocked the door with the keys the lawyer had given her. The shadowy interior smelled stale. When her eyes adjusted, she saw that everything was much as she remembered: one large room with a kitchen and living area, a sofa opposite an oak table and chairs. There was a current calendar on the wall: August 1990. Her mother must've been there recently.

Above the sofa hung one of her mother's excruciatingly accurate paintings, a still life of fruit in a crystal bowl. Perfect, but soulless. She never understood her mother's mania for detail, obsessively adding color, then removing it until she was satisfied with the result. Well, other people must've appreciated it, because her art sold. Franny preferred the interpretation of reality, impressionistic scenes. This was a bone of contention between them. Her mother had sneered at Franny's pastel-colored landscapes with the ambiguous horizons, extrapolating from them that her world view was diametrically opposed to her own. "Grow up," she said, "and accept that life is dog-eat-dog. Come down to earth if you want to produce real paintings that people might buy."

Franny had put some distance between them in order to keep a modicum of self-respect. A gallery in Montreal liked Franny's work and hung three of her imagistic landscapes, though none had sold yet. Meanwhile she worked as a waitress, and every now and then an ad agency sent some freelance design work her way.

Pulling aside the flowered curtains, she opened the windows to let in some air. She would find a local real estate agent to sell the place because she couldn't afford to pay the capital gains tax.

She noticed a piece of paper by the phone. Names and phone numbers in her mother's precise handwriting: the gas station she'd passed on the highway, a Chinese restaurant in the nearby town, a hardware store, Franny's number, and the number of someone with the initials F.C. What was the name of the man the lawyer had mentioned? As executor, he had found that her mother had been sending monthly cheques to a man unknown to him. Franny had never heard of him either. She fished in her purse for the name she'd scribbled down. Floyd Cameron. Why was her mother sending this guy two hundred and fifty dollars a month?

Franny ducked her head into the studio with its canvases leaning against the walls. No answers there. She was more likely to find clues in the bedroom. The old flowered comforter on the bed in the tiny room made her grimace, reminding her of her mother. She opened the drawer of the night table. An old black-and-white photo stared up at her. With a shock, she recognized her father. She had seen only a few pictures of him besides her parents' wedding photo, which her mother liked to hide. Franny had his longish face and square jaw, the same wave in her dark hair. Did Franny remind her mother of him? Remind her that he had left her after five years of marriage? Her mother avoided the subject and balked when Franny, aged ten, started asking about him. She had been persistent in her quest for answers until one fateful day a letter arrived for her with no return address. She still remembered her father's typed words, no surprise since she had read them over and over. It was the only thing she had left of him.

Dear Franny,

I am sorry things turned out like they did. But all of that is behind me. I am happy now with a new family so don't look for me. You will understand when you are older.

Daddy

Her father was the real reason for the bitterness between her and her mother. A few years earlier she had tried to find him, hoping he was still alive, but with so little information, she kept bumping into dead ends. She recalled her father had a sister, Aunt Rose, but didn't know her married name. They hadn't kept in touch after her father left. When Franny asked her mother for the aunt's surname, she became unreasonably angry, screaming into the phone. That was when Franny had stopped talking to her. Water under the bridge.

Deeper inside the drawer, Franny found her mother's unique wedding band made of brushed two-tone gold. She had stopped wearing it years ago. Nearby, she saw an old black iron key. Beneath it lay a yellowed newspaper clipping. An obituary.

> *Stan Timinsky died peacefully on May 20, 1985 in Etobicoke General Hospital after a brave battle with cancer. Beloved husband of Rose (née Callum), brother-in-law of Arthur Callum and Charlotte Callum, loving father of John and Linda. Visitation at . . .*

Bingo! Franny checked the date of the obituary again. 1985. Only five years ago. Maybe she could still find her. Maybe Aunt Rose could help her find her father. The longing for him that had never left now irresistibly surfaced.

She ran to the kitchen and looked in the cupboard for a phone book. Along with the local one, her mother had kept an out-of-date Toronto directory.

She flipped through impatiently: Timinsky, Timinsky. A half dozen but only one with the initial R. She dialled the number, heard it ringing through. A woman answered.

"Is this Rose Timinsky?"

"Who's this?"

"I'm Charlotte Callum's daughter. Franny. Your niece."

Silence. Maybe she had the wrong person.

"Artie's girl?"

Franny smiled. "Yes. Artie's my father . . ."

"Well, well. I remember you when you were three or four years old. How old are you now?"

"Thirty."

"It has been a long time . . ."

"Yes, it has. I thought you might want to know—my mother just died."

"Oh, I'm so sorry. Was she ill?"

"Sudden heart attack."

"Haven't seen her in years. She was a talented woman."

Franny counted a few beats before going on. "I was wondering . . . Well, I was wondering if you knew where my father was."

A moment of silence. "I hope you don't take this the wrong way—I have nothing against you, mind. But the next time you speak to him, give him a message from me: he's the most selfish bastard in the world. After all these years, not to bother to pick up a phone—"

"When was the last time you spoke to him?"

"1964. I called to wish him a happy birthday. He was already drunk."

Franny thought her mother had exaggerated about the booze. "Did he say he had plans to go somewhere?"

"Not outright. But he owed people money and asked if I could lend him some. Imagine the gall! He was always short of cash. Wouldn't be surprised if he ripped somebody off, high-tailed it out of the country with the money."

Franny didn't know what to say to that.

"Wouldn't put it past him. I'm sure he's very happy somewhere. Who needs a brother like that?"

***

Franny tossed and turned in her mother's bed that night, wishing she hadn't located Aunt Rose. She preferred the fanciful image she had of her father to the real thing. Finally, she fell asleep toward dawn, but her dreams were full of shadows and eyes. When the sun was barely up, she startled awake. Someone had climbed the stairs to the porch.

She flew out of bed in her pyjama sweats, moved the curtain in the living room an inch to see out. An old guy wearing a plaid shirt and a baseball cap over a long white pony tail stood there. He caught the movement of the curtain and nodded. Now she had to open the door.

"Where's Charlie?" he asked.

With a start, she realized he held a dead rabbit by the legs in one hand and a rifle in the other. "Who?"

"Woman that owns this place."

"Oh. Charlotte. That's my mother."

He squinted at her. "You used to come here when you were a kid?"

She nodded. She vaguely remembered the creepy old neighbor, only his hair and beard had been dark then. What was his name? Ronnie?

"She likes to make rabbit stew." He raised the dead animal in explanation.

Franny kept her eyes off it. Her mother would not be making any more stews. "She died a few days ago."

He lowered the rabbit, the colour draining from his face. After a minute, he said. "I'm sorry . . . how?"

"Heart attack."

He shook his head. "We were friends. I knew her a long time." He looked down at the bleeding rabbit. "I'll leave this with you then."

She waved her hand vigorously. "I'm vegetarian."

He gave a crooked smile. "You're not much like her. What's your name?"

"Franny."

"That's right. She talked about you. I'm Floyd, your neighbor." He rested the rifle on his shoulder.

"Floyd? Floyd Cameron?"

He stared at her.

"But my mother called you 'Ronnie.'"

"Nickname."

"My mother has been sending you cheques every month."

His small eyes widened in surprise. "You know about that?"

"Her lawyer told me. What are they for?"

"I . . . I take care of the place for her. Maintenance and such."

So he was the gardener. "It seems like a lot of money for that."

"She is . . . was a generous woman."

"Not the person I knew." Franny could've used that money.

He watched her and seemed to guess what she was thinking.

She felt uneasy about the rifle. "What did she say about me?"

"Oh, this and that. She said you turned into a beautiful young woman." He squinted at her. "She was right."

Franny thought, she never told me that. "She ever talk about my father?"

"Not really. Good riddance, I say."

"You knew him?"

"Enough to know she was well rid of him."

"Because he drank?"

"Because he was a mean drunk."

Could she trust what this man said? "What did he do? When he drank."

He looked past her into the cabin, making her more uneasy.

"Don't recall."

He was lying.

After mumbling some parting words, he stepped down from the porch and across the clearing before disappearing into the woods. Fast for an old guy. He recalled, all right. Why wouldn't he say?

When she was sure he was gone, she headed for the back of the yard where a bench stood on a small flagstone patio. The stones had seen better days, some shifting out of alignment in the sandy soil. She sat down on the bench, trying to erase the picture of Floyd Cameron with the dead rabbit. The man had his nerve, bad-mouthing her father.

***

Franny warmed up a tin of vegetable soup from the cupboard for breakfast. She ate while staring down at her mother's drawing of the cabin. The lawyer had presented it to her wrapped in tissue paper inside a leather portfolio, as if it were a precious work of art. Which it sure as hell wasn't. The will specified that Franny could do whatever she wanted with the paintings in the rented Toronto apartment—she had dropped in for a quick look around before driving north—but she was to hold on to this drawing. Her mother had singled it out. What was so special about it?

She couldn't put her finger on why, but it seemed imprecise, unlike her mother's paintings. Despite the solid lines of pen and ink, the scene was dreamlike and oppressive. When she screwed up her eyes, she could detect a face like a gargoyle peeking out from the top of one of the trees. A gargoyle? Dropping her spoon, Franny snatched up the paper and stepped outside.

She stopped beside the house where her mother would have stood, trying to find the perspective of the drawing. An obvious error astounded her. Her mother had badly misjudged the crawlspace delineated by the stonework along the bottom of the cabin. In reality, the stonework only extended about a foot above the ground. In the drawing, her mother had exaggerated it to three times its height. A conundrum, considering her obsession with accuracy. She wouldn't have made a mistake like that. What was down there?

She told herself she wasn't climbing into the crawlspace on a stupid hunch. The place was dark as pitch.

Franny walked back into the house, into her mother's studio. She lifted the rag rug from the floor. A shiver skipped across her. There it was: a square of wood in the linoleum, the hatch to the crawlspace. She tried to lift it but it was locked. Too bad. Then she remembered the old iron key in the drawer.

She fetched it from her mother's night table. Fumbling with the key in the lock, she turned it. The hatch creaked open, stiff, like an arthritic joint. A rickety ladder reached down into the murky black.

She found a flashlight on a nearby shelf and aimed the beam down. From where she crouched, she could see a few boxes amid the dust. Why was she doing this to herself?

Gripping the sides of the ladder, she eased herself down, cursing. She shone the flashlight beneath her, watched a centipede scurry away. Once on the bottom, she had to move around on her knees. It wasn't called a crawlspace for nothing.

She opened two cardboard boxes, raising up dust. Both held old

National Geographic magazines. She pointed the flashlight through the shadows, her eyes falling on a leather case from her school days. She unlatched the lid and found her ancient manual typewriter. Stashed inside were some folded sheets of paper. They appeared to be drafts of a typewritten letter with lines struck out, some words written in her mother's hand. When she read the first one, she stiffened.

> *Dear Franny,*
>
> *I can't help how things turned out. Don't look for me. I have a new family and am happy now. Forget about me.*
>
> *Daddy*

Another page:

> *Dear Franny,*
>
> *It wasn't my fault how things turned out. Don't ever look for me. I am happy now. Goodbye.*
>
> *Daddy*

Franny had the final version at home in her drawer. Her mind could not get around it. Unsettled, she searched the floor with her flashlight, the beam landing on an old cookie tin. She opened the lid. Inside, sat another sheet of paper and a rubber stamp. The printed letter was word for word the one she had received from her father. The rubber stamp was set to a date: September 10, 1970. The day her father's letter had been stamped, supposedly by the post office. The letter he had never sent.

It had all been a sham. Her father had never cared enough to send a letter. Why had her mother done it? To get Franny off her back.

She realized something was left in the cookie tin: a slim leather wallet. She opened it and found a business card in one of the slots: *Ace Motors, Yonge Street, Toronto*. Beneath, it read *Arthur Callum, salesman*. Her shoulders tightened. In another slot she found a social insurance card with his name on it. Her hand trembled as she pulled out the driver's licence with a tiny photo of him. Signed by Arthur Callum. Expired in 1965. A year after he had run off. Had he left behind his identity as well as his family?

When she got back upstairs, she found a magnifying glass and held it over the photo in the licence, the longish nose, the square jaw. With a chill, she leveled the glass over the gargoyle in the drawing. It hovered in the branches of the pine tree, the nose and jaw too familiar, only made of stone. And amid the pine needles, behind the head, stone wings.

Franny took the drawing outside, heading for the pine. It had grown taller in the back corner of the yard. She looked up into the branches where the gargoyle would have floated, trying to position herself beneath it. She found herself stepping onto the flagstone patio. The stones were so loose, she kicked one of them aside. Then another. And another. Her heart raced. She pushed the bench off and worked for fifteen minutes, heaving and sweating. She stared at the exposed soil, horrified at what she was thinking.

Looking around the yard, she found a rusty shovel and began to dig down into the earth. She couldn't believe she was doing it, but she dug down one foot, two feet. She stopped a minute for air. When she was nearly three feet down, the shovel hit something besides earth. She cleared the soil away carefully with her hands until she touched something hard. Something yellow-white. A bone, large and contoured. Could it be an animal? She kept moving earth away from the area with her hands until she came across more bones. This time, several thin bones together. Something glinted among them. Catching her breath, she lifted a ring from the soil. A band made of brushed two-tone gold. Someone screamed. She realized it was her.

The bushes moved apart and Floyd Cameron stepped into the clearing.

She jumped up, crying, "You killed him!"

He took off his baseball cap and stared at the bones, unsurprised.

"You were in love with her and you killed him."

He shook his head dolefully. "You got it all wrong, missy. She did it."

"What?"

He looked at her with pity. "She had every right—he was beating on her."

"No . . ."

"Might've killed her one day. More to the point, she was afraid he would start beating you, too."

"Beating me . . .?"

"I hoped I'd never have to tell you. He was mild when he was sober. Not a prince, mind you. But when he started drinking, watch out."

She shook her head. "That can't be . . ."

"I'm sorry . . ."

All those years of waiting for him to walk through the door. The fantasy of him loving her.

"People aren't always what you want."

She stared down at the bones, feeling sick. "What happened?"

He stroked his beard, gazing past her. "One night I heard a commotion going on, louder than usual. I knew how he was, so I came running. They were screaming at each other on the porch. Her face was bleeding. He'd hit her. She went inside and I thought that was that."

He put his cap back on. "But then she came out again, this time with a cast iron frying pan. He was lunging at her when she hit him in the head. Went down hard. She hit him again. And again. Strong for a woman."

Franny could barely breathe. "How could she . . .?"

"She was afraid for you. You were a little thing. She was afraid he would go after you next. She told me. She did it for you."

Franny shook her head. "For me?"

"She loved you."

Franny felt tears sting her eyes, the first for her mother. "She never showed it."

"She wasn't the type. She was a funny woman, your mother. Proud and prickly. But she loved you."

Everything she'd ever thought about her mother, every memory was wrong.

"I wish that . . ." She shook her head. There was no point wishing, she almost heard her mother say. "Then what happened?"

"I buried the body."

He picked up the drawing from the bench. "She drew this right after. Wasn't herself for weeks. Then I took the stones from the walkway and built the little patio, like a kind of memorial. We prayed here. That made her feel better. After a while, she could let it go.

"She insisted on sending me money. 'Consider it a pension,' she said. Gratitude for helping her, not judging her. Said she got her life back after that."

Franny burst into sobs, grieving for the first time. Her mother was sending her a message in the drawing. She knew Franny would figure it out. She wanted Franny to know the truth.

Floyd took her in his arms gingerly and patted her back while she wept.

"I'll get him out of there," he said. "Bury him in the bush."

In a moment of clarity, the mystery of her mother mingled with the mystery of the glacier and Franny could finally picture the two-kilometer-thick swath of ice, could hear it thunderously carving out the hills and dales where the forest would take root. She loved the huge murky scale of it, the diminishing in size of human troubles. Her father, unknowable to her forever, would transcend whatever he'd been in his short life and merge with the forest.

She wondered what color paints she would need to depict ice. Her mother would have a good supply of oils in the studio. Franny could count on her for the important things.

MAD ABOUT YOU

by G. M. Malliet

Destination: Axebury Cove, England
In a remote English village by the sea, an American visitor encounters a seemingly happy family, a strange old woman, and unexpected deception.

We got off the ferry at Axebury Cove, a village along England's Jurassic Coast. People always say a village "nestles" along a coastline but honestly, this one does. Little cottages overlook the water, as if they were carved in place at the dawn of time and painted blue and pink and yellow to match the sky. There's a promenade, a small rocky beach dotted with warnings about riptides, and a shambolic-looking pier. It was all charming, and this time of year the village was nearly deserted. Perfect.

I doubted if even in summer Axebury Cove got a lot of visitors, not with brighter lights just down the coast road. But now England was tipping into winter and some mornings required wrapping up as if we were off to scale the Alps.

We were there on a roots journey—his, not mine. I'm American made and that's all I needed to know. I taught history, ancient and modern, at Grover Cleveland High School and my interest in the past pretty much ended when I retired. Personally, I'd much rather not know a lot about my ancestors, and I feel Douglas would be wise to follow my example.

Douglas is also a retired teacher—high school Phys. Ed. He would never admit it, but he cherishes the secret hope he's descended from nobility, and that one day we'll get a letter informing us we've inherited a vast estate along with the income for its upkeep. And an invitation to Buckingham Palace for his investiture. Some years ago Douglas had a coat of arms done up by some online outfit. It features boars and dragons and bars sinister and a host of other nonsense, all of it clearly made up. He had it mounted and framed, and if the house caught fire, that coat of arms is the first thing he'd save.

***

The village is not easy to get to. We'd driven a rental car from the dock at Southampton to Weymouth, and from there we'd caught the car ferry that chugged over to Axebury Cove rather than risk the winding narrow roads. We'd reserved a room at the top of the Seafairer Hotel, converted from an old manor house when the last lord died off. The conversion did not include the installation of an elevator, unfortunately, but the view from our bay windows over the sea made it worth the hike up three floors. Douglas, on the basis of nothing whatsoever, had already decided this once had been his old family mansion, although the lord of the manor had been named Parishmann.

"A Swinletter by marriage," Douglas insisted.

Whatever. I was determined to make the best of things, snapping photos for an album I planned to put together for him for Christmas. A big compensation was the hotel's full English breakfast: fried eggs, fried bread, bacon, sausages, tomato, mushrooms, and black pudding. I knew what black pudding was and left it tucked to one side of my plate, but the rest of it I devoured, ravenous from climbing up and down scenic hills. On Thursday's agenda was a fun romp through the village churchyard, pulling back the weeds to peer at indecipherable gravestones. But we never got that far on Thursday.

The hotel's dining room was furnished in rickety bamboo painted white to suggest the tropics, and while it was clean it was very old, the kind of musty-old that had nooks and crannies and corners impossible to reach with a duster. The window ledges were lumpy with layers of paint, so future historians could easily replicate the paint color from 1765 or whenever. A fake potted palm sat in one corner, but each table was decorated with a small vase of real red and white carnations.

We were first down to breakfast each day and generally had only an elderly woman for company. She sniffed at our morning greeting and hid behind a newspaper at a corner table. I wouldn't at first have known she was elderly because her hair was a deep shade of auburn, but when she lowered the paper to reach for her coffee and clawlike, misshapen fingers emerged from her long black sleeves, it was apparent she was wearing a wig. She was the aging Elizabeth I brought to life. I wondered if, like the Queen, the woman had lost her hair to age or illness, or to damage caused by wearing a wig all the time. She looked very old, on-her-last-legs old.

***

I should tell you about the cliff and the tree, since they were prominent landmarks that feature in the story I'm about to relate. The tree clung precariously to a cliff, quite near the edge, and it so clearly was ancient that Douglas just knew it was woven somehow into an ancestor's story. I suggested that perhaps a Swinletter had been hanged from it, a joke that didn't go over too well. Anyway, the tree was spooky—enormous, bent, lopsided, and missing several limbs that had either been sawn off in attempts to save it or torn off during a storm. It leant back from the cliff as if recoiling from the wind that had pushed at it for hundreds of years, projecting the sort of ghostly image favored by designers of Halloween cards. The sea encroached, gnawing away at the underside of the mealy cliff. It was only a matter of time before the tree roots were exposed and the whole thing tumbled into the waves below. A few more centuries and the hotel might follow—potted palm, carnations, and all.

It became part of our morning routine to climb one of two paths up the hill, one steep and one winding. We'd stand at the top and gaze out over the sea in a proprietary way, taking in the view and the fresh air. Wooden steps led down to a thin strip of beach to the left of the cliff, but straight below was water. Endless seas of roiling water. It made me think of fishermen who set out from Axebury Cove and never made it back. Douglas was much taken with the riptides, explaining that if you were caught in one you had to swim sideways out of it. That sounded to me like the nonsensical advice to turn your car wheel into the spin on icy roads, but I nodded.

Douglas took my picture as I stood beneath the tree, my hair blown about by the wind, with the sea visible in the background. It is still a favorite photo, capturing the eerie spirit of the place. It was not a good setting for a couples' photo, not to my mind, although the hotel sitting room had an album stuffed with wedding pictures, some professionally taken, of couples standing there smiling. Obviously, nuptials kept the place going during the slower months. The couples all were wearing their finest for the big day, many of them apparently not having the wherewithal to hire a good tailor or seamstress. More than one bride looked as if she were making it to the altar just in time, if you get my drift. Why, under the circumstances, they all insisted on wearing tight-fitting white satiny sheaths is anyone's guess.

As we walked down the hill that morning, the old woman with the frightful wig was coming up the steeper trail. I thought she'd have trouble making it to the top at her age—the trail was slippery, with few rocks or flat areas to use as stepping stones or resting places. Once launched on the decision to head up, there was little choice but to keep going or slide ignominiously back down. She moved like someone well aware of the fragility of hipbones, with a limp that suggested knee or hip surgery, but she made it to the top by herself, like an aging billy goat. She stood there a long while.

***

For our third dinner at the hotel we were seated at a table with a view overlooking the distant promenade, perhaps in deference to our foreigner status. There were only three window tables, highly prized, and the table next to us was taken by a handsome couple and their child, a little girl of about three with enormous eyes and dark curly hair like her father's. She was a well-behaved little thing, glowing with contentment and charm—one of those British babies with the rosy red cheeks that make you wonder what on earth they feed them.

We had met this family only once in passing, as they seemed to come down to breakfast long after we'd left to look at gravestones or paw through the archives in the local library. The woman was rather maternal in appearance, with a pouter-pigeon breast and hair worn in Charlie's Angel's layers. Makeup enhanced her large blue eyes; she shared her daughter's rosy cheeks and didn't require further camouflage, but her style was old-fashioned—a floral dress with gathered skirt and a matching cloth belt. June Cleaver wore that sort of thing as she stirred the brownie mix and admonished Wally to be nicer to the Beav. The shoes, worn with nylons, were like something the Queen would wear, low-heeled and flesh-toned. She looked earnest and wholesome, and excited to be on vacation with her little family, as if a holiday at the ends of the earth were a rare treat.

I heard her call him Stanford, which suited him; she was Caroline. He had a patrician look about him, although he may not have been the brightest patrician in the kingdom. Balding on top with curly dark fringe and wearing a lot of gold at the wrist. He was dressed for vacation but in carefully creased trousers; over a polo shirt he wore a blazer. Color him "at a loss without my suit and tie." He looked at least a decade older than she, and I pegged him as some kind of lawyer or banker. They both wore plain gold wedding bands.

He made heavy work of chatting with his little girl, as if he were unused to being around children. But he was polite and attentive to Caroline, helping her into and out of her chair and passing the bread basket. His only vice that I could see was a single cigarette he allowed himself after the meal.

I thought she may have had to give more than he did—he had that air of fatuous self-importance that told me this was true.

I couldn't hear everything they said, although I did try. They seemed to be talking about their walk around the local sights, the cleansing breeze off the ocean, and I heard her mention Bradford, as in, "It's nice to get away from Bradford."

Bradford, I happened to know, was in Yorkshire. A favorite author of mine used to live near there. I pretended to have accidentally dropped my napkin, leaning over for a moment so I was closer and could hear a bit better.

"I know," he said. "It's a relief."

"So nice. Becky is thrilled to spend some time with you." It might have been an admonition or a complaint, but it came across as a happy declaration of fact.

"I know." His tone was defensive. "I wish things were different, but at least I'm here now. This new job . . ."

"I know, I know," said Caroline. She batted her eyes adoringly; they actually glistened. It was either allergies or infatuation.

"Look at those two," I whispered to Douglas. "They're just devoted to each other; you can tell. I wonder what their secret is?"

Douglas and I had met in college. Now, two children and a grandchild later, we were . . . comfortable.

"Dunno," said my husband, not much interested. "Separate bathrooms?

***

After-dinner coffee was served from a sideboard in the sitting room, and guests chose seating as they could find it. Stanford and Caroline took their coffees to a rattan loveseat on the enclosed side porch, sitting with their backs to us as they looked out over the promenade. Little Becky ran in circles for a while until her mother gently admonished her to sit still. To my amazement, she did. It was never thus with my two boys who responded only to bribes and threats.

Douglas and I sat indoors by the stone fireplace. The elderly woman walked in from outside, leaning heavily on her cane, and with a smile I gestured for her to join us, as most of the other seats were taken. I had not seen her in the dining room and guessed she'd taken her meal at the village pub. I sensed that it was more out of politeness than willingness that she took the chair opposite our sofa. She sat with her back to the sea view.

We did introductions and she told us her name was Delphine. Mrs. Delphine Knowlton, visiting from Australia. She said she had just buried her mother somewhere in Kent and was driving around on her own. "Having a little vacay," was how she put it. We were given to understand, without her actually saying so, that the travel was being underwritten by her inheritance.

"I've been away so many years," she said. "I'm nearly seventy now. England's like a foreign country to me. I'm just another tourist passing through."

The mention of age is usually a cue for the listener to say politely that the speaker doesn't look her age. But Delphine Knowlton did look her age and I couldn't bring myself to tell the polite lie, so I just gave her a wan smile. She looked a hundred, haggard and worn. I'd spotted a wedding ring, so I said, "You went to Australia with your husband, did you? For his job?"

It was the wrong thing to say, from the way her face froze and her coffee cup stopped halfway to her lips.

"No," she said. "I am a professional woman. I went there to teach in the schools."

Well, that was me put in my place. But there had been something about Delphine that spoke to me of a woman who had put her husband's needs and interests above her own for all of her life, who had indeed regarded marriage as the apogee of feminine achievement. Someone who took pride in starching and ironing her tablecloths and frilly curtains, in canning her garden-grown tomatoes and cucumbers. Who gauged her social status by her husband's achievements rather than her own. My own mother had been such a woman and I felt I knew the type well. Now I saw that I had missed the ramrod-straight posture and the keen gaze beneath that terrible wig that spoke of something more. Something, if truth be told, rather odd. It was in the intense glitter of her nearly black eyes beneath thick straight brows, and her expression as she pulled her head back and tucked her chin down. Stubborn, I thought. Used to getting her way. God help any of her students that stepped out of line.

I started to tell her Douglas and I had been teachers, too, when she cut me off.

"I think," she said as she rose, having finished only half her coffee, "I'll retire early. I tire easily these days. I bid you good night." With a curt nod and no further ado she left the room. She walked slowly up the steps, that hitch still in her gitalong.

She didn't retire, though—at least, she must have changed her mind and come back down. I had left my reading glasses in the lobby, and when I returned to retrieve them I could see her sitting quite alone on the porch, on the loveseat recently vacated by Becky and her parents, staring out to sea.

***

The accident happened the next day.

At least, I prefer to think it was an accident. We couldn't prove otherwise so why, as Douglas said, make a fuss? We were strangers in England and we weren't either of us sure what had happened.

And he was right. Murder is not a word to be tossed about lightly.

After breakfast we happened to follow Caroline as she climbed the winding path to the oak at cliff's edge, holding her daughter's hand. Because Becky was so small, it was slow going, but Douglas and I didn't mind. We exchanged some joking references to treadmills and stair climbers as we panted our way up the steeper path.

Behind us came Becky's father, so on this Douglas and I were later in complete agreement: Stanford had nothing to do with what happened next.

We reached the top of the cliff to find Delphine Knowlton already there, a scarf wrapped around her head. Confusingly, she was holding the child. I saw at once the very edge of the cliff had broken off, leaving the roots of the old oak exposed, and taking perhaps four square feet of soil.

Douglas and I stood frozen for a moment, our eyes swiveling between Delphine and the child and the cliff, looking at the empty space that should have held Caroline. Did I only imagine it, or had I seen the top of her head vanishing, like Wile E. Coyote in a Road Runner cartoon?

Douglas's account jibed with mine except as to whether Caroline had screamed as she fell. But Douglas is deaf as a post for the high notes, and I myself wasn't sure if I'd heard a gull's cry or a woman's. We both thought we heard the crunch of soil and rock as the cliff edge gave way.

But I did not imagine that in that second I saw Delphine leap back from the edge, pulling the child (and herself) to safety. There was no safety rail. We were not in America, where the area would have been thick with posted warnings aimed at people with no common sense.

Douglas and I inched as near the cliff edge as we dared but we couldn't get close enough to see anything. Caroline might have been swept out to sea. She might have been sprawled, dead or injured, at the bottom of the cliff.

Douglas ran over to the wooden steps leading down to the strip of beach, Stanford now following. I did wonder what had taken Stanford so long, but he had been dawdling and couldn't see from below what had been happening.

I turned to Delphine, not sure what to do.

"What," I said, "happened here?"

The docile Becky seemed content in Delphine's arms. But something was off. Delphine wasn't even breathing hard from the climb, the excitement, or the rescue of Becky. I was, but the elderly

Delphine was not. She had to have been waiting at the top. Waiting, rested, and for some time. But, waiting for Caroline? Why?

A sudden breeze caught at her scarf as she turned into the morning light, pulling it away from her face. Her heavy makeup was obvious in the daylight—the lined forehead, the heavily drawn brows, the dark shadows beneath the eyes. She didn't seem to register my shock at her appearance but brushed past and started down the steps to the beach, still carrying Becky. I could only follow, puzzling out what it all meant, uneasy that she had her arms around the child.

Below, Douglas had stripped off his coat and waded into the water waist high while Stanford stood about wringing his hands. Seeing me approach, he splashed in after Douglas, thrashing about to no purpose.

"I can't swim," he told Douglas. "It's my heart. I can't . . ."

I didn't believe him. I turned to Delphine and was astonished to see on her face, beneath the stagy makeup, a look of triumph. Instinctively I reached for Becky and pulled the child away from her.

And just then I saw Caroline's head bob up out of a far wave, her face a pale oval against the blue sea. She threw her head back, choking and gasping for air. I willed her to start swimming and finally she did. Straight into the riptide.

Douglas waved his arms, pointing to his left, crying, "Swim out! Swim out of it!" I could see now that if she continued on her current path, the tide would keep pulling her back until it wore her down like sea glass.

The horizon shimmered as I stood, shaky and trembling with anxiety, but managing to hold on to the now-crying little girl. I suspected in my heart what had happened, but I could never prove it. An argument, a struggle, a loss of balance. A push?

Douglas swam out to her from the beach at a slow crawl, the waves against him. In her panic Caroline fought him at first, but finally, exhausted, allowed him to guide her in at an angle to the shore.

Where, gasping and coughing, she pushed away the hand Stanford held out to her. I might have heard "you bastard" carried faintly on the breeze.

I could almost swear Stanford had stalled around rather than do anything to help. But she survived, Caroline did. She was fine. Although . . .

I turned to Delphine, who had pulled off that awful wig. Beneath was a full head of shiny dark hair. She threw back her shoulders, losing the dowager's hump. Beneath the now-obvious makeup, she was not much older than I was.

The cane was gone. Perhaps it had gone over the side with Caroline.

***

That night, Douglas was in the bathroom changing for dinner when from our window I saw Caroline drive off, Becky with her, strapped into her safety seat. The car's tires kicked up gravel as they spun out of the hotel's circular driveway. Becky's dark curly head turned and she seemed to look in my direction. I willed her to see me, but I knew she could not.

Douglas and I had not stopped talking about what we had seen, what we might have imagined, and what we should do about it all. Caroline's leaving put an end to it. We decided it was up to her to report it—whatever it was. Then and only then could we try to fill in the blanks for the authorities.

The surprise was that we knew as much as we did. I felt sure Delphine had been unaware of our daily hill-climbing routine, or she would have chosen a better moment in which to act.

And Caroline would be dead now.

Had it been an attempted murder? I still couldn't take it all in.

***

We spent the next day on our usual ramble, but greatly subdued and avoiding any cliffs. That night at dinner, Delphine and Stanford sat together at a window table. I wondered only at my lack of astonishment. If Caroline had drowned, I had no doubt "Delphine"—undoubtedly not her real name—would have vanished. And all Douglas and I could have told anyone who asked was a story about an elderly woman who had told us she was visiting from Australia.

That look of triumph had not left her face. The sheepish look had not left his. He also looked—what? Relieved.

He went out for his smoke after dinner and I wasted no time going over to her where she sat by the fireplace. I was not going to let her off so lightly. She was dressed in a silk sheath and pearls, unrecognizable as the wizened old woman of yesterday.

I had one simple question for her. "Why?"

"Why forgive him?"

Actually, that had by no means been my question, but I was so amazed she didn't tell me it was none of my business I kept mum.

"Why not? Because he's all I have. Because I'm fifty-five and I don't want to be alone. Because we have thirty years together and two children and a big house and you don't throw that away for an . . . indiscretion . . . four years ago."

The cherubic Becky—an "indiscretion." And anyone could see the affair with Caroline had been ongoing, not a one-time-only occasion. She even had worn a wedding band—to enhance the deception when they were out in public, sure, but might it have been a gift from him, to show his love?

The lies we tell ourselves when we don't want to see what's under our noses. For doing this to me, Douglas would have found his belongings waiting for him on the front doorstep, starting with his copy of Debrett's and that stupid coat of arms.

"You're just finding out?" I asked her delicately, for truly, it was none of my business, except in the broad way attempted murder—possible attempted murder—is everyone's business. But she was eager to talk, even euphoric—now that the crisis was past and her cowardly husband returned to her.

"He told me his stepbrother had died, and as there was no one else, he had to go handle the arrangements. He forgot to take his phone and I saw the text messages from her. I followed him out here. I brought my makeup kit with me so I could observe what went on, unobserved. I'm an actress, you see."

Of course by now I'd realized the wrinkles we'd seen in the dim light of the fireplace had been latex, glued on and painted over, as were the clawlike, horror-show hands.

She added, as if it explained everything, and perhaps it did, "Stanford was always a weak man."

You got that right, lady.

She read my look. "I've stood by him through everything. Other affairs, sure. Passing flings. But this time was . . . different."

Yes, Becky's birth made a huge difference. I wondered if the child had been in danger, too, if only for an instant. Had Caroline handed Becky over for some reason? Had the child been rescued from falling just in time? Somehow, I knew that would have been her cover story, if push came to shove—"I was the rescuer, not the attacker." I eyed her closely as she went on.

"I had to know, this time. I finally had to make him choose. This woman, or me? What did he really want? And—you saw. He chose me, my family, our family. You saw; he chose us. He didn't care if that woman died. He didn't lift a finger to try to save her." She smiled complacently. I wondered if she was completely unhinged. "He'll never see either of them again."

My thoughts returned to the image of Becky being driven away. And I thought, she's better off.

"She might have drowned," I said.

"I'm an expert swimmer. I would not have allowed that to happen."

I doubted that. She didn't need the elaborate disguise to prevent a drowning or death from hypothermia. She needed it to commit a murder.

I could not resist. The woman was as deluded in her way as poor Caroline had been. The real question was why she would stay with such a creep. I said, "And you believe he has chosen you?"

"I know it."

"There's Becky to think of. I assume she's his."

"We've no proof of that," she said, coldly.

Her blindness to anything but her own wants angered me to the boiling point. "Caroline will ask for help. For money, support. Especially now that the affair is in the open. And she'd be well entitled."

Delphine scoffed at that. "She's already tried a spot of blackmail to try to get him to leave me. That's the kind of woman she is." Caroline did not strike me as being that kind of woman at all, but I let Delphine run on. "We'll see," she said. "We are well off and I'm prepared to be generous. If . . ."

If Caroline agreed to forget the whole thing, she'd be compensated. Got it. As things stood, she'd be better off taking the money. And staying as far away from her lover and his noxious wife as she could get.

Would Caroline really be that wise? Somehow I doubted it. Remembering the adoring way she looked at Sandford, she might try again, once the shock wore off. Motivated perhaps even more by having met his appalling wife.

"Do you really think she'll go for that?" I asked. "Being bought off?"

"She already has."

Again I didn't believe her. Would she just go quietly, given what had happened? I could think of only one thing that would frighten her.

Becky. The thought of losing Becky.

Delphine nodded. "The threat of a team of lawyers lined up against her is powerful. To someone of her class, particularly."

God. She had played the one card that would work. In case bribery alone wasn't effective, in case physical intimidation didn't frighten her off—only make her angry, as it would me—there was the threat of taking Becky away from her, using some made-up accusation that she was an unfit, single mother. I'd seen more than a few of my students at the heart of ugly custody battles to know how that game was played. The threat of losing Becky was guaranteed to terrify Caroline.

"She wanted sole custody, in writing," said Delphine, again

with a sneer that made my fingers itch to reach out and shake her until her brains rattled. "As if anything else were ever going to happen. The woman's delusional. She's more than welcome to custody."

Would Caroline call Delphine's bluff? I doubted it. She wouldn't have the money to fight in court, for one thing. Just some money doled out, nicely judged to keep her away, to pay for Becky's basic needs. It wasn't blackmail, of course, but I'd be willing to bet Delphine would portray it as such.

I remembered the feel of Becky's soft little body as I'd held her yesterday. She was the casualty here.

"They won't be bothering us again."

The "or else" hung in the air.

I stood. Like Caroline, I couldn't get away from her fast enough.

WHAT GOES AROUND

by Kathryn Johnson

Destination: Chicago, Illinois
The World's Columbian Exposition attracts visitors and exhibitors from all over the world. A bridge designer, patent medicine entrepreneur, and young married couple find themselves sharing lodgings, until one of them turns up dead.

June, 1893—Chicago

"That is a perfectly dreadful idea!" Polly Thompson gave her neighbor, May, a stern look.

"Not at all. You'll rent rooms in no time, close as we are to the Exposition."

The World's Columbian Exposition, celebrating four hundred years since Columbus landed in America, had just opened, and every hotel room in Chicago was booked.

"Mama, you've said my secretarial pay isn't enough to meet our expenses," her daughter Sarah pointed out.

Now they were ganging up on her?

"Anyway, this place is far too large for just you and Sarah." May flung her arms wide as if in demonstration of the spaciousness. "Letting out a few rooms is the perfect solution."

Polly's head throbbed. "Do you have any idea how much work taking in boarders will mean?" On the other hand, she couldn't ignore the logic of May's suggestion. In the year since Adam had passed away, they'd barely scraped by.

Sarah lowered her voice conspiratorially. "The Kolinskis let out two of their rooms, fifty dollars for each, per week!"

Polly stared at her. "Each?" She envisioned cooking for strangers, laundering their dirty linens. She shuddered. And what of her cherished privacy?

"Listen, Sarah and I can help. I'll cook the evening meal. Sarah can strip the beds and wash sheets. You'll do that for your ma, won't you, dear?"

"Of course!" cried her daughter, making it sound like a game. A game her darling eighteen-year-old girl would likely lose interest in far too quickly.

"Fifty dollars a week." Polly pressed her lips together. She was having one of her you'll-live-to-regret-this feelings.

***

The first boarder arrived in response to the tasteful sign Polly placed in her window.

"Doctor Franklin T. Morgan," said the red-whiskered gentleman in a dignified black frock coat, introducing himself. He grasped a carpet bag in one hand, and a gold-tipped walking stick in the other. "What a lovely home you have."

"Come this way." Polly beckoned him inside. She liked his eyes—playful they were, the color of periwinkle flowers. And his manners—impeccable! The prickliness of meeting a stranger eased. She showed him the middle room at the top of the stairs.

"I serve a light supper at six o'clock sharp. Breakfast, buffet-style, available by seven a.m. Most visitors to the fairgrounds take their midday meals there. I haven't gone myself, but my friend tells me there's an astonishing variety of international foods on the Midway Plaisance."

"Excellent! I expect I shall be far too busy at my booth to return until late in the day." He smiled his approval and advanced her two weeks' rent.

Perhaps she had been foolish to not come to this arrangement sooner. A hundred dollars—just like that! It seemed almost too easy.

Not an hour later, a young couple appeared at her door.

"The name is Wesley. Alan Wesley. And this is my wife, Winifred. I wonder if you might have a suitable room for us?"

Polly looked them up and down. Their clothing was neither elegant nor shabby—store-bought, surely, but so were her clothes. They seemed clean, respectable persons. But one never knew. The newspaper had warned of pickpockets and confidence men—attracted by the moneyed fair crowd. But these two didn't look shifty or dangerous.

The woman fingered a simple silver locket, dangling from a silk cord around her throat. A plain wedding band graced her left hand, but that might be a contrivance. Should she ask for a marriage license as proof they were lawfully wed? Such a touchy issue. She didn't want to play host to disreputable goings on.

"For how long will you want the room?" she asked.

Mr. Wesley glanced at his wife. "I should say two days will suffice."

Mrs. Wesley dipped her head in silent agreement.

Polly decided they were likely too poor to afford more than two nights in the city. She led them up to the largest of the remaining rooms, Sarah's bedroom before they became hoteliers.

"You aren't from around here," she said, thinking she'd heard a subtle difference in the man's speech. "Boston, is it? New York?"

"No," the man said. "We're from—"

"Canada," his wife supplied.

***

"Only one room left to let." May nibbled one of Polly's soda biscuits, fresh from the oven. "See how easy that was!"

Polly stood at the stove whipping potatoes with milk and butter to go with May's meatloaf for their supper. "Did I tell you the doctor is also an inventor?"

"No!" May's eyes widened.

"He's come to sell his patented tonics and educate people about modern treatments for their ailments. He gave Sarah a sample."

"How wonderful!" But the gleam in May's eyes quickly dimmed. "By the by, have you heard? Two more houses were broken into. The police think they're getting in through unlocked windows or doors. Used to be, no one saw the need for locks."

A brisk tap on the front door interrupted meal preparations. Polly patted her hands on her apron.

Bookended by two pots of bright red geraniums on her stoop stood a stranger of extraordinary appearance. His beard and mustache clearly had not been trimmed in days. His worsted wool waistcoat and trousers appeared far too heavy for such a mild day. But it was the disturbing intensity of his dark eyes that made her retreat into her foyer.

"I need a large, quiet room," the stranger stated forcefully before lunging, uninvited, through her door. "At the rear of the house, if you please, madam." He thrust a business card at her.

"Oh!" She blinked at it, hesitating before taking it from him.

George Washington Gale Ferris, Jr.
Engineer - Metal Bridge Designs & Inspection
Pittsburgh, Pennsylvania

"I'm sorry, um, Mr. Ferris," she managed with some relief. "The only room I have available overlooks the street. It isn't much bigger than a closet." Good. She didn't want him under her roof. Not for another minute.

"Bother!" he grumbled. "Well, it'll have to do. The terms, madam?"

With reluctance, she recited her rules, the price of room and board, and the fact that he'd be sharing a bathroom with her other boarders. He muttered further complaints, but reached into his trouser pocket and pulled out sufficient bills to reserve a week's stay.

"Are you building a bridge hereabouts, Mr. Ferris?" She held up his card when he looked confused. "Or do you also have a booth on the Midway, like one of my other boarders?"

"A booth? Good lord, no!" He laughed. "Would that my life were that simple. No, no. I'm here to supervise the final stages of construction of my wheel."

"Wheel?" Then she recalled the oddity she'd heard would be the centerpiece of the Exposition.

"Yes, the Paris Exposition had its tower, designed by Mr. Eiffel. Chicago will have my magnificent Ferris Wheel. Come by next week, I'll give you a free ride." He leaned in, eyes electric-bright, approaching madness in their enthusiasm. "When your car reaches the top, you'll be over two-hundred-and-sixty feet in the air."

"Oh, my!" She touched her fingertips to her throat.

***

It was while they were gathered around the dining room table that evening when things started to go terribly wrong.

Mr. Ferris, looking exhausted and distracted, shoved his meatloaf around on his plate, eating little of it. He rudely refused to respond to inquiries as to his day at the fairgrounds. Apparently, things had not gone well.

Thankfully, Dr. Morgan took up the conversation. He spoke eloquently about the virtues of patent medicines. "All my nostrums, tonics, and salves are very popular on the Midway!"

"And what are they good for?" Sarah asked. "I haven't yet tried the sample you gave me."

"What are they not good for, you might as well ask." He winked at her, making the girl blush. "Rheumatism, female complaints, colic, anxiety, soreness of muscles, indigestion, and more."

"Bollocks!" snarled Mr. Ferris. "Nothing but a damned snake oil salesman, that's what you are, sir."

The Wesleys sat stone still. Polly thought she saw the glitter of tears in Winifred's eyes. Then again, it might have been a trick of the softly hissing gaslights.

"Stop it!" Mr. Wesley whispered urgently in his wife's ear. He looked around as if suddenly aware the others could hear him.

"I–I'm sorry." Winifred rose unsteadily from her chair and fled the room, taffeta skirts rustling like dead leaves.

"Oh dear," said Polly.

Alan Wesley laid his napkin on the table. "Excuse us, please. She's very sensitive about, um,"—his gaze landed on Ferris—"bad language." He followed his wife out of the room.

"Well, now," Dr. Morgan chortled, "I dare say a good dose of my tonic would steady the lady's nerves."

Ferris glowered at the man then turned to Sarah, seated beside him. "Don't let him bamboozle you, miss. His potions are worthless concoctions of grain alcohol, laudanum, and—"

"Yet I grow richer by the day." The doctor regarded his accuser over clasped hands. "The public loves me, while they think you a fool for your metal sky-wheel. What will they say about you when it comes crashing to the ground?"

Ferris's face flushed a deep, purplish red. "You are nothing but a fraud, sir! And a dangerous one at that." He pushed to his feet and stalked out of the room.

Polly released a held breath. How had her guests come to hate each other . . . and so quickly?

As if Dr. Morgan sensed her discomfort, he reached across the table and patted her hand. "Don't be concerned, dear lady. Some folks fight progress. One would think they'd rather suffer than change their old-fashioned ways."

***

Polly bolted upright in bed. Voices! She was sure she'd heard voices. She reached out in the dark, felt her daughter's warm body beneath the quilt beside her, and let out a sigh of relief.

Then another shout came from somewhere in the house. Whoever it was, they sounded furious.

Polly pulled her robe from the bedpost, stepped into her slippers, and opened her bedroom door. The dark hallway appeared empty. With considerable trepidation, she moved along the carpeted landing.

"Is anyone there? Hello?" She paused and listened. Nothing.

Polly clutched the front of her robe at her throat, trying to calm herself. She remembered the break-ins May had told her about. Was there a thief in her house?

Ever so slowly, Polly descended the stairs. She reached out and turned up the gaslights as she went. An amber glow lifted away the darkness.

Comforted by the light, she walked through each room on the ground floor—kitchen, pantry, dining room, parlor. Nothing seemed to have been disturbed, and there was nothing missing. But what of the voices?

If she called the police, would they think she'd been dreaming? Imagining things? She checked all the doors and windows on the main floor. All were locked, except for the back door that led out to the garden. She threw the latch, telling herself she must be more careful in the future. Was this how he'd got in? And left?

But an intruder would have to be very stupid to make so much noise. Perhaps one of her guests had surprised the thief and scared him off.

Polly hated to wake her boarders, but she felt duty-bound to check on everyone.

Ever so softly she rapped on Dr. Morgan's door. His sleep-gruff answer came. "Yes? What?"

"Are you all right, Doctor?"

"Fine."

"So sorry to have disturbed you." She moved on to the next door. Knocked.

"Mr. Wesley?"

Winifred responded almost immediately. "He's sleeping, Mrs. Thompson. I hate to wake him. Is it important?"

"Maybe not, dear, but, you see—"

The couple's door cracked open. "Those awful noises woke you, too?" Ms. Wesley, bundled in a floral nightgown, peeked out at her. "Is everything all right?"

"It seems to be. No one has entered your room tonight?"

"No. I'm sure I would have known. I'm a light sleeper."

Polly crossed the hall to Mr. Ferris's room and knocked. "Mr. Ferris. Are you quite well? There has been some trouble and I—"

The door flew open and she found herself facing a fully-clothed man who looked as far removed from sleep as any human being could be. Books, blueprints, and charts were spread across the bed behind him. He glowered at her through bloodshot eyes. The skin above his mustache shone ghastly pale in the dim gaslight.

"What the devil, woman! First your rowdy tenants. And now you pounding at my door."

"I'm so very s–sorry. I—"

"Another disturbance and I shall be forced to find alternate accommodations. A bloody park bench would be an improvement!" He slammed the door in her face.

***

The next morning, Mr. Ferris and the Wesleys quietly helped themselves to griddlecakes, scrambled eggs, bacon rashers, and homemade applesauce. Dr. Morgan hadn't come down yet.

Conversation around the table was barely civil. Polly supposed her guests were as tired as she was after the previous night's interruptions.

While her boarders finished eating, she and May started

washing up the cooking pans. Polly asked Sarah to make up the rooms. "And see if the doctor needs fresh towels."

"Must I?"

Polly frowned at her daughter's reluctant tone. "Yes, you agreed to help." Was the girl so soon trying to dodge her share of the chores?

Moments later, an unearthly scream from the floor above sent a pan flying out of May's soapy hands.

***

The police arrived within the half hour. Residents and guests of the house sat in the parlor until the two officers came back downstairs. Polly's hands hadn't stopped trembling. The Wesleys looked stunned. Ferris, stoic. Poor Sarah kept breaking into sobs, so traumatized was she by her discovery of Dr. Morgan's body.

"Miss," the younger of the two officers said, "it would help if you could tell us why you went into the doctor's room."

"Because I sent her to tidy up, of course," Polly said. "And she told you—the poor man was on the floor, already dead."

"Quite, madam," the second, not-so-young or nice police officer snapped. "But if he didn't respond to the young lady's knock, why did she enter his room alone?"

"Oh, good grief!" Mr. Ferris snarled. "What are you implying, sir? Miss Sarah was simply doing her job."

Polly stared at the engineer, shocked that he'd come to her daughter's defense.

The young officer cleared his throat. "Miss Sarah, we're not accusing you of anything. In fact, it appears the doctor suffered a heart attack." He looked at Polly. "Mrs. Thompson, perhaps a cup of tea would be calming for everyone? If the rest of you will wait here in the parlor while we do what needs to be done, that will be a great help."

Polly couldn't help noticing the grateful look Sarah gave the young officer. Nor did she miss the bashful smile he sent her daughter.

***

It wasn't until the next day that Polly understood the worst was not over. The two police officers returned with a Detective Clive Evans, a rail-thin man with wolverine features and a complexion that approached gangrenous.

Detective Evans interrupted her surviving guests' breakfasts to explain that his men, the previous day, had found a pistol in Mr. Ferris's room and a hunting knife in the Wesleys' room. He asked for an explanation from each.

"I always travel with a pistol for protection," Ferris said. "I regularly carry substantial amounts of cash to pay casual laborers on construction sites."

"And you, Mr. Wesley?"

The Canadian shrugged. "If you have any experience traveling in the Northwestern wilderness, you know that a good knife often comes in handy."

The detective made no comment and turned away abruptly, heading upstairs. When he returned to the dining room, Polly could no longer restrain herself.

"I don't understand why you'd even ask about a gun or a knife, Detective. If Dr. Morgan died of natural causes—"

"The coroner considers the gentleman's death to be entirely unnatural." Evans shot her a sharp look.

Mr. Ferris perked up noticeably. "Are you saying the man was murdered?"

"I am, sir."

"But how?" Sarah burst out. "I saw no . . ."—she looked nervously at her mother— ". . . no blood."

"Poison," stated the detective, turning to her. "Madam, please tell me exactly what you prepared for the doctor for his last meal."

"But we all ate the same thing," Ferris interrupted, "served from shared serving platters at table. Wouldn't we all have been poisoned, or at the very least sick if the food had been tampered with?"

Evans tapped his foot, considering. "Then the poison must have been introduced through other means. Mrs. Thompson, did you bring the gentleman anything to eat or drink later that evening?"

"No. Nothing."

Sarah shifted on her chair just enough to draw everyone's attention. The girl's pretty blue eyes filled with tears. She stared down at her hands clutched in her lap, then at Polly, seated next to her at the table.

"Well, my girl?" the detective prompted solemnly.

"Oh, Mama!" She crumpled into an astonished Polly's arms.

"What is it, dear? What's wrong?"

Detective Evans took a step closer to the Thompson women. "What did you do to the man, miss? You might as well confess rather than make us work for the truth."

"I–I didn't do anything to him," Sarah wailed. "It was h–h–he that—"

"The bounder!" shouted Mr. Ferris.

Polly suddenly understood. "You must tell the police everything. No matter how embarrassing."

Sarah took some time to compose herself. "The day he arrived, after supper, he stepped into the upstairs hallway, saying he needed to show me something. As soon as I entered his room, he closed the door and he . . . he—"

"Horrible, horrible man!" Mrs. Wesley cried.

"Let the girl continue," the detective commanded. "Go on, miss."

She stared down at the table. "He pushed me against the door and . . . pressed his mouth over mine."

"Oh, my precious girl!" Polly gasped.

The young officer stepped forward. "Did he hurt you, Miss Sarah?"

"Oh, no! I was so shocked, you see, I didn't know what to do. Then it just happened."

"What happened?" the detective took a step toward her.

"I laughed."

"You laughed?"

"Yes, sir. I know I probably should have screamed and fought him off like any respectable woman. But it all seemed so absurd—an old man like that, and him knowing other people were in the house. What was he thinking?"

Good girl, Sarah. Humiliate the bugger! Polly thought.

The detective persisted. "You must have worried he'd interfere with you. Is that it, young lady? He tried to corner you again, later that night?"

Sarah's head snapped up. "No, sir!"

"You wanted to punish the man for taking liberties."

"Stop it, Detective." Polly stood and moved between him and her daughter. "When I asked Sarah to clean his room the next morning, she was clearly nervous but didn't say why. Now I know."

Evans' eyes narrowed. "Or maybe she thought it less incriminating for someone else to discover his body."

***

Over the next few days, the young Chicago police officer—Frank Milton—returned with updates on the investigation. He always asked for Sarah.

According to the coroner's report, a quantity of poisonous fluids had been ingested by the victim. Given their nature and potency, and the amount consumed, Dr. Morgan would have quickly lost consciousness and died during the night.

"So, it was suicide, not murder?" Sarah said.

Frank shook his head solemnly. "Oh, no, ma'am. Our Detective Evans, he's eliminated that possibility. People say the doctor was ever such a cheerful and charming fellow, and doing so well with his business. No. Murder most foul it was. Detective Evans believes the victim was forced to drink the vile stuff."

"Forced?" Polly gasped. She thought of the voices and shuddered. Had she heard the murdered man's cries for help? Perhaps the doctor woke to discover the neighborhood thief and he shouted out an alarm to the household. But would a burglar take the time to wrestle poison down a man's throat before fleeing? And why would the doctor have so calmly answered her through his bedroom door—saying he was fine when he was dying?

"Hard to imagine anyone would have willingly drunk that foul mess." Frank screwed up his face. "Chemist says there was turpentine, morphine, sugar syrup, and Lord knows what else."

"Then whoever killed him must have planned it, and brought the poison with them," Sarah said.

Frank shook his head. "It was one of the doctor's own tonics. We found four empty bottles returned to a crate in the closet."

***

"I don't understand why the police insist we remain in Chicago," Mr. Wesley complained. "It's not as if we could be suspects!" He stabbed his fork viciously into the chicken breast on his plate.

"Damned inconvenient," Mr. Ferris agreed. "I should be back in Pittsburgh by now."

"Is your wheel complete?" Sarah asked. "I want a ride if it is."

"Oh, do you really think it's safe?" Polly realized, too late, that its inventor might take this as an insult. "I'm sorry, sir. It's just that the newspapers—"

Ferris waved away her concern. "Of course, journalists always sensationalize. We've tested the wheel. Put on my own people yesterday. Perfectly sound."

"Oh, I must see it, Mama! Everyone is talking about Mr. Ferris's Great Wheel." She rushed on. "My friend Agatha says everyone who has visited The White City says it's breathtaking. Greek temples spread over acres of parkland. Pretty canals with electric boats shuttling people about."

Ferris beamed proudly. "Come as my guests, ladies. Name your day." He waved toward the Wesleys. "You as well, of course. A pity you don't have children; it would be quite the treat for the little ones and . . . Oh, dear! Have I said something wrong?"

Polly turned to the young couple. Indeed, Mrs. Wesley's face had gone utterly white. Her husband looked little better.

"It's nothing," Winifred whispered, her eyes filling with tears. "I had thought that once we . . . I mean, if it weren't for—"

"My wife and I can't have children," Mr. Wesley stated. "I'm afraid Winnie is sensitive on that subject." He helped her to her feet.

"How sad," Sarah said when they'd left the room.

"I wish I hadn't spoken. Far too personal." Ferris stared at the doorway through which the couple had departed. "It's just that . . . when one shares a roof with people, if only for a short time, you begin to—"

"Feel as though they're family," Polly murmured. "I'm sure the Wesleys realize you meant no harm, Mr. Ferris."

It was then that the night of the murder snapped back into her mind with shocking clarity. And she thought she knew what had happened. Although, if she was right, it made everything worse.

***

The next morning Polly explained her suspicions to May.

"But suspecting and knowing are two different things," May objected. "I mean, you can't just accuse a body."

"That's why I need proof . . . and your help."

"I just can't believe . . ." May shook her head. "I mean, matters of the heart can drive a person to extremes. But murder? And by so violent a means?"

"I know, dear. I know." Polly sighed.

Soon, Mr. Ferris left to join his crew on the Midway. Sarah went off to her typist's job downtown. Mr. Wesley headed out for his morning walk through the park. The sound of running water announced that Winifred was preparing her customary morning bath.

Polly and May put down their teacups and stood up from the sofa as if drawn to their feet by a single string.

They climbed the stairs to the second floor without speaking. May positioned herself between the shared bathroom at the end of the hallway and the Wesleys' bedroom door. Polly let herself into their room.

As soon as she closed the door behind her, she felt a wave of guilt for snooping. She reminded herself that she was on a mission: to learn the truth.

The room was furnished simply: a double bed, single bedside table, tall oak chifforobe, and mirrored vanity table with a cushioned stool. On the table lay a lady's tortoise-shell brush, comb, and hand-mirror. In the pink crystal dish lay Winifred's rings, locket, and silver earrings.

Polly reached for the locket, fingers trembling. As she had suspected, on closer examination, the dark cord wasn't silk at all. It was finely braided hair, meant to be worn in memory of a loved one. Mourning jewelry.

What she must do next was too awful to contemplate. She felt as though she were exhuming a body. But she had to know, didn't she? Only then could she go to the police.

Just then she heard May's voice, raised in alarm. "No, Mrs. Wesley! I'll fetch your bath salts."

A softer voice answered. Hurried footsteps. And then the bedroom door swept open.

***

Winifred Wesley stared at Polly. "What are you doing, Mrs. Thompson?" Her lovely eyes shot to the locket.

"Cleaning the room!" May squeaked.

Polly winced at the hopeless excuse. "I suppose we should talk, Winifred," she said gently.

Below, the sound of the front door opening and closing and heavy treads on the stairway announced Alan Wesley's return from his constitutional. The three women froze. A moment later, he appeared in the bedroom doorway. The couple exchanged significant looks.

Wesley's face darkened. "I don't care what the police say. We're leaving. Winifred, pack!"

His wife—still transfixed by the locket in Polly's hand—seemed not to have heard him. "You have no idea what we've been through," she murmured.

"Please don't, darling." Wesley stepped toward his wife, but at the last moment spun to face Polly. His eyes brimmed with fury. "Whatever you may believe, you have no proof."

Polly sighed. "You poor, poor people."

The woman jumped as if she'd been shot. "Alan, she knows! Oh, Lord, she knows everything."

Polly stepped toward her. "Your husband is right. I have no proof. Other than what's inside this locket." She placed it tenderly into Winifred's palm. "This is your baby, isn't it? Your precious child?"

Wesley touched his wife's arm in warning, but she collapsed backward onto the bed and sat clutching the locket to her breast. "Jenny. My little Jenny Ann," she whispered.

He steadied himself against a bedpost, resignation replacing anger in his features.

"What happened to her?" Polly whispered.

Winifred snapped open the heart-shaped locket and held it out to Polly. In one half rested a sepia miniature of a little girl, no older than two. In the other was an inscription: Our precious Jenny. Lost but never forgotten. Forgive us, dear.

Alan Wesley had said they couldn't have children. A lie, it

would seem.

The tragic story spilled out.

Wanting to soothe their baby's terrible teething pain, the couple sought recommendations from friends. Several mentioned Dr. Emmanuel's Healthful Restorative, which advertised cures including calming fussy children and inducing peaceful sleep. Desperate, they tried it on Jenny and put her back to bed. Minutes later, to their relief, their child's cries ceased. But when they checked on Jenny during the night, their baby had stopped breathing.

They requested an autopsy. The coroner told them that the tonic they'd given their child was laced with morphine, far too much for a toddler. Combined with the high alcohol content, the mixture was deadly to a child so young.

"But why blame Dr. Morgan for an inferior medicine that isn't his?" May asked.

"Morgan is, or was, Dr. Emmanuel," Wesley explained wearily. "Although I don't believe a medical degree exists for any of his aliases. He leaves town, changes his name, appearance, and bottle labels to avoid arrest."

Polly watched Winifred caress the silver heart resting in her lap. "I see."

"The man was the devil himself." Wesley wiped at his own damp eyes with the sleeve of his jacket. "Our Milwaukee police issued a warrant for his arrest, but he fled before they could catch him. We tracked him down under a different name in Ohio," Wesley continued, "then again in Michigan. But he continued to elude us."

"Until we finally followed him to Chicago," Winifred said softly.

"But how did he not recognize you? Surely your daughter's death would have made the newspapers."

Wesley grimaced. "We borrowed one of his tricks. We changed our name, and altered our appearances."

"Mr. Ferris was right," Winifred whispered. "He called the man the devil himself. Our baby isn't the only child to have suffered from his greed. So many have died, or become addicted, made terribly sick . . ."

"I honestly don't think the man cared who he hurt." Wesley stared pleadingly at Polly. "You must see that we couldn't rest until he was stopped. Leaving it to the police simply wasn't working."

***

The crowded Midway Plaisance stretched out before Polly as Sarah dragged her from one display to the next.

They'd spent the morning at the Women's Pavilion, then the Palace of Fine Arts and Louis Comfort Tiffany's glorious chapel. Moving sidewalks and trams comfortably transported visitors across more than six hundred acres of fairgrounds with exhibits contributed by forty-six nations.

As evening fell over the transformed marshlands, electric lights flickered magically on, and Polly began to feel the pleasant weariness of a day well spent.

She had pieced together that fateful night. Alan Wesley had been in the doctor's room when she knocked. He had answered her through the closed door, mimicking Morgan's voice. Winifred pretended that her husband was with her, sleeping. The anguished voices that had awakened Polly belonged to Wesley and Morgan, locked in a combat of wills. Wesley threating the other man with his knife, forcing him to drink quantities of his own vile potion until he passed out.

Polly was incapable of lying to the police. But she could remain silent. Without proof, the case would remain unsolved.

And so, she had hugged Alan and Winifred, and out of her home they had walked. No promises to write. No addresses exchanged. But she held them in her heart, the three of them—father, mother, and precious baby Jenny.

SUMMER JOB

by Judith Green

Destination: Camden, Maine
Crewing on a passenger schooner seemed a perfect summer job for a college boy. But Jared finds not everything is idyllic aboard: not the hard work, not the contempt shown by the experienced deckhand, and not the mystery surrounding his predecessor's abrupt departure.

Jared snapped awake. *Where am I?*

The thin light of dawn poked in through a porthole. The air was heavy with moisture and the smell of unwashed clothes. From all sides came a gentle sloshing sound.

Oh, right. Maine. The harbor in Camden. The schooner.

With a gurgling snort, Rex turned over in the opposite bunk. "C'mon, College Boy. We gotta get to work."

"Huh?" Jared sat up in his bunk. "But I thought we didn't take off until after breakfast."

Rex was on his feet now, his head nearly grazing the ceiling of their tiny cabin. "After *their* breakfast." He jerked a thumb in the direction of the galley. "We sail as soon as the passengers are done eating."

Jared rolled out of his bunk and pulled a T-shirt on over his head. "So whatever happened to the other deckhand? Why'd he quit?"

"Who, Jimmy?" Rex shrugged. "Wouldn't know. Let's go."

"Coming!" Jared hustled after Rex up the ladder and out into the bright Maine morning.

A stiff breeze snapped the pennants on mast tops, and ruffled Jared's hair. The tang of the salt air, the sparkle of the sun on the water, the cling-clang of rigging against metal masts as the boats rocked at anchor all around them in the picture-postcard harbor . . . Oh, man, this was the life!

He'd seen the ad: the *Mary Josephine* needed a deckhand for the rest of the summer. They must have been desperate, because Captain Endicott had hired him sight unseen, and could Jared get his ass up to Camden—now! "Last guy jumped ship in Castine and left me flat!" the captain bellowed. "And I got twenty-three people boarding tomorrow evening!"

So Jared hit the road. By the time he'd negotiated the narrow, winding streets of Camden and found the dock, all the greeting he got from the captain was, "Hurry up and get on board. Rex'll tell you what to do."

The schooner was smaller than Jared had expected, hardly more than a hundred feet long, everything below decks small and cramped. But there was plenty to do: loading enough food for an army, cleaning the toilets, hauling the passengers' luggage aboard and stowing it in their miniscule cabins—everything performed at a dead run before he and Rex fell into their bunks long past dark.

But now, this morning, came the big moment: getting the schooner's sails up, and the anchor, and who knew what else. Jared didn't Know The Ropes—ha, ha—so he'd have to depend on this know-it-all Rex. For everything.

The hatch cover over the galley cabin was tipped up, and through the open space came the tinkle of silverware and a genial hubbub of conversation . . . and the aromas of coffee and bacon, and fresh-baked bread. Jared hadn't met the cook yet, but she must be great. He pictured a sort of ocean-going Mrs. Santa Claus. Suddenly his stomach growled so loudly that he expected the tourists on the dock to turn and stare.

"First we pull in the gangplank," Rex announced. "And don't scratch the paint, or the cap'n'll eat you for lunch. On three. *One. Two* . . ." And he started to lift.

Jared was caught off guard. The gangplank slipped through his fingers and slammed to the deck.

"Watch it, College Boy!" Rex roared. "What, you were all the cap'n could find to replace Jimmy? The only person actually breathing? I'll bet you don't know the mainsail from the jib! You're gonna be lots of fun out on the bowsprit!"

Bowsprit. That was a word Jared did know. And he couldn't help glancing toward the front of the ship, where the spar stuck out and out, twenty feet at least over the open water. And, he realized with a shudder, it had a sail wrapped around it. A sail that would have to be *un*wrapped by—

The deckhands.

He was beginning to understand why Jimmy had quit.

"Ready to cast off, boys?" rumbled a voice behind them. And they were off again, vaulting onto the dock to untie the huge lines, leaping back aboard to coil the lines and stow the bumpers. Then—

"The mainsail's a piece of cake," Rex said over his shoulder as he picked his way through the passengers, now all milling about on the deck. "There's always some guys like to help with the yo-heave-ho stuff."

The ship had pulled smoothly away from the dock and was motoring out among the moored boats, as the busy town slid away behind them. The captain stood at the ship's enormous wheel, one big hand gripping a spoke, the other thrust casually into the pocket of his rumpled jacket.

"Anybody want to help, just grab the line," Rex called to the passengers, pointing to the rope that trailed across the deck. And sure enough, a few of the men happily lined up, as if getting ready for a game of tug-of-war. "Haul away."

They hauled. Rex started to sing in a mellow baritone, some ancient sea chantey, and the four men pulled together while beside them the enormous pile of canvas on the boom stretched up and up in an ever-broadening triangle. The sail took on life, snapping in the wind, bright in the morning sunshine. Up and up, huge now above them, powerful. Jared felt his heart beat faster as his arms reached and pulled, reached and pulled, in time with the other men. This was the life.

"OK, now the jib." Rex's voice lasered into Jared's thoughts. "Let's see how you do on the bowsprit, College Boy."

It was as bad as he thought, wrestling with the stiff sailcloth, feet planted on a single rope, balanced above the gray-green water that churned fifteen feet below him on its way to being sliced by the ship's heavy wooden bow. But at last the sail was ready, and they were set to haul away—and he was back on board.

"Well, well, Rex," the captain called from his position at the wheel. "Trying out the new guy?"

"Uh . . . yes, sir, Cap'n," Rex said, and dove down the companionway.

The captain nodded. "Rex usually gets the jib ready before we leave port," he told Jared. "Easier that way. But you did OK, Sullivan. Go get your breakfast."

He'd done OK! Rex was messing with him, but he'd done OK! Glowing with pride, Jared stepped onto the ladder.

The galley was low and dark, lit only by a row of tiny windows under the hatch—how had twenty-three passengers fit in here? Rex lounged on a bench at one of the tables, using the ship's hull as a backrest, eating a biscuit slathered in butter. Beyond him, a huge woodstove glowing with heat hunched against one wall. In a cast iron skillet atop the stove, half a dozen eggs sizzled alongside slices of bacon.

And at the counter stood a young woman, mincing onions with an enormous knife. She was slim with blond hair caught up in a rubber band, wearing a cotton dress washed to colorlessness. Her eyes, as she turned to look at him, were large and dark over high cheekbones. Oh, man! She was *beautiful!*

"I'm Anna," she said, her voice so low that he almost couldn't hear her. Her hands went on mincing the onions. She didn't even need to look. "You must be Jared."

"Yes. Um . . . Jared Sullivan. The new deckhand." The glow from his triumph on the bowsprit was gone. "But . . . um . . . you knew that."

"Yes." Anna tipped the cutting board over a pot. "Stew for lunch," she explained, and glided to the stove to slide the eggs and bacon onto two plates. "Coffee's fresh. Cups are over there," she added, gesturing with her perfect chin toward a cup rack on the counter. A plate in each hand, she turned toward the nearer table.

Rex stood up to block her way. "Only three eggs this morning?"

Anna tried to step around him. "You want more, I'll cook more. There's plenty of biscuits."

Rex slipped an arm around her waist and pulled her to him, plates and all. "That's not enough to keep a real man going." Anna struggled to pull away, but Rex's arm tightened around her. He tilted her face up toward his. "Makes it so all a man wants is—"

"Let her go!" Jared squawked.

Both Rex and Anna turned to stare at him. Even the fried eggs seemed to look at him, goggle-eyed on their blue china plates. "Well, I mean, come on," Jared stammered. "She doesn't like it."

"Shh, both of you," Anna whispered, and rolled her eyes toward the open windows over their heads. "They'll hear." She wriggled out of Rex's embrace, set the plates on the table, and retreated behind the counter.

Rex dropped onto a stool and used his fork to trowel butter onto another biscuit before applying himself to his eggs. Anna picked up her knife and began crushing cloves of garlic against the cutting board. Jared found himself watching her, gazing at the line of her cheek against her narrow shoulder as she leaned on the knife.

"Thank you." Her words were so quiet that he felt them more than heard them. She looked up at him then, and her eyes were deeper than the ocean.

"You gonna eat?" Rex cut in. "Or just look at the scenery?"

Anna dropped the knife and turned to load a chunk of wood. "Man," Jared said, casting about for something—anything—to say. "Why do you have a wood stove? Isn't fire dangerous on a ship?"

Rex grinned at him around a mouthful of egg. "Propane could blow a hole in the side—down we go. Or were you thinking of electric, with a re-e-e-ally long extension cord?" He shoved a last chunk of biscuit into his mouth and stood up. "Well, you two have fun. *Some* of us have work to do." And he disappeared up the ladder.

The galley suddenly seemed very quiet, in spite of the chatter of the passengers on deck, and the waves sloshing by inches away on the other side of the hull. Jared ate his eggs. Anna minced the garlic. The silence grew.

Anna glanced at him, then back at her cutting board. The knife went on mincing, mincing.

"So . . . I'm curious," Jared said. "Do you know why this Jimmy guy quit? Did Rex scare him off?"

Anna shrugged, a tiny, helpless movement of her slim shoulders. She wouldn't look at him.

***

The afternoon passed languidly by. The schooner had the entire circle of ocean to herself, in glorious solitude. The dome of sky was an azure blue, punctuated here and there by a fluffy white cloud which would have been perfect in a child's drawing. The sails filled lustily with the breeze; the ship scudded through the waves; the sunlight sparkled on the ever-shifting water in a million, million points of light; the passengers took photos, or sunbathed, or, overcome by so much fresh air, dozed.

Jared dashed about below decks, cleaning the bathrooms, swabbing the warren of corridors, delivering fresh towels to the passengers' cramped cabins as well as a mid-afternoon snack of cheese and crackers, cookies, brownies, iced tea, beer. "Do you ever get a moment off from cooking?" he asked Anna.

"The passengers have to eat," she murmured.

Later, as he stood at the rail watching a miniature island slide by, not much more than a craggy rock encircled with surf and capped by one solitary pine, he could hear Anna moving about down in the galley: the *thunk* of wood into the stove, the rattle of a pot lid. Then a song began to unfurl and lift through the open sidelights under the hatch cover. Anna was singing to herself down there as she worked: a Gaelic melody, by the sound of it. Her voice was sweet and pure.

It was quite possibly the most beautiful thing Jared had ever heard.

***

Evening, purple dusk gathering along the far horizon. They motored into a little harbor in the lee of a lonely island: a few houses clinging to a hillside, a dock, somewhere in the distance a dog barking. Rex and Jared stood ready with the enormous anchor while the captain chose his mooring. Jared tried to watch for the captain's signal, but suddenly Rex called out "Now!" and the anchor ripped out of his hands and plunged into the water.

Jared jumped away as the chain leapt overboard after the anchor, uncoiling with a metallic gnashing like teeth that could tear off fingers or a whole arm in a flash. Or drag an unwary deckhand overboard and down to the bottom. He shivered. "Isn't there a safer way to do this?" he asked Rex.

"Wuss," Rex said.

After supper, Jared washed the dishes on the deck, and passed them back down the companionway to Anna. He could see her face upturned to him, luminous as the moon, and her hands, when they brushed his, were slightly roughened and cool.

***

Morning again. Kicked awake by Rex. Anchor up, sails up, breakfast. Had Jared ever had any other existence?

They sailed to a green cupcake of an island with a classic rocky headland and a cove sheltered by dark green pines—how many islands did Maine have, anyway? Thousands?—to let the passengers walk on the beach. Jared gathered wildflowers and brought them back, slightly wilted, to present to Anna.

Of course Rex saw them. Of course Rex had to comment. "Oh, goody! Look what College Boy picked for our cabin!"

Jared tucked the bouquet under his arm and turned to help hoist the dinghy up to the divots. "It's for the galley."

"Hah! You think Anna's into you?" Rex jerked on his line, sending the dinghy swinging, so that Jared's line burned through his hands before he grabbed it and pulled back.

A guy can hope, Jared thought. He scooped up the scattered flowers from the deck and ran the gauntlet of lady passengers murmuring "Oh, how sweet" to clatter down the galley ladder into the aroma of tomato sauce and baking bread.

Anna was chopping lettuce into an enormous salad bowl. "I brought you these from the island," Jared said, holding out the bouquet.

"They're beautiful." She laid her knife down, and slipped the flowers into a jar. "Thank you."

He watched her hands arranging the flowers in the jar. He wanted to feel her fingers entwined with his.

***

The day passed, full of golden light, and always high above them the huge sails full of wind. Jared had just finished cleaning the bathrooms, and had come up on deck for a moment in the air, when Rex was at his elbow. “C’mon, College Boy. We got company.”

Jared looked around at the unbroken circle of horizon. Nearby a lonely island poked out of the waves, but that was all. “Out here?”

“Yup. Tonight’s the lobster bake. And here,” Rex added, as a boat lumbered out from around the island, “come the lobsters.”

The boat was shabby, nothing but a sort of small cab over an open deck, and a big winch which Jared supposed was for hauling up the lobster traps that were stacked in the stern. With a throaty roar that testified to its being powered by a truck engine, the boat pulled alongside. “They’re a long way out.” Jared tried to see the name of the boat in its traditional spot on the stern, but the paint was chipped and unreadable. “Where are these guys from?”

“How should I know?” Rex said. “C’mon.”

The passengers had gathered along the schooner’s rail, and chattered excitedly as the two men on the boat heaved the first of the wooden crates up to Jared. Reddish-green seaweed poked out between the slats of the crate, and water dripped from the lowest corner.

“Oof.” Jared let the crate hit the schooner’s deck with a thud. “Why do they pack these things so heavy?”

“Watch it!” Rex cried. “You wanna have lobsters crawling all over?” Now Jared could hear the rustling and clicking of the lobsters as they scrambled over each other inside. “Let’s get these crates down to the galley.”

“All right, all right.” Jared hefted a crate and pushed through the crowd of passengers, which parted like the proverbial Red Sea, while behind him the lobster boat roared away.

When he clambered awkwardly down the ladder, Anna wasn’t at her usual spot behind the counter in the galley. The pots and pans hung neatly from their hooks, the knives marched in a row across their magnetic holder, and the counter was scrubbed clean. The curtain was drawn across her bunk, just down the corridor beyond the big Victorian-looking icebox. Was she inside resting? He couldn’t tell.

“Move it!” Rex crowded behind him in the narrow space, carrying two crates, of course, just to show him up. Jared wrestled with the antique brass handle of the icebox until the heavy door swung open, engulfing him in cold air. He stepped in, set down the crate with a thud, then shoved it back against the shelves so that Rex could set down his double load. Inside the crates the lobsters continued their mysterious journeys, clicking across each others’ shells.

***

Jared threw himself on his bunk, desperate for an afternoon nap, but moments later came Rex's bellow: "Let's go, College Boy!" Jared hauled himself off the bunk and dragged himself up the ladder.

The ship was approaching a cluster of islands, one with a lovely curve of beach, with waves crashing blue and lacy white on the headland like something out of a painting. But there was no time for gazing. He and Rex were at it again: dropping the sails, helping the passengers into the dinghy, carefully, carefully, and rowing them to the beach in groups of four and five. And one last run back to the ship for dishes, and firewood, and an enormous cauldron of coleslaw. And on top of the load, the crates of lobsters.

"That's weird." Jared stood, balanced in the dinghy, as Rex passed down the crates. "These things feel lighter than they did this afternoon."

"The lobsters're packed in seaweed, doofus. The seaweed gets dry. Move it! Shove that crate against the thwart, or we'll never get everything in." Rex dropped onto the seat and grabbed the oars.

"Hey, what about Anna?" Jared had been waiting to lift her down into the dinghy. He could almost feel how it would be, his two hands about her slim waist—

"What about her?" Rex headed for shore with short, snapping strokes. The little dinghy practically leapt out of the water with each pull.

"Isn't she coming? To cook supper?"

"Nah," Rex said. "Lobster dinners on shore, we're the cooks."

So while the passengers strolled about the island, or collected wave-smoothed pebbles on the beach, Rex and Jared built the fire, boiled the water, massacred the lobsters, laid out all the fixings, gobbled when they could, heaved the lobster shells into the ocean, gathered everything else back into the boxes and crates, counted the passengers as they drifted back to the landing, and ferried the whole lot back to the ship.

Jared crawled back into his bunk bone-weary, and dreamed about Anna.

***

And woke in the middle of the night with the terrible feeling that she was in danger.

He lay still, listening to the waves lap against the hull just inches from his head, and thinking about the unmarked lobster boat, so far from shore . . . the lobster crates . . .

The lobster crates weren't lighter because the seaweed had dried out. What kind of idiot did Rex think he was? Whatever *else* had been in those crates was still on the ship.

He slipped out of his bunk. The floorboards were cool under his bare feet as he slid his phone out of his duffle, inched the door open, and stole out into the corridor. Maine was perfect for smuggling, he thought, as he crept toward the galley. All those coves and inlets and lonely beaches . . . Maine had as much coastline as the whole rest of the country put together. And it was close to Canada.

The elderly schooner moved and creaked like a live thing, masking his footsteps. But the door to the icebox—he'd forgotten how difficult it was to open. And suddenly Anna was standing beside him, ghostlike in her pale cotton nightgown.

"Where are the lobster crates?" Jared whispered.

"The empty crates?" Anna stared up at him. "Rex put them in the icebox to get them out of the way."

Empty. Of course. Then where—

Jared yanked again on the icebox handle, and the door swung open. The lobster crates were stacked neatly on the floor—empty. Next to them, flour sacks and bags of potatoes—still sealed shut. Jared started to paw through shelves loaded with vegetables, milk jugs, cartons of all sizes. Where—

"What are you looking for?" Anna asked.

"Wait." By the dim glow of the nightlight in the corridor, Jared spotted two black plastic garbage bags in the corner, full and fat. "What're those?"

"Trash? Rex put them there after the lobster bake. He said . . . he said not to . . ."

Jared hefted one of the bags. It was heavy. He tore it open, dug through a layer of kitchen scraps and slimy seaweed until he found them: packets. Thin, white packets. Hundreds of them.

He drew out one of the packets and turned it toward the light to read the label: *fentanyl 100 mg.*

"Fentanyl patches! Oh, my God, Anna, do you realize what this stuff is?"

"No," she whispered. "What is it?"

"This stuff is dangerous! It's been all over the news lately. It's for cancer patients, people who are in constant pain—but addicts are drying the stuff and smoking it—and they don't realize how strong it is. People are *dying*!"

"But Rex—"

"Rex is bringing it into the country. And that guy Jimmy . . . Jimmy must've caught on. And he ran for it. Or . . . or did he get—"

Jared turned back to the ghostly figure in the corridor. "Oh,

Anna, we've got to stop Rex. I've got my phone. I'll get some photos . . . and we'll call, get the police out here."

"There's no service out here," Anna whimpered. "Not until we're almost to the dock in Castine. But then . . . with him watching, I wouldn't dare. Rex would—"

"I'll call," Jared said. "Don't worry. I'll call. The police'll be waiting for him, and . . . I'll keep you safe!"

Anna melted into his arms. As the ship rocked gently beneath them, he could feel her slim body shuddering against him with silent sobs.

***

Morning. Threading among islands. Jared checked his phone every chance he got, but Anna was right: no service.

And suddenly they were coming into a harbor. Rex barking orders: mainsail down, jib stowed, ready to throw the anchor.

Jared felt his heart racing. He had to make that call! But it seemed as if Rex was hanging over him, watching every move he made. As soon as he got ashore, then. "Where are we?" he asked Rex.

"Castine, man. This is home for me. And this kid's got shore leave. Cap'n said I could go visit my grandma. Let's hurry up and get everyone ashore, OK, dweeb?"

The passengers were already lining up to be ferried across to the landing, faces alive with the promise of shopping, and space to stretch out. As he rowed back and forth with load after load of passengers, Jared, too, gazed at the town, the gracious tree-lined streets, so restful and green after the endless glare and motion of the ocean. One last load, and then he'd—

"How did *that* happen?" the captain bellowed. He was standing on the deck, staring up at the mast. "Sullivan! I don't know what you two idiots did when you got the sails down, but the main halyard is wrapped around the backstay. Get up there in the bosun's chair and get it *un*wrapped. You hear me?"

Jared eyed the forward mast, towering above the deck. And that bastard Rex was disappearing into town, probably making contacts with his fellow drug runners! "In a sec, Cap'n. I just need to—"

"*Now*, Sullivan!" roared the captain. "I'll take those folks to the dock."

OK, Jared thought. *Fix the halyard thing. Then call.*

The bosun's chair turned out to be a sort of sling with a safety harness, and pulleys arranged so that he could haul himself up . . . and up . . .

Sunlight sparkled on the waves that wrinkled the harbor. A light breeze fluttered the pennants at the mast-tips of the pretty little yachts anchored nearby. A seagull flapped by, sleek and elegant against the blue, blue sky.

Jared listened to the creak of the pulleys above him as he hauled himself higher. And higher. His heart thundered in his ears. *Hurry! Hurry!*

Almost to the top of the mast. The bosun's chair swung around, twisting in the wind, and he slid sideways in the seat. Tipped. Fought to get turned back around again to where the halyard was caught. Grabbed for the backstay.

He heard her voice. A small, thin sound in all the slap of waves against hulls, and ropes dinging against masts, and the swish of cars passing under the giant oaks in the town. She was singing one of her Gaelic songs.

He looked toward the galley hatch, and saw her coming along the deck. Even from that distance, he could see her familiar cotton dress, her narrow shoulders, her braids curving over the top of her head. He wanted to call out to her, tell her that in moments he would make that call, that she would be safe—

Now she was below him, her face a pale moon as she looked up at him. "I'm sorry," she said. Her voice was so quiet that it was almost lost in the jumble of sounds of the harbor, but he could see her lips move, forming the words. "You're very sweet, but . . ."

His heart crunched inside his chest. "Anna?"

"Rex knows how to keep his mouth shut," the quiet voice went on. "And Jimmy . . . well, I wish you'd run, like Jimmy." And she looked up, up, at the line coming out of the pulley above his head.

He glanced up. Saw the delicate, almost invisible knife slits in the rope. "Anna!" he cried. "Anna! No! I won't—"

But she walked quietly away. And he heard a pop. A tiny pop, inches from his face. As the first strand broke.

He lunged for the rope. But under his hands, he felt the strands break, one after another.

He tried. Oh, he tried. He threw himself toward the mast, reaching, reaching—

But he knew he was going to fall.

DEATH IN A STRANGE AND BEAUTIFUL PLACE

by Leslie Wheeler

Destination: Reykjavík, Iceland
Grief and the need to see where her husband died bring a widow to Iceland, where she makes a heart-stopping discovery.

Am I crazy to visit the place where David died?

Megan Norcross braced herself for the landing at Keflavík Airport. The jet's wheels hit the runway hard, bounced, and found purchase. Reversing engines roared in her ears. She flattened herself against her seat and tightened her grip on the arm rests.

If she'd taken the same flight from Boston to Iceland a year ago, her husband would have been there to hold her hand. But at the last minute, her mother had become dangerously ill. Megan had stayed behind to be with her parents. To her relief, her mother had recovered. But then, in a cruel twist of fate, David had died alone in Iceland.

The noise diminished and the jet taxied smoothly to the gate. I can relax. Yet even as Megan thought this, she felt a niggling worry. No turning back.

On her way to the baggage claim area, she passed long lines of young people waiting for their departing flights. They wore hiking boots and carried backpacks. In their fresh, eager faces, she saw herself and David as they'd been twenty-some years earlier. Her light brown hair was shorter now, her face no longer unlined, and she'd added a few pounds to her slender frame. Otherwise, she didn't look much different from the person she'd been: a somewhat reluctant companion to her adventurer husband. If she'd gone with David on what had turned out to be his final adventure, might it have ended differently? She felt a stab of guilt.

In the baggage claim area, she watched for her bag while keeping an eye out for the man who'd promised to meet her. She'd just spotted her suitcase when she heard her name spoken. The next moment, Bruce Wilder's arms enveloped her.

Megan clung to him as to a lifeline. Which was exactly what he'd been during the difficult months since her husband's death.

Family and close friends had been supportive, yet it was Bruce who comforted her the most. Bruce, whom she'd never met in person, and knew only from David's messages, then from speaking with Bruce himself.

The call from the man at the American embassy notifying her of David's death had come as such a shock to Megan that she barely heard, let alone comprehended what he'd said. Contacting her soon afterward, Bruce had filled in the gaps and answered the questions she hadn't thought to ask.

In the long conversations that followed, first over the phone and later via Skype, a certain intimacy had developed between them. Bruce was ever ready to lend a sympathetic ear to her outpourings of grief, while reassuring her there was nothing she or anyone else could have done to prevent the tragic accident that had taken David's life. When all else failed, he managed to lighten her leaden mood with an amusing tale about some incident in his life.

It had been months since a man had held her, and Megan welcomed Bruce's embrace. "You look good, Meg," he said when he released her. "Even better than on Skype."

"You look good, too. But with all your time at the beach, I'm not surprised."

He grinned. He was a big, burly, bearded man with red hair, and freckles peppering his face.

"Where's Ashley?" Megan asked.

"Ash isn't feeling well. Must've picked up a bug on the plane yesterday. I'm sure she'll be fine by tomorrow." He glanced around. "No luggage yet?"

"There—the one with the pink ribbon." Megan pointed to the conveyor belt, and her suitcase that was about to disappear into the chute. Bruce sprang onto the platform in the middle of the belt, grabbed her bag, and heaved it onto the floor. He moved with the ease of someone accustomed to hefting heavy objects, which she knew he did as the owner of a bike and surf board shop in Laguna Beach.

Megan found herself comparing him to David. While Bruce seemed almost reckless in his platform jump, David would have proceeded with caution, perhaps waiting for her bag to come around again. Which made his accidental death all the more surprising.

***

There were few lights on the road from Keflavík to Reykjavík. The little Megan could see from the car window revealed a barren and pockmarked landscape like the surface of the moon. Jagged masses of black rock bore witness to the island's volcanic past, and funnels of steam rising into the night sky from various hot spots were evidence of continued instability.

In a message David had described Iceland as a "strange and beautiful place." He was right about the strangeness, but Megan wasn't sure about the beauty yet.

***

Ashley joined Megan and Bruce for breakfast in the hotel dining room. Ash blonde with large gray eyes, skin so pale it was almost translucent, and fashion-model thin, she fit her name to a tee. Her ethereal beauty drew attention from a few men as she made her way slowly and unsteadily toward them. Bruce had explained that Ashley's "drunken sailor" walk stemmed from an inner ear problem that affected her balance, making it impossible for her to take part in hikes and other strenuous activities the couple had once enjoyed together.

Ashley spoke little and barely touched the ample Scandinavian breakfast of cold cuts, cheese, smoked salmon, eggs, yoghurt, granola, and fresh-baked bread. Her distant manner made Megan uncomfortable. She wasn't sorry when Ashley said she wouldn't be accompanying them on a walking tour of the city.

David had written enthusiastically about Reykjavík. So, despite her grief, Megan was primed to enjoy it. The city tour and sightseeing elsewhere in Iceland were also ways of putting off the visit to the site of his death. She'd made a list of David's favorite places, which Bruce promised to show her. Now as then, the late August weather, sunny with an autumn crispness in the air, was perfect for sightseeing.

As if in defiance of the months of total darkness that lay ahead, Reykjavík was a riot of color. There were flowers everywhere, and houses and shops, especially in the older part of the city, were painted vibrant reds, yellows, and blues. Like David, Megan loved the mix of old and new: from the stone ruins of a Viking longhouse at the City Museum, to Harpa, the mammoth, modernistic concert hall whose façade consisted of hundreds of angled panes of glass.

Bruce was an obliging guide, agreeing to climb the hill to the Hallgrímskirkja church, even though he was clearly tired and readily admitted "churches weren't his thing." Inside the church, which David had described as "a rocket about to launch, with walls designed to resemble volcanic pillars," Megan slipped into a pew. Gazing up at the steeply vaulted ceiling, she said a silent prayer for her husband. Lowering her gaze, she was aware of Bruce watching her, his expression unreadable. The next moment, he glanced at his watch and said, "Time for happy hour. And I know just the place to enjoy it."

Over Viking lagers—David's favorite beer—at an outdoor café on the shore of a lake in the middle of the city, Bruce described meeting David for the first time. "He was sitting over there." Bruce pointed at a nearby table. "His nose was in a guidebook, so we knew he was a tourist like us. I went over and introduced myself. Turned out we were both doing the self-drive tour in the same direction and staying at many of the same hotels. 'How about we travel together?' I said. 'You won't be by your lonesome, and I'll have a companion to do stuff with that my wife can't anymore.'"

Megan had heard the story from Bruce before, but now the vision of David seated close by was so real that she almost rose and joined him. If only she had come with him, maybe . . .

"Don't be sad." Bruce's voice broke through the drumbeat of regret in her head. "Dave was a great guy. And he had a great life with a wife and a job he loved. Blew me away when he told me he was an environmental lawyer. He was so smart. As a guy who barely squeaked through high school, I feel privileged to have known him. I miss him. Always will. I know you will, too. But we have to go on with our lives. I hope this trip will help you do that."

"I hope so, too," Megan said.

Bruce gestured at her half-empty beer glass. "Let's finish up here, go back to the hotel, pick up Ash, and get some dinner. I'm thinking a fish place, where you can try a local specialty. How does pickled shark sound?"

Megan laughed and made a face. Bruce always seemed to know how to tease a smile from her.

***

The next day they set off on the southeasterly route around the island that Bruce, Ashley, and David had traveled the previous year. At Bruce's suggestion, Megan sat in front, Ashley in the back. When Bruce and Megan left the car to get a better view of the sights, Ashley usually stayed inside. If she did get out, she didn't walk far and used a cane for support.

At Þingvellir National Park, which David had described as "a place of such rugged volcanic majesty, it's no wonder the Vikings chose it for their parliament," Megan couldn't wait to explore. Ashley, however, remained in the car. Upon Bruce's and Megan's return, Ashley said, "I'm sure Bruce showed you the Drowning Pool, where women found guilty of adultery were killed. It's one of his favorite spots."

Megan didn't know what to make of the comment, but she heard the edge in Bruce's voice when he replied, "I showed her the Hanging Rock, too, Ash, where men got theirs."

"But not for adultery," Ashley said. "I find it interesting that women were the ones punished for adultery, and men rarely were, if ever."

***

Later that day at Gullfoss, hailed by David as "Iceland's answer to Niagara Falls, only wilder and grander," Ashley walked to the overlook at the top while Megan and Bruce descended a steep, spray-drenched trail that brought them close to the water thundering over a fault into the gorge. Overwhelmed by the brute force of the falls, Megan felt the water pulling her toward it, closer and closer, until . . . Without realizing it, she must have stepped too near the edge. Bruce flung an arm around her, and pulled her back. She leaned into him, heart pounding. "I wasn't going to . . ." she stammered into his chest.

"'Course not." Still, he kept his arm around her, and when he did finally release her, he held her hand as if he didn't quite trust her to make the climb to the parking area. Glancing up, Megan spotted Ashley watching them, a black-hooded figure in spray-wet rain gear.

The waterfall they visited the next day was more beautiful than terrifying. Standing on wet, slippery rocks behind the falls, Megan recalled David's words about the same spot: "If only you'd been with me, watching the water descend in delicate, lacy curtains." She felt such an intense yearning for him that, closing her eyes, she willed him back with all her might. In this country with its fantastical landscape, she could almost believe, as Icelanders did, in "hidden people." If an evil troll had spirited David away, perhaps a good fairy would return him. For a moment, it seemed her wish had been granted. Arms encircled her, and someone kissed her on the mouth. She jerked away. "No, Bruce, I can't."

"I'm sorry, Meg. You looked so lovely and sad, I just—I don't know what came over me. It won't happen again."

***

A couple of hours later, they stopped along the coast so Megan could see the black sand beach, basalt columns, and large sea cave David had raved about. While Ashley took a seat at an outdoor café at the edge of the beach, Megan and Bruce set off across the sand. They ascended the step-like columns and peeked into the mouth of the cave. But when Bruce said he wanted to scale one of the big slabs of basalt that stood in the water near the shoreline, Megan left to join Ashley.

Two unfamiliar men were talking to Ashley, who smiled up at them—the first time Megan had seen her smile on the trip. As Megan approached, Ashley waved a dismissive hand at the men and they drifted away. Ashley's smile vanished with them.

"Where's Bruce?" she asked languidly, toying with a strand of blonde hair. Megan told her. "Figures," Ashley said in the same slightly bored manner. They sat in silence while Megan searched for the right words. "You don't seem all that happy to be here," she said finally. "I hope it's not because Bruce and I—"

"Bruce and you what?" Ashley trained a gray eye on her.

"We've been spending a lot of time together. He's being kind to me because I wasn't here when my husband died."

"Really?" Ashley said, still playing with her hair. "I thought he was doing it to punish me."

"Punish you!" Megan blurted, startled. "Why would he do that?"

"Ask him." Ashley picked up her cane and walked back to the car.

After Bruce returned from his climb, they started the long drive to Skaftafell National Park. In the gathering darkness, they drove across a seemingly endless wasteland of black sand and volcanic debris left behind when a volcano erupted inside a glacier. A volcano within a glacier? Megan found it hard to imagine, but in this land of fire and ice anything was possible. The desolate landscape suited her mood. Skaftafell was where David had died.

***

"Welcome back, Mr. Wilder." The man behind the desk at the Glacier Guides booking office in Skaftafell greeted Bruce. He was tall and lean with blue eyes, a deep tan, and a tuft of blond hair sticking up in front.

Bruce peered at him. "You're Einar . . . something?"

"Olivirsson. I was your guide on the glacier walk last August, and later, as a member of the ICE-SAR, I took part in the attempted rescue of—" He broke off at a warning signal from Bruce. Megan had heard enough to know he'd been about to mention David. She wobbled on legs turned to rubber. Bruce looked concerned. Olivirsson moved swiftly to her side. "Are you all right?"

"Yes, I . . . I am David Norcross's widow," she managed finally.

Olivirsson's blue eyes brimmed with sympathy. "I am sorry we could not do more for him. And now you have come to . . .?"

"Megan wants to see the place where her husband . . . where it happened," Bruce said. "I'd like to confirm our reservation for this afternoon's glacier walk."

Olivirsson peered at the ledger. "Yes, party of two."

***

Megan and Bruce spent the morning taking a leisurely stroll along a scenic trail to the edge of another glacier. Part of the walk was wheelchair accessible, but when Bruce offered to bring Ashley to the overlook, she said, "I've already seen it. David wheeled me there last year, remember?"

It was the first time Ashley had mentioned David by name, and the peculiar emphasis she placed on his name, combined with her needling tone, made Megan's skin crawl. Bruce responded with stony silence.

When they were alone, Megan seized the opportunity to ask him about a previous remark of Ashley's.

"Yesterday, Ashley said she thought you were paying so much attention to me to punish her. What did she mean?"

Bruce sighed and kicked a stone from the path. "When Ash first developed her balance problem, she felt I was neglecting her, so she had an affair. I was hurt and angry when I found out. We went to counseling and came to an understanding. Ash wouldn't have any more affairs, and I'd spend more time with her. I've tried to keep up my end of the bargain, and I think she has, too. I'm not sure what this is about."

Before Megan could question him more, Bruce pointedly changed the subject by calling her attention to a peculiar rock formation.

***

They met Ashley at the visitor center's cafeteria for lunch, taking their trays out to the patio. Afterward, Bruce drove Ashley back to the hotel, and Megan stayed behind. Tilting her head toward the sun and closing her eyes, she tried not to think about the glacier walk ahead of her.

"May I join you?" Opening her eyes, Megan saw Olivirsson standing nearby with a lunch tray. She smiled and gestured at an empty seat. After he'd taken a few bites of his sandwich, he asked if she had any questions about the hike.

"Actually, I do. I've never walked on a glacier before, so I'm kind of nervous."

"There is nothing to worry about," Olivirsson assured her. "The walk is easy, so we will not use ropes or harnesses, but you will wear crampons and carry an ice axe."

"How far will we go?"

"A short distance up the glacier and back."

"What about crevasses and ice holes?"

"There are no crevasses on the hike, but there is one hole, which I will be sure to point out."

"It still sounds dangerous. If my husband, a skilled mountaineer, could fall into a hole and—"

"Skilled mountaineer or not, your husband should not have

ventured onto the glacier without a trained guide. Especially in bad weather with limited visibility."

"What? I thought he had you for a guide. Didn't you just say so to Bruce?"

"I was Mr. Wilder's guide, but your husband was not part of our group. He was on the list to come with us, but canceled at the last minute."

Megan felt the ground shift beneath her. This wasn't what Bruce had told her. "If David didn't go with your group, when did he go?"

"Early the next morning, after the weather had turned nasty, Mr. Wilder and your husband went out by themselves. After your husband fell into the hole, Mr. Wilder hiked back to the visitor center to report the accident. That was when I became involved as a member of ICE-SAR."

Olivirsson looked at her, his expression somber. "Again, I am sorry we could not do more for him. Our first goal is to rescue people in trouble. Failing that, it is to recover their bodies for those they've left behind. In your husband's case, we could do neither. If it had been a crevasse, where he managed to get a hold, we might have been able to save him, or at the very least, recover his body. But falling into a mill well is extremely dangerous. Because it is a channel or chute that glacial melt water runs into, you can become trapped under the glacier, making rescue or recovery nearly impossible. Sometimes we must weigh risk against return. In your husband's case . . ." He shook his head.

"Risk, yes," Megan said slowly. "David would have understood that. He was all about assessing the risks involved before he did anything that might be dangerous. That's why his death seems so strange."

"There was something odd about it," Olivirsson said. "Another man fell into the same mill well and died two springs ago. A German tourist was foolish enough to hike onto the glacier alone without proper gear, and paid the price. His story became a cautionary tale I share with all my groups while showing them the mill well."

Megan tried to make sense of this. "So, Bruce knew? No, that can't be true!" She raised her hands, palms out, as if to shield herself from such disturbing thoughts.

Olivirsson met her gaze steadily, until something behind her caught his attention. Glancing over her shoulder, Megan saw Bruce approaching.

"Mr. Olivirsson was giving me tips about how to walk on the glacier."

"Excellent." Bruce clapped Olivirsson on the shoulder. "We don't want to make this any harder for Meg than it already is."

***

As the group gathered for the walk, Olivirsson drew Megan aside and told her he would halt their party a short distance from the mill well to allow her a few minutes alone there before he showed it to the others. She thanked him for his consideration. She'd already decided to wait until after the walk before confronting Bruce. She didn't want anything to get in the way of her visit to David's grave. To clear her head and focus on this goal, she imagined that she and David were hiking, that he'd gotten ahead of her, and had stopped to call to her. I'm coming, David, I'm coming, she imagined herself responding, as she often had on the trail.

The words became a mantra she used to blot out concerns about Bruce, and the non-stop noise from a Chatty Cathy in their group on the bus ride, and later on the hike to the edge of the glacier. There, she halted her inner monologue to pay attention as Olivirsson demonstrated how to fasten their crampons onto their hiking boots and hold their ice axes. He told them to balance their weight evenly so that all sixteen spikes of the crampons engaged, and to climb in a zigzag pattern rather than a straight line.

The part of the glacier they were to walk upon was a striated slope of dirty ice with patches of white showing through. I'm coming, David, I'm coming, Megan repeated, as she climbed carefully, keeping her eyes on the ground. Only when they reached their destination at a point where the dirty ice gave way to a seemingly impassable pile of broken-up, blue-green ice, did she realize how far they'd come, and wonder how they'd get down again.

Didn't matter. She was where she wanted to be. While Olivirsson spoke to the group about glaciers in general, Megan spotted an opening in the ice and went to it. Although she'd imagined this moment many times, nothing had prepared her for the torrent of emotions that swept over her as she peered into the mill well. She felt a sadness and yearning more intense than before, but also surprise at the well's beauty. The surrounding ice was a lovely light blue, and the water looked crystalline and inviting. But its allure was deceptive. She could almost picture a beautiful but dangerous creature emerging from the water and beckoning to the hapless traveler before disappearing into the depths. The hapless traveler was David, who'd been lured into the well, never to return. Anger at the glacier for taking him burned within Megan. But she was being irrational; the glacier was a force of nature, not a conscious actor in his death.

Even as she thought this, she heard Olivirsson and the rest of the group approaching. Olivirsson drew a circle around the opening with his axe and, cautioning the party not to get any closer, he explained what the well was and why it was dangerous. “I heard a couple of guys fell into this well and died last year,” Chatty Cathy volunteered. Ignoring her, Olivirsson picked up a moss-covered stone and started to talk about it.

“What happened with those guys?” Chatty Cathy interrupted. Olivirsson continued to ignore her, while Bruce, who now stood beside Megan, frowned and shook his head at the woman. “Aw, c’mon, I wanna know about the guys who got killed,” she persisted.

Megan could contain herself no longer. “One of those guys was my husband, and the story I was told by his friend, this man here,” —she indicated Bruce—“was that my husband fell into the well by accident when he became separated from his group. But now it seems there was no group, only his friend who knew about the well, because Mr. Olivirsson warned him about it the day before.”

Bruce’s face erupted in red blotches that spread until his entire face screamed scarlet. “What the hell? Dave was my friend. I’d never harm him. You’re a goddamn liar for suggesting that!” he shouted at Olivirsson.

“I did not accuse you of anything,” Olivirsson shot back. “All I did was tell Mrs. Norcross the truth.”

“Why did you lie to me, Bruce?” Megan demanded.

“Meg, please! Dave was a good friend. How did I know how he’d react when I told him not to hit on Ash?”

His words struck Megan like a sucker punch. “Hit on Ash?” she echoed after she’d gotten her breath back. “I don’t believe you!”

“He’d been making moves on her behind my back from the get-go. But I didn’t find out until I came back from the glacier walk and found Ash in tears. She said he’d tried to force himself on her.”

David forcing himself on Ashley? Her straight-arrow husband? Ashley had to have been lying. “Then what happened?” she asked through gritted teeth.

“I was gonna confront Dave on the spot, but Ash said to wait till I calmed down. She wanted Dave and me to go someplace where we could be alone and have a quiet, rational talk.”

“Good advice,” Olivirsson chimed in from where he stood on the other side of the mill well from Bruce and Megan. “But you should not have taken your friend out on the glacier in bad weather, when you knew it would be treacherous. And then lie about it to his wife.”

Bruce glared at him and raised a fist. “You keep out of this!”

“I will not be silent where possible wrongdoing is involved,” Olivirsson replied sternly.

The color drained from Bruce’s face. “There was no wrongdoing. It was an accident! You believe me, don’t you, Meg?” He looked at her pleadingly. But in that moment Megan didn’t know what to believe.

Bruce glanced wildly around at the other members of the group, as if seeking support. But the men and women began to back away. Bruce glared at Olivirsson again. For an instant, Megan thought he’d leap over the well and attack the guide, like he’d leaped over the airport conveyor belt. Instead, yelling, “Damn you to hell!” Bruce hurled his ice axe at the guide.

Olivirsson ducked and the axe sailed over his head. Carried forward by the momentum of his throw, Bruce came down hard on a patch of ice at the edge of the well. It gave way under his weight, and he slid into the water.

“Dav–Bruce, no!” Megan cried. She tried but failed to grab him. She had a last glimpse of his horrified face before he disappeared down the well.

“Are you just gonna stand there while that poor man drowns? Do something!” Chatty Cathy shouted at Olivirsson.

“I will call ICE-SAR. But it is probably too late.”

***

“I know it’s hard, but you’re gonna be all right,” Chatty Cathy, whose real name was Jean Hawkins, assured Megan as she and her husband Leo bade Megan goodbye at Keflavík Airport several days later.

Megan had spent those days lost in a haze of pain and grief, haunted by the vision of a man who was sometimes Bruce, sometimes David, vanishing into an icy grave. If Jean hadn’t taken Megan under her wing, and made sure she at least went through the motions of living, Megan might never have gotten to where she was, about to board a flight back to Boston. She was enormously grateful to the couple for all they had done.

“You’re gonna beat this!” Jean gave Megan another hug. “Isn’t that right, Leo?”

Leo, who was as silent as his wife was talkative, nodded.

“Get a load of her!” Jean gestured toward a couple heading for the security line. “That’s one lady who hasn’t wasted time hooking up with another guy.”

Megan turned to find herself looking straight into Ashley’s smirking face. Beside her stood Einar Olivirsson. The couple leaned into each other–sharing a kiss? Olivirsson stroked Ashley’s shoulder and left. Ashley stared at Megan, her lips curled in a triumphant smile. Then, Ashley walked in a perfectly normal manner to the security line.

The fog that had enveloped Megan since Bruce's death lifted. She saw clearly how Ashley had played them all. Only happy when surrounded by admiring men, Ashley probably set her cap for Megan's handsome, accomplished husband. When David didn't respond, she lied to Bruce about David coming on to her, pitting the two friends against each other in a showdown that ended in David's death. Later, jealous of the attention Bruce gave Megan, Ashley tried to create a rift between them, too.

Megan would never know what had happened between Bruce and David on the glacier. Still, she now saw Bruce less as a villain, and more a victim of his wife's deceit. As for Olivirsson, by playing the grieving widow, Ashley had won his sympathy—and perhaps much more.

Megan's gaze returned to the security line. Ashley had gone on her merry way, undoubtedly thinking she was done with Megan.

But Megan was far from done with her. Gripping her carry-on with grim purpose, she strode briskly toward the security checkpoint.

Not so fast, Ashley, I'm coming, I'm coming!

WE SHALL FIGHT THEM

by Carla Coupe

Destination: Stepney, London, England
New toughs trying to move into Kaiser Bill's territory aren't welcomed by his suppliers or customers. Bill may be young, but he knows how to deal with intimidation tactics.

Dusk blurred the outlines of buildings and deepened shadows as Wilfred Billings picked his way through the fallen bricks and charred timbers in what was left of a row of homes on Bromley Street. His greatcoat flapped in the brisk March wind, and with his good arm he clutched his parcel close. Skirting the corner, he edged along a garden wall and into a small yard. A slump-shouldered woman wiping her hands on her apron answered his knock on the back door.

"'Ello, Kaiser," she said, a smile briefly lighting her face.

"Rosie." He tipped his hat and gave a quick nod. Stepping closer, he handed her the parcel. "Three tins of tongue and a quarter pound of bacon."

"Thanks, dear. The lads appreciate it. Poor things, they're really feeling the hunger, especially Jim." She handed him a few banknotes.

"Lad that size needs filling up." Kaiser glanced around and tucked the notes away. "We're close to blackout. Are you headed to the shelter?"

Rosie frowned. "I don't think so. Alf said he wanted to sleep in his own bed tonight, Nazi bombs be damned."

"Take care then."

"You as well."

She closed the door, and he melted into the shadows. He had made his last unofficial delivery for the day, and his bad arm ached. A pint would go down a treat, he decided, before it was time to meet Doggo.

Blackouts didn't bother him. After living in Stepney thirty years—his whole life—he knew these streets, knew the alleys and yards and passages. The bombs left holes and gaps and mountains of rubble along his way and the stench of smoke and mortar dust hung in the air. At least the bloody Nazis hadn't touched the George Tavern, not only his local but also his home for the past year.

Kaiser knew when to be grateful.

Sticking to the growing pools of blackness, as was his habit, he walked noiselessly down East Arbour Street, almost deserted now. A few searchlights already crossed the sky, and many people had taken refuge in the shelters. Only the Air Raid Precautions wardens patrolled the streets, enforcing the blackout. It was just a matter of time before the bombers showed up for their nightly runs. Up ahead, the ruins of St. Thomas loomed jagged against the darkening sky. The church had just celebrated its centenary three years earlier, and now it was a heap of blackened rubble. Damned incendiaries.

As he neared the church, he heard a gasp and the murmur of voices. A soft thud followed by another gasp made him pause. Boys playing in the rubble? At this time of night? Not likely. He crept forward until he could see several shadows move, heard a second thud, a groan, then a sharp, brittle laugh that raised his hackles. Not a trace of humor in that laugh.

The drone of approaching bombers was just audible, then the wail of the Carter sirens began, rising and falling. More searchlights crossed the sky. In the distance, anti-aircraft gun batteries fired round after round. The shadows froze for a moment, then melted away in a flurry of footsteps. A moan from beside a half-fallen wall drew him forward.

"Bleedin' sods," wheezed a familiar voice.

"Doggo?"

Explosions sounded in the distance.

A gasp, a groan. "Kaiser. Why the hell weren't you here a quarter hour ago?"

Kaiser pulled his Ronson lighter from his pocket and, using his body as a shield to avoid drawing the wardens' attention, pressed the button. He squinted in the light of the wavering flame and muttered a ripe curse. Doggo was done up like a kipper, looking like he'd gone a couple rounds with Hitler's goons.

"Whose husband did you cheese off this time?" Kaiser doused the flame and pocketed the lighter before he carefully knelt on broken slabs of stone. He fished out his handkerchief and handed it to Doggo. The sounds of explosions grew fainter. Must be blanketing the south for a change.

"Ta." Doggo tried to laugh, but stopped short with a grunt. "Think they broke a rib. I didn't cheese off no one, I swear. I just finished fixing that little problem with Rafe Thomson and was going to the George when these three pillocks come out of nowhere. They asked if I knew you—"

"Me?" Kaiser sat back on his heels.

"Asked for you by name—Kaiser Bill—and before I could hook it, they dragged me here. Two of 'em held my arms, and the other one took a dozen swings." The Doggo-shaped shadow moved as he slowly sat up.

"You know them? Seen them before?"

"Never. The two gits who held me called the other Shef—he's a right manky sod—and barking mad. Laughed as he hit me, called you a crip, and said to tell you he's taking over your patch."

"Oh, he is, is he?" Kaiser frowned and rubbed his bad arm. It had never grown right, not since he was born. Kept him from serving, too, but a cripple? Not him. When a couple chavs gave him his moniker after they learned about Kaiser Wilhelm's withered right arm, he welcomed it. Besides, Kaiser was a better name than Wilf any day. "Looks as if he knows who runs with me."

"Too right. And Gladys said some bullyboys bothered her on the street yesterday afore the warden came by. Could be these tossers."

Kaiser balled his fist. Bothering his Gladys as well as pasting Doggo? Action was called for. "She should have told me."

"Eh, you know Gladys. Thinks she can fix anything on her lonesome."

Kaiser grunted his agreement. "Can you stand? We'll knock up Doc Pruitt—he'll be at home. He hates the shelters."

"I think so."

Slowly, and with a considerable amount of swearing, Doggo struggled to his feet, Kaiser supporting him as he straightened. Well, this put the kibosh on his plans. No time for a drink now. No, he had a full dance card. First, get Doggo to the doctor. Second, find out more about this Shef and his mates. Third, decide how to take care of these pillocks who wanted to invade his turf. No better than the Nazis, they were. If England could stand more than six months of nightly bombing and not give in, he and his mates could stand up to these wankers.

What had Churchill said? "We shall fight in the fields and the streets . . ."

Too right.

***

After the all-clear sounded the following morning, Kaiser made toast and tea in his room. Wasn't much to look at, just a bed-sit in the upper floor of the George, but the building hadn't been hit, which was more than could be said for a lot of others in London. No work today. His job at Whitechapel Station was deemed casual and didn't pay much. Still, enough "damaged" goods, especially cigarettes and silk stockings, found their way into his hands and then on to his customers that he'd managed to save a tidy sum.

Gladys had visited her mum the night before and wouldn't be at her job until later in the morning, so he had time to look up some of the local lads first. They knew the lay of the land as well as he did, and he gave them a milk run—just find what they could about this Shef and report back.

"Stay low," he said, giving them all the stink eye, especially Tommy Wilson, who at fourteen had more nerve than sense. "No dust-ups, y'hear? Just ask about, report back what you hear, and let me an' my lads take it from there."

After that, he made his way to Weiss's newsagents, where most of his cartons of cigarettes ended up. Blond, buxom Gladys Newbury—thirty-five if she was a day, but admitting to twenty—presided behind the counter. Mrs. Weiss wouldn't take over until late afternoon. Hat in hand, Kaiser waited until the shop emptied and then leaned against the counter.

"Thought you'd like this," he said and handed Gladys a small, newspaper-wrapped packet.

"Fell off the turnip wagon, did it?" she asked, unwrapping it just enough to see the contents. "Silk knickers! Very nice." She re-wrapped it and slipped the packet into her apron pocket.

Kaiser tipped her a wink and grinned.

Gladys returned his grin and leaned over the wooden counter, giving Kaiser a prime view of her assets. "Thanks, dearie."

Kaiser eyed her cleavage and sighed. First class, that. "You should charge a penny a peek. You'd be set for life."

She sniffed and straightened, patted her apron pocket. "Come 'round tonight. Maybe you'll get lucky."

"I'm always lucky when I'm with you." Kaiser hesitated. "Heard you had some aggro from a couple berks yesterday. What happened?"

Her eyes narrowed. "Nothing I couldn't handle. A wide boy and his two tossers stopped me on my way to work. Thought I was a scrubber and made noises about taking turns. I put a flea in their ears and sent 'em on their way."

"Recognize any of them?"

"No." She chewed her lip, her gray eyes flickering over Kaiser's face. "What's up?"

He lowered his voice. "They gave Doggo a right pasting last night. Asked about me and said they were moving into my patch."

She blew out a slow breath. "Gits. If I'd've known that, I would have done more than give them a piece of my mind. How's Doggo?"

"I took him to Doc Pruitt. Doggo's got bruises and a cracked rib, but before they could do worse the siren went off, and they legged it."

"I'm not going to thank the Nazis for that." She frowned. "You'll need descriptions if you want to track them down. The gaffer's young—maybe eighteen or twenty. Brown hair, blue eyes, trying to grow a thigh tickler, but it's a poor showing, not a spot on yours." She smiled, and her finger gently traced Kaiser's neatly trimmed mustache. "Flash clothes. Bright lad, does all the talking. The other two are older, just muscle. A blond and a ginger."

Kaiser caught her hand and gave her fingers a quick kiss. "Did you hear any names?"

Gladys thought for a moment, then shook her head. "No. I'll ask some of the girls to have a butcher's and let me know if they spot them. What's your plan?"

"Dunno yet. Just doing obbo."

The bell on the door rang, and two men walked into the shop.

Gladys stepped back and smoothed her apron. "Have a care, dearie," she said softly. "Whoever he is, he's a right vicious berk. You'll have to take him down fast, or he'll be back, causing more than just a dust-up."

Kaiser nodded. "Ta, Gladys. See you tonight."

With a quick smile and a pat on her apron pocket, Gladys turned to her customers. Kaiser put on his hat and hurried out the door.

***

Kaiser rounded the corner onto Stepney Way. The shell of a bombed-out building stood across the road, bricks still damp from the fire hoses and smelling of smoke and burnt timbers. Balancing on a pile of rubble, Tommy Wilson threw broken bricks at a line of tins, whooping as he knocked down each one. When he finished, he clambered from the pile and spotted Kaiser.

"Oi, Kaiser!" Tommy dashed across the busy road without looking. Hoots and curses followed him.

Kaiser stopped and leaned against the sun-warmed wall. What a cabbage. He'd be surprised if Tommy lived until he was old enough to grow some sense.

"I found—" Tommy began, panting.

Kaiser grabbed his arm and gave him a shake. "Don't shout my business to the world, you git."

"Sorry."

With a jerk of his head, Kaiser led the way around the corner to a quiet spot. "Now, what did you find?"

"I asked around—carefully, like you said—an' Mr. Martin says they was in the Anchor, their gobs flapping. The gaffer goes by Shef Steele. Comes from Rotherhithe, wants to make his name on this side of the river."

"Any news on his bullyboys?"

Tommy frowned. "Not much. Fair one's Johnson, and the ginger's McDonald, but they don't say much." He looked at Kaiser, sandy brows raised expectantly.

"Good work." Kaiser fished in his pocket and handed over a threepenny bit. "There's a bob in it for you if you can find his crib."

"Ta, Kaiser. Will do." Tommy sketched a salute and hurried off.

He watched the boy go and shook his head. Too much energy, too few brains. Tommy was going to land in more than a spot of bother if he wasn't careful. At least he was too young for national service; knowing him, he'd probably step in front of a bullet his first morning out. Kaiser sighed. Damned Nazis.

Time for business.

***

Rob Austin looked up as Kaiser slipped in the back door. "You're running late."

Kaiser carefully moved around the hanging carcasses and worktop covered with a quartered pig. He breathed through his mouth—the iron-tinged smell of blood gave him the collywobbles—then perched on a stool in the corner of the butcher's shop. "Been trying to track down a nob who calls himself Shef Steele. You hear of him?"

Rob grunted, his cleaver neatly separating ribs from flank. "Was in here yesterday with his two bullyboys. Said he'd give me a better price than you, and if I didn't like it, his boys would change my mind."

"What'd you say?"

Another chop with the cleaver, and Rob gave a dry laugh. "I called for Perce."

Kaiser snorted. Constable Perce Austin was well over six foot tall and correspondingly broad, with hands like hams and a mind as simple as a clear summer sky. Placid, too, which was a blessing in a man that large, and loyal as Greyfriars Bobby. "And when he showed up, they scarpered?"

"Like the rozzers were up their bums. Still, wouldn't put it past 'em to report me as a black marketeer or smash the glass out front."

Kaiser nodded agreement. "Nasty pieces of work."

Pausing for a moment, cleaver raised, Rob met Kaiser's gaze. "What'll you do? Nazis are bad enough, can't have tossers like these moving into Stepney." He brought his cleaver down with a thunk. A spatter of blood covered the table.

"I'm working on it." Kaiser frowned and rubbed his chin. "Tell you what. If they stop in again, and I'm certain they will, let 'em think you're interested. Find out what you can about this Shef's plans, who he's leaning on, who he thinks will flip, that sort of thing."

"Don't take too long. This wanker's not a patient man." Rob jerked his head to a pile of neatly wrapped parcels. "Bacon and sausages. For you."

"Ta." Kaiser stowed the parcels in the capacious inner pockets of his greatcoat. Come summer, he'd have to devise another way to transport his goods. If they were all still alive. "Afternoon, Rob."

Rob wiped his hands on his bloodstained apron. "Tomorrow then, Kaiser."

Kaiser slipped out the back. Housewives with hungry families were waiting.

***

"Mmmmm. What time is it?" The bed creaked as Gladys rolled over and smiled.

Almost boneless with pleasure, Kaiser reached across the blankets and dangled a scrap of pale peach silk on one finger. "Time to find another pair like these, if that's the greeting I get."

"Worth the effort." She stretched slowly, her arms pale in the dim light.

Kaiser just laughed and leaned over, planting a kiss on her shoulder.

With a satisfied hum, Gladys ruffled his hair. Her smile faded, and she propped herself up on one elbow. "Have you decided what to do about that Steele berk?"

His lethargy fled as fast as water through a drain. He lay back, staring at the ceiling's cracked plaster. "I think so."

"You going to off him?" Her tone was matter of fact, but he felt her quickly repressed shiver.

"Me? Not a chance." He turned his head and met her gaze. "You really think I could do that?"

She hesitated, then shrugged. "There's a war on. All of us do things we never thought we would."

"True. But I'd rather the rozzers get him. And I think I've worked out a way for that to happen."

Her brows lifted, and a soft smile touched her full lips. "Yeah?

Now that's the Kaiser I know and love. Spill, dearie."

"First, I'll need your help . . ."

***

Kaiser shivered and glanced down Commercial Road. A chill drizzle fell and ice seeped into his bones, keeping all but the hardiest souls inside.

"You're clear, right? Keep to what I told you to say." He handed Tommy half a crown. "If you bollocks this up, I'll have your hide."

"It's a doddle, Kaiser." Tommy pocketed the coin and winked, then loped down the street in his thin jacket, heedless of the cold and damp.

Huddling deeper into his coat, Kaiser turned the corner onto West Arbour Street. He quickly made his way to the ruins of St. Thomas and slipped behind a half-collapsed wall. After navigating the uneven floor, he reached a stone arch, cracked and soot-blackened but standing. Steps led into darkness. Kaiser pulled a torch from his pocket and switched it on, then cautiously made his way down.

He had to set aside the heavy torch before he could pull a big brass key from his pocket and unlock the massive oak door. It swung noiselessly on well-oiled hinges. Kaiser had taken care of that as soon as he'd discovered this corner of the crypt was still sound; you never knew when a bolt hole might be useful.

Picking up the torch, he swept the light over dozens of cigarette cartons, packets of silk stockings, and bolts of cloth. He hated losing so much of his inventory, but needs must. Any less and his trap wouldn't look genuine. He ripped opened a pack of cigarettes and stuffed them into an inner pocket.

The next time a shipment arrived at the train station he could start replacing his inventory. He closed the door and slid his torch back into his pocket. As he clambered up the steps, he dropped a few cigarettes on the worn stones as bait. Kaiser threw another couple by the half-wall, making sure they were just visible. Then he made his way to the George, where a pint and a fire awaited. He had an hour or two to kill and might as well be comfortable.

***

It was going on half three by the time Tommy poked his head around the door and caught Kaiser's eye. With a glance at the busy barman, Kaiser joined Tommy at the rear door.

Tommy was practically bouncing with news. He leaned toward Kaiser and whispered, "They went into Austin's and stayed a couple of tics. Came out smiling like they was cats with cream. They seen Gladys just now and are heading this way."

"They didn't bother her or Mrs. Weiss, did they?"

"Nah. The shop was doing a roaring. Too many customers for them to act up."

Kaiser nodded. "Give me ten, and then you know what to do."

Tommy hesitated. "You sure I can't follow you? See them take the bait? I can hook it if there's a problem." He looked up at Kaiser expectantly.

"And your aunt would have my arse for grass if anything happened to you." Kaiser shook his head. "Just do what I said and stay clear."

Tommy frowned, but gave one sharp nod before he left. Kaiser put on his hat and coat, turning up the collar against the chill. He stepped outside. At least the rain had stopped, although heavy clouds still threatened.

Kaiser strolled along Commercial Road, nodding to friends and acquaintances. No bombs had hit along this stretch of the street. If he ignored the ARP wardens, the men and women in uniform, the haggard and lined faces of those he passed, he could briefly convince himself that the war was just a nightmare. That he'd wake up to peace and security.

Kaiser gave a dry chuckle. He was off his head if he believed such tosh. He stopped for a minute at the chemist's, staring in the window. The reflection showed the bustle on the pavement behind him. Across the road, two men lounged against a shop front.

The young one fit Steele's description, and according to Gladys and Tommy's information, the blond must be Johnson. But there should be three of them.

Kaiser shifted, scanning the reflection for McDonald, the ginger. Where was he?

"'Ullo, Kaiser."

A young woman with a warden's hat and satchel stopped and smiled at him. Despite the cold, she wore a cropped jacket, and her short skirt fitted her curves like a glove.

"Afternoon, Sally. How's your da?"

"Well as can be expected," she said, rubbing her hands together. "Thanks again for the . . . gifts. Da says he won't forget your kindness, and if ever you need a favor . . . think of him."

"Ta, Sal."

She shivered. "Must dash."

He turned to watch her leave. Nice view, especially in that tight-fitting skirt. But more importantly, he could scan the pavement opposite without Steele or Johnson twigging he'd spotted them. They quickly showed their backs as he turned, but there was no sign of anyone who could be McDonald.

He'd worry about that later. Time to move on.

As soon as Kaiser turned onto West Arbour, the pavement grew quiet. Only the occasional harried housewife hurried off to the shops before they closed. Kaiser headed slowly toward St. Thomas. When he could, he checked that Steele and Johnson were still following. But where was that sod McDonald? There was no sign of him.

Kaiser approached the church. He stopped and glanced around before slipping into the ruins. Rounding the corner, he stopped short, biting off a curse.

McDonald—with that ginger hair, it must be him—stood beside the stone arch holding Gladys's arm. Her coat gaped open and he pressed a wicked-looking knife to her side.

"Well, if it isn't Wilfred Billings," said a smarmy voice behind him. "Or should I call you Kaiser, like the Jerry toff who lost the last war?"

Kaiser glanced over his shoulder. Well, the gits had followed him, as he'd planned.

Johnson moved close behind, and a sharp point poked Kaiser's back through his coat. At least it wasn't a gun. Steele walked to his side and smiled, showing all his teeth. Kaiser met his gaze. He'd seen eyes like Steele's before: glittering, sparkling. Filled with madness.

"Mr. Billings suits me just fine. How're you holding, Gladys?" He turned to her.

"Sorry, dearie," she said with a grimace. "'is Lordship here jumped me when I left the shop." She glared at McDonald, who blinked impassively. "If you slice this dress, I'll see you in hell." McDonald gave her a perfunctory shake.

Kaiser clenched his fists but didn't move. He wouldn't help Gladys by getting killed. Yet the torch in his pocket weighed heavily against his hip.

Steele strolled over to where Gladys stood. "You've a smart mouth, I'll give you that." With a chuckle, he slowly looked her up and down. His gaze lingered on her bosom. "Nice form, too, for all you're mutton dressed as lamb."

Gladys's eyes widened for a heartbeat, then she snorted. "Well, this mutton could teach you a thing or two." She inhaled. Her chest rose, straining against the thin fabric of her dress. Steele's and McDonald's eyes followed the movement. "Care for a lesson?"

Kaiser frowned. What was Gladys up to? And was Johnson, standing behind him with the knife, as distracted as the other two? He surreptitiously inched his good hand into his coat pocket. His fingers closed on the torch.

Steele licked his lips. "Tempting, but what about him?" He jerked his head at Kaiser.

"A girl needs a bit of fun now and again," said Gladys with a shrug. "But I've got to think of my future, too. A rising tide lifts all boats, after all." She wiggled a little. Somehow her cleavage grew even more impressive. "Ever thought about me doing two of you together?"

Steele's eyes went glassy. McDonald breathed heavily through his mouth, the knife falling from her side.

"Now!" she yelled, twisting out of McDonald's grasp.

Kaiser didn't hesitate. He pulled out the heavy torch and turned, bashing Johnson's bonce. The man grunted and collapsed. Kaiser turned back to help Gladys.

She didn't need help. Both Steele and McDonald lay unconscious at her feet. A rising lump and trickle of blood on Steele's temple matched one on McDonald's onion. Tommy—damn him, Kaiser had told him to stay away—scrambled over the stones. He hefted a good-sized piece of brick, about the same size as the one that lay beside Steele.

Gladys dropped the stone she held and dusted off her hands. "I saw Tommy creeping around while the git was talking. Seemed our only chance. You good, then?" she asked Kaiser. At his nod she twisted, pushing aside her coat to check her dress. "One rip on this dress, and I'll give his head another bash."

Tommy panted up to Kaiser. "I popped him on the first try, Kaiser!"

Kaiser sighed and shoved the torch back into his pocket. He liked that torch. Good British steel taking out bad British Steele.

Tommy continued. "I know I wasn't supposed to follow you, and you can rip me off a strip later. But I tipped off Perce, and the rozzers are on their way. We've got to scarper!"

"Right." Kaiser glanced at the three men on the ground. They were all breathing, which was something. His plan would still work. "There's a door at the bottom," he said, pointing to the stair. "Bring up a few cartons of cigarettes. We'll leave 'em beside these gits: black marketeers all wrapped up as a present for the Old Bill."

Tommy hurried down the stairs, Gladys following close on his heels.

"Leave the door open," she said, her voice echoing hollowly. "I'll put a couple cartons on the stairs, too, in case they need a Belisha beacon."

In a moment they were back. Kaiser arranged the cartons beside the men. Gladys also carried a few packets of silk stockings, which she dropped next to the cartons. Then she reached down and opened one, stuffing the stockings into her décolletage.

Kaiser lifted an eyebrow.

"My compensation," she said. "For pain and suffering."

A few minutes later, they were away from the ruins and watching the police from across the square. They waited until Steele, Johnson, and McDonald, as well as the cigarettes, stockings, and fabric, were loaded into the Black Maria and driven away.

"What's to stop 'em from grassing on you?" asked Tommy as they turned toward Commercial Road.

"Oh, they'll give it a go." Kaiser shrugged and wrapped his good arm around Gladys. "But I know a thing or two about some of the muckety-mucks, enough to keep 'em from looking my way. They like their bacon and eggs, as well as silk stockings for the missus. And they like keeping it local. I'll be good this time."

"So we've won!" said Tommy, his grin as wide as the Cheshire Cat's.

Kaiser shook his head. "The battle, yeah. But the war? Don't know about that yet."

"Remember what Mr. Churchill said." Gladys pressed close to his side.

Kaiser nodded. "'We shall fight them,' he said. 'We shall never surrender.'" He gave Gladys a quick kiss on the cheek. "Too right."

MARIGOLD IN THE LAKE

by Susan Thibadeau

Destination: Long Island, New York
Is personal assistant Daisy just accident prone or has her employer's popular blog put Mrs. Marigold Greenway and Daisy in danger?

This was my second time in the emergency room since I'd started working for Mrs. Marigold Greenway three weeks ago.

"Goodness, Daisy, you're accident prone," Marigold said as we waited for the doctor to come in. My swollen and bruised wrist ached so much I couldn't answer. I tried to recount what had happened but all I remembered was pushing Marigold out of the way as a flowerpot plummeted toward her from the rooftop above. I must have used my hand to cushion us as we tumbled to the pavement. It was all such a blur.

After the doctor came in and x-rays were taken, I got the good news that it was only a sprain. Nonetheless, the doctor bandaged it and ordered up a sling. "Rest this and ice it," she said and then looked into my eyes. "I don't want to see you back here again."

"Don't worry, Doctor, I'll make sure she's more careful," Andrew, Marigold's son, said from the doorway. The doctor turned and even though I couldn't see, I knew she was smiling at him, maybe even blushing. He'd had that effect on every woman I'd seen him with, myself included.

At the moment I was worried I'd lose my job. What good was a personal assistant with a knee brace and an arm in a sling? I jumped up from the table to show how nimble I still was. Unfortunately, the weight on my knee, badly scraped and sporting a few stitches due to a run-in with a runaway cart, left me breathless with pain.

"Hold on," Andrew said, maneuvering around the doctor to get to me.

He was too late, though, because Marigold was already by my side, patting my shoulder. "Daisy, Daisy, you have to go slowly. Heaven knows if you hadn't been so fast last week you wouldn't have stepped in front of that loading dock cart."

I was in too much pain to manage anything but an "Uh huh."

Andrew regarded me in silence, as if considering a weighty issue. I feared he was trying to come up with a way to tell me I was fired. Instead, he turned to Marigold. "Mother, maybe it's time for you to work on that story you hinted at in your blog last month."

Despite Marigold Greenway's being almost sixty-seven, her online blog was the toast of New York City's young, hip crowd (as she called them). She'd typically post once a week and her fans eagerly awaited the tell-all gossip Marigold effortlessly acquired. But every once in a while she'd post a brilliant and fully formed news story.

"About Tim's murder?" Marigold asked.

"Yes." Andrew smiled at me. "Maybe you should go on location. A little time for both of you on Long Island might give Ms. Fields a chance to heal."

Through the haze of pain, I felt a blush coming on and couldn't tell if it was because of Andrew's impossibly perfect dimples or my relief at not losing my job.

"We'll go tomorrow!" Marigold wrapped her arm around me and nudged me forward. "Let's go pack. You can help pick out my outfits!"

"Now, Mother," Andrew stepped in front of us, "perhaps you should drop Ms. Fields at her apartment. I think she could use a night to rest and pack her own things."

Marigold agreed, apologizing for her enthusiasm. "My driver and I will pick you up at eleven tomorrow morning. If you have time between now and then you should Google Tim St. Titus."

***

My wrist felt a little better the next morning when I sat down at my laptop and typed in Tim St. Titus's name. Several old newspaper articles came up describing the young actor last seen swimming in Lake Ronkonkoma during the early summer of 1982. Even after an exhaustive search, St. Titus's body was never found. His companion, a Miss Marigold Meadows, described in great detail their evening together, culminating in the skinny-dipping episode that turned tragic.

"One minute he was there, the next gone," she was quoted as saying.

The photo of that companion, said to be an up and coming actress in one article, was very familiar. I enlarged the image on the screen, studying the patrician nose and the sweetheart chin, all features I knew well in my employer.

I printed out the articles as I collected clothes and the book I was re-reading, Hardy's *Far From the Madding Crowd*, and threw them all into the only suitcase I owned, a holdover from my student days. It was hard to believe I'd been out of school for eight years, trying to make it in a world that didn't seem to want what I had to offer. Perhaps if I'd studied something useful, instead of English Lit, I'd be set now in a well-paying job instead of worrying about losing the one I had.

By the time Marigold's car arrived I was packed and ready. I'd neglected to ask where, exactly, we'd be staying on the Island, imagining some modern architectural masterpiece on the shore. After all, the Greenways had money—lots of money. With that in mind, after saying "Good Morning" to Marigold, I sank into the limousine's plush leather seat and closed my eyes. But something nagged at the edge of my consciousness. For a minute it bobbed about, then slowly came into focus.

I sat up. "Marigold, did you say 'murder' yesterday? Did you say Tim St. Titus was murdered?"

Marigold adjusted her Kate Spade cardigan. "Yes, dear, I did."

"But the newspaper articles said he drowned. They even quoted you as saying he drowned."

"That's what I thought back then, but . . ."

There was a dramatic pause. Even though Marigold had given up the theater when she married, she still employed many of the skills she'd acquired on stage.

"Two months ago the sister of an old friend Emma Allenton called and read me a few pages from Emma's diary," Marigold continued. "The diary was in an old trunk the sister found in the attic when she was getting the house ready for remodeling. It's a bed and breakfast now and we're going to stay there." She clapped her hands together enthusiastically. "It's on the North Shore. Of course, I've always loved the South Shore, but won't it be fun to stay in a hundred-year-old house?"

My dreams of ocean vistas seen through wide expanses of glass evaporated.

"It will be, don't worry." Marigold patted my good hand. "I bet you want to know what was in the diary?"

"Uh-huh," I answered.

"Well, Emma died that very same summer, soon after Tim drowned. It was a hit and run. So heartbreaking." Marigold paused again until I nodded in agreement. "It turns out Tim was dating Emma, too. I never knew. Anyway, in her diary Emma wrote she was afraid someone would try to kill Tim."

"Who?"

"Emma didn't say who—or why." Marigold bit her lip. "You know, when her sister contacted me, I was so busy with my blog, and"—she smiled at me—"looking for a suitable assistant, that I didn't take it all that seriously."

"What changed your mind?"

Marigold bit her lip again. "I guess, in thinking more about it, I began to wonder. Tim was a lifeguard at the lake, after all. You wouldn't expect him to drown."

I shifted in my seat to stare full on at Marigold. "You think someone drowned him? But wouldn't you have heard that happening?" I shivered. "Wouldn't whoever it was have drowned you, too?"

"Well," Marigold's gaze dropped, "the truth is, I was very tipsy by the time we jumped in the water. And it was cold. I got out pretty fast and huddled under my towel."

"But Tim never got out?"

"No. He never did. All that was left of him was his clothes. The lake being so deep, they never even found his body. At the time, I believed what people told me—that he'd simply drowned. That the Lady of the Lake had come to take him for her lover."

Marigold spent the rest of the car ride telling me the legend of the lake. An Indian princess, kept from her true love, a white man, took her canoe to the middle of Lake Ronkonkoma where she slid into the water and drowned herself. But her ghost remains. The legend says each year she drowns a man to make him her lover, so they can be together in the spirit world.

"Of course," Marigold added, "I didn't really think it was a ghostly Indian maiden that drowned him—although it's strange that so many men have drowned in the lake. I guess the legend did predispose us all to think he'd accidently drowned."

I'd been so interested in the story I hadn't noticed we'd gotten off the Long Island Expressway. On my right I thought I saw a glimpse of blue water.

"That's Lake Ronkonkoma," Marigold said. "We're going a little farther north."

I craned my neck but couldn't see any more of the lake. Fifteen minutes later we pulled into a long driveway. At its end sat a white house, Victorian in style. As we approached, we saw a gaping, charred hole in its side. The car slowed. Marigold jumped out, purse and all. I followed as she ran up the steps and crossed the porch to the front door. She stepped inside. I hesitated, looking down at my wounded wrist and knee, then walked in after her. Soot covered the walls of the foyer and layered items on the small round table at its center. The smell of burnt wood roiled my stomach.

Marigold stood in front of the table, hands on hips, studying the stairs. Before I could warn her against mounting them, a voice boomed behind us.

"This house is off limits, ladies."

It's worth noting that, given three weeks with Marigold, I'd grown immune to loud noises and startling events and so didn't jump out of my skin but, instead, calmly turned to see a middle-aged cop in the open doorway. As he escorted us back to our car he filled us in on the fire that had destroyed almost half of the newly renovated B&B and put its owner in the hospital's ICU.

"We'd better get a hotel room. I know just the place," Marigold said, once we were back in the car. She gave directions to her driver.

"It's too bad we won't be able to see your friend's diary after all," I said. "Even if it didn't burn up in the fire, we can't get into the house to get it."

Marigold rummaged through her purse. "I *did* find something on the table." She pulled out a soot-smudged envelope and tore it open. A small cassette dropped out.

I picked it up. "Well, it isn't a diary." The plastic looked old, the tape inside tired. "I don't suppose you have something to play this on?"

***

Marigold took a two-bedroom suite in a nearby hotel, part of an upscale chain. Its concierge, a fan in awe of my employer, found us a cassette player, which was delivered to the suite along with complimentary wine and slices of chocolate cake.

"Lovely young man," Marigold said as she speared a piece of cake with her fork. I slipped the tape into the player.

"It's Tim," Marigold said as we listened. "He had a wonderful voice."

It was true. His voice was rich as maple syrup, marred only by how he'd sometimes stress the wrong syllable in certain words. He said "*a*dore" instead of "a*dore*" each time he told Emma how he felt about her. He said "*co*caine" instead of "co*caine*" each time he explained to Emma why he feared for his life.

When the cassette was done, I poured two glasses of wine. "You never knew about him and Emma?"

"No, not until her sister called and read me the diary." Marigold's smile held a hint of sadness. "Anyway, it was so long ago. And, truthfully, I didn't really take Tim seriously. We'd acted off-Broadway together. He was very handsome but I never felt all that romantic toward him. I guess a part of me never trusted him."

"Do you think Emma made the recording because she thought he was going to ask her to marry him?"

"It certainly sounded like that's what she was expecting. She sounded so hurt at the end." Marigold sighed. "Emma always was sentimental. Of course she'd want a recording of that special moment. Instead, she found out the man she loved owed a lot of money to a drug dealer."

"Why didn't she come forward after he'd drowned?"

Marigold's pregnant pause lasted longer than usual. Finally, she answered. "I guess she didn't want to sully the reputation of the man she loved by telling about his drug use—or the fact that he'd been selling, too."

We finished our cake in silence, watching through the window as rain fell.

"We should visit Emma's sister," Marigold said as she put her empty plate on the tray.

I agreed, and went into the smaller bedroom to pull out my slicker. I heard part of Marigold's phone conversation through the open door.

"I'm an old family friend, why can't I see her? Oh, I see. Will you call me when she's allowed visitors? Oh. Oh. Well, thank you."

Marigold walked into my room, cell phone in hand. "No visitors allowed right now." She tugged at the hem of her sweater. "Put on your rain jacket. Let's go to the lake!"

***

"Across the way, there. That's where it happened." Marigold pointed to a heavily wooded part of the shoreline. "Even though it was private property, everyone went there to swim at night."

It started to rain harder. I pulled my slicker tight around me.

"Officially, this isn't really a lake at all. It's a kettle hole," Marigold said when I didn't respond. "During the last glacial period, a chunk of ice detached from the retreating glacier and left a deep hole after it melted. The hole was so deep it tapped into the underground water table, guaranteeing it would always be filled with water." Raindrops rippled the lake's surface, creating an odd textured pattern of light and dark.

I shivered and pulled my slicker tighter still. We were alone, the lake seemingly abandoned, the Lady of the Lake left bereft of young men to suffocate with her love.

"Did you hear that?" Marigold snapped around, her handbag plowing into my bandaged wrist.

I hadn't known I was so precariously perched, my body hovering over the water as it was. Startled by the shooting pain in my wrist, my wounded knee buckled beneath me and my other heel shot out, meeting the lake. The rest of me followed. Cold water engulfed the lower half of my body.

"Daisy, Daisy, you should be more careful," Marigold said as she squatted and reached both arms toward me." Behind her a gaggle of geese came briefly into view, then out again. "Here, take my hands."

With her help, I managed to climb out of the water.

"I think our next step is to check old newspapers. Maybe we can find out who else sold cocaine back then." Marigold frowned. "I've checked before for other stories. Some of the archives of the local papers aren't up online yet." Her gaze swept over me as I stood shivering under the pounding rain. "Are you too wet to go to the library?"

"Of course she's too wet," a voice said behind us.

Marigold spun around again, nearly sending me back into the water. "Andrew! Darling! What are you doing here?"

Andrew opened a large umbrella and held it over me as he answered his mother. "I called your driver and heard about the fire."

"Well, darling, you shouldn't have come. We've already found another place to stay."

"I know, Mother. But what you don't know is that the police think the fire was started on purpose."

"Why didn't that nice policeman tell us that?" Marigold asked.

"I spoke to someone higher up the chain of command," Andrew said. "Come on now, let's get back to the hotel and get Ms. Fields out of these wet clothes." He hesitated for a moment. "I mean, let's let Ms. Fields get some dry clothes on."

Andrew followed us back to the hotel, where I quickly changed and rejoined him and his mother in the sitting room.

"Andrew is going to help us at the library," Marigold said. "Won't this be fun?"

***

Four hours later we were back in the sitting room. Two pizza boxes and multiple bottles of water littered end tables while photocopied newspaper articles were spread out in front of us. The library excursion had been hugely successful, due mostly to Andrew. He'd so charmed the librarian that she'd conducted most of the search herself, finding us a wealth of news articles on a cocaine ring operating near Lake Ronkonkoma the summer Tim drowned.

"What have we learned?" Marigold asked, poking through the scattered pages.

"We learned the cocaine ring had racked up millions of dollars," I said. "And we learned there was a blood bath among the dealers that summer. The ones left standing were rounded up by the police."

"But no money was ever found," Andrew added.

"Well, it's obvious," Marigold said. "Tim's was the first death in that turf war. Poor Tim. He always struck me as someone willing to bend the rules. It looks like the lure of big money caught him in a trap."

Andrew picked up a slice of pizza. "Except for the tape, you have nothing to tie Tim St. Titus to the cocaine ring. He wasn't named in any of the articles. We may be at a dead end."

"Nonsense!" Marigold said. "We're making great progress." She took the last slice of pizza and closed the box top, revealing a flashing red light on the room's phone.

After calling the front desk she turned to Andrew. "They said the hospital phoned to let me know we could come in now and talk to Emma's sister."

As Marigold gathered her handbag and raincoat, Andrew helped me up. "We'll take my car."

I would have preferred curling up on my bed with my book. There was something about the way Thomas Hardy wrote that I found irresistible, much as his character Boldwood found the beautiful Bathsheba. Instead, I threw on my slicker and followed Marigold down to the hotel lobby.

"Wait here, I'll bring my car around," Andrew said.

"Nonsense." Marigold headed for the doors. "We're not invalids, are we, Daisy?"

Andrew looked at me and shrugged. I smiled up at him and was rewarded by his dazzling smile in return. Perhaps our gazes locked for a moment as we caught up to Marigold outside. I can't exactly remember. It all became such a jumble. The flash of silver at the corner of my eye, the sound of an engine growing ever louder, that sound becoming a roar, Andrew's yells, me throwing my body toward Marigold, a heavy weight—it turned out to be Andrew—landing atop of us.

***

Marigold pushed back the curtain that separated Andrew and me, and pulled a chair between our emergency room gurneys. "That driver must have been drunk. Thank goodness we weren't killed."

The truth was, I felt half dead.

"What did Emma's sister have to say?" Andrew asked as his mother sat down.

"Darling, I still couldn't see her. They say no one from ICU called. Isn't that odd?" Marigold pulled out her cell phone and typed. "I've texted my driver. He's on his way."

"You folks were very lucky," the ER doctor said as he walked into the room. "It looks like bruising and some scrapes. You'll both feel stiff and sore. If that persists, see your physician. I'll have the nurse bring your discharge instructions."

The doctor was right. It was luck that we hadn't been plowed over outside the hotel. In the ambulance, the EMT told us witnesses said it looked like the car didn't want to risk running into the building and shied away enough so we could jump out of its path.

After the doctor left, Andrew sat up. "Mother, I think we'd better go home. Back to the city."

"But darling, why?"

"Because it should be obvious by now that someone is trying to hurt you. It's only thanks to Daisy that you haven't been seriously injured yet." He jumped off the gurney and crossed his arms like the principal at my elementary school used to do. "I think your blog may have gone too far."

"My blog?"

"Yes, Mother. Someone you gossiped about is trying to get even with you. We should go back to the city. I thought you'd be safer here, but I was wrong."

"But . . ." Marigold stopped for a second, as if debating with herself. "I never write anything about anyone unless I clear it with them first."

"What?" Andrew's arms dropped open.

"These are all my friends, or friends of friends I talk about. I'd never really tattle. They like to have naughty things written about themselves—as long as they can decide what those things are. It's just like reality TV."

Andrew looked like he might sink back onto the gurney but pulled himself together. "Someone is trying to hurt you, Mother. Someone lured you out of the hotel and tried to run you down."

"Darling, this is all just a string of coincidences." This time it was Marigold who crossed her arms. I half expected she'd stomp her foot, but she relented. "Though I suppose Daisy and I can work on the story back home, online and over the phone if needed."

After the nurse sent us on our way, Andrew guided Marigold and me down the hospital corridor. On the way, I realized I'd forgotten my jacket. I sent them ahead and went back to get it.

The light had dimmed automatically in the air-conditioned room. Its chill gripped me. I crossed quickly to where my slicker hung over a chair, grabbed it and just as quickly left, my knee and wrist and newly bruised shoulder complaining loudly. Despite that, I still had to force myself to walk, not run, down the hallway. Around me, the low hum of equipment married with hushed conversations. Some serious: "Another IV, Doctor?" "Looks like a compound fracture." "Set up a CT scan, Nurse." Others, less so: "How about lunch?" "*Ex*cuse me, I must have taken a wrong turn." "Where do I pay for parking?"

Even after I passed through the ER doors into the hospital's lobby, the chill remained, in fact it intensified.

"There you are." Andrew limped toward me. "I've tucked Mother into the limo. She's insisting on going back to the lake before we leave to soak in its atmosphere. We'll drop you at the hotel and pick up my car. You can rest while we're gone."

***

At the hotel, I grabbed my book, went down to the café and settled into a booth with a pot of very hot coffee, and some toast and eggs. We'd been in the emergency room all night. I was hungry and tired and I'd begun to wonder if I'd ever feel warm again. Happily, the cold that had gripped me slowly dissipated under the spell of Hardy's novel. Things were working out for the heroine. She'd marry her rich neighbor who clearly adored her, even if we knew she loved someone else. She'd be safe. She'd be—

The coffee cup clattered onto the saucer. I'd read this book in high school, and then again in college. Bathsheba can't marry Boldwood.

I pulled out my cell. Marigold didn't answer. It took me a minute but I found Andrew's number. He didn't answer. I called the police. Although they promised to send a car to the lake, I could tell they didn't believe what I was saying. I ran into the lobby. Marigold's driver was there, talking with the concierge.

"The place where people used to go to swim naked at night," I said. "I have to get there, quick!"

The concierge gave us directions and ten minutes later we pulled onto a wooded lane. As the road curved, Andrew's car came into view.

"Wait for the police," I told the driver but he refused and, truthfully, I was relieved. We stepped onto the path beyond Andrew's Mercedes. Although my body ached, I managed to move quietly through the woods, Marigold's driver in tow. Finally we came to the lakeshore.

Twenty yards out, a small rowboat rocked precariously. A man was standing up in it, looking over the side as bound hands reached up from the water. The man lifted an oar high overhead, readying to hit the owner of those hands. At the same time, Marigold rose up in the stern of the boat and launched her handbag into the air. It hit the standing man squarely, the thud reverberating across the water. The man pitched forward into the lake. A second later, Marigold's driver dove in and swam toward the now violently rocking boat. I called the police for the second time.

***

"I'm not sure I could have held out much longer. I couldn't swim with my hands tied. Well, actually, I can't swim at all." Andrew's momentary embarrassment brought a lovely blush to his not-usually pale complexion. "It seems a miracle you showed up. How did you know?"

I'd pushed back the curtain and dragged a chair between Andrew's and Marigold's gurneys. "My book. Bathsheba couldn't marry Boldwood because her husband was still alive. He'd faked his drowning death."

"Thank goodness you were an English major," Marigold said. She sat up as the doctor walked in. "Can we go now, Doctor?"

He frowned. "We need to keep both of you for a few more hours, just to be sure. You both sustained blows to the head."

Although Marigold looked disappointed, she perked up when her driver walked into the room, the driver who fought off Tim's attempt to push Andrew under the water after he fell in, thus rescuing his employer's son.

"Tim almost got away with faking his own death," Andrew said.

"We were all so ready to believe Tim had drowned. Lake Ronkonkoma's legend fed our imaginations. And, of course, the lake is so deep. And so dark. It was understandable back then that divers might not find his body. It was a brilliant plan. He was the one who scooped up the cocaine ring's cash. While everyone else fought he just walked away with it. Brilliant." Marigold slumped back onto her pillow. "But poor Emma."

After Marigold's driver fended him off, Tim swam to the other side of the lake. The police picked him up there. They told us he'd confessed to trying to stop Marigold. He was the one who set the loading dock cart careering toward us, the one who sent the flowerpot crashing to the earth, and the one who set the B&B on fire, hoping to destroy the diary Marigold had mentioned in her blog. He was the one at the wheel of the silver car that tried to run us down. He was at the lake when I fell in. And he was at the hospital, too. "*Ex*cuse me," I'd heard that maple syrup voice say without realizing it, "I must have taken a wrong turn."

"Without your blog, Emma's killer would never have been brought to justice," I said to Marigold.

"That's true, Mother," Andrew agreed.

Perhaps Tim read Marigold's blog because it reminded him of a life he'd had to leave behind. The police told us when Tim read about Marigold's plans to investigate his death he started to worry it would get the case re-opened. He was afraid the drug dealers and distributers he'd stolen the money from and who were now out of prison would come after him. He was afraid the police would put the pieces together and realize he'd killed Emma. It was Emma who'd picked Tim up the night he and Marigold skinny-dipped. Once he stole the money, he killed Emma to make sure she couldn't tell anyone he was alive.

"Well, Mother," Andrew said, "this is going to be one great story on your blog."

Marigold nodded, then paused for a moment. "I know, dear. But I think you and Daisy will get a byline, too."

MURDER ON THE NORTHERN LIGHTS EXPRESS

by Susan Daly

Destination: Ontario, Canada
A reunion of university friends aboard a northbound train leads to unexpected revelations—and danger!

13 October 1961
Miss A. C. Berlin
59 Beech Avenue
Toronto 2, Ontario

Dear Miss Berlin,

Thank you for letting us see your proposal for Banners over Quebec: The Seven Years' War and Its Aftermath.

We have read the outline with great interest, but we regret that we must decline your offer to submit the full manuscript.

While there are many aspects of your project that would be appealing in the academic world, an examination of your outline and list of chapters suggests that it covers the same ground as a work published earlier this year by Borealis University Press.

Flames Along the St. Lawrence *has not only received great acclaim in the academic community, it is so well written, and has such universal appeal, that it has become a bestseller on the popular lists as well.*

While we at the University of Kingston Press would have been pleased and proud to be the publishers of such a book, we cannot take the chance that *<u>two</u>* *books about the Seven Years' War as it pertains to Quebec would find equal favour with the public.*

Wishing you the best of luck in your future endeavours,

I remain, very sincerely yours,

J. Raymond Wayne
History Publications Division

P.S. I am surprised, with all the research that you presumably put into your work, you were unaware of this landmark publication.

P.P.S. The department secretary has pointed out that you are Alice Berlin, authoress of several popular historical romances. I suggest you stick to this proven formula instead of attempting such an ambitious serious history project.

I crumpled the letter into a ball and threw it in the general direction of the waste basket, then addressed the absent Mr. Wayne.

"First of all, you fathead, it's *Doctor* Berlin. Didn't you notice all those letters after my name? And they are *not* romances. They're highly acclaimed historical novels."

As for the non-word "authoress," I decided to ignore it before my brain exploded.

So much for Plan B, submitting under my own name. I knew it was a mistake. If only plan A hadn't been such a tragic failure.

Well, on to Plan C.

Except there wasn't one. Since some other Seven Years' War aficionado had beaten me to it, my master work was of no value: commercial, literary or academic.

Curse the luck.

***

One month later

"Attention, passengers. The Northern Lights Express, departing at 8:30 for Gravenhurst, Huntsville, Burk's Falls, North Bay, Cumberland Bridge, and Borealis Bay is now boarding at Track 3."

I stood in the great hall at Toronto's Union Station as the announcement was repeated in French. A maelstrom of passengers surged all around me: all-night travellers emerging into the morning rush of the big city, people arriving for business meetings or leaving for a rendezvous. Rapturous reunions with grandchildren.

There was still time to back out. I could just vanish into the crowd and let the train leave without me. If I went home now, no one would—

"Alice?" came a voice behind me. "Alice Berlin!"

Too late.

I turned to see the woman who had been my best friend all through university. Even after twelve years, Maggie Talbot hadn't changed a bit. I found myself swallowed up in her overwhelming embrace, all furs and perfume and excitement.

I *had* missed Maggie. Something I hadn't planned on.

"I can't believe you're coming, too." Maggie released me and stepped back, taking me in. "Wait till the others see you. They'll be so excited."

Not all of them.

"It's great to see you again," I managed to say. And it was true, mostly. "Who else is coming?"

"The usual suspects. Jack and Gareth are probably already on board, checking out the bar car."

"What about Roger?" We were all his guests on this celebration journey.

"He's joining us at Huntsville. Come on, let's go find Track 3 and get settled."

I grabbed my case and we headed for the platform.

Point of no return.

***

"I can't believe it's been twelve years since I last saw you," Maggie said as we leaned back against the plush seats opposite each other. The click of the wheels over the rails and the slight swaying of the carriage offered a sense of comfort as the late autumn fields and farms north of the city rolled past us.

"I know," I said. "Are you back in Ontario now for good?"

Maggie drew on her cigarette and blew a cool smoke ring.

"For good or ill. After all those years in Vancouver, I've found my niche at McMaster. Hamilton's not so far from Toronto, so we can get together. Have you seen the boys much?"

"Christmas cards, mostly. I haven't really seen them socially for a few years now. Except Walter."

Her faced clouded at the mention of Walter.

The last time I'd seen the others was at Walter's funeral.

Maggie rallied. "And now we're all successful in so many different fields."

Gareth was editor of a literary magazine, while Jack was now head of research at the Canadian Broadcasting Corporation. As for Roger . . .

I didn't want to think about Roger.

"Especially you." Maggie ground her cigarette butt into the tiny excuse for an ashtray in the arm of the seat. "You've gone on to fame and fortune. And now Roger—"

Before she could expand on Roger's achievements there was a general clamour of male voices from the front end of the carriage. Jack was the first to catch sight of us.

"Alice! Maggie! By all that's holy!" He yanked me to my feet and enveloped me in a generous hug, followed by Gareth, who greeted me with his usual subdued and courtly manner.

"This is great!" Jack said, giving Maggie an equal hug. "Here we are, the shining stars of the class of '49."

We weren't all exactly shining stars. But from the first day of

Canadian history class at Borealis University in the fall of 1946, we'd formed a tight study group and a tighter social group. We'd stayed together until graduation, then gone our separate ways in the wider world.

Today, for the first time, the five surviving members would be all together again, aboard the Northern Lights Express.

And, I knew, for the last time.

***

The Northern Lights Express is a misnomer. It certainly isn't an express, since it makes numerous stops along the way. As for the Northern Lights, well, considering the train leaves Toronto in the morning and Borealis Bay in the afternoon, the chances of seeing the Northern Lights are slim. But the name has a romantic ring to it, and the train runs through three hundred and fifty miles and five hours of some of the most spectacular scenery on earth.

Its passengers comprise a mix of northern residents coming into the city or heading back home, workers going up or back from their long stretches of well-paid isolation jobs, and tourists—hunters, fishers, and sightseers—on a northern getaway.

The fourth flavour of passengers are the academics, because the last stop on the line is the home of Borealis University, on the northern shore of Lake Temiscaming.

There weren't a lot of passengers that day. Mothers with young children, couples, solo travellers were dotted around the car. The four of us had the far end to ourselves, so we spread out over two double sets of seats, all facing each other.

Maggie produced a large thermos of coffee to share, and as Jack passed around his flask of Northern Spirit Rye, I found myself recapturing the give and take of old times. If I could just forget the reason for this trip.

Roger had invited the four of us to travel back to Borealis University for a ceremony on Wednesday, when he would take up his appointment as head of the history department, the first department head who was also a graduate of the university.

We all knew it was exactly what he'd set his sights on, right from the start of his academic career. And now he wanted his old friends there for it.

We took advantage of Roger's absence to talk freely about his new career.

"Impressive anywhere," Gareth said, "but especially at Borealis."

Our alma mater boasted the finest history school in the country, especially for Canadian history, which still seemed to be criminally neglected elsewhere across our country, and nonexistent everywhere else.

"It sure ought to impress the in-laws," Jack observed.

"He's married?" I asked.

"Engaged. She's the daughter of the vice-chancellor at the University of Ottawa. The parents have a country place near Huntsville, so that's why he's joining us from there."

"He's so young," Maggie said. "How qualified is he, really?"

"Not surprising they were ready to snap him up, after the publication of his book," Jack said, producing a copy from his leather satchel.

The sight of the blue and gold jacket sickened me.

Everyone had read it. Including me. After my rejection, I'd bought a copy of *Flames Along the St. Lawrence.* The first shock was seeing Roger Morrissey's name on the cover. But even then I hadn't the stomach to read it, until I got his invitation and couldn't put it off any longer.

That's when I got my second shock.

The book was everything that fathead at U. of K. Press had said: that extremely rare commodity, a crossover work that found equal favour in two worlds. It was not only unreservedly acclaimed in the academic world, but also remarkably popular with the general public, without a hint of having been dumbed down.

Maggie frowned slightly. "We all love Roger, and we know he's capable of dazzling everyone with his way with words. But really, he never struck me as smart enough to produce a work like *Flames Along the St. Lawrence*."

"It's been winning awards," Gareth said. "And it's been hailed as the new definitive work on the subject."

Jack looked at Maggie. "Are you suggesting if an intellectual work is popular with Wednesday afternoon book clubs, it must be short on academic merit?"

"I didn't say that," Maggie pointed out. "I'm saying I never expected *Roger* to write such a book."

Jack shook his head with a sad smile. "And I never expected to hear what sounds like professional jealousy coming from you, Maggie. What about you, Gareth? Are you as surprised as Maggie?"

"Not at all." Gareth drew on his pipe. "He certainly shone in history when we were undergraduates together."

"Yes, modern American history," Maggie pointed out. "Medieval European history. The British Raj in India. He knew many things about many periods. But he was never interested in the Seven Years' War or the Capture of Quebec." She glanced my way. "More Alice's line, actually."

Jack laughed outright at this. "Oh come on, Maggie. I admit our Alice has made a name for herself with her historical romances—"

"Historical *novels*," I pointed out automatically.

"Yes, all right," Jack said. "But let's face it, they're *not* the same as a work like *Flames*."

"No," I said. "But I think Maggie was pointing out my fascination with New France in the eighteenth century, and its fall to the British in the Seven Years' War. It was *my* period."

"I've read all your books, Alice," Maggie said, "and I love them."

"So have I," Gareth said. "They're historically accurate *and* entertaining."

I thanked them both.

"As for Roger," Gareth went on, "I never doubted that someday he would produce a work as brilliant as he did. I'm delighted he's had such a success with it, and it's got him this new position. It's what he's always wanted."

As he delivered this testimonial, the train began to slow and people in the carriage gathered up coats and bags, getting ready to disembark.

As we pulled to a stop at Huntsville, Maggie leaned against the window and called, "Look, there's Roger. Yoohoo! Roger!" She banged on the glass, and the others joined her. Roger, standing on the platform with two suitcases, caught sight of us and grinned and waved. He grabbed his bags and ran down the platform toward the door.

***

We were north of Burk's Falls when the talk turned, as it must, to Walter.

"If only old Walter could have been with us," Jack said. He leaned back and pulled a second mickey of rye from his jacket pocket and offered it around. The sun still wasn't past the yardarm.

"Walter," Maggie said with a sigh. "He was such a sweet guy. Always willing to hold a door for a lady, or hold her head when she'd had a night on the town."

"Or cover your, uh, derriere when you were out after curfew," Jack added.

Or help an old friend try and get her book taken seriously by a publisher.

"A real gentleman," Roger agreed. "More to the point, willing to lend his class notes or read over an assignment for spelling and grammar."

Gareth nodded. "Even though he wasn't the highest achieving

student in the class."

"Here's to Walter." Jack raised his coffee mug. "A solid B student but an A-plus friend."

"To Walter," we chorused.

Maggie drained her spiked coffee. "Just what did happen, anyway? I heard about his death when I was out west, but—was it some kind of fall?"

The guys looked at each other, perhaps waiting to see who would take the lead. I kept my mouth shut. I really, really didn't want to talk about it.

Gareth volunteered by clearing his throat. "It was about two years ago. He lived alone in the upstairs flat of an old house. Slipped on the icy steps one night, coming home late, and banged his head on the concrete."

"His landlady found him," Jack added, "but it was too late."

"That's so sad," Maggie said. "No one to keep an eye out for him. He was teaching, wasn't he?"

"Yeah," Roger said. "History and English at Jarvis Collegiate. Remember his funeral? Alice, you were there. What a crowd, eh?"

"Yes. All his students, past and present. He had no family, but so many friends, since he was such a nice guy."

There are worse epitaphs.

***

I needed to speak to Gareth alone. As we headed for the dining car for lunch, after leaving North Bay, I held him back. We stood in the vestibule between the cars.

"What's up, Alice?"

"Were you serious when you said it was no surprise Roger had written a book as good as—" I nearly choked on the title—"*Flames Along the St. Lawrence*?"

He frowned and took a long draw on his pipe before answering. "Yes. Absolutely. Are you joining Maggie in doubting his ability?"

I looked through the window in the sliding door that led to the next car. The rest were out of sight.

"Oh, I have no doubts at all. He didn't write that book."

He raised his eyebrows. "That's a pretty severe accusation. Based on what evidence?"

"I know that Walter was working on that book."

"Wait." Gareth tamped out his pipe and slipped it into his jacket pocket. "Are you saying that Walter—*Walter?*—wrote it?"

"Well, yes." That's what I was *saying*.

"And that Roger knew about it, and when Walter died in that bizarre accident, Roger took advantage of it and stole the manuscript?"

"I saw the manuscript myself. And I know that Walter was going to send it to someone—you or Jack or one of our old professors—to take a look at it, get some advice about where to submit it."

Gareth looked straight into my eyes, clearly rattled by my revelation, but he seemed ready to hear more.

"I've got a few questions about this," he said. "Assuming any of this is true, why now? The book was published almost a year ago."

"I'd heard about Roger's book from—from someone in publishing, but I didn't read it until last week. After I got Roger's invitation to help him celebrate."

That had been my second shock. Reading my own words published under Roger's name.

"Why not go to Roger directly?"

"Because I haven't a clue how to approach him. I'd already accepted the invitation, but ever since I read the book, I've been sick with wondering what to do. Go to the university directly? The dean of history, maybe?"

"Kind of rough on Roger, wouldn't you say, not giving him a chance to defend himself first."

There *was* no defence, but I didn't feel like continuing the discussion. Gareth didn't seem to be taking it seriously enough.

"You go on," I said. "The others will be waiting for you."

"Aren't you coming?"

"I have a sandwich in my bag," I lied. "I really don't want to face Roger right now."

"I understand. What do Maggie or Jack say? Or have you asked them about it?"

"No. Just you."

"Probably wise. Let me think about this a bit before you say anything to anyone else."

I went back to my seat. For a while I just stared out the window at the dramatic landscape of rugged rocks and bare trees of late November. It should have lifted my heart, but all I could think was, had I done the right thing in talking to Gareth?

Why hadn't I just cancelled my trip and written to the university? How much of a fool would I feel now if I tried to talk to the dean or vice-chancellor or whoever. They'd think I was crazy.

The best thing, I decided, was get off at the next station and wait there until the Northern Lights Express made its return trip later in the day.

Then I'd get my hands on a lawyer.

***

It was easier than I'd expected. The others were still lingering in the dining car when we reached Cumberland Bridge, about half an hour before Borealis Bay, so I was able to slip on my coat and get my bag from the rack.

As the train slowed and the station was announced, I realised I couldn't simply vanish from the train. I had just enough time to scribble a quick note to Maggie saying I needed to return to Toronto and had got off at Cumberland Bridge. I folded the note and left it on her seat. Completely devoid of logic, at least it would let her know where I'd gone.

Cumberland Bridge was a more popular station than Borealis Bay, due to logging and mining in the area, so a fair number of people got off. I was relieved to be in a crowd, rather than standing alone and visible on the platform. I watched the train rumble across the steel bridge over the Montreal River. It disappeared around a curve.

Within a few minutes, the families and workers and visitors had all been collected. The platform now stood deserted under the grey sky, surrounded by the silence of the forest on all sides. I'd have a good three hours wait, so a little fresh air and a walk along the river, after all those hours in the smoke-filled carriage, would do me good. Help me work out the next step in this weird situation.

I headed toward the river and began to walk along the high bank. The peacefulness of the late autumn air and the tang of the pines began to soothe me.

"Hey, Alice!"

I turned to see Gareth running to join me.

Hell. Where had he sprung from?

He caught up with me. "I was worried about you. When I saw you get off I thought someone should look out for you."

"You didn't need to. I just couldn't carry on being nice to Roger."

I stood there uneasily, despite Gareth's would-be reassuring smile.

"You could have just waited at the station in Borealis," he said.

"I'd rather wait here for the returning train. Even if it means waiting alone for hours."

"Sure, I understand."

Did he? We stood there on the edge of the high bank looking down to the rushing water.

"What I don't understand, though," Gareth went on, "is why you care so much that Walter's work get the recognition you feel it deserves. After all, it can't do him any good now, whereas Roger can, and has, benefited greatly from it."

"You can't be serious! Even putting aside the concept of academic recognition, which I won't, there's the matter of Roger cheating his way into a post at Borealis. A highly responsible post at that. But even if he were the lowest teaching assistant, I still wouldn't let him get away with it."

Gareth shook his head slowly. "Leave it, Alice. Just leave it."

I shivered, not from the fall air, or the sight of the water rushing past below. But I stood my ground.

"What's it to you that Roger should become a big name academic?"

"What's it to *you* that Walter's name should live on? I don't recall you two being particularly close."

"We were friends. Like I thought we were all friends. But now I'm not at all sure about you. If Roger can be such a low-life, and you're defending him . . . I don't even know how Roger got hold of that manuscript anyway. I thought Walter would show it to you or Jack or—"

"Walter *did* send it to me." Gareth's words were so casual I almost missed their import.

"He did?"

"Of course. No way would he consult Roger on anything like that. He knew as well as I did Roger was always willing to pay out big money for a well-written essay on any assigned topic."

"So he *did* cheat, even back then. And you helped him?"

"I did, Jack did, and half a dozen other hard-up students did. We all needed the money. Even your pal Maggie did it once or twice, though in her case, I think it was a matter of his charm and lovely blue eyes. Only you and Walter seemed immune."

"He never asked me to," I murmured, while thoughts of truth and consequences raced around inside my head.

"Of course not. He knew you were sea-green incorruptible. Which is why, as you all observed, Roger had no record of excellence with the Seven Years' War. That was *your* particular field of study. Ironic, isn't it, how his fame is now based on . . ."

His discourse trailed to a stop and he looked at me with dawning knowledge and wonder and—was I mistaken?—respect.

I stepped back from him, but he grabbed my wrist and stopped me.

"It was *your* work, wasn't it? No wonder you were so sure it was stolen. So ready to go to bat for it."

"Let me go," I commanded, trying to pull free. He gripped me all the harder. He was above me on the incline, so I didn't want to struggle, considering the loose gravel at our feet, angled toward the steep rocky bank and the rushing water.

"It begins to make sense," Gareth went on, still in a tone of quiet discovery, amusement almost. "Except why? Why would you have Walter front your book?"

"Oh, come on, Gareth. Because I'm a woman, of course. Women always get short-changed when it comes to academic credibility. Or maybe you never realised that. Add to that I was already known as a writer of popular historical novels—'romances' some people like to call them. People who haven't read them."

"I told you they were excellent, remember?"

I ignored this. "Walter and I came up with the plan that he would do all the up-front work of finding a publisher. We'd keep my name out of it until everything was set to go, and then I would reveal myself to the publisher as A. C. Berlin, MA, PhD."

He grabbed my other arm, but still sounded eerily calm and reasonable.

"Well, Alice, since you've levelled with me, I'll do you the same courtesy. Roger, as we all knew, always had his heart set on a brilliant academic career. Heaven knows why, since it doesn't pay anywhere near as well as, say, a bank president, though certainly much higher than an editor at a struggling literary magazine. But that was his glorious dream. Unfortunately, while he had the ambition, he had neither the brilliance for it, nor the inclination for hard work. He had, however, the money."

Let him keep talking.

"So he just kept on doing what had always worked so well. Pay others to do it for him. He proceeded through graduate school and into his recent position at the University of Ottawa."

"I'm sure his students must be thrilled to have such a mediocre teacher."

"They *love* his classes. You know what a charmer he can be. He's an excellent lecturer, though I suspect he cribs those as well. And then, of course, he hit the jackpot. Or rather, I did."

"When Walter sent you the manuscript." I really didn't like where this was going.

"Roger always kept an eye out for the Big Chance, and he had me looking around, too. As usual, he was willing to pay big for this one. Walter's book—I beg your pardon, *your* book—just fell into my lap. Terrible title, by the way, but I like to think I came up with a better one. *Flames Along the St. Lawrence.*"

"Pretty derivative, actually," I said, forgetting I should keep him calm and sane. "*Drums Along the Mohawk* was a second-rate movie."

He ignore the jibe. "He had to pay me handsomely for it. As I said, an editor's pay isn't all that great. I held out for half of the advance and royalties. But I'm kind. When he got the offer at Borealis, I said the salary was all his."

"But you'll always own him," I pointed out. "How fortunate for both of you that Walter fell on his steps at just the right"—my voice caught for an instant, then I forced myself to continue—"time to be of use to you."

His tone remained calm. "Yes. Very fortunate."

The rapid flow of the Montreal River was too close for comfort, but tenuous foothold be damned. I twisted my arms within his grasp and broke free and gave him a shove. As he fell, he grappled for a hold on the rocky bank, and I turned to scramble up to the path. He grabbed my ankle, and I found myself sliding down the bank with him. Gravity was relentless against us, and I finally did what I should have done when I'd first encountered Gareth.

I screamed. Long and uninhibited. Pausing only long enough to gulp in a breath and resume screaming.

And I kicked. We were losing ground rapidly, but I flailed my leg, determined to shake him off.

Gareth hit the water, never letting go of me. At the last moment I twisted myself sideways and wedged my body against a boulder at the water's edge. I was already half in the water, fighting the icy flow, but I clung to the rock for my life. I could see Gareth struggling to keep his head above the surface of the deadly current, still gripping my ankle.

I might have held us both safe, but I had a flash of Walter being pushed on the ice-covered steps outside his apartment, hitting his head, and losing his life.

Because of *my* book.

God forgive me, I gave a hard twist to my leg. Gareth's grip loosened and I watched the river claim him. His face surfaced for a moment. A choking cry— and he was gone.

***

Roger was a wreck. Emotionally, psychologically and, of course, academically.

The four remaining stars of the Class of '49 sat huddled in the dean's study at Borealis University after endless hours of rescue work and failed rescue attempts and police questioning, after interrogation from the dean of history and long complex explanations from me and broken confessions from Roger.

The dean had his personal staff provide us all, especially me, with hot food and hotter drinks. Finally, he'd left us alone.

I was still shivering, despite a change of clothes and the fire in the room. Maggie sat close beside me, her arm around my shoulders. She and Jack kept trying to express their bewilderment over everything.

"I still can't believe it." Maggie's voice was steeped in misery.

"Gareth . . ." Jack murmured in disbelief. "Walter . . ."

Roger remained silent, looking sick and miserable.

Finally he spoke up, repeating what he'd already said in many different ways.

"I didn't know anything about it."

"You didn't know it was supposed to be Walter's book?" Maggie snapped. "Didn't know Gareth had killed him?"

"No. *No*! All right, yes, maybe I suspected it was Walter's book. Gareth didn't say so, but he told me it was written by someone who would never claim it as his own. But *Walter* never wrote anything like that. He didn't even write half decent essays at university. That's why I never—" He cut himself off.

"Why you never paid him to write one for you?" Jack asked.

He didn't respond to that. "My career's in the toilet now. The one thing I wanted more than anything in the world is gone. My fiancée . . ." He shook his head. "Maybe she'll stand by me."

"Why should she?" Maggie asked.

But Roger kept on at his mantra.

"You have to believe me. *I didn't know*."

***

Well, maybe Roger didn't know. I've never been entirely sure. Just as sometimes, in the dead of a sleepless night, I'm not entirely sure Gareth did, in fact, kill Walter. Or was trying to kill me. Maybe Walter's death *had* been an accident. And maybe, on the river bank, Gareth had been struggling for his life.

Like me.

CZECH MATE

by Kristin Kisska

Destination: Prague, Czechoslovakia
Living "Prague Spring" proves hazardous when the newly-granted freedom of the press comes under renewed Soviet threat and student Pavla Lašková finds herself torn between family and friend.

Summer 1968
Prague

The bells of St. Nicholas chimed, startling the flock of pigeons which guarded the statue in the middle of Prague's cavernous old town square. The birds fluttered past Pavla, causing her to trip and scatter her stack of newspapers across the cobblestones.

Do prdele! Oh, hell. The documents, special edition copies of a freedom manifesto signed by seventy Czech and Slovak intellectuals, would be crumpled. Her brother, Karel, was waiting for her at Charles University so they could distribute them to students that morning before classes began. Now she'd be late. Knuckles scraping raw against the granite pavers, she scooped the papers into a haphazard pile.

No one ventured near the Baroque church to help Pavla gather her mess. She couldn't blame them. The Party had controlled religion for enough generations that most Czechs were now agnostic. Stuffing the wrinkled newspapers—which a mere two days ago could've gotten her expelled from her university—into her satchel, she dashed to make up for lost time.

"Stop, citizen!"

She'd attended enough Youth Communist League meetings to know that the clipped tone of voice could only mean one thing.

Secret police.

Pavla froze, not daring to turn around. The pile of manifestos burned a hole through her messenger bag into her back. What had possessed her to risk walking through the center of Prague from the printer? Freedom of the press had been in existence for less than twenty-four hours. No one had tested yet whether the Party would honor the liberty.

"Identification papers." A second voice, gravelly—suggesting years of chain-smoking unfiltered cigarettes—barked the command. The metal tips of his boots clicked on the bricks and stopped a few paces behind her shoulder. Grateful the police officer couldn't see the frustration on her face, she slipped her wallet from her jumper's pocket. His gloved hand confiscated her personal documentation.

The street lamp shone down on her like an interrogation spotlight, but not a whisper of air stirred in *Staroměstské náměstí*. Somehow, even the few pre-dawn pedestrians in the Old Town Square had evaporated as quickly as her hope. No nearby alleyway offered escape. Just the massive wooden church door of St. Nicholas stood by challenging her, agnostic that she was, to beg God for help. But if her mother's prayers hadn't saved her father, why would He answer hers now?

"Lašková, Pavla. Student. Charles University." Boredom laced his statements as he read her identification, but they all recognized the power he wielded. "Turn around."

Pavla forced a neutral look on her face, obliterating any trace of fear or guilt before facing them. Both police officers sported leather jackets despite the summer's warmth. While her hands hovered midair, she prayed—yes, prayed—that her brother would show up to intervene. That she'd see her mother again.

"Comrade Lašková . . ." The policeman paused to light a cigarette with the flame from a brass lighter. Her pulse hammered the cadence of a death march. If the police searched her, they'd find the stack of manifestos in her messenger bag and arrest her for treason. ". . . explain why you, the daughter of a political prisoner, are in front of a church. A subversive—"

"Pavlínka, there you are!" A loud, energetic voice fractured the otherwise silent square as a tall young man jogged toward them, his straight hair bouncing into his eyes with each step. She didn't recognize him. "Silly *holka*, we were supposed to meet under the astronomical clock."

Whoever the hell he was, this man must be her angel. If she believed in angels, which she didn't.

"Papers . . ." The smoking police officer, who'd assumed command over his partner, held out his free hand to inspect the intruder's documentation. Pavla used the distraction to inch her messenger bag further from view. "Novák, Marek. Broadcast assistant. Radio Prague. What is your business here, Comrade Novák?"

The young man—Marek, she now knew—towered over her. He pivoted as he spoke to the policemen at a quick clip, some excuse about meeting Miss Lašková to tutor her in applied physics. How did he know her name? Or her engineering curriculum?

Behind Marek's back, which only Pavla could see, he flashed three fingers. Then he moved his hands away.

In her peripheral vision, a figure shifted, camouflaged by the shadows of the massive statue in the center of the square. A third policeman.

Pavla's gut churned. Her brother always said there are no coincidences. With so many police officers together at this early hour, her arrest must have been coordinated. Premeditated. She was trapped just like her father had been. At twenty years old, she was a dissident. The proof was tucked inside her bag, in the copies of the freedom manifesto she and Karel had planned to distribute at the university.

But the secret police backed off. They returned both of their personal documents and departed without another word. Marek, her guardian angel, had intervened. He'd saved her from her father's fate.

He guided her toward the medieval astronomical clock, a cluster of overlapping golden dials. Inside her jumper pockets, she balled her hands into fists to keep them from trembling. Once they were out of sight of all three officers, she stopped dead.

"Thank you." She breathed her words, not sure she'd articulated them.

"Be careful, Little Rook." The apostles in the medieval tower began their mechanical march. Marek spirited away as the clock's figure of death tolled the time.

Why had the police left them alone? How did he know her family's nickname for her? Or that she'd needed help?

"Wait. Who are you?"

***

Pavla squinted against the August evening sunshine reflecting off the brass saints as she raced across Charles Bridge. The Baroque statues reminded Pavla of her father's beloved chess set pieces. Hovering beyond the Vltava River was Prague Castle, big rook to her Little Rook.

Since it was summer break, instead of taking classes at Charles University, she'd been working this past month retooling machines at the same factory as her mother in the outskirts of Prague. But every Saturday, she trekked the hour-long tram ride into the city to meet her university friends.

Despite the billowing cigarette smoke inside the pub, she plowed through the crush of students anticipating a chilled, frothy Pilsner and spirited debate. The hot topic was the new Action

Program, reforms to their country's communist regime that First Secretary of the Party Dubček introduced a few months ago. He dubbed it "Socialism with a Human Face." Czechoslovakia now enjoyed freedom of speech, freedom of movement across the borders, a multi-party government, and, granted almost two months earlier, freedom of the press.

The people—she—had a voice. Finally. They could speak their minds. Even Radio Prague's broadcasts were stripped of Soviet propaganda. Pavla could travel to Germany or Austria. She, her brother Karel, and most every other university student welcomed these changes like springtime after a decades-long oppressive winter.

They were living Prague Spring.

Pavla squeezed into an open space at the bar. With her fingers curled around the edge of the worn mahogany, she leaned forward to flag the bartender. Instead, she noticed a familiar face sitting alone. It was the same young man who'd saved her six weeks earlier from the secret police.

Bypassing her friends' table, she plopped three beers in front of him, sloshing foam down one of the glasses.

"I found you, Marek Novák." She dragged a stool from a nearby table. "May I join you or are you too busy tutoring strangers in applied physics?"

"Please stay. Why three?" Half standing, his smile revealed a dimple she hadn't noticed when he'd intervened on her behalf.

"One beer for each policeman who let me go." Pavla clinked his glass as she looked him in the eyes and took care not to cross arms—silly Czech superstitions, but she couldn't afford to tempt fate. "*Na zdraví!*"

"Cheers, Little Rook. To the health of those three . . . clowns." His fingers dwarfed the pilsner glass. They were beautiful in their strength, which lead to solid wrists and the arms straining his sleeves. Was it getting warmer in here? She gulped her beer to hide the telltale blush creeping up her neck.

"Did we ever meet before that morning on *Staroměstské náměstí*?" Not a chance. She'd have remembered him if they had.

"I met someone from your family. He holds you in high esteem."

Karel. That explained his knowing her nickname and her classes. Attending the same university as her overbearing big brother had been suffocating. Even her mother had tried to temper his protectiveness. But if Karel had recommended her to this Czech Adonis, then perhaps he'd backed off his guard. Slightly.

"Don't believe everything he told you. I can be trouble when pressed, as he knows firsthand." Pavla poured the third beer into each of their glasses, trying not to stare at Marek's lips as he laughed at her quip. "So tell me, are you a university student also?"

"Used to be. I work at Radio Prague now."

"You report the news?" She straightened, leaning toward him. She and her mother tuned into the state radio station whenever the anti-communist Radio Free Europe frequency was jammed.

"Not quite. I started in January, right after Dubček began his reforms, but they won't let me broadcast without censoring. Though if our new freedom of speech prevails, I hope to report live someday."

His voice. Oh, she could listen to that deep timbre every night on the radio. And in person. "Why were you—"

"Forget about me. I'm boring. Why did you decide to study engineering? Not many women choose that field."

"Don't change the subject, Marek. Why were you in the square that morning? You weren't too scared to help me. I tried to find you these past few weeks to thank you, but I couldn't."

"Meet me for dinner. Tomorrow."

"I can't. I live outside Prague when the university isn't in session."

"Next Saturday, then. Here." His knee grazed hers, launching shockwaves through her. His sandy hair, square jawline, hazel eyes, and of course that dimple were an intoxicating combination.

She glanced away, remaining silent. Not because she didn't want to accept his invitation. In fact, this moment was perfect. But she didn't want to curse him. Bad—tragic—things happened to people she cared about.

Then again, he might be different. He possessed a defying sense of courage she'd never witnessed. All her progressive, freedom-fighting friends were vocal in support of their country's recent changes, but no one had ever challenged the police directly. Except Marek.

She nodded and held up three fingers.

"Pavlínka! Don't talk to him!"

The grip on her arm spun her off her chair, away from Marek, and through the crowd before she could inhale her next breath. Her brother, Karel, dragged Pavla outside the pub into the balmy summer evening and whipped her around. Though quite late, the sun had yet to escape the horizon. Hundreds of spires stood silhouetted above them in the faux-dusk.

"Let. Go. Of. Me." After ripping her hand from Karel's grip, she shoved, sending him scrambling backward. "So what did I do wrong this time?"

"You were almost arrested the morning we distributed copies of the *Two Thousand Words* manifesto?" Though only a couple years older, his frown lines had been etched into his brow ever since the day he'd inherited the title head of the Laška family. "Why didn't you tell me?"

"*Ježíš Kristus*. You're not my father. Besides, that was six weeks ago." Pavla crossed her arms but drew a shaky breath. As children of a political prisoner, both she and Karel were branded with invisible bullseyes. It was a matter of time before they'd be suspected of contributing to the anti-Soviet resistance, a charge that would be easy to prove. "How did you find out?"

"Gossip gets around. Trust me." He spat his words. Gone was her patient big brother who helped her fine-tune her skills at chess—the game of strategy their father, a master chess player, had taught them both before he was arrested.

"I got away. Case closed, Karel. You must have some other reason for embarrassing me in front of my friends."

Karel placed his finger on his lips, then motioned for her to follow him around the corner. Peeking in through a sliver separating the smoke-stained curtains, Pavla watched Marek order another beer.

"Why were you talking to that scoundrel, Pavlínka?" Perspiration beaded on the bridge of Karel's nose, fogging his wire-rim glasses. He wiped them on the hem of his button-down shirt.

"This is ridiculous. I can talk to whomever I want. Besides, Marek said you spoke highly of me."

"Lies! The only thing I've ever told him was to stay away from our family. Plus, your *friend's* name isn't Marek Novak. It's Zdeněk."

"That . . . cannot be true." She frowned at him sideways. But her rational-to-a-fault brother fidgeted with his glasses, a nervous tic he'd acquired after their father disappeared, evidence that as much as she didn't believe it, Karel did.

"Zdeněk Stiburk. He was a few years ahead of me at the University. He was arrested as a dissident and sentenced to a labor camp."

"Impossible, Karel." Her voice sounded hollow inside her head as she replayed every conversation with Marek. "He's here in Prague. No one has ever returned from prison. Not even Father."

"Exactly!" Karel grabbed her shoulders but released them before she could shove him off. Again. "How did Zdeněk escape? Was he miraculously granted clemency? Ridiculous. There's only one way. He bought his way out. With information."

"Are . . ." Blood pooled to her feet. She steadied herself against the building's cinder block facade while trying to process Karel's accusation. "Are you telling me Marek is a party spy?"

"*Do prdele*, Pavlínka. You may be book-smart, but your naiveté will get us all killed. Why do you think Zdeněk was crazy enough to intervene once the police had stopped you? Anyone else would've been arrested for obstruction of justice." His face twisted as if he'd bitten into a tart lemon. "Look, the Soviets have planted informants everywhere. In our police force. In our communist party. In our university. On every street corner in Prague. They don't trust Dubček's changes. They believe Czechoslovakia is going soft on communism."

"But Dubček's been meeting with the Soviets about Prague Spring all along." She shook her head. If her brother was wrong about the political situation in the country, maybe he was also mistaken about Marek. "Brezhnev knows every change made to relax the police state. Czechoslovakia hasn't eliminated communism; we're adding a human face. Just like it stated in that manifesto we distributed."

"Wrong!" The vein in his neck throbbed. "The Warsaw Pact nations are meeting in Bratislava this very minute. What are they discussing? Reining in our new liberalization policies. Condemning the *Two Thousand Words* manifesto. Restoring censorship."

Pavla stared at him, at a loss for words. Could the freedoms the Czechoslovakian people recently gained be at risk?

"There are no coincidences, Pavlínka. If Zdeněk is on probation, the only way he can remain safe is to expose citizens who are resisting the Soviet regime. He even tried to corner me several times over the past few months."

"I don't believe you!" She shifted away. Marek's name was Zdeněk? Czechoslovakia's Prague Spring could end? Nothing Karel said made sense.

"You want proof?" He took a deep breath before dropping his voice a notch and placing his hands gently on his little sister's shoulders. "Look up Zdeněk's name in the university's registrar's office. They keep photographs of all former students. You won't find a record of Marek Novák anywhere."

Pavla shook her head, thoughts colliding in her mind. "But he saved me."

"Mark my words, Little Rook. The Soviets will regain power." He slipped into the shadows, backing away. "You have to protect yourself, no matter what the cost."

***

"You lied, Marek. Or should I call you Zdeněk?" Pavla leaned over the same table where they'd chatted the previous week, hissing at him. She'd considered skipping their rendezvous that night, but couldn't override her curiosity. "Why?"

The din of students crowding every inch of the beer pub may have diffused the audibility but not the acid lacing her accusation. Her words hit their mark. He paled, standing as if an accused prisoner facing his sentence.

Marek's height and sheer mass dwarfed her, but she stood her ground, gripping her fists, still incredulous that Karel's bizarre theory about Marek had been correct. How could she have let a dimple and broad shoulders influence her perception? "Why didn't you tell me the truth?"

"I'm glad you came, Pavlínka. I can explain everything. Let's go to a restaurant—"

"No. I'm not going anywhere with you." Her chin quivered, her nose flaring with each breath. "How do I know you won't alert the police?"

"I didn't when you were carrying copies of the Two Thousand Words manifesto. Why would I now?"

"You knew I had the papers?"

"Yes. And if you look at the bottom of the declaration, you'll find my signature on it with the other sixty-nine intellectuals." He waited for her to respond, but she pressed her lips tighter. "Forget dinner, but at least give me five minutes to defend myself."

He pulled out the stool she'd occupied the week before, but she flinched and shifted aside. How could one piece of furniture embody loss? In that one gesture, her romantic hopes evaporated into the grim reality of secret police and neighbors betraying neighbors. Instead, she borrowed a chair from a nearby table and sat as far away as possible, crossing her arms.

Waiting.

"*Tak.* So, what would you like to know?" He placed his hands on the table and trained his eyes on her.

"Why did you lie to me?"

"About my name?"

"About telling me that my brother spoke highly of me."

"I never said that."

"Yes, you said, 'I met someone from your family. He holds you in high esteem.' That could only be Karel."

"I meant your father."

Pavla's throat ran dry. Her father was dead. How dare he invoke his memory? She stood to leave, never to set eyes on Marek again.

"Your father—Václav—saved me. I was sentenced to the same

forced labor camp. For two years he gave me half his daily food rations. Apparently, I reminded him of Karel."

"He's . . ." She stopped mid-turn and swallowed, grasping for some thread of truth among the lies and propaganda. "My father's still alive?"

"He was when I left in January. He asked me to find you and your family. To make sure you're safe. To send his love. He reminisced about you every day. I tried to tell Karel several times, but he wouldn't talk to me."

"Prove it." Pavla sank into the chair, trying but failing to absorb all this new information that seemed to fit together seamlessly. What was she missing?

"A month before your father was arrested, he took you to your forest chata. Outside the cabin, you got between a mother boar and her piglets. Your father heard the squeals and grabbed you just before she charged. You both escaped by climbing a tree, but the boars wouldn't leave. The night grew colder, so your father wrapped his shirt around a stick and lit it on fire with his cigarette lighter. He used the torch to scare them away."

"Did he mention how old I was?" Searching Marek's eyes, framed by squint lines etched like wings, she found honesty. She'd never told anyone outside her family what had happened, but those boars had terrified her almost as much as the secret police.

"About five years old. Your father misses playing chess with you, Little Rook. I'm surprised he survived all these years. The labor camp is worse than you can imagine."

Still not able to face Marek, she forced her fists to relax. "Few are released from the forced labor camps. So why you? Why not my father?"

"Because new evidence proved I was innocent. I changed my name to protect my family." The vein pulsed on his forehead. She could relate. Sharing a name with a convicted political prisoner was its own circle of hell.

Marek glanced at his watch, revealing a jagged scar on his wrist. "I know you have more questions, but I must cancel our plans for tonight. Forgive me. I'd still like to take you to dinner. Soon. I can pick you up . . ."

There it was again. That dimple.

She paused. "Tomorrow."

After he had departed, she peeked through a slit in the curtain. On the street corner, a man wearing a dark leather jacket lit a cigarette.

The police officer with the gravelly voice.

***

Pavla and Marek had lingered far too long over dinner and three beers—always three—at the restaurant. Every night this past week, he'd driven out to her mother's flat in the outskirts of Prague to meet Pavla for dinner. After hearing stories of her father at the labor camp and poring over their family photographs with Marek, her mother was as attached to him as she was. Karel would accept him, given time.

Who needed sleep? It was late-August, and this was Pavla's last week working in the factory before the hops harvest began. Then her university classes and her political activism meetings would resume.

In the night's silence—strolling hand-in-hand with Marek along the street lamp dotted boulevard—she found peace. She pressed her lips against his. They kissed under the waning crescent moon.

Finally.

Humming in the distance grew louder until the air vibrated. A squadron of military airplanes flew low overhead. In the dim silvery moonlight, the silhouette of parachutes floated to the ground like the puff seeds of a dandelion.

"*Ježíši Marie*!" Marek grabbed her hand. "Come!"

They raced back to his rusty Škoda and fumbled to unlock the doors, not daring to glance behind where Prague's airport lay. Marek almost ripped the stick shift out of the floorboard while changing gears as the tires rumbled over the cobblestone roads.

"Paratroopers?" Pavla gripped the dashboard to keep from hitting the windshield.

"Soviets."

"Because of Dubček's reforms?" Karel had warned her that Brezhnev didn't support Prague Spring. His tolerance of Czechoslovakia had apparently run out.

Marek clenched his jaw.

"Where are we going?" Pavla swallowed bile as they bulleted toward Prague's center.

"Radio Prague. We need to inform the people. So they can prepare."

Minutes after midnight, the radio station's phone rang. Soviet tanks had crossed several borders into Czechoslovakia. Rumors circulated that this invasion could be the largest Soviet deployment of military force since World War II.

They, together with a small crew of night-shift employees, drafted statements to read to the country. Marek's radio broadcast went live—realizing his dream. He and the other journalists were on a constant news loop with updates and a message from Dubček.

The Russians are invading. Stay calm. Don't fight back.

"Marek!" Pavla squeezed his arm when it seemed he had a moment to catch his breath. Karel's warnings were coming true. "Brezhnev's irritation escalated after Dubček allowed freedom from censorship and the press. One of his first objectives of the occupation may be to take control of the television and radio stations."

"What are you suggesting?"

"Do you have any extra radio equipment? I can set up an underground station to continue broadcasting if they attack the station."

"Brilliant, Pavlínka." He graced her with a flash of his dimple while shoving a box in her arms. Together they raced around the station gathering coiled wires, metal boxes covered with switches and knobs, and headphones.

She followed Marek and his colleague, Jiří, into the dark street, schlepping her burden against the flow of people chanting and marching through the streets. Why didn't they go back inside? While she fought the instinct to hide and protect herself, the crowd swelled to thousands in the dark of night. The Czechoslovakian people shared one mission.

Resist the Soviet occupation.

After stowing the gear in the trunk of his Škoda, Marek stopped her from sitting in the passenger seat. "Pavlínka, no. You can't go. Defying the Party is treason. The Soviets will find the underground station."

"Too late. We're all dissidents now." She kissed him, then snatched his keys and hopped in the car with Jiří. Unrolling the window, she yelled back as they sped off, "Keep broadcasting from Radio Prague, Marek. The people need you!"

***

After jerry-rigging a makeshift underground radio station in her empty dorm room, Pavla left Jiří behind and joined the Czechoslovakians' nighttime pilgrimage toward Prague's epicenter, *Václavské náměstí.* At every corner, people tore down street signs and flipped the arrows to misdirect the Soviets.

Regardless, by dawn, an endless stream of tanks plowed into Prague. Tens of thousands of demonstrators waving Czechoslovakian flags swarmed around the tanks. Soviet soldiers fired guns at protesters, but the crowd refused to disperse.

As Pavla draped a discarded flag over a lifeless, bloodied victim, someone turned up the volume of a portable radio. Marek's voice pierced the chaos, advising protesters to remain calm. The Soviets had arrested Dubček and were flying him to Moscow for questioning. He ended his broadcast with an anti-Soviet call: "We are with you. Be with us, too."

I'm with you, Marek. He was still broadcasting from Radio Prague. Thank God, he was safe. She closed her eyes, his voice projecting strength while everything she held dear collapsed. Her country. The democratic reforms she, Karel—who must be somewhere among the protesters—and her father had risked their lives to promote.

Pavla struggled against the mob to return to Marek. She skirted past collapsed building facades, flag-covered bodies forgotten on street corners, and trucks loaded with flag-waving Czechs.

Tanks stood sentry, facing the station's building. Through the haze of gun smoke and chanting, she crept behind the Soviet soldiers aiming at the unarmed protesters who'd formed a human barricade to protect the radio station. More bodies littered the ground.

Scrambling around one of the tanks, Pavla tripped on a loosened cobblestone. White hot pain exploded through her knee. Breathing through the pain, she struggled to stand, but combat boots stepped in her way, blocking her.

"Comrade Lašková. We meet again." That gravelly voice.

Behind the gun's barrel pointing at her head was the same secret police officer who'd almost arrested her two months before when she'd dropped the stack of manifestos. The same one who invaded her nightmares ever since. Now, he was dressed in a Soviet military uniform.

As she raised her hands in surrender, a single file line of radio reporters exited the station. All were handcuffed, except one.

Marek.

Somewhere in the mob, several portable radios blasted a continuous stream of static, the result of the now-occupied Radio Prague. The noise sputtered, then Jiří's voice rang clear from the radio waves. Live. He repeated the word craved by every Czechoslovakian—*Svoboda*. Freedom.

The commander motioned Marek over. Why wasn't he handcuffed? Karel's warnings flashed through Pavla's brain like a warped montage. Was he a spy?

"How is Radio Prague still broadcasting?"

Marek faced the commander unblinking, a duel.

"Agent Novak, where is the other studio?"

Seconds ticked by as if each one held an eternity. Still, Marek wouldn't speak. A soldier shoved him to his knees, face-to-face with Pavla. Why wouldn't he save himself?

Marek's eyes met hers, and she knew. To save himself, he had to betray her. And he—her guardian angel—refused, but she could save him. They were pawns in this twisted game of chess, but every Soviet bullet was real.

"I did it." Each syllable condemned her for life. Perhaps she would be reunited with her father. "I set up the other radio station."

Pavla was dragged into a standing position, shocks jolting through her split knee.

"Don't believe her," Marek ordered as handcuffs were clicked around his wrists. "Comrade Lašková knows nothing. She's innocent."

She shook her head. The satellite radio had been her idea, her crime. Not his. Why risk returning to the forced labor camps?

"Agent—no, Prisoner—Novák, you failed every task of your mission. You were assigned to infiltrate and disable Radio Prague."

"I performed my assignment." Marek slumped, squeezing his eyes shut.

"You fed us counter-intelligence and interfered with recruiting members of Prisoner Vaclav Lašek's family. Now, this? You undermined last night's Soviet Operation Danube by broadcasting from Radio Prague." The commander stepped between them and pointed his gloved hand at him. "The Party does not tolerate double agents."

"I'd rather die than return to the forced labor camp."

Marek craned his neck, searching over his shoulder until he found her. Behind his back, tethered in handcuffs, he held three fingers. "Boars, Pavlínka. The Soviets are like wild boars, but you're smart. Fight them. Use their weapons against them."

I love you, she mouthed, wishing she could teleport back to twelve hours earlier when her life had been perfect.

"Re-education may have been an option had you not signed the *Two Thousand Words* manifesto." The commander placed the barrel on Marek's forehead.

No!

The tanks' clanking and the peoples' yells disintegrated into nothingness. Silence washed over Pavla until all she could hear was her heartbeat, much like her father's chess clock. Her strategy materialized.

Her move.

Pavla snatched a nearby soldier's gun and aimed at the commander's head. Anyone who believed a pawn couldn't take the opponent's king hadn't played against her.

"Don't shoot him, Pavlínka."

From behind, cool metal pressed against the back of her head followed by the telltale clicks of a trigger being cocked open, creating a broken triangle of death.

"I warned you to stay away from Zdeněk, Little Rook." This voice she'd loved for forever. But why? How?

"Karel?"

"Checkmate."

KEEP CALM AND LOVE MOAI

by Eleanor Cawood Jones

Destination: Easter Island, Chile
Taking an evening walk to enjoy the sunset behind the Moai without a flashlight or charged phone battery has surprising consequences for Sarah when she makes a new acquaintance and finds herself involved with a missing person . . . and danger.

Our tour guide, Rico, was speaking in Portuguese for the benefit of my companions while I took a good look at the small opening carved into the hill above the rocky coastline. Entire families had lived there over the centuries. It didn't look like a great place for people who loved their creature comforts, but maybe they hadn't known what they were missing, being busy surviving and all.

Rico repeated himself in English. "With a single small opening, you had a good chance of keeping out attackers and animals. They would have had to enter one at a time. You might have a sharpened rock to stab them. Or if you were sleeping, you might use your pillow."

"Pillow?" Gisselle was perplexed.

"Si." Rico nodded at her. "They slept on a flat slab of rock. If they couldn't use their weapon, or had broken it, WHAM, pillow over the head."

Ouch, right?

Gisselle involuntarily moved closer to her new husband, Fernando. They were on their honeymoon and excited about exploring the world. They were young, beautiful, and in love. I quite liked them anyway.

"Great place to hide a dead body," said Boo-Boo McNash.

I cringed on the inside and kept my poker face on the outside. I hoped. Boo-Boo never missed a chance to tell the world about his chosen vocation as a mystery writer. If I counted the number of times he'd mentioned his career since we set foot on this island in the middle of nowhere the previous afternoon, I would have already run out of fingers and toes.

I'd decided the best way to handle him was to have no reaction.

At all. If you encouraged Boo-Boo, he kept talking. We'd learned that one the hard way.

So Boo-Boo's comment was met with stony silence, which was either appropriate or ironic, depending on your point of view, since we'd all arrived there hoping to learn more about how the Easter Island ancients had dealt with the one artistic material they'd had—the rock they had used over the centuries to craft the stunning statues known as Moai. The world mostly knew them as statues of giant stone heads, but most came with giant stone bodies as well.

Rico drifted back into Portuguese as he pointed toward the coastline and the islet of Motu Nui and talked about the legendary Birdman culture, which he'd already treated us to in English. My mind drifted, too, as I contemplated my companions.

I should probably clarify that Boo-Boo's given name wasn't actually Boo-Boo. (As far as I know.) He had introduced himself to the tour group at the airport in Santiago, Chile, where our party of six had met on the plane. The travel agent had booked our seats together, so it was only natural we would introduce ourselves and share our excitement about our exotic destination.

"McNash," he'd announced. "Robert McNash. Perhaps you've heard of me, if you read at all. But you all can call me Bob."

It wasn't technically his fault that he had a voice and shape reminiscent of Yogi Bear's erstwhile companion, Boo-Boo Bear: shortish and beefy, big nose, heavily lidded eyes, and darned if he didn't have on a bright blue bow tie. So you can't blame him, but you can't blame me either for mentally rechristening him Boo-Boo on the plane ride over.

Other than wanting to be more famous than he was, Boo-Boo seemed like a nice guy. He was traveling alone, as was I. The rest of the group consisted of Gisselle and Fernando, our beautiful Brazilian honeymooners who spoke three languages, and a lovely retired couple from Portugal who spoke little English. Boo-Boo, from Britain, and I, the quintessential American tourist, were mostly limited to English.

It was a really great group, but I couldn't wait to ditch them when we arrived at the Easter Island airport and go exploring on my own. The guided tours would start soon enough.

Did I mention how charming Mataveri International Airport is? No? It's a wooden shed built in the shape of an upside-down boat. Baggage is put in a single room so you can grab and go. It's a bit disconcerting as the runway is simply gigantic. NASA enlarged the runway in the mid 1980s to provide an alternative landing spot for space shuttles. When the shuttle program ended, Easter Island was left with a runway long enough to land gigantic Boeing 700-family aircraft. We'd all flown here on the one available jet out of mainland Chile, a 787 Dreamliner. (If you're a plane geek at all, you'll know that's really going in style. Real china and silverware for airline meals, too.)

So I hurried ahead of everyone and caught the hotel shuttle to the island's only five-star resort, an eco-style village consisting of rather luxurious metal pods. (Sunken bathtubs. Big porches. Meals included.) This was my fiftieth birthday trip and I'd saved up for years. *Meals included* meant safe food and plenty of it. Five stars meant great service and someone who would speak English to the tourists. I wasn't sure if I'd have time for the sunken bathtub, but it was a great idea in theory.

Being a child of travelogues and nature specials brought to me via our color television, and parents who supplied travel books by the likes of Thor Heyerdahl and Osa Johnson, this trip was the stuff dreams are made of. When I got to my room and opened the sliding glass porch door and could see a row of Moai across the harbor from the hotel, I knew I'd arrived. After a quick change of clothes, and liberal application of insect repellent and sunscreen, I grabbed my phone and backup charger and headed out for a hike over to the giant stone heads.

I ducked behind a pillar when I heard Boo-Boo's voice booming from several pods over. I waited until he entered his room and closed the door before I ran down the twisty sidewalk and out to the main road. Nothing against Boo-Boo, but I didn't want him bellying up to me. Not that my guy back home had anything to worry about—the one who had no understanding of why I wanted to come to an island quite literally in the middle of nowhere for my birthday instead of lounging in the Caribbean with him and a few rounds of umbrella drinks—but I wanted time alone to absorb the island atmosphere.

The front desk clerk was charming and helpful. (I had no idea when I would meet someone from Chile who wasn't charming. I wanted to bring them all home with me.) "It will take you thirty minutes to walk all the way to the Moai," she told me. "You will see the most beautiful sunset there. Just stay on the main road around the harbor and through the village. And you'll need this." She handed me a bottle of water, and I was off to explore the harbor and the island's only village, Hanga Roa.

"Moai, like Hawaii. Three syllables," I reminded myself, practicing the pronunciation out loud. I loved the Polynesian custom of pronouncing each letter in a word distinctly. "Mo. Aye. Eee," I said again. Perfect. Maybe.

I had to stop and take pictures of the shoreline, the waves, and, as I progressed, the nature center, natives, tourists, birds, village cricket field, more waves . . . The upshot is, by the time I wound my way around the harbor, almost two hours had gone by and I could see I would have to run to catch the sunset from the best spot.

I dashed off the main road and cut behind the cemetery filled with statues and flowers, and past some creepy shoreline carvings of obviously recent design.

Side note: I should work out more.

By the time I crossed over the hill between the main road and the shoreline, I was out of breath, red-faced, and completely happy when I saw my first close-ups of the spectacular Moai. My map told me I was at Ahu Tahai. I crept closer to the statues, dodging tourists, tripods, and a handful of native dancers filming a documentary. The sunset was coming. It was going to be spectacular, and I had my phone ready for pictures.

It was a festive atmosphere as everyone on the grassy hill relaxed, took pictures, or posted on social media as the sun went down. The five Moai, or what was left of them, shone up splendidly against the rocky shore, unbelievably blue water, and peachy pink clouds.

Paradise. I checked my phone for a signal and logged on, posting a quick selfie of me in front of the Moai, captioning it "Rapa Nui." This was too good not to share. I had a great signal. Only 2,300 miles off the nearest mainland and my internet connection was better than the one at home.

The phone rang almost immediately, and an alert popped up that I had ten percent battery left. I really should have brought a portable charger.

"Hey, Sarah! You got there!" My guy, stalking me on social media. "Great picture! Looks like it's kind of hot, though."

"I wish you were here! It's amazing!" I sat down on the lush grass and gazed at the dregs of the sunset. I barely noticed the other tourists packing up and heading for the field and the long walk back to the main road.

"Um," he said. "It does look nice. But what's Rapa Nui?" This was the guy who'd offered the Caribbean and had no interest in giant stone heads, I reminded myself. He'd probably be getting off work and rounding up someone to go to dinner with soon. He seemed a million miles away. (5,013 miles to be precise. I'd looked it up. I love the internet.)

"It's what the natives call Easter Island, you know? It's also the native language, close to Tahitian. Official language is Spanish, of course." I wished for the billionth time I had an ear for languages.

"Ha ha. You must have a great connection to Google there. I bet you just looked that up."

"Busted!" I agreed. "But hey, I'm here at sunset, and I have a super low battery. How about if I call you when I get back to the hotel?"

"Low battery and a million photos?" I could hear him smiling. "Sure. Be safe and I'll talk to you later tonight."

"I'll be safe," I promised. "Enjoy dinner." He could probably hear me smiling, too. But I had just enough time to get a few more snaps before the sun sank below the horizon.

That was when I realized how dark it had become and that everyone had left the hill while I lingered. I could see the lights of the village in the distance, and I knew the general direction of the main road, but it was suddenly a little disconcerting. (I refused to use the word frightening. Easter Island is known for being relatively crime-free.)

Besides, I had the flashlight on my phone to help me navigate my way through the tall grass, which was pockmarked with footprints, dips, and holes. It really was dark, and I chided myself for getting caught out here alone. I didn't want to ruin my trip by twisting an ankle.

I flipped on the phone's flashlight and started gingerly picking my way over the next rise. That's when the battery died, the light went out, and I was left standing there while my eyes tried to adjust to the dark. I took a deep breath, shoved the phone in the back pocket of my shorts next to the useless plug-in phone charger, and resolved not to panic or shed a tear.

At least I could see lights in the distance and had a sense of the direction to go. Five Moai loomed to my right. I could sense rather than see them. They were strangely comforting and at the same time stoic.

"This island is only so big," I said out loud. Where had everyone gone, and so rapidly? How had it gotten dark so suddenly? "This island loves their tourists. Nothing will happen, it just may take a couple of hours to walk back to the hotel is all. Hopefully I won't miss dinner."

I was so busy staring at the ground and talking to myself I didn't see the man standing in front of me. I gasped.

"English? French?" He startled me again when he spoke. He was quite a young man. I could tell that much in the dark. He was wearing jeans and carried a knapsack on his back. He was a good six inches taller than me and rail thin.

"English," I agreed. "Lost," I added sheepishly. He didn't scare me. I didn't know if that was wise or foolish.

"Come," he said, holding out a hand. "I need you."

I need you? Maybe that meant he wanted to help me. Sometimes you have to just turn it over and trust, I thought to myself. I won't deny I sent up a quick prayer. I grasped his warm, sturdy hand, and he pulled me up over the next rise.

"Not much English," he said. "Road to Hanga Roa?"

"Eco hotel?" I tried.

"Road," he said firmly. He held me up as I stumbled, and slowed down a bit.

"Thank you," I told him. OK, so I was a little frightened. But he seemed harmless, and only about fifteen or sixteen. Just a kid.

"No French, Spanish?" He sounded hopeful.

"Sorry."

A long silence followed. I concentrated on keeping my footing.

"You like the president? Which American president you like?"

Seriously, I'm lost in the middle of nowhere with a beautiful Polynesian (I assumed) kid leading me out of the deserted field I'd been boneheaded enough to get lost in after dark, and he wants to talk politics?

I laughed out loud. "I came here to forget about politics," I told him. "I like them all."

He laughed, too. "I bet you do not like them all. You are polite."

We were near the road. I could see a streetlight. My companion stopped suddenly and released my hand. "You go on. Hotel. Censo. No food in village tonight."

I knew what censo was. The national census. The whole country of Chile closed down for it once every five years. Today was that day and apparently the village was no exception. I'd had to fill out a form at the airport so they could count me as a tourist.

"Are you coming?" He'd made no move to go forward, and in fact stepped back.

He waved his hands. "Go on."

I could see him more clearly now. The beat-up knapsack, weathered clothes, the fact that he was too thin. He smiled at me and turned to walk back down into the field.

I realized he must be sleeping down there. He'd probably helped me out of the field to rid me from his sleeping space. Well, no matter.

"Gracias! Thank you!" I called after him. "Merci!" I added for good measure. I meant it.

It was a slow, dark walk home. I was accompanied by four of the island's stray dogs almost the whole way, which was both sad and sweet. I didn't have any treats for them but they seemed to be fairly well fed. Just a little lonely. Like me.

I was a hot, sweaty mess when I got back to the hotel dining room ten minutes before the kitchen closed. I found a waiter and asked him to bring me whatever was easiest. I also found Boo-Boo, who was a little drunk and sitting on a patio by the ocean, alone at a table for four. I sat with him to be polite but, to be honest, probably wouldn't have if he hadn't seen me first. He ran through a drunken litany of books he'd written and famous people he knew. I nodded and ate. I was back in the room and asleep an hour later, forgetting to call home.

***

"Miss Sarah?" Rico's voice interrupted my reverie. I really had drifted off, thinking about the night before. I hoped I hadn't missed too much of his lecture about the Birdman competition. That was the crazy (from my point of view) way the leader of the Rapa Nui had been chosen each year until around 1860. It involved months of physical training and swimming to a distant island to find the first bird eggs of the season. The eggs of the sooty tern, or *manu tara*, to be precise.

People got up to the most interesting things before television came along to suck up all their time, didn't they? But Rico's voice brought me back to the present moment, which was not bad at all. We were standing on the edge of the enormous volcano Rano Kau, and it was quite impressive.

"I wanted to know if you would like a bottle of water," my tour guide said, smiling at me. "You were in the daydream."

I saw the other members of the party over by the tour van, digging into a picnic basket. I accepted the water. "When do we see the Moai with you, Rico?"

"Always the question," he smiled. "Tomorrow morning we go to Ahu Akivi. There the Moai are farthest from the shore and we will learn why. You will see them with me or one of the others. I am the bottled water distributor here on the island and I must make a big delivery first."

Another van had pulled over and two men wearing the same tour company shirt as Rico had joined the picnic. We walked over and feasted on apples, cheese, and crackers. Soft drinks were available but I chose to stick with water. I saw Boo-Boo downing two different sodas. No one was talking much, and it wasn't just the language barrier. Sightseeing in such a beautiful place is tiring.

***

It was going to be another beautiful evening, and tonight's sunset was shaping up to be even more spectacular than yesterday's. I resolved to find my way back over to the village

Moai, but get out of the vast field before dark this time.

After a quick change of clothes back at the hotel, I had the front desk call me a cab. I had to laugh when I slid inside the little, beat-up vehicle and recognized the driver as Kiko, one of the tour guides I'd shared a picnic with a few hours earlier. "Does everyone on the island have two jobs?" I teased.

"At least!" he agreed. "We make our money how we can."

"Rapa Nui. You are survivors!" I told him. The native population had been down to fewer than two hundred at one point. Remarkable group of people. I sat back and stuck my hand in my pocket to make sure I had plenty of local currency and felt several folded Chilean pesos.

I meant to look out the window at the harbor as we zoomed by, with stray dogs trying to keep up with the car, but my eye was caught by a small picture clipped to the windshield visor on the passenger's side.

"I think I know that guy," I said.

"Impossible," Kiko said. He sounded sad. "That is my nephew. He has been missing these three months."

I thought hard. "I think I saw him last night, on the hill, after the tourists left. It was dark. He helped me. He really looked just like that picture, I think. It was dark, and I only caught a glimpse of him in the streetlight."

I didn't know how much of what I said he understood, but he grew quite excited, bouncing up and down in the seat in his agitation.

"You must take me to him," he said. "We are so worried. We thought he had drowned. We have been wondering whether to have the ceremony and place the marker."

I felt funny. If I was right about who the kid was, he was obviously trying to stay hidden. "I don't know," I said slowly.

"Please." Kiko was driving slowly now. He looked at me in the rearview mirror. He had tears in his eyes.

I caved. What business of mine was it anyway?

"Meet me at the bottom of the hill by the Moai as soon as it is dark," I told him. "I will show you where I saw him and maybe he'll be there again. But I got the feeling he wants to be left alone, and, hey, I'm not even sure it's him."

He nodded and we pulled up beside the coastal cemetery. I left him in the cab, jabbering rapidly on his phone, and walked over the hill toward the Moai. The sunset was indeed so spectacular that I was all over social media in an instant, posting the pictures of a lifetime. And I texted several back home to my guy, along with plenty of XO's so he'd know I missed him. I rolled my eyes at myself, but it was such a romantic moment and I wanted to share it.

Then Gisselle and Fernando wandered by, hand in hand, and I took romantic shots of them as well. They invited me to have dinner with them, but who wants to interrupt a honeymoon, right?

Finally, everyone drifted off and I was left alone in the dark. I was nervous, but at least this time I'd saved plenty of battery for my phone flashlight.

"Tuki!" Kiko had come up behind me and was calling softly. "You must come! It is Kiko!"

I heard a voice from behind the Moai. "No. It is not safe."

They spoke rapidly in another language I couldn't follow, and the exchange grew heated. I could tell young Tuki was crying. Finally Kiko grabbed my hand and led me behind the Moai, closer to the coast. We heard waves crashing, and I saw an opening beneath the smallest statue of the five, under the platform which had once held many more. We crossed over the ropes meant to keep out the tourists and grew closer to the platform. It looked like someone had dug out a small cave, and a rock had been pushed away from the entrance.

"Come!" Tuki's voice. Kiko bent down and slithered into the opening. I followed him. I would be filthy for dinner. (Go figure I'd think of food at a time like this, but the hotel really did have excellent red snapper with sautéed vegetables. And don't get me started on the molten lava cake.) With any luck, the joyful family reunion would be over soon and I could get back to being a tourist.

I stood up inside. The small opening belied the sizeable cavern beneath the Moai. Kiko turned on a little flashlight and shined it on his nephew's face. "Tuki," he said. He sounded sad again. But why? He should be ecstatic.

"Nowhere is safe!" Tuki was openly sobbing now.

I heard a noise behind me in the cave entrance, and another flashlight clicked on. "Boo-Boo!" I breathed. "What are you doing here?"

He spared me a confused glance—he did, after all, have no earthly idea who Boo-Boo was—and turned his attention to the two native men as he slid further into the cave.

"You were right to call me and tell me to follow you, Kiko. As for you, Tuki . . . Son, I told you not to interfere." The British accent was gone, and Boo-Boo suddenly looked less doughy, more tough. No bowtie, either.

And a gun in his left hand. I'd watched enough cop TV shows to recognize what a silencer was, too. We all froze. It crossed my mind to wonder how he'd gotten a gun on the airplane, but then I realized there were boats, and no doubt other ways outside my naïve scope of possibilities. I also realized this was probably not Boo-Boo's first trip to the island.

This was not good. "What is going on, Kiko? Tuki?"

"I swear, I will never say anything!" Tuki could barely get the words out through the tears. "I am sorry I tried to interfere! I just want to go back to my life!"

"Kiko, what have you done?" I didn't understand, but it seemed clear to me Kiko had ratted out his nephew.

Oh my God. Whatever was going on, it was all my fault. And I was too shocked for words.

Tuki sobbed, and I was about to follow suit. "Tuki," I said helplessly.

"You should not have tried to stop the drug shipment," Boo-Boo said. "It was none of your concern. And your telling my captain you would go to the police and the mayor. You were wise to hide, but your island is small. You scared off my captain, who has disappeared. Now I must start over. And you have delayed my distribution long enough. You are a loose end."

I doubted Tuki and Kiko understood all of that, but I sure did. I moved closer to Tuki and squatted beside him where he lay on the ground, sobbing. I reached behind him to comfort him with a hug, and my hand felt something round and heavy on the ground. A sharp edge sliced into my finger. Some sort of tool, maybe? A rock. Definitely a rock.

"He told me he would kill my son if I didn't help him to find you, Tuki." Kiko was subdued and I could barely hear him. "That was the choice he gave me. My son or my nephew. I didn't see how you could have gotten off the island but I could not find you."

I'm going to stop right here and go back to the part where this was shaping up to be All. My. Fault. I'd led them straight here, to this innocent young boy.

"The threat against your son holds, Kiko." Boo-Boo's voice was hard. "You will be my local distributor. You will not say a word about me to anyone. You will not say a word about what happened to your missing nephew. You will not say a word about this tourist. You dropped her off at the Moai for sunset and she mentioned she was thinking of going swimming in the dark afterwards. Look at her. She is far from fit. It won't be hard for people to believe she swam out too far and drowned."

Seriously? Boo-Boo was judging MY physique? And for the record, he had no clue how to pronounce "Moai."

"You knew this moment would come, Tuki. And you seem a pleasant, if odd, sort of person, Sarah," Boo-Boo said. "It's a shame to have to do this to you. But you've already witnessed too much."

I stood up. "Funny, you don't sound sorry at all."

I'd wanted a birthday trip, not a starring role in a made-for-TV action movie. But needs must. Not for nothing was I star pitcher on my high school softball team that went all the way to the state championships.

I doubt Boo-Boo saw what was coming. But I gave my throw all I had and struck him square on the temple with that sharp-edged rock. He pulled the trigger on the way down, but the gun fired harmlessly into the wall of the cave.

Kiko kicked the gun out of Boo-Boo's hand and bent down to check his pulse. Just like the cops on TV. There was a trickle of blood at Boo-Boo's temple and I couldn't tell if he was breathing.

"I work part-time for the police some nights," Kiko said to no one in particular. "We have never had much crime to deal with here." He paused and looked at me. "He is quite dead."

He wasn't kidding about how many jobs everyone had around this place, was he?

Kiko turned to his nephew, who shook his head and turned his back on his uncle.

We were going to have some explaining to do, and I wasn't sure of anything. (Except that Christmas at their house was going to be really awkward.)

So we sat down and discussed it. Then we dug a hole in the cave and put Boo-Boo in it. I felt sorry for Tuki, having to stay in the cave and sleep with the body, but we needed to figure out the best way for him to show back up to his family. Kiko wanted to make sure the captain of the boat was truly gone. And I wasn't sure Tuki would ever be safe on his island again.

Kiko took me home in his cab. I surprised myself by still having an appetite, and enjoyed an excellent dinner.

The next day's tour was to the enormous Moai across the island at Tonariki and the amazing Rano Raraku quarry nearby where the statue carving took place over all those centuries. (Which kind of puts paid to the whole "aliens carved them" conspiracy theory, once you've seen it.)

We had agreed never to talk about what happened again. I was going to let Kiko make the call on to how handle things and whether to bring in the police. I was going to disappear back to the mainland. I also secretly decided to find a way to sponsor Tuki to come to the States and find him work, and got his contact information from Kiko.

And before I knew it, it was time to leave.

It was a great plane ride home. Bit long, of course. Two

connections. But I amused myself making notes on my phone and in my handy new notebook from the Easter Island Eco Hotel gift shop. (It says Keep Calm and Love Moai on the cover. I am calm, mostly. I love the Moai, definitely. Perfect.)

Lots of notes, as it turned out. By the time I was nearing my home airport of Dulles International outside Washington, D.C., almost twenty hours later, I had a fully fleshed-out plot going. One with giant statues and caves and plenty of island mystique. And a certain not-so-fluffy pillow, which, in fiction at least, makes a much better murder weapon than a plain old rock.

Boo-Boo McNash wasn't the only mystery writer in town, you know. And one does change names and alter facts to protect the innocent, doesn't one?

ISAAC'S DAUGHTERS

by Anita Page

Destination: America

In 1911, Malke and her daughters undertake the grueling voyage from Russia to America in hopes of reuniting with the husband and father who abandoned them. Superstition and nightmares are only part of the baggage they bring with them.

My grandson David, dear man that he is, comes for dinner every Friday, and every Friday urges me to get out more and mingle. Once, to make him happy, I had lunch at the senior center and it was one long organ recital—heart problems, reflux, constipation. This was not for me. Besides, I'm not lonely. I take my walks, gossip with the doorman, drink tea with a neighbor, and, at the end of the day, I have my ghosts for company.

After dinner, I talk about the past and my grandson listens, claiming he likes to hear my stories as much as I like to tell them. Next summer it will be seventy-five years since I came to America from Russia—the year was 1911 and I was fourteen years old—so I can't swear to the accuracy of every detail. David says not to worry. Facts are one thing, truth is another. As for repeating myself, which I'm sure I often do, he says that a good story is always worth hearing again.

***

My mother, who believed in the Evil One, took precautions to keep her daughters safe. She tossed our fingernail clippings into the fire so that his demons couldn't collect them, spit three times on the ground if someone was foolish enough to comment on Miriam's beauty or my cleverness, and warned us not to look at the river when we passed it after dark. Demons might be lurking anywhere, but, as everyone knew, water at night was always to be avoided. This is to explain why, before we left for America to get our father back, my mother took us to see Grusha Karpovna—the witch, we children called her, though never to her face.

Years later I still dream of that morning, the sweet smell of mown fields, Miriam's hand warm in mine as we followed our mother on the road to Grusha's cottage just outside our village. In my dream I'm ignorant of the future which, like the distant hills, is obscured in haze. Also in my dream I worry that our father, the free thinker, would disapprove of this expedition. Our father, who hadn't sent for us as he'd promised, who'd barely written in three years.

***

The last letter from America came from a cousin of my mother's who'd left Russia years earlier. My mother, who could read some Hebrew but barely any Russian, asked me to read it aloud.

And so I did, unprepared for the storm that would follow: *I am sorry to be the one to tell you this, dearest Malke, but you should know that your Isaac has taken up with a whore from Galicia.*

My mother, famous for her explosive temper, outdid herself that day, pounding the table, banging her head against the wall, demanding that God tell her what she, a pious and faithful wife, had done to deserve this. Then she rushed off—to see the father of the letter-writing cousin, we later learned—leaving Miriam and me terrified and bewildered.

That night, in our bed in the attic, my innocent sister, who was ten, whispered, "What's a whore from Galicia?" I wasn't sure but told her that I thought it was a woman who kissed men even if they were married to someone else.

***

Grusha greeted us at the door of her house that morning, a pretty child clinging to her skirt. Miriam and I were told to wait outside and mind the girl, but little Anna only wanted her mother, so my sister and I were left on our own.

Miriam walked off to explore the garden, but I remained close to the house, idly listening at the half-open door when my mother made this request to Grusha: "Give me something to make my husband love me again." That surprised me since I'd never thought of love in connection with my parents. When the women came out a short while later I saw my mother tuck a blue paper packet up her sleeve and guessed that was the love magic. Would it work, I wondered, if my father, the rationalist, didn't believe in it?

The girl was still clinging to her mother, but Grusha's attention was on my sister, exclaiming at her beauty: the lips like rosebuds, the brown eyes with specks of gold, just like her Anna's. I, Sarah, the impatient one and not the beauty, grabbed Miriam's hand to leave.

At that moment, Grusha stepped between us and slipped something over my sister's head, telling my mother that she was smart to be careful, that this little one would certainly attract the demons. Then she turned to me and said, "Don't worry, I have one for you, too." The string necklace had an evil-smelling cloth bundle attached and I started to protest but was silenced by a sharp word from my mother.

That was when Grusha Karpovna leaned close, her spicy smell mingling with the smell of the amulet. She whispered to me as if she could see into my soul, "I'll tell you a secret, my girl. The demons don't care whether you believe or not."

***

Our journey to America began weeks later when our uncle, the father of the letter writer, came before dawn to take us to the train. I remember the rhythm of the horses' hooves and the smell of hay in the back of the wagon where Miriam and I huddled against the cold. To this day I can hear my sister's sweet voice as she sang, "Good-bye, little house, good-bye, river." I remember the stars disappearing as the sky turned gray, and the gentle way my uncle lifted us down from the wagon when we got to the train—this big gruff man of whom I'd always been shy. I remember, too, the weight of his hand on my head as he prayed for our safe passage.

As for the train ride, my memories are like snatches of light in a dark room. The crowded platforms, the hours of waiting. The filthy cramped compartment, the smell of my own sweat, the stale bread, the hard-cooked eggs that toward the end made me gag. The boredom, the fear that this journey had no destination, that this was what the rest of our lives would be like. And then to cheer us up, there was my mother's litany of worries: we would be robbed; we wouldn't be allowed on the boat because our papers were incomplete; our father wouldn't meet the boat and we would be sent back to Russia.

We lodged for two nights in Hamburg while we waited for the boat that would take us to England, sleeping on our baggage on the floor because the bed was crawling with bugs. In Liverpool, where it never stopped raining, my mother was told that the ship on which we'd booked passage to America was delayed. No one explained why or how long we'd have to wait, so my mother stopped eating except for bread and water because she was afraid our money would run out.

On our last day in Liverpool when we were on our way to the pier, I had to stop to tie my bootlaces. When I ran to catch up with my mother and Miriam, I saw them as if they were strangers, two fragile figures weighed down by their baggage in the crowded street. At that moment I admitted to myself for the first time that I hated my father for leaving us.

***

By our second day on the ship, I forgot how miserable I'd been on the train and remembered only that if you looked out the window you saw clouds and hills and sometimes a blazing sunset, and once, horses running in a field. In the women's steerage, we were packed like cattle, sleeping on shelves stacked one above the other. Here it was always night and you had to take it on faith that time was passing, that there was more to life than babies crying and the thrumming of the engines, the watery soup and herring, the stink of unwashed bodies and foul breath, the smell of people being sick, the suffocating smell of the ship's bowels.

What made it worse was my mother's refusal to go up on deck. This was what people did in order to move about and get some fresh air, but not her. Someone might steal the baggage, those precious rags we'd brought from Russia. When I begged her to let me and Miriam go alone, she looked at me as if I was insane, which was close to the truth because she was driving me mad.

Finally, a few days into the trip, Mrs. Lebovitch, a talkative, cheerful woman who'd attached herself to us, came to our rescue when she offered to take Miriam and me on deck with her. She swore to my mother—and gave us a wink that my mother didn't see—that she wouldn't let us out of her sight.

We clattered up the iron stairs, I silently urging stout Mrs. Lebovitch to move quickly so that our mother couldn't call us back. And, oh, the feeling of freedom, the bliss of being able to breathe the sea air when we stepped onto the deck. Despite her promise, Mrs. Lebovitch let us go off on our own, begging us not to go for a swim because if we did our mother would have her head.

As we made our way to the railing, I was struck by how many people were camped out on deck with their baggage. One family, with three dark-haired girls, sat in a close circle as their mother passed out food, the youngest girl staring at us as we went by. How I envied the girls their cozy family and a mother who let them sleep under the stars rather than suffocate below.

Miriam and I found a spot at the railing, our shawls wrapped tight against the stiff wind. This was our first view of the open sea, and on that brilliantly sunny day I was mesmerized by its vastness and its beauty. My mother, I knew, would have muttered an incantation to ward off the evil spirits lurking beneath the waves, but I was not her.

Looking to the horizon I had a sense, for the first time, of how far we'd traveled, too far to ever go back. On impulse, I pulled Grusha's foul-smelling amulet over my head and tossed it into the wind, shouting, "Good-bye, Russia."

When I saw the look of panic on Miriam's face, I told her not to worry, that our mother would never notice the amulet was gone. Although she nodded to make me happy, I saw the look in her eyes and realized that our mother's anger was only part of her fear. Like my father, I believed in the rational world, but she was her mother's daughter, depending on Grusha's magic to protect us from the unseen demons.

I took her hand as we left the railing, regretting my impulse and angry at my mother for planting these ideas in my sister's head. We'd stopped near the gate that separated the steerage deck from the rest of the ship, and as we talked I noticed the uniformed guard glaring at us as if we intended to trespass. I immediately puffed out my chest and mimicked the man's sour face, strutting and barking orders in a gibberish foreign tongue, glad to hear my sister laugh for the first time since we'd left home.

***

The next morning my mother was convinced that Miriam, listless and pale, had caught a chill. That meant she was condemned to stay below and breathe the foul air, just the thing to improve her health. Since only a selfish girl would leave her sister when she wasn't feeling well, it was expected that I would stay with her. I'd been accused of selfishness so often that I accepted it as part of my character and refused to be deterred. Besides, I knew Miriam was only tired because she'd had a restless night, crying out two or three times in her sleep. Nightmares were an old story with her, even more so since we'd left Russia.

And so I made my escape with Mrs. Lebovitch, again leaving her to stroll the deck on my own. The dark-haired girl I'd noticed the day before was lying with her head on her mother's lap, and I thought how lovely it would be to have a mother who let you do that.

As I approached the gate at the end of the steerage deck, I expected to see the big-bellied official who'd glared at us the day before, but the gate happened to be unguarded at that moment. I hesitated for barely a second before I slipped past, driven partly by curiosity but mostly by hunger. It was midday and I was sure the passengers on the other side of the gate wouldn't be eating herring and boiled potatoes.

So there I was, a fourteen-year-old girl so ignorant of life that I was unaware of how shabby I looked until I found myself on the second-class deck where well-dressed people stood talking quietly in groups or sat comfortably in chairs—no one here reclining on their baggage—taking in the sun.

For a second I was tempted to scurry back to the safety of steerage, but when a gong sounded and the passengers began to move in a leisurely parade, I thought only of food. I followed, hanging back when we arrived at the entrance to the dining room, intimidated by a glimpse of white-jacketed waiters and gleaming china. Hunger, however, was more powerful than shame, and so I rewrapped my shawl to hide my dress and went in. I quickly found a seat at a half-filled table, relieved that the others were too busy eating and talking to notice me.

Almost immediately, a waiter put a bowl of chicken soup in front of me, fragrant and glistening with fat. It was a wonderful soup, a beautiful soup, and I wished I could bring some back for Miriam and my mother, but how can you carry soup? However, I did manage to slip two rolls into a napkin, and then a third for Mrs. Lebovitch.

When the waiter took away the soup bowl and set slices of pot roast on my plate, I cut a piece for myself—what a pot roast that was!—and, when his back was turned, unfolded my napkin and began to fill it with meat. "Such an unselfish daughter," I imagined my mother saying to Mrs. Lebovitch.

Then the chatter at the table stopped, and I looked up to see the waiter glaring at me, a tall man with bushy eyebrows and ears like jug handles. I tried to hold onto the napkin, but he grabbed it from me, spittle spraying from his mouth as he berated me in words I didn't understand. I didn't care that everyone at the table was staring when he yanked me to my feet, but my tears flowed at the sight of the beautiful white rolls tumbling to the floor.

***

When my mother demanded to know where I'd been, I told her I'd been on deck, and that Mrs. Lebovitch must have missed me in the crowd. I tried to look contrite but in fact I was only sorry that I'd been caught and that I'd worried Miriam who burst into tears when she saw me.

Later in bed, after our mother was safely asleep, I told Miriam about the chicken soup and the pot roast and the lost rolls. I mimicked the waiter, hoping to make her laugh, but her only response was to tell me in a shaky voice that she'd been afraid I wasn't coming back.

"Did you think I'd grown wings and flown to America without you?" I asked, a big mistake because that only brought on more tears. Eventually I was able to pull from her the reason for her fear. The demon who visited her dreams had threatened that if she, Miriam, didn't go with him, he would take me. Since she'd refused to go, she thought that when I didn't come back . . . and here she began trembling and couldn't go on.

I held her and told her that she was a dear sister to worry about me, but that the demon was only a bad dream. I promised her that once we got to America the dreams would stop because in America demons were not allowed. I hoped that would make her smile, but it didn't, so I kept stroking her hair, forcing myself to stay awake until I heard her quiet breathing, furious with my mother and Grusha who'd put such thoughts into her head.

***

Later that night something woke me—a sound, a stirring, a sense of the warm empty space next to me. And then came the foreboding that drove me out of bed, barefoot, in a thin shift, not bothering with my shawl. Quietly, quietly past the sleeping women, panicking when I got to the stairs and heard the clanging of footsteps on the flight above. I raced up the steps, at first whispering "Miriam," then calling out, not caring if I woke the whole ship.

The sleeping passengers stirred and muttered on the moonlit deck as I shouted my sister's name. I tripped over someone who grabbed my leg but I kicked my way free, still shouting. When I saw the ghostlike shape running toward the railing, I screamed "Miriam!" but Miriam kept running.

"Please," I screamed, getting closer, but not close enough. I screamed again, no words, just terror as Miriam climbed the railing, her shift billowing in the wind as she flung herself overboard. A second later I was at the railing, wanting only to join her in that vast black sea, fighting the strangers who pulled me to safety.

I remember only fragments of the rest of that night: men shouting orders; the mother of the three dark-haired girls speaking a language I didn't understand as she wrapped me in a shawl. Then I was back in steerage where Mrs. Lebovitch held me, both of us crying, and where my mother, wild with grief, refused to look at me. I couldn't bear lying in the half-empty bed, so I sat up the rest of the night wrapped in the gray blanket that smelled of Miriam.

Between me and my mother in the days that followed there was only an accusing silence, each of us needing someone to blame.

***

Mrs. Lebovitch, whose sister was already in America, had prepared us for Ellis Island. She told us that we would be poked and prodded by the doctors and questioned by the examiners to make sure we weren't sick or feeble-minded. If we passed the examinations, we would be welcome in America, once my father came for us.

"And if he doesn't come, they send us back to Russia?" This had been my mother's great fear since we'd left home.

"He'll come, don't worry," Mrs. Lebovitch said, which was like telling my mother not to breathe.

***

We arrived at Ellis Island on October 4th, 1911, and after hours of standing in lines we were declared healthy enough and smart enough to stay in America. At that point, we joined the others who were waiting in the Great Hall to be claimed. Night came, but not my father, so along with the other unclaimed passengers, we were fed, assigned cots, and given soap and clean towels so that we could scrub the ship's filth from our bodies.

The next morning we were back in the Great Hall, my mother praying silently as I was sure she'd been doing all night. After a couple of hours, our name was called and we hurried to the gate through which we'd watched people disappear the day before.

In the corridor beyond the gate I looked for my father, ignoring the clean-shaven American who approached us. When he said, "Sarah, it's Papa," I stood stiffly, unable to meet his eyes. "I hardly know you," my mother said to him, and he said, "You look the same, Malke."

Then, looking around, he asked, "Where's my Miriam?"

My mother, afraid of his reaction, planned to tell him that Miriam had died of a fever, but before she could do that I told him the truth because I wanted him to suffer as we had.

He stared dumbly at me, and then screamed at my mother: "What kind of woman can't take care of her own child?" Then to me: "And you, the sister? Where were you?"

"We were with her on the boat," I spat back at him. "Where were you?"

I thought he was going to hit me but instead he turned away and, without a word, picked up two of the satchels. My mother and I gathered the rest of the parcels and followed him down the stairs and out the wide doors to the ferry landing, to America.

***

He'd found an apartment for us on Attorney Street on the Lower East Side of New York, four flights up, three small rooms, one with a window. When he made it clear that he wasn't going to sleep in the apartment, my mother said, "Your wife and your daughter come all this way, and you're going to your whore?"

We were in the middle room, the kitchen with its grimy unlit stove and bare wood floor. The light was dim here, although outside the sun was shining.

My father said, his voice breaking, "You let the ocean swallow my Miriam, and you think I'm going to spend one night with you?"

Not a word from my mother as he slapped money on the table

and walked out. When he was gone, I said, "It's my fault for telling him the truth."

"He would have left anyway." My mother sounded as exhausted as she looked. "His daughter's death is only an excuse."

***

He came back two days later to tell us that arrangements had been made. My mother would do piecework at home for the same ladies' garment factory where he himself worked. Also, he would stop by the next morning to take me to my school. In the evening, I could help my mother with the sewing, but school had to come first. We were standing in the kitchen while he made these pronouncements. If he noticed the scrubbed floor or the clean oilcloth on the table he didn't mention it. Neither did he ask how the pot of soup came to be simmering on the stove when he'd left us without a crumb in the house. If not for Mrs. Curran upstairs, an Irish lady with a few words of Yiddish, who'd made sure I didn't get robbed by the pushcart peddlers on the noisy, crowded street, we might have starved.

After that, he came every Friday to deliver and pick up the piece goods. He would put the money we'd earned in the cracked teapot my mother used as a bank, and then quiz me on my English. My mother avoided him, remaining in the front bedroom where she did her sewing.

One cold, wet Friday toward the end of winter, about five months after we'd arrived in America, my mother joined us in the kitchen for the first time. I assumed she had a quarrel to pick with him, but instead she invited him to have a glass of tea. I noted that she was wearing a fresh shirtwaist and a clean apron, and noticed, too, how she flushed when my father, adding sugar to his tea, joked, "All these years we're married and your mother still doesn't know how sweet I like my tea."

Some weeks later, when the days had grown mild enough to leave the front room window open, my father announced during his Friday visit that a distant cousin of his had recently arrived from Russia. With my mother's permission, he would like to bring him for Shabbat dinner the following week.

"Since when do you need permission?" my mother asked as she set out glasses for tea. "I'm your wife."

***

When my father ushered the cousin, Jacob, into the apartment, proclaiming, "You see how my Malke turns our modest home into a palace," I understood that the dinner was nothing more than my father's chance to impress this shy young man fresh off the boat. My father had abandoned us in Russia, and again that first day in

America. Now, after raising my mother's hopes, he would abandon us again.

Still, later that evening, as my father and Jacob lingered at the table, I allowed myself to imagine that we would once more be a family. As if to encourage that fantasy, my father announced that he had not eaten honey cake like his wife's since he left Russia, and, on top of that, for once his tea was sweet enough.

That night, my father stayed and insisted Jacob stay, too. Over his protests, I gave up my cot and made a bed for myself in the kitchen on two chairs pushed together. As I lay there fully dressed, shy of my cousin on the other side of the wall, I was aware of the sounds coming from my parents' room. Not that long ago I'd been an ignorant girl from the old country. Now, educated by my new American friends, I understood what those sounds meant.

***

My mother's screams woke me. I leapt out of the makeshift bed, stumbling in the dark as Jacob, a step ahead of me, pushed aside the curtain that blocked the entryway to my parents' room. I shoved past him to see my mother sitting up in bed, moonlight spilling onto the covers, her hands covering her face as she screamed my father's name. My father, lying next to her, was still as death.

I ran to get Mrs. Curran, who sent for a doctor. Jacob, who'd held a small mirror to my father's mouth, said it was too late for a doctor, that Isaac's soul was with God, but Mrs. Curran said this was how it was done in America.

The four of us waited in the kitchen while the doctor examined the body. Mrs. Curran explained that the doctor had to sign a paper before we would be allowed to bury my father. Nothing to worry about, she said. This was the procedure.

But the doctor didn't sign the paper so quickly. First he wanted to know everything the deceased had to eat or drink that night. I said we'd all had the same things and named the dishes my mother had prepared.

When my mother realized that her food was being blamed for Isaac's death, she became hysterical. That was when Mrs. Curran pleaded with the doctor, "For God's sake man, let these poor people bury their dead."

***

A few days after the funeral, while sweeping the apartment, I found a packet among the fabric scraps under my mother's sewing table. As I dusted it off, I realized it was the blue packet my mother had slipped into her sleeve on Grusha Karpovna's doorstep. "Give me something to make my husband love me again," my mother had begged and Grusha had obliged.

At that moment I thought of our Shabbat dinner with the cousin and remembered my mother's words as she poured the tea: "This glass is for your father." I'd assumed that meant she'd put extra sugar in his tea, but now understood that she'd also added Grusha's love medicine. I understood, too, that I'd lied when I told the doctor we'd all had the same things to eat and drink. Only my father had sipped tea from the glass I'd handed him.

That moment of realization and the questions it raised have stayed with me my whole life: Had the tea killed him? Had Grusha intentionally given my mother the wrong powder? If so, why, since she had no reason to want him dead?

I opened the packet, not looking for answers but simply because it was in my hand, and carefully brushed aside the residue of powder that clung to the paper. There, tucked into one of the folds, like a message waiting to be found, was a tiny braid of hair, fine silky strands that could only belong to a small child—to Grusha's Anna, I assumed.

At that moment I was back in Russia, holding my sister's hand as Grusha exclaimed at her beauty: the lips like rosebuds, the brown eyes with specs of gold, just like Anna's.

And just like Isaac's, I now realized.

I held the braid in my palm as I whispered, "My dearest Miriam, you and I and our mother aren't the only ones our father abandoned."

***

Every year, on the anniversary of my sister's death, my mother and I took the train to Coney Island. There, at the ocean's edge, we recited the traditional mourner's prayer and then remained for a while, each of us lost in memory. On the trip home I would think about going to Russia to look for my half-sister, but then wonder what I would say to Anna if I found her. That her mother murdered our father and drove Miriam to her death with her talk of demons?

Not that I believe Grusha alone was responsible for my sister's death. If my father hadn't abandoned us, if my mother hadn't taken us to Grusha's, if Grusha hadn't provided the amulets—if I hadn't terrified Miriam by throwing my amulet overboard—my sister might still be alive.

In the end, as I often tell my grandson, we were all guilty.

A DIVINATION OF DEATH

by Edith Maxwell

Destination: Burkina Faso
In a country where divination is a part of daily life, the solution to the death of a young man may depend on a dying statement and a fortune-teller's ritual.

The round hut, dark and cool, held mysteries I would never know. We had come with only one to solve.

It was a scant week since Issa Diallo—Mariama's brother and my new love—had been killed on his motorcycle here in southwestern Burkina Faso. The police had ruled it an accident, but I wasn't so sure. Mariama wasn't either.

She and I had driven this Saturday to visit a fortune-teller in Gouinduguba, a tiny village in the dry quiet of the region. Usually we laughed and talked as we traveled the countryside. Not today. Mariama, my research assistant and translator, was subdued with grief, and my own heart also hung heavy. I still couldn't believe Issa was gone. He and I had been friends, and for the last month, lovers, too. Tall, with both a brilliant smile and an adorable dimple, the university-educated scholar had returned to his hometown to teach teenagers.

Mr. Ouedraogo, the holy man we'd come to see, looked like a little old Japanese farmer sitting in the January heat under a big shade tree, with his hooded eyes that twinkled, his long dark hand-sewn robe, his crocheted skull cap with an incongruous yarn pouf at its peak. His jaw was edged with a white-gray beard like a rim of grizzled cotton.

He ushered us into his divination hut. Every diviner's office I'd seen was small, as if the compact space concentrated the fortune-teller's power. The high threshold was worn smooth from decades of bare feet passing over it. Eland horns, a dried gourd on a string, a bunch of dusty herbs, and a bird's tail feathers hung from the thatched roof. Cracks crept like snail trails along the mud-plastered walls of the cylindrical structure.

The old man reclined on his side and threw a handful of cowrie shells onto the ground, picking up three. He selected a page from a dusty unbound book written in an arcane script. He murmured over the shells, then asked me a question in Joula, his gaze intent on my face.

"He wants to know if you are having a fight with somebody over money, Aiseta." Mariama translated into English for me, but used my Burkinabe name instead of Alice, the name my parents had given me twenty-eight years ago. She smiled, her smooth dark skin glowing beneath a purple damask headscarf tied like a turban rather than a hijab.

I thought. "Yes." I was an anthropology doctoral student studying diviners and their objects, and I'd been living in the small town of Banfora for a year. I knew by the time the two years on my research grant were up I'd only have dented the surface of the diviner culture. Issa's sudden death had slowed things even further. I was going to have to defend my need for a funding extension of at least a year.

Mr. Ouedraogo told me to perform a sacrifice. "Take a live ember, pour water on it, and pick it up. Speaking to your heart, say the person's name three times, then bury the ember in the ground."

I nodded that I understood and that I would do it. Mariama whispered that the actions of the sacrifice are related metaphorically to the problem. In the States we bury hatchets, in Burkina Faso they bury embers: same difference.

"Ask him," I prodded her. We'd agreed on the way over that she would see if the diviner had something to say about Issa's death.

She took in a deep breath. Sadness was written in her drooping eyes as she spoke softly in Joula. I caught only her brother's name.

The old man threw the shells on the ground again, tapped two that fell apart from the rest, and turned the pages of his book. He reached for the gourd on the string, loosening the string until the gourd moved freely on it.

"Lift it all the way up," he commanded.

Mariama obliged. She stared at the pale gourd.

The old man spoke directly to the gourd in his low divining voice, different from the one he used when he talked to us. "If Issa's death was a violent one, come down," Mariama translated in a whisper.

My palms grew sweaty. She had to be nervous, too, but I kept my gaze glued to the gourd. What should we do if it dropped? The gourd descended halfway down. I gasped.

"If you're lying, and the death was accidental, come down all the way," the diviner said to the gourd. It stayed put. He asked Mariama to try to push it farther down or move it up, and she couldn't make it move. The old man smiled, a sole top tooth remaining in the middle of his pink gums.

Mariama, college-educated like her brother, finally glanced at me, her eyes wide. Consulting the diviner is a routine part of people's lives in this region. They need to find out what is causing an illness, whom to marry, or why the millet crop failed. They seek help with impotence, incompetence, infertility, and infidelity. Everyone does it, even in the big city, even Christians and Muslims. My assistant was no different.

"Do you know what this means?" she whispered to me.

"Not really." It could mean the gourd got it wrong. It could mean a little old diviner was pulling a scam. Or it could mean we were right in thinking Issa was murdered. I had no idea which of those was the case. I suspected the last.

"What are those rings?" I asked the diviner, pointing to a bowl holding twisted metal hoops.

"Those are to prevent accidents, and these prevent poisoning." The diviner warned me that poison might not be the same in my country, and Mariama explained that poison could mean someone wishing you ill, or giving you the evil eye, or other non-ingested means of harm.

"I'm going to ask him one more question," she said.

I nodded. Mr. Ouedraogo first shook his head in response, then held out his palm. Mariama laid another 100 CFA coin on the ground in front of him. He took her right hand in his. With his left hand he shook a gourd that rattled, and clinked a large ring on a metal knife in rhythm as he chanted. He stopped, then prescribed a sacrifice that would tell her what she wanted to know. Mariama translated as the diviner told her she should buy a silver ring and then put four coins on the ground.

"Pass the ring over the coins four times, give the money to a girl, and wear the ring," he said. "Do this on a Sunday and you will have your answer."

We thanked him and stepped out of the hut. On our way to the car we passed a woman sitting against the wall under a tree, but Mariama did not greet her.

"She's a sorcerer," she whispered to me. "This woman did bad things to people. You know why her leg is bandaged? She has a sore that never heals because of an evil spell she cast on someone."

We climbed into the car and I pointed it back toward Banfora.

"If only Issa had been wearing a ring like this one." Mariama extended her hand as we drove, showing off the anti-poisoning ring I'd bought each of us. "He might still be alive."

"Did you believe the diviner's gourd?" I asked.

She nodded slowly. "Do you know what I asked him at the end?"

"No."

Her voice came out a hoarse whisper. "I asked him who killed Issa."

***

Along the way Mariama pointed out sacrifices—a few palm fronds and a hoop of vine, a white chicken recently killed, an upturned pot topped with feathers and roof straw, a pile of kola nuts—I never would have seen otherwise. The sacrifices that the spirits ask for can be endless, she told me, since the spirits are quite capricious. Just like humans.

"How will doing the sacrifice tell you who the murderer is?" I glanced over at her.

"I don't know. But I am going to carry out his instructions. On Sunday."

Tomorrow.

"Aiseta," she continued. "I didn't tell you this before, but when I went to the hospital, when Issa was dying, he whispered something to me."

I whipped my head to the right to stare at her. "He did?"

She nodded, gazing straight ahead. "He said, 'Killed me.' When I asked him who killed him, he whispered something like 'Sa'—but his voice was so weak I could barely hear him. If there was more to the name, I'll never know." Her voice broke. She shaded her forehead with her hand as her shoulders shook. After a minute, she sat up straight again and wiped her eyes. "It was the last word he spoke."

"So all we have to do is find someone, whose name begins with Sa, who wanted Issa gone?"

Mariama nodded. She pointed to a small road coming up on the right. "Turn into that *quartier*. We have to visit my mother."

I slowed. "Are you sure you want me along? Your mother must be deeply mourning Issa's death."

"We all are, but I know she likes you. It will help her for us to visit."

I made the turn and we bumped down a dry dirt road with ruts so deep it was an inverted obstacle course to drive around them. I parked under a baobab tree massive enough that a dozen people holding hands wouldn't reach around its trunk. We walked slowly and greeted people as we passed by tidy round houses connected by adobe-plastered walls. Flowers splashed color on a building in one compound next to corn flour spread out on a piece of plastic to dry.

Mariama's mother sat on a low stool in the shade of her house.

A woman in her twenties squatted beside her, picking small stones out of a basket of peanuts.

"That one was Issa's girlfriend before you," Mariama murmured to me before we reached the women.

My eyes widened. Issa had told me his ex was furious with him for ending things with her, and she blamed me. He'd said she was pressuring him to marry her, and that was why he'd broken off with her, not because of me.

Mariama greeted her mother.

"Please tell her I am very sorry for her loss," I told Mariama, and listened as she spoke.

The mother held out a hand for mine, her sad rheumy eyes gazing at my face. I gazed back as we exchanged four rounds of the ritual greetings.

"This is Salamatou." As Mariama introduced me to the woman cleaning peanuts, she shot me a quick glance, as if she was trying to tell me something.

My insides turned cold. *Sa.* Salamatou. Could she have been so angry with Issa she killed him? But how?

Salamatou barely glanced up. "*Bonjour*," she said in heavily accented French. Such curtness was the epitome of rude in this part of the world.

A girl in her mid-teens sat on a mat nearby. She laughed and cast her wild happy eyes around: the village idiot. Mariama said her name was Yabil. As I greeted the girl and shook her hand, she chortled with delight and uttered only, "*Herebe*," in a high-pitched, almost robotic voice.

I responded with the ritual, "*Here doron.*" Peace only. I remembered some wrapped candy I had in my bag and handed her a piece. She whooped like she'd won the jackpot, tearing off the paper and popping the sweet into her mouth.

"I think we should examine Issa's motorbike," Mariama whispered. "Maybe somebody messed with it."

My eyebrows went up, but I nodded. She led the way to a lean-to at the far corner of the compound. Yabil tagged along, tossing her head to peer grinning at a plastic bag caught on a tree branch overhead. Mariama pulled off a tattered tarp covering the bike. I winced to see the scraped-bare metal, the twisted fork, the flat front tire, all evidence of a bad crash, and my eyes filled.

I caught Yabil watching me. With a suddenly sad look on her face, she reached out to touch my arm. Her rough fingers stroked my skin with a feather touch. I gave her a gentle smile.

"How can we tell if someone tampered with it?" I asked, not entirely sure why I was whispering, too.

"The police said it hadn't been messed with. But my uncle? He's a mechanic. He thinks there might have been sand put in the gas tank."

"That would make the engine malfunction, causing Issa to crash."

She nodded. "My mother won't let Tonton take the bike apart, though. She treats it like a shrine."

She covered it again, and we visited with Mariama's mother for a little longer before making our way back to the car.

"Yabil almost died at birth," Mariama told me as we strolled. "Her brain was a bit damaged, that's why she's, how do you say *fou*?"

"Crazy?"

"Yes, but not bad crazy. Just empty. Simple."

"She seems happy, though," I said.

"She is. She even has a job. She cleans the floor at the bar in town."

Once we reached the road again, it was only two more kilometers to Banfora. My mind roiled with thoughts of Issa's death.

"Mariama, where was Issa before he died? I mean, I know he was out on his motorcycle after dark. But where had he been, and where was he going?"

"He was teaching the adult literacy class. It's held at the same school where he teaches children during the day."

"And he was riding home from there?" It wasn't easy to navigate these roads at night, even in a car.

"The police said he'd been drinking."

"He must have gone to the bar after class."

"*Oui.*" Mariama nodded. "I think we should go to the bar. Ask them what they saw. But first I have to buy a silver ring."

I steered the car through the narrow streets of Banfora until we reached the only bar in town, which was next to the open market. As I climbed out, the day's third call to prayer floated out from the mosque tower a block away, a haunting melodic chant that would always sound like Africa to me. The irony of the bar's location was obvious. Devout Muslims wouldn't be caught dead at an establishment serving alcohol.

Mariama and I wandered into the market. Five o'clock was late in the day for commerce, with many of the permanent stalls already closed, but she walked straight to a nearly hidden merchant tucked in a corner. By his lighter skin, narrow face, and blue Arabic-style tunic and pants, I guessed he was a Tuareg, one of the nomadic people from northern Mali and Niger. They were known for their silver craftsmanship.

She spoke in French with him, and after a few back and forths of bargaining, she came away with two shiny silver rings. She handed me one. "Here."

"You got me a present?"

"Mine matches, see?" She held up the ring clasped between her index finger and her thumb. The ring widened in front and featured an intricate pattern etched in black. "We will remember Issa with our rings."

I gave her a hug.

"To the bar?" she said, squaring her shoulders.

"To the bar." I was ready for a cold beer. Inside I paused, letting my eyes adjust to the mostly empty cool darkness. A couple of men perched on stools at the bar, and only one of the tables around the edges of a dance floor had people sitting at it. The plastered walls had been painted blue a long time ago, judging from the cracks and the faded color.

"You coming?" I murmured to Mariama.

"Let's do it."

I smiled to myself. It always sounded funny when she used a slangy English phrase like that. I followed her to the other end of the bar from the two guys. Mariama was already exchanging greetings with Celestine. The bartender was a robust woman in a green print dress, a matching headscarf tied with a flourish. She looked at me expectantly, so I started the round of greetings in Joula.

"Peace among you," she answered.

"Peace only. How are you?"

"There's no trouble at all."

"Ah. The family?"

"There's no trouble at all with them."

"Ah. Good. Peace," I finished. No quick *hi-howareyas* around here.

"Do you want a Castel?" Mariama asked me.

"Twist my arm."

Celestine brought over two local lagers and frosty glasses. She said something in Joula to Mariama, but I understood only Issa's name.

"She's saying she's sorry about his death," Mariama said.

The bartender switched to French. "If I had known that night was Issa's last, I would not have accepted his money." She leaned closer. "I think somebody poisoned him."

"Poisoned?" I asked in alarm.

"I didn't see it," Celestine said. "But it's easy enough to drop poison in a drink. I can't watch every glass all the time."

Mariama sucked in a breath. I thought about the effects of almost any potent drug combined with alcohol and a motorcycle at night on bad roads.

"Was he here alone?" I asked.

Celestine made a *tsking* sound. "No, he was with Samou, and the tall *toubabou*."

Samou was a friend of Issa's, and I knew the Joula word for foreigner. "Do you mean Brian?" He was an American who'd been fired from teaching at the International School in the capital and had thought he'd landed the teaching job here that Issa snagged instead. I was surprised Brian was still allowed to be in the country, unemployed as he was. Or maybe he was here illegally.

"Brian is not the name," Celestine said.

A *toubabou* could be any European or Australian, anybody with pale skin, really. Just because I wasn't aware of the dude didn't mean he didn't live here, or hadn't stopped in as part of a trip.

"Look, Samou's over there," Mariama said. "You know he's Salamatou's twin, right?" She pointed to the other end at the nearer of the two men, whose back was to us.

She might as well have pointed to her brother's dying words. *Another name starting with Sa.* I hadn't even thought about Issa's friend's name. I barely knew him and wasn't aware he was the twin brother of the woman who'd felt wronged by Issa breaking up with her.

Mariama called to him. The slender man turned and raised a hand in recognition. He lifted his bottle and moved down to our end.

After a couple of quick rounds of greetings, Celestine urged, "Samou, tell Aiseta about that night. The night Issa had his accident."

"I met him here, you know, for some beers." Samou spoke to his reflection in the big mirror behind Celestine, smoothing his hair.

"With Salamatou?" Mariama asked.

I shot her a quick look. Why was she asking about his sister?

"No," Samou said. "She doesn't like to drink."

"I've been trying to find my friend Brian," I said. "Was he here, too?"

Now I had Samou's attention. He turned to look at me, but when he spoke his gaze slid over my left shoulder.

"Our local *toubabou*? Yeah, he was here. He bought us a couple of rounds."

"Did he find a job?" I asked. I hadn't seen him in a few weeks.

"No." Samou checked himself out in the mirror again. "He's staying with me now."

"His name isn't Brian," Celestine interjected. She set her fists on her ample hips. "Not the *toubabou* who comes in here and puts more beers on his account than he can pay for."

I wrinkled my nose. That sounded exactly like the Brian I knew.

"That's because his Burkinabe name isn't Brian," Samou said to his reflection with a tired air, as if he couldn't believe we didn't know.

"What is it?" I pressed.

"Sawadogo."

***

I stood next to my car outside the bar, but my hand shook so much I couldn't fit the key into the lock. After what Samou said, I had laid money for the beer on the bar and rushed out. I had to talk to Brian, *aka* Sawadogo—another name starting with the syllable Sa. But what if he'd killed Issa?

Mariama appeared at my side. One look at me and she grabbed the keys. "Come on. We're going to visit the *toubabou.* Samou's apartment is only two blocks that way."

In my upset, I'd forgotten where I was. I let her lead me along the quiet streets that smelled of meat roasting on the ubiquitous charcoal brazier mixed with a hint of sewage from the barely covered ditches at the sides of the road.

As we walked, Mariama murmured, "I picked up an interesting fact from Celestine after you left."

"Oh?"

"Not now." She rapped on a blue-painted door set into mud-plastered walls, announcing, "*As-salamu alaykum*," an Arabic greeting that persisted even in this corner of West Africa that was more Christian and animist than Muslim.

The door creaked open to a yawning Brian, barefoot, sandy hair mussed, and clad in an undershirt and tie-dyed drawstring pants. He started the expected response of, "*Alaykumu as . . .*" but trailed off when he saw who it was. "Hey, Alice, Mariama. What's shakin'?"

Now that we were here face-to-face with him, I didn't know what to say. 'Did you kill Issa?' wasn't quite the effect I was looking for. Luckily, Mariama stepped into the breach.

"We were just over at the bar and Samou told us you were staying here. Celestine says you're devastated about Issa's death."

I stared at her. She had?

Mariama went on. "As we all are." She paused, as if expecting to be asked in.

Brian finally got it. "Of course. Um, come on in." He backed into the darkened room. "It's kind of a mess right now, sorry about that."

I stepped in as he threw open the shutters, revealing a veritable pigsty. The air smelled of dirty socks, marijuana, stale beer. Clothes were tossed on the cement slab floor, and a ratty blanket trailed off the rattan piece that was trying to be a sofa with no cushions. I didn't go any farther in.

"Sorry, I'm sleeping on the, uh, couch for now," Brian offered. "But I'll probably get Issa's job, now that he's gone."

He didn't even notice Mariama wince at his thoughtless remark.

"Then I can get my own place," Brian went on.

Mariama stayed in the entrance, her lip curled ever so slightly. "My mother has hired a *griot* to memorialize Issa tomorrow and she wanted to be sure you and Samou were invited to the feast."

I blinked at her. *Feast? A praise singer? Tomorrow?*

"Me?" Brian looked as surprised as I felt. "OK, sure. I'll ride over with Sam. What time?"

***

The next afternoon Mariama and I again sat with her mother in the shade. Salamatou painted her nails nearby, and Yabil sang softly to herself, rocking from one foot to the other, happy eyes focused on a vulture perched on a neighbor's roof. No praise singer—*griot*—was in evidence, nor a feast. Mariama had asked me simply to trust her. I rubbed the back of my new silver ring with my thumb.

A motorcycle's putt-putt grew nearer until Samou pulled into the opening in the wall. Brian rode on the back. Both, expecting festivities, wore nice shirts and slacks, now slightly dusty from the ride.

Brian slid off and looked around with a bewildered air. "Where's the *griot*?"

"And the feast?" Samou directed his question to his sister, who shrugged.

Mariama rose and grabbed two more stools from the house, then gestured to the men to sit. My heart pounded in my chest.

"Yabil?" Mariama called to her. Yabil laughed at the vulture before joining us. She squatted in front of Mariama.

Mariama drew out the four coins and the silver ring. We all

watched as she laid the money in a square on the ground. She passed the ring over them four times with a solemn air, her lips moving to the words of a prayer, an incantation, or something else I couldn't fathom. She slid the ring onto her right hand and picked up the coins. She took Yabil's hand, and closed the girl's palm around the money.

"Those are for you. Yabil, can you tell me who poisoned Issa?"

Yabil nodded. Brian swore in English. The girl looked around the circle, from Salamatou to Brian to Samou. Samou's eyes narrowed. Salamatou examined her nails as if nothing special was happening.

The tension was unbearable. Did Yabil really know? And if she did, could she communicate it?

Yabil pointed to Samou.

"I didn't!" He stood knocking over his stool. "She's crazy, everybody knows it."

Yabil then moved her finger to point at Salamatou. Yabil's face looked worried, but her hand didn't vary, didn't shake.

Salamatou pushed up to standing. "I was right here when Issa was killed. I had nothing to do with it." She tossed her head.

Yabil crossed her middle finger over her index finger in the sign for twins and pointed at both siblings, back and forth. The next time she pointed at Salamatou, Yabil cupped her hand around her ear.

Mariama stood and clapped her hands. Two uniformed police officers emerged from the dark of her mother's house. "Yabil is telling us she heard Salamatou tell her brother to spike Issa's drink so he would crash on his way home. Celestine at the bar said she saved the glass Issa was drinking out of that night. Yabil was there cleaning, and she saw Samou put poison in Issa's glass. I think you'll find Samou's fingerprints on it and traces of something toxic inside. If you search Salamatou's room, you'll probably discover the drug she gave her brother to use."

Unlike Yabil or his sister, Samou was shaking. "I didn't want to kill him! He was my friend." His voice was desperate. "Sala told me it would just make Issa sick, that she wanted to teach him a lesson."

"Liar," Salamatou shrieked. She stalked toward her twin, her face a mask of fury, but one officer caught her arm, handcuffing her hands behind her back, telling her she was under arrest. His colleague did the same to Samou, and they marched the two away.

Mariama's mother just nodded to herself, unfazed by any of it. Yabil grinned at the coins in her hand, stroking each in turn.

I looked admiringly at Mariama. "Your talents are wasted as a translator, girl. You should be a detective."

She smiled. "Maybe I will be. But don't you think I should consult Mr. Ouedraogo first?"

PAYBACK WITH INTEREST

by Cheryl Marceau

Destination: Taos, New Mexico
Christmas Eve at the pueblo, a time for ancient rituals—and, sometimes, modern mayhem.

A flaming piñon log collapsed into the tallest bonfire, showering sparks on the throngs gathered waiting for the sacred ritual to begin. The crowd's excited chatter subsided to a soft murmur as the procession emerged from the candlelit church into the firelit night.

Somber men carrying long rifles led the way, two by two. The crowd dropped back to make room. Torchbearers and singing worshippers followed, accompanying a statue of the Virgin of Guadalupe as she was borne along a route established centuries before. On a cue that only they seemed to hear, the men stopped, lifted their rifles, and fired into the heavens. The roar of the gunfire drowned out the sounds of crackling wood and voices raised in song.

Rita rubbed her hands together for warmth. The take on Christmas Eve the last few years had been better than she'd eked out for a living for the rest of the year combined. Amid the local folks and new-age spirituality seekers, whom she left alone, stood tourists in fur and cashmere whose pockets begged to be picked. Who wouldn't notice anything missing until they reached for their wallets to pay for dinner back at their fancy Santa Fe restaurants a couple hours later that night. Rita took nearly as much pleasure from embarrassing these rich people as she did from counting her earnings. She felt satisfaction in balancing the scales of life. The rich had far more than they needed, whereas she'd never had enough. She was careful never to steal the wallet of anyone who did not appear to be wealthy, and over her years here in Taos, she had developed a discerning eye for wealth.

She made her way through the crowd, careful to stay back from the many small and large bonfires that burned brightly across the plaza. The pueblo was beautiful at any time, but to Rita it was magical on Christmas Eve, and not just because of the money she would take home.

Two multi-story adobe structures, each made of dozens of

rooms and still intact after nearly a thousand years, stood to the north and south of a large open plaza. Taos Mountain towered over them in the distance, its snow-covered peak glowing in the moonlight. An adobe wall surrounded these buildings as well as several others including the pueblo church, over a century old, and the ruins of an even older church destroyed more than a hundred and fifty years before that. A tall gate next to the church opened to the parking lot and the road leading out. Very few people actually lived in the pueblo now, but most Taos tribal families maintained apartments in the compound for use on occasions like this.

"It is a fine night."

Rita jumped when she heard the voice so close behind her. She'd been studying a target in the crowd and had lost track of everything else. She was getting careless. She wouldn't be able to do this much longer if she didn't pay closer attention. The tribal police had banned her from the pueblo after an earlier incident. Christmas Eve was now her only opportunity to sneak into a festival here, under the cover of darkness.

"Very cold," she answered. Her well-worn leather jacket gave only token protection against temperatures which were nearing zero on this clear winter night. If not for the bonfires, her fingers would be too cold to do her any good. The voice seemed familiar, but the man stood out of the glow of the firelight, his face hidden in the shadows. "I can't remember it ever being this cold."

"I have not missed this ceremony once since I was a boy, many years ago now. My daughter has hot chocolate waiting for me." The old man pointed to the north adobe building, where several first-floor doorways were lit by battery-powered lanterns. "I am sure we know each other."

"You must be thinking of someone else."

"I do not forget a beautiful face. You are welcome to come and have hot chocolate with me."

"Thanks for the generous invitation, but no." She couldn't tell if it was simply a friendly gesture or if the old man was hoping for something more. The days when she'd turned heads were behind her, but she was still a handsome woman.

The man shrugged. "Your loss. My daughter makes the best hot chocolate. She uses chocolate syrup, none of that powdered stuff." He melted into the crowd and was gone.

Rita looked for other familiar faces. She'd select her targets carefully, paying more attention to who was nearby. It wouldn't do to be recognized again, or worse, for someone to catch her as she worked.

The procession made its way along the winding route through

the plaza, moving slowly and hypnotically. After a short distance, the marchers stopped and the riflemen repeated their salute. This provided Rita with excellent cover. No one would pay attention to her while the report of the gunfire echoed around the adobe walls.

Rita wormed into the middle of the crowd, away from the light of the bonfires. She smelled an expensive men's cologne. Her thumb and forefinger grasped a thin leather wallet and inched it out of a back pocket, then slid it into the hobo bag on her shoulder as she eased away from the target. She never looked to see what she'd taken until she was well away from the scene. Before anyone knew their belongings were gone, she would have cleaned out the cash, wiped prints off the wallets, and dumped them. Then she'd head home, to an old hippie commune miles away on the mesa. As long as nobody recognized her, Rita was confident there was little chance of being caught. An aging hippie chick, however attractive, wouldn't interest most people tonight. She was merely part of the scenery.

The procession halted and the riflemen readied to fire their salute once more.

Rita closed in on a man with movie star looks, wearing an expensive down jacket. His companions had equally expensive attire, particularly a brunette wearing gemstone studs as large as her earlobes.

"You can sense the sanctity and peacefulness of this place," the man said to his friends as Rita's fingers grazed his wallet. "But watch out. I come here nearly every year when I'm not on location somewhere, and twice I've been robbed."

"Here of all places!" one of the others said.

The movie star nodded. "It's disgraceful that this sacred ceremony is contaminated by such evil."

Rita stifled a snort at the phony spirituality, but at the same time the comments worried her. It was the first she'd heard of anyone directly connecting their losses to this place. Maybe it was time to stop working Christmas Eve at the pueblo and stick to the flea market or the big art fairs in Santa Fe, where the crowds were packed so tightly you could prop up a corpse and no one would notice. After tonight, she'd lay low for a while.

The procession stopped, and again the riflemen took aim. Rita worked a wallet out of the man's pocket, pleased to see that he didn't even twitch, and tucked it into her bag. Just as gunshots reverberated around the plaza, she felt something heavy slump against her legs. She choked to see the man whose wallet she'd just lifted sprawled at her feet.

"Give him room!" one of his friends shouted. "Is there a doctor here?"

The tribal police ran from their positions around the plaza to where the man now lay, his head cradled by the brunette. "You'll be OK," she said over and over, rocking and crying.

Rita edged away, slowly and with as little apparent intent as she could manage. She didn't want anyone to suspect that she was running from the scene.

Once she was behind the northern pueblo building, she paused. Sirens screamed in the distance, probably the ambulance from the town hospital as well as town police to back up the tribal officers. Rita made her way as quickly as she dared to the old ruins, and from there hugged the low adobe walls as she crept to the plaza gates and out of the pueblo.

Back on the main road, she climbed into her old VW microbus and threw it into gear. The van hesitated then pulled onto the road. Rita headed for the Rio Grande Gorge west of Taos and the mesa on the other side of the river. She wanted to be as far from the pueblo as possible. If the movie star was dead, and she was fairly sure he was, she didn't want to take any chances that she'd be identified in connection with him.

As soon as she was well out on the mesa, she pulled the van off the road and stashed the wallets in a hidden compartment the prior owner had created as a safe place to store weed. Even if the cops pulled her over, or someone spotted her at the pueblo and fingered her, they'd never find the wallets. She'd deal with them in the morning.

***

Home was the remains of a hippie commune built at the end of the sixties, where Rita's parents had met and where she was born. No one lived on the compound now except Rita and the few goats and chickens she kept. The old straw bale house had survived the breakup of the commune and years of weathering, waiting for Rita to return and make it her home more than thirty years after her small family disintegrated. Her artist mother had been thrilled to learn Rita had returned. Her father, now a property developer, refused to support her in any way as long as she stayed in what he called "that hovel."

Rita was awakened just before sunrise by the sound of gravel crunching outside. She tensed, her heart pounding. Bears were just about the only creatures out here big enough to make that much noise, and it was the wrong time of year for bears. She threw on jeans and a sweatshirt and peered out the window. A rusty old sedan with a two-by-four for a back bumper was parked out by the goat pen. Rita noted the license plate, standard New Mexico red-on-yellow. She tried to read the number, but could only make out the last three digits.

"I see you are awake," someone called.

Rita recognized the voice immediately as the old man from the pueblo. She froze, like an animal that has been spotted by a predator, hoping to avoid detection.

"Go away or I'll call the police," she yelled when it became apparent he intended to wait her out.

"I do not think you will." He came nearer. "I have very important business to discuss with you."

She grabbed the flashlight she kept by the door, then stepped outside.

"I know who you are," the man said. "I saw what you did at the pueblo. I want the money you stole or I will tell the police you killed that man. I think they will believe me."

"I had nothing to do with that!"

"That is your story, but I have proof."

"Proof of what? You've got nothing," Rita said, desperately trying to remember every detail of the prior night's events.

The man smiled. Rita could see his expression in the growing winter daylight. "You forgot this in your hurry to leave," he said, holding out a bundle wrapped in a rag. Pulling away one corner of the rag, he revealed a gun.

"I've never owned a gun. Never touched one in my life."

"The prints have been wiped from it. The police will find it is the same weapon that shot the man. They will locate it on this property after they get an anonymous tip."

"You can't prove it was mine."

"The police will have the proof they need."

Rita stared at the man in disbelief. "I didn't get anything last night. That guy got shot and I ran away. There's nothing to give you."

The old man continued to approach until he stood in the beam of the flashlight. He was no longer smiling. "You give me the money from last night, or the police get a call."

Rita shivered. In a flash of recognition, she knew why he'd seemed familiar the night before. The old bastard had pointed her out to the Taos tribal police at the Feast of San Geronimo a couple of years back. He'd accused her of stealing a silver bracelet from him. She'd been wearing the only silver bracelet she owned, one her mother had given to her. The police found stolen wallets in her bag, so the man walked away with her bracelet and the police took the wallets. She was surprised it had taken her so long to remember him. He'd worn a huge felt hat that day, obscuring his eyes, but it was the same guy. He must have known she was the woman living in the old commune, which any longtime Taoseño could tell him how to find.

She'd have to give the old man what he wanted, then find a way to keep him out of her life. "I don't have the money with me," she said. "It's stashed somewhere else."

"I will come with you to get it."

"No, it's my special place. I go alone."

"In that case, I will stay here in your lovely home and wait for you. I will make sure that nothing bad happens while you are gone. It would be terrible if the propane stove started a fire and burned it down."

Rita frantically tried to think of another ploy as she climbed into the van and drove north on the mesa. She was sick at the thought of this man defiling her home, possibly burning it to the ground. The police would believe whatever he told them. She already had evidence of that.

***

The old man's threats shook her badly. She left people alone, mostly, and wanted to be left alone herself. If he needed money, he should steal from rich people himself. What would she do if he turned her in? The thought of a life on the run was almost as bad as life in jail for a murder she hadn't committed. At least New Mexico didn't have the death penalty. That was some comfort.

It was Christmas Day. The wallets were stowed in their hiding place. Rita needed time to plan her next move. She decided to risk going into Red River, a ski resort town where there'd be a lot of strangers and she could pass unnoticed. She'd sit somewhere warm, have a badly-needed cup of coffee, and ponder her options.

The sky was a brittle blue, the air so cold Rita could feel her nostrils freeze when she breathed. She parked in front of a diner with a flashing OPEN sign, and walked past the newspaper kiosk by the door. A bold black headline covered the front of the *Santa Fe New Mexican.* The words blurred. She was afraid to look. Then something registered and she swiveled to look again.

ACTOR JOHN MORRIS SURVIVES HEART ATTACK AT TAOS PUEBLO. Next to the headline was a photograph of the movie star who had collapsed at her feet.

Rita seized the handle on the kiosk and shook it. Nothing happened. She crouched to read the top half of the front page.

"That no-good lying bastard!"

***

She drove back the way she came, stopping well before the turnoff to her home, and dug out the wallets. She pulled out most of the cash, leaving a little in each wallet, and wiped off her prints. It hurt to give up even a dollar, but the old cheat had to be convinced he'd won.

A plume of smoke curled up from her kiva fireplace when she returned. He'd made himself at home all right, burning the firewood she'd worked so hard to collect.

"Did you bring me the money?" he asked, stepping outside.

"Can't I get you to walk away?" she pleaded. "Look around. Do I look like I have anything to spare?"

"You are smart, you will find a way to get more money. Now give me what you promised me."

She handed him a tattered plastic goat feed bag with the wallets, eleven in all. "Here. Take a good look. I wouldn't want you to think I cheated you."

The man set the bag on the ground, pulled out a wallet, and peered inside. He grunted and threw it back, then grabbed another. "This is all you got?"

"Everybody uses plastic now. Pretty soon I won't score any cash at all."

He opened his car door and tossed the bag inside. "Do not forget. Next month you better find a way to get more money. I will be back."

Rita watched the plume of dust that trailed his car until he was far away, then pulled her cheap cell phone out of her jeans pocket.

Her call was answered in a flash. "Taos County Crime Stoppers."

"I saw a guy pickpocketing at the pueblo last night, just spotted him again. He's driving an old Ford, dark brown, two-by-four on the back bumper. New Mexico license plate ends in 497."

She smiled and flipped off the phone. Karma's a bitch.

ISLAND TIME

by Laura Oles

Destination: Port Alene, Texas
When her youngest son gets into serious trouble, Diane Davis has a difficult choice to make. Will she let her beloved business go to satisfy her son's debt?

Diane Davis pulled her car into the parking lot, squinting through the hazy film covering her Honda's windows. A regular clash between the coastal town's ever-present humidity and her older vehicle's tired air conditioning meant Diane always had "wash car" on her to-do list. Although it annoyed her, she realized it was a small price to pay for being able to live in Port Alene, Texas.

Until recently, Port Alene had remained one of the few island towns on the Gulf of Mexico that managed to escape the attention of wealthy city dwellers searching for that perfect vacation home, and investors devouring holiday spots to buy and sell for inflated prices. Changes were coming, though, and locals were already complaining of the inconveniences that came with an invasion of new residents. As a business owner, Diane felt conflicted about the growth. More customers meant more revenue, but the benefits were dampened by the reality that Port Alene was in danger of losing its island town charm.

As Diane stepped out of her car, she checked her watch, noting the shop lights were on but Max's truck was nowhere to be seen. She unlocked the front door and was met with a burst of cold air, the chill a strong contrast to the warmth outside.

"Where's Max?" Diane asked. Her eldest child, Anna, was busy stocking the pastry cabinet for the café. The family business, Island Time, had been Diane's brainchild, and over the last decade had grown from a small coffee shop into one of the island's premier gathering spots for locals and tourists alike. Diane relied heavily on her three children to manage the daily operations and staffing. Max, the youngest at twenty-two, had proven the least reliable of her offspring.

"I woke up early and couldn't get back to sleep, so I thought I'd check in here, which was a good thing because"—Anna waved her hand at the empty café—"the place was dark, and he was nowhere to be found. I think he takes the island time attitude to an extreme." She sighed. "We need to discuss removing him from the business, Mom. He can't expect to benefit if he's not willing to work. It's not fair to me and Tom." She pointed to a wall behind her. "Oh, and I pulled that electrical cord out of the socket. It keeps sparking and I'm afraid something's going to catch fire back there."

"Thanks, hon. I really need to get the electrician to check on it."

Diane knew her daughter was right about Max but she just wasn't ready to have that difficult conversation. "We'll discuss the brother situation later, Anna," she said, her voice calm and soft. "For now, let's just get things ready to open. Most of the tourists are gone, so you can clock out early." Diane hoped the small gift of an afternoon off would appease Anna until she could figure out what to do about Max's latest misstep. As the eldest and a stereotypical overachiever, Anna could be counted on to pick up the slack, no matter what the situation. And Max took advantage whenever possible.

Diane stepped behind the counter to give her daughter a hug. She then looked Anna in the eye. "I promise that we'll get this sorted out, OK? You shouldn't be covering for him all the time." Diane wanted her daughter to know she had been heard, and that she would put her foot down. Max was going to have to answer for his behavior.

***

Monday passed without so much as a word from Max. Calls from Diane and Anna had gone straight to his voicemail, not uncommon as Max often claimed his cell phone battery needed charging. They knew it was code for "I'm avoiding your call," but he usually responded the same day. Neither Tom, the middle child, nor Anna had heard from their brother, and Diane wondered if she had misinterpreted Max's lack of response for something more serious. She decided to go by his apartment once she finished her run.

Diane loved running the loop by the ferry landing. She enjoyed watching the boats travel across the channel between Port Alene and its sister town, Rockville Heights, and the pelicans and gulf birds perched on wooden posts. The ocean always offered a breeze. Sometimes it was light, taking the edge off the blistering heat, and other times it brought enough force to blow hats off heads. She stepped into her stride, propelled by the sound of the barges and the feel of the salty residue that clung to her skin and wrapped itself in her hair.

Diane cleared her first mile just shy of eleven minutes, her second mile coming even more quickly at ten and half. Her worry about Max had pushed her pace, her body needing to rid itself, even if only for a few moments, of the anxiety that came with keeping tabs on her youngest.

She walked to her car, sweaty and with labored breath, and removed her cell phone from her armband. She checked it to find no texts from him but one from Anna saying all was well at the cafe. Diane reached for the water bottle inside her car and drained half of it. She plopped down in the driver's seat, her legs sticking to the leather, her body heavy from exertion. She turned on the air conditioner full blast, tilting the vents to her face.

Diane headed for Max's apartment before going home, a quick ten minute drive from the ferry landing. Early morning traffic in Port Alene was often light, and since it was not yet eight, Diane found herself mostly alone on the road. She turned off Pelican Point onto Beachcomber Trail and pulled up to Max's duplex. The structure was built on stilts like so many others in the area after countless storms had flooded dozens of homes. She would likely find him asleep in bed, pizza boxes on the floor and the television on in the background, a living cliché of bachelor life.

She pulled into the parking lot and noticed that Max's truck was gone. She claimed his parking space and walked up the steps. Maybe a friend had driven him home after a late night out.

"Max, are you in there?" she called, then knocked on the door.

Silence.

Diane placed her ear against the door. No television, no movement. She waited and knocked once more. Again, no response. Without a key to his apartment—Max had scoffed at the idea of his mother having unfettered access to his place—she wasn't sure where to search next. Max didn't have a girlfriend, and she couldn't imagine where he would be if not at home, especially this early.

She started to worry.

***

Diane returned home for a quick shower, then gathered her laptop and work files and left for Island Time. She had to park farther away than usual, the off-to-the-office crowd now in line for the daily caffeine and pastry they required to get through the first part of the workday. Four women exited through the front door with to-go cups in hand. Diane recognized them from a local real estate and vacation rental firm in town. Permanent housing for locals was scarce because so much of the demand catered to vacationers and 'snowbirds,' the very valuable retired visitors who would leave their cold climates in the winter months and head for

Port Alene's more moderate temperatures. Diane knew she had been fortunate to find her place a decade earlier. The task would be more difficult and expensive now.

As she stepped inside Island Time, she smiled and greeted each customer waiting in line. There were five in the queue so far, with Anna and Tom both behind the counter tending to requests. Diane knew Tom hated working front of the house. He was much more content to handle the books and behind-the-scenes needs of the shop, but with Max still missing, the other two siblings were left to handle the café.

"Hi guys." She gave each of her children a quick touch on the shoulder as she walked behind them toward her office door. Anna offered a tight smile and Tom nodded, his attention firmly focused on the blender as he tossed a fresh banana and a few strawberries in for a smoothie.

Tom called to her as she opened the office door. "There's something I need to talk to you about once we get through here."

"Sure. I'm just going to make a few calls. Come in when you can."

The rush dwindled to a trickle as the clock neared eleven. Anna turned her attention to cleaning tables and straightening the customer coffee supply bar while Tom disappeared into his mother's modest office.

"Have you heard from Max yet?" Diane asked. "Any texts, updates, anything?"

Tom shook his head. "Not a word." He plopped down in the small cushioned chair across from his mother's desk. "I mean, we know Max is irresponsible but this is off the charts for him. I need him with the customers. He's better at all the small talk than I am." He hesitated and then said, "And I think we have a problem that might be related to Max."

"What is it, Tom? You look worried."

He pointed to a small cabinet behind Diane's desk. "I went to put some business files in the safe . . ."

Diane turned to look at the cabinet, the safe still hidden behind its closed doors. "And what?"

"And the emergency cash is missing."

Diane stood up slowly and took a few steps toward the cabinet, kneeling down to open its doors to reveal the small safe. Turning the dial left, right and left again, she heard the click and opened the steel door. Atop her paper files rested a small cash box. Diane opened it and found . . . nothing.

"How is this possible?" Diane asked. "Why would he need ten thousand dollars? That's our entire emergency fund!" Diane slammed the box shut and returned it to the safe. "This isn't normal, Tom," she said. She slouched in her chair and covered her mouth with her hand. "Why would he take the money?"

Tom stood from his chair and moved toward his mother, giving her a hug. "I don't know, Mom."

"Of course, I don't have any of his friends' numbers." Diane realized that even though Port Alene was a small town, there was still a great deal she didn't know about her youngest son's life. Carter and Dale were Max's casual friends, good for fishing and drinking beer, but what else had he been doing with his time?

Something that required stealing ten grand from his family, apparently.

Diane left Tom in the office and, laptop in hand, went into the dining area of the now empty café. She took a seat by the window in her favorite spot in one of the two large leather club chairs separated by a small wood end table. Anna brought her mother a hazelnut latte, placing the large ceramic mug on the table. She sat in the opposite chair as her mother explained what Tom had discovered.

"What could he possibly need ten grand for, Mom?" Anna asked, her eyes wide. Her hands reached for a nearby napkin. She crumpled it and tossed it on the table. "I can't believe it."

"So, you don't know anything about what Max has been up to?" Diane asked.

Anna shook her head. "You know how he is. Everything's great, all small talk. He's not one to share his problems." Anna tapped her finger to her lip. "There's one thing but it's a long shot. I mean, it's lunchtime, but I know he hangs out at the Tarpon Taproom sometimes. Carter's got a crush on one of the waitresses there, and the bar food's cheap, so . . ."

"It's worth a shot."

Anna nodded. "It's worth a shot."

***

Diane drove down Pelican Point, leaving the comfort of the sunny, clean local businesses for a section of town known by locals as Alibi Alley. Alibi Alley was home to businesses known for cheap spirits and anonymity. If the places made any money, it sure wasn't being put back into the buildings' exteriors. Several watering holes all in a row shared weather-weary signs with paint peeling from the edges and some letters missing entirely. The harsh Texas sun had taken its toll. Diane found the Tarpon Taproom at the end of the block on the corner of Sunny Sands Lane and Sea Breeze Street. Desperate Drive and Shady Street is more like it, she thought. As she pulled into the parking lot, she noticed there were a half dozen cars in the parking lot.

Including Max's silver Ford F-150.

Diane breathed a sigh of relief but she was still angry.

She pulled open the front door of the Tarpon Taproom, her eyes narrowing from the sharp change of piercing daylight to a dim bar interior. It was surprisingly warm inside, no sharp slap of air conditioning, an indication that the owner went cheap on comfort as well as on alcohol. Two men glanced in her direction from a pool table, cigarette smoke snaking from their lips to the lighted Shiner Bock sign hanging above them. Their attention quickly returned to the game at hand.

At the far corner of the bar, a man hunched over a draft beer, his face tilted as he watched the replay of a football game. He wore a baseball cap, a black T-shirt, and cargo shorts. Diane made her way over to him, her presence causing him to turn in her direction.

Carter.

"Hey, Ms. Davis," Carter said, his words coming quickly. "Uh, what are you doing here? Doesn't seem like the kind of place you'd be hanging out."

Diane pointed to the door. "Where's Max? I saw his truck outside. I need to talk to him."

"Uh, he's not here," Carter said. He reached for his beer and took a long drink. He avoided eye contact, instead glancing at the television and then back to his glass.

"What do you mean, he's not here?" Diane asked. "Where is he and why are you driving his truck?"

"Uh, he's not feeling well so I borrowed the truck to pick up some food for us."

"He's at his apartment then?"

Carter shook his head. "No, he's kind of . . . hiding out."

"Hiding out?" Diane's anger gave way to a churning fear, her pulse now pounding in her ears. A waitress carrying a large brown paper bag smelling of fried food interrupted their conversation.

"Here you go, Carter," she said. "See you next time."

Carter nodded, his smile forced. He inhaled deeply and then pushed the words out. "He's in some trouble, Ms. D."

"You're darn right he is," Diane replied.

"No, Ms. D.," Carter corrected her. "He's in real trouble."

Diane pointed to the food. "Grab that and let's go. I'll follow you."

Carter nodded.

Diane left the dark seclusion of the Tarpon Taproom for bright daylight and the reality that her son had somehow gotten in way over his head.

***

Diane followed Carter to the ferry landing. The line was short, and they waited only a few minutes for the next ferry to dock. The loud clang of the metal drive ramps connected, allowing the cars to pull up in order. Port Alene had four ferries on duty, each capable of holding twenty cars. Diane followed Carter in line and waited for the chance to board. It took just a few minutes for the *K.L. Derringer* to max her load. The ferry master signaled for the cars to turn off their engines, and then they began the short journey across the water to Rockville Heights. Diane rolled down the window and rested the crook of her elbow on the door. She listened to the sounds of churning water under the barge mixing with the calls of the gulls. Sticky salt residue had begun collecting on the fine hairs of her forearm in the short few minutes it took to get to Port Alene's sister town. Once docked, she waved to Carter ahead of her, and waited for the ferry master to release the chains and direct them down the ramp.

Diane was far less familiar with Rockville Heights, and was dependent upon Carter to navigate to Max's destination. Five minutes later, they turned into a park with two large playscapes and bench seating for picnics. At the far end of the park, Diane spotted her son underneath a bench canopy, watching the two vehicles coming towards him.

Carter exited Max's truck and Diane followed behind him. Max wore sunglasses and a cap, and as she got closer, she saw bruises on his face. One eye had turned marbled shades of purple with hints of green on one side.

"Max, what happened?" Diane asked. She touched his face. Max flinched and leaned back. She resisted the urge to reach for him a second time.

"It looks worse than it is," Max said. He looked to his friend, who handed him the paper bag of food. "What's wrong with you? Why would you bring my mom out here?"

Carter shrugged, shoving his hands in his shorts pockets. Diane spoke for him. "I was looking for you and found him at the Tarpon. Why haven't you been returning my calls? Tom's calls? Anna's calls? What is going on with you?"

Max gestured to the metal bench across from him, placing the paper bag on the table. "I was hoping to figure out a way to fix this without you knowing about it. I should have called and told you I was sick with the flu or something. I just . . . panicked."

"You took ten grand from my safe and you're telling me that you should have lied about having the flu?" Diane's hands shook, her anger threatening to unleash full force. “What happened to your face? And why did you need my money? Our money?”

Max hung his head. Not making eye contact, he said, “I had hoped to put it back before you realized it was gone.” He then looked up over his sunglasses. “It was Tom who found out, wasn’t it?”

Diane ignored his question and instead offered her own. “What did you need the money for, Max? Why would you steal from us?”

“Borrow, Mom,” he corrected her. “I was going to put it back.” Max nodded at Carter, who was standing off to the side of the table.

“I’m going to, uh, go take a walk. Be back in a few.” Carter left, giving the two time to discuss Max’s peril in private.

“I found out about this underground poker game,” Max started, “and I was doing really well. I made about twenty grand last month, which is a lot considering how much I earn at Island Time.”

Diane inhaled deeply. “Wow. Twenty grand? Playing cards?”

He nodded. “Yeah. It’s a real rush.”

“It’s also very dangerous.”

“I know, Mom. It’s just . . . I was making a lot of money, and when they asked me to buy into the higher tier, I needed more cash.”

“So you took the ten from my safe?”

He nodded. “I figured I would double my money and put it back, maybe a little extra on top . . .”

“And then you lost it.”

Max reached for his cap and took it off, brushing the sweat forming on his brow, his sandy blond hair matted from the rim of the hat. “I lost big, and I lost to the wrong guy.”

Diane sat quietly for a moment. “How much? And who is he?”

Max waved his hand in the air. “He’s not the kind of guy you want to know, and certainly not someone you want to owe.”

“How much, Max?”

“Two . . . hundred.”

“Two hundred thousand?” The words echoed in Diane’s ears. “Max, I don’t have that kind of money. None of us do. How are you going to pay that back?”

Max removed his sunglasses to wipe a tear threatening to stream down his face. He sniffed, rubbing his hand on his shorts before returning his sunglasses to serve as cover for his bruises.

“I don’t know but I need to pay it off soon. If I can’t, he keeps adding interest. I’ll never get out from under it. This guy has a reputation, and I didn’t know until it was too late. He owns businesses, some he's gotten from people who can't pay."

Diane felt the blood run cold in her veins. "He knows about Island Time?"

He nodded. "Yeah, he does. I ran my mouth some before and . . ."

"He wants it to wipe the debt clean."

Diane hung her head in her hands, her chest so tight she could barely breathe. She sat quietly with Max, absorbing the choice she was now being forced to make.

"So, it's your safety or my business. Is that what you're telling me?"

She then leaned toward her son, putting her hand on his. "Island Time is more than your job. It's what I want to pass along to you, Tom, and Anna. You know that. I'm planning on opening a second location once I get some of the debt paid off . . ."

Max reached for his mother's hand and squeezed. "I keep trying to think of another way out of this, and I don't know what to do. "

Diane waved to Carter in the distance to return. She tapped on the table. "You need to come back to the café and we'll meet as a family. This affects all of us, not just me."

"I know, Mom. I'm sorry."

"I'm sorry, too," Diane replied. She got up from the table and went around to the other side, then hugged him close. Max nestled his head into his mother's shoulder, his sobs pulsing against her. Diane had to tell Anna and Tom that the family business was at risk.

There looked to be no way out.

***

Diane and Max drove in silence all the way back to the café. Diane had texted Anna and Tom, told them that Max was safe but that she needed to call an emergency family meeting. When they arrived, the shop's sign indicated they were closed.

Diane unlocked the door. Max followed her inside, his shoulders hunched. His two siblings greeted him with concern. Anna gasped when she saw Max's bruised eye.

"What happened to your face, Max?" Anna said, reaching her hand to touch his injury. "Let's get some ice on that."

He waved off her offer. "I'm fine, Sis. Really."

Tom kept his arms crossed, worry on his features but also frustration showing through. "What did you get into this time, Max?" He looked to Diane. "How bad is it?"

The four sat together at one of the wooden tables in the café. Max fidgeted in his chair as he explained the poker network and the payment he now owed for his losing streak. Diane watched Anna's face, which went through the same emotions she had experienced just hours before. Tom's expression remained stoic, unflinching.

Diane said, "This family now has a very real problem because Max owes two hundred grand . . ."

"Two hundred grand?" Tom stood up, the wooden chair scraping on the floor. He wiped his brow, put his hands on his hips, and shook his head. "What were you thinking? What is wrong with you?"

Diane continued, "Getting angry won't help. Max owes two hundred grand, and they want Island Time as payment."

Tom remained standing, his body rigid, his jaw clenched. "This is his mess. He needs to clean it up."

Diane replied, "All three of you are living in apartments, and I don't have enough equity in my house to cover the debt. And the business is already leveraged from all the improvements we did. I can't get enough cash out of it right now."

Max remained slumped in his chair, the lid of his cap grazing his crossed hands on the table. "I was winning at first," he explained. "I had no idea I could lose so much so fast. They kept fronting the money to me when I was down, and before I knew it, that was it." He then added, "This isn't just about me. They're going to go after Mom if I don't get them their money."

"Can't we go to the police?" Anna asked.

Max shook his head. "I don't have any proof, and they have all kinds of power. Did you know he owns Barry's Laundromat now?"

Diane sat back in her chair. "What? No, they don't. Barry retired and sold it."

Max shook his head. "No, he gave them the business to cover his debts. He didn't retire. He was forced out. That's why he moved." Max rubbed his hands together, cracking his knuckles. "The cops can't help us. I wish they could."

Hours passed as the family struggled to find another solution. In order to buy Max's safety, Diane would have to hand over the one thing she loved more than anything, save for her children. She would have to sacrifice Island Time. She placed her head in her hands and sobbed.

After a few moments, Diane wiped her tears with a brush of her palm and straightened her posture. "I'd like some time alone here in the shop, so I'll lock up. Go home and we'll talk tomorrow." She hugged each of her children and then locked the door behind them. She glanced around the café. All the years she had spent building her business, and for what? To hand it over to someone who didn't love it the way she did, and who certainly didn't deserve it. Still, she knew it was time to let it go.

Her dream had died.

***

Diane woke to the ring of her cell phone. As she reached for it on her nightstand, she checked the time on her clock. It was almost four in the morning. She pressed the screen and placed the phone to her ear.

"Hello?" she answered, the sleep still evident in her voice.

"Hello, is this Diane Davis?" A man's voice asked, the tone deep and all business.

"Yes, it is. Who is this?" Diane sat upright in her bed now, brushing her hair away from her face. Her eyes adjusted to the darkness of her bedroom.

"This is Assistant Chief Robert Mayers with the Port Alene Fire Department. I'm sorry to report that we've been called to your business due to a fire."

Diane asked, her voice heightened. "A fire? How bad is it?"

"Your location being a standalone building is a plus in this instance, but I'm sorry to tell you that the property is badly damaged. You may want to get here so we can give you more details."

"Yes, sir, I'll be right there." Diane ended the call, quickly brushed her teeth and dressed, tucking her hair into a baseball cap. She then called all three of her children to tell them about the fire. They agreed to meet at the café. As she drove, she could see the smoke and flames from a distance.

When she arrived, she was greeted by Assistant Chief Mayers and told that, while they couldn't determine anything for certain yet, it appeared to be an electrical fire. Diane covered her mouth with her hand, observing her building now in ruins. Everything she had worked for had been reduced to smoldering walls and ash. Her beloved Island Time was lost.

Diane stood at the edge of the parking lot as her children arrived one by one. Once they had all gathered, they stood together, their arms around one another, watching the fire department put away their equipment.

Anna asked, "What are we going to do now?"

Diane stared at the business she had worked so hard to build and sighed. "The insurance money should cover Max's debt and then, from there, I don't know what we will do."

Anna stood staring at the fire, as her mother watched her expression change. She had connected the dots. "Mom, did you . . ."

Diane held her hand up to signal quiet. She struggled to get the words out. "They can have our money, but Island Time will always remain in the family. If we can't keep her, they can't have her either."

IF IT'S TUESDAY, THIS MUST BE MURDER

by Josh Pachter

Destination: Belgium
A bus tour through Belgium. Twenty-two passengers including one charming single gentleman and five single women, fans of E. F. Benson and Ellery Queen. Surely a murder must be on the itinerary . . .

Phillida Marlowe leaned forward and carefully applied her lipstick. Then she grinned at her mirror image, flipped her hands out to the sides and, channeling Roy Scheider in *All That Jazz*, announced "It's showtime!" to her otherwise empty hotel room.

She dropped her makeup kit into her duffel, zipped it closed, and set it outside the door for Jeremy to collect, ducked back in to make sure she hadn't left yet another phone charger behind, and headed down to the bus.

It was Tuesday, day three of Westminster Travel's eight-day, seven-night *Life in the Lowlands* excursion. Airfare from Heathrow to Zaventem and Schiphol back to Heathrow, four-star hotels every night, all breakfasts and box lunches included, welcome and farewell gala dinners (with unlimited beer, wine, and soft drinks), admissions to all local attractions, and the services of a charming guide (i.e., Phillida, who was advertised as being fluent in Dutch and Flemish but wasn't, though who cared, really, because the natives all spoke quite good English).

They'd now done their two days in Brussels—welcome gala at Chez Léon in the Rue des Bouchers, the Royal Palace, the Atomium, the obligatory pilgrimage to Manneken Pis, the Grand Place by night—and were off to Bruges this morning for a canal-boat ride, a walking tour, a pint of Straffe Hendrick at De Halve Maan . . . and then tomorrow, across the border and into Holland for the usual stops at the Keukenhof for the tulips and Kinderdijk for the windmills before winding up in Amsterdam, where they would have another Royal Palace and another ride in a canal boat, plus the Van Gogh Museum and Rembrandt's "Night Watch" at the Rijks, a brown café in the Leidseplein and their farewell gala at the Five Flies before heading home to Cheltenham or Market Snodbury or wherever it was they'd come from.

As usual, Phillida was the first one on the bus.

"Bloody Peter!" she muttered in frustration, when she saw the half-empty packet of Walkers cheddar-and-bacon crisps on the dashboard. She'd *told* their driver again and again to keep his bloody awful crisps in the glove box when he wasn't actually stuffing his face with them, but Peter rarely remembered. It was a wonder the man was able to stay focused long enough to get them from Point A to Point B without first rambling through the rest of the bloody alphabet.

She put the packet where it belonged and did a quick check of the rest of the bus, pleased to see that Jeremy had as usual swept the floor and run a dust cloth over the windows, inside and out. Although there was no assigned seating on her tours, her generally elderly group members generally staked out a claim to a particular seat on initial boarding and stuck with it for the duration. Some of them went so far as to mark their territory, like cats, leaving some personal possession on "their" seat at the end of each leg of the journey. There was Juliana Jordan's *Fodor's Guide to Belgium* at 3B, for example, and Lucia Caldwell's knitting—what on earth *was* that monstrosity? A scarf? A sweater for her Corgi?—at 7C, Emmeline Paxton's Ellery Queen paperback at 9B, Nathaniel Steele's thick hardbound compendium of six E.F. Benson novels at 11D, and Alicia Moncrief's dog-eared collection of word searches at 14C.

She left these items where they were (far be it from her to interfere with the territorial imperative!), but picked up the empty Lion Bar wrapper Mrs. Satterthwaithe had left behind at 6A and used it to protect her fingers from Mr. Satterthwaithe's wad of used tissues—the man had a simply revolting habit of hacking up gobs of phlegm at every turn of the road—at 6B.

After properly disposing of the rubbish, she glanced out the window and saw her sheep approaching across the meadow that was the Auberge Dehouck's parking lot. She squeezed out of the aisle to make room for them, and greeted them with a professionally assumed imitation of cheerfulness as they mounted the steps and filed past her to their seats.

In the lead came Jonathan Arbuthnot (tall, brush mustache, military bearing) and his traveling companion Jasper Cornwallis (squat, stocky, dirty fingernails)—in the privacy of her thoughts, she had christened them the Major and the Miner. To avoid paying the single supplement twice over, they claimed, they had chosen to share a twin-bedded room, but who did they think they were fooling, the silly old poofters?

Close behind them came the Tomkins and the Timkins, who

lived in side-by-side cottages in the Cotswolds and, as if they didn't see enough of each other fifty weeks out of the year, apparently took all their holidays together. Basil Tomkins was a head taller than his wife Samantha, and Camilla Timkins a head taller than her husband Nigel. Why didn't they simply swap spouses, Phillida wondered, to even things out a bit? Or perhaps they *had*, once upon a time, or were more evenly matched back in Quivering-on-the-Edge but livened things up by changing partners—as in a square dance—whilst far from home.

Then came Casey and Malvika Talwar, who had emigrated from the Punjab to Hammersmith ages ago. Casey couldn't possibly be an Indian name, could it? Perhaps those were his initials, K.C.—for what? Krishna Chaudri? Karma Chameleon? Kentucky Chicken?

They were followed by the Agnellis, the Epsteins, and the Federers, boarding as if by pre-arrangement in alphabetical order.

Poor Mrs. Walker—who actually *used* a walker, and whose first name was apparently protected from disclosure under the Official Secrets Act—brought up the rear, and Jeremy interrupted his stowing of the baggage to assist her up the steps.

There, that was all of them. As they settled themselves into their seats for the forty-two-mile drive to Bruges and Peter switched on the engine and adjusted his rear-view mirror, Phillida stood at the front of the bus like a queen surveying her troops on Flag Day and performed the obligatory headcount.

. . . eighteen, nineteen, twenty, twenty-one.

No, that was wrong, there were supposed to be twenty-two of them. She must have been distracted and missed one out. She started up again with Mrs. Walker in 1A and recounted.

. . . nineteen, twenty, twenty-one.

Bloody hell, one of them was missing! Annoyed, she reached for her clipboard and compared the names on the list to the faces eying her inquisitively, wondering what was delaying their departure.

Mrs. Walker in 1A, check.

The Major and the Miner in 2C and 2D, check.

Juliana Jordan in 3B, check . . .

. . . Emmeline Paxton in 9B, check.

Fred and Lila Epstein in 10A and 10B, check.

And there he was—or, rather, wasn't: Nathaniel Steele in 11D.

Most of Phillida's ladies and gentlemen were retirees traveling in pairs. This time around, Nathaniel Steele was the only gentleman traveling alone, and he had been made quite the darling of Juliana Jordan, Lucia Caldwell, Emmeline Paxton, and Alicia Moncrief, the four solo women on the tour. (Technically, Mrs. Walker was also a solo woman, but she alone had seemed completely immune to Mr. Steele's considerable charms.) He had probably lost track of the time, was still standing before his bathroom mirror adjusting the toupee he seemed not to realize everyone in the group knew full well he affected.

Well, there was nothing for it, if they were going to remain on schedule. With a long-suffering sigh, Phillida climbed down from the bus and trekked back across the parking lot to the hotel, climbed the broad flight of stairs to the second floor and knocked on the door of room 213.

"Mr. Steele," she called. "Wakey wakey!"

There was no response.

She rapped again, more sharply this time. "Time to go, Mr. Steele! We're all on the bus!"

Silence.

Truly wound up now, she rattled the doorknob to get the old fool's attention—and was startled when the door swung open at her touch.

Hesitantly, not wanting to embarrass the man if he was still in his smalls, she peeked into the room.

Nathaniel Steele was lying stretched out on the bed, fully clothed but sound asleep, his suitcase open beside him, a folded city map of Brussels clutched in his hands.

Phillida marched over to the bed and tapped his shoulder.

He did not awaken.

She shook him purposefully, hard enough to dislodge his toupee, which slid from his head onto his pillow and lay there like a dozing Pomeranian.

Mr. Steele slept on, and it was only then that Phillida noticed his chest was not rising and falling with his breathing, and there were angry bruises on his throat, and he *wasn't* breathing, and he was dead.

***

"I am sorry to keep you all waiting like this," said Detective Inspector Bavo Van Laerhoven, his English accented but perfectly understandable. The twenty-four faces that stared at him wore an assortment of expressions: frustration at the long delay, boredom, curiosity, and of course horror at the knowledge that one of their number had been strangled to death.

"We have completed our examination of the—ah, of the deceased," he continued, "and I'm afraid we will have to try your patience a bit longer."

The next hour was spent taking statements from each of the

twenty-four of them—twenty-one passengers, Peter the driver, Jeremy the baggage handler, and Phillida the tour guide. By the end of that time, a clearer picture had begun to take shape.

Nathaniel Steele—a lifelong bachelor—had spent thirty years doing something both terribly uninteresting and yet terribly important in the Civil Service. Now, in his retirement, he had decided to see a bit more of the world than his sheltered corner of Whitehall, and he had signed up for his first organized tour, *this* tour, Westminster Travels' *Life in the Lowlands*.

He had kept himself to himself on the bus, slowly reading his way through his thick collection of E.F. Benson novels, but he had been affable enough during the various sightseeing expeditions and mealtimes of the past two days and had in fact paid courtly attention to the group's five single women, even the uninterested Mrs. Walker.

The medical examiner would not have much to say about the time of Mr. Steele's demise until he had completed his postmortem examination, but the indications he had been able to observe at the *locus delicti*—body temperature compared with room temperature, rigor mortis, lividity—suggested that death had occurred no more than twelve and no less than seven hours before the discovery of the body—thus between eight o'clock last night and one o'clock this morning. The victim had been seen in the hotel bar the previous evening, and had enjoyed a pint of Trappist beer with the Epsteins before the three of them had gone up to their rooms at approximately eleven, which narrowed the death window by a further three hours.

Between 11 p.m. and 8 a.m., each of the couples alibied themselves for the relevant time period: the Agnellis, the Epsteins, the Federers, the Satterthwaites, the Talwars, the Timkins and Tomkins, even the Major and the Minor. By eleven o'clock, they were all tucked up in bed, and two by two, like animals trooping onto Noah's Ark, they'd gone down to breakfast at seven and hadn't been out of each other's sight except for the occasional brief trip toodle-oo.

That left the five single women, Peter, Jeremy, and Phillida unaccounted for—and the M.E. had concluded from the size of the bruises on the dead man's neck that his killer had small hands, which seemed to let out Peter and Jeremy.

"When are you thinking it will be possible for us to be leaving for Bruges, sir?" asked Casey Talwar timidly.

"*Je suis désolé*," the inspector replied, "but this bus isn't going anywhere until the murder has been solved."

"But," Lucia Caldwell protested, "we're supposed to be at the

Basilica of the Holy Blood in Bruges at two this afternoon for the veneration of the Relic of the Holy Blood!"

"I expect you're going to miss it, madam," said Van Laerhoven.

"But we can't! It's the most important part of our whole trip!"

"Not any more, I'm afraid. The most important part of your trip as of this moment is determining who strangled your Mr. Steele."

A heavy silence descended upon the bus and its passengers.

"I've no idea if this will help," said Phillida, "but I've just realized something."

"Yes?" the inspector drawled.

"His clothes," said Phillida.

"I am—how do you say it?—entirely ears."

"Well, the clothes he was wearing when I . . . when I found him were the same clothes he wore to dinner last night, and—"

"—And he was such a meticulous man," interrupted Juliana Jordan. "Surely he wouldn't have worn the same outfit two days in a row!"

"Men don't wear *outfits*," Basil Tomkins harrumphed. "We wear *clothes*."

"Either way," the inspector mused, "that suggests that he must have been killed before undressing for bed, closer to the early side of the medical examiner's estimate of time of death. Thank you, Miss Marlowe, that's a useful point. But now we—"

"Why don't you use your little gray cells, like that Belgian in that movie with Ingmar Bergman?" said Gino Agnelli.

"Ing*rid* Bergman," Lila Epstein corrected him primly. "Ing*mar* Bergman was a director, and he didn't direct *The Murder on the Orient Express*."

Inspector Van Laerhoven blinked. "I have no idea what you're talking about," he said.

"Hercules Porrot," Mr. Agnelli explained. "How can you not know him, he's a famous Belgian policeman?"

"Pwah-ROW," said Emmeline Paxton indulgently. "Air-KYOOL Pwah-ROW. And he was a fictional private investigator, not an actual policeman, although, according to the backstory Agatha Christie provided for him, he—"

The inspector cut her off with a shake of his head. "Never heard of him," he said.

"Oh, you *must* read him," said Emmeline Paxton. "I adore classic detective fiction."

"I don't read fiction," the inspector murmured. "It bores me."

"But you're missing so much," Miss Paxton protested. "The red herrings, the deductive reasoning, the impossible crimes, the dying— Just a moment. What if Mr. Steele left a dying message behind?"

Van Laerhoven's stolid face was completely expressionless. "I have *no idea* what you're talking about," he said again.

"A dying message," Jeremy jumped in, eager to help. "I know about that—my mum's got the 'ole Ellery Queen series on DVD. It was on the telly about a fousand years ago."

"And—?" the inspector prompted.

"And a dying message is somefing they done all the time. Some bloke gets chopped, but before 'e expires 'e writes down some mysterious clue to the name of 'is killer."

"And why doesn't he simply write the *name* of his killer?" Van Laerhoven asked, his interest piqued.

Jeremy's face twisted. "I—I dunno. 'E just *don't*."

"If he did," Emmeline Paxton explained patiently, "the killer might come back and see it—and, of course, then he'd destroy it. *Did* Mr. Steele write anything before he died?"

"Nothing," said the inspector flatly. "We found no paper in his room, not even a newspaper."

"Unless he wrote something on that map of Brussels he was holding," said Phillida.

The inspector shook his head. "No pen or pencil, either. And there was nothing written on the map."

"Well, perhaps the map *itself* was a message," Phillida said slowly. "After all, there was no reason for him to have it in his hands when he died."

"His suitcase was open on the bed beside him," said the inspector. "He was packing. Perhaps he was putting it away when he was attacked."

"Nonsense," rumbled Jonathan Arbuthnot. "If someone attacked the chappie, he'd've dropped the map and defended himself."

"Perhaps it *was* a message, then," said Frannie Satterthwaite. "The killer choked him and left him for dead. But he *wasn't* dead. He regained consciousness, but he knew he was dying and wanted to tell the police who'd attacked him."

"He had nothing to write with," her husband picked up smoothly, "and nothing to write *on*. But he saw the map he'd been packing and was able to grab it before he died."

"But what does it mean?" asked the inspector, intrigued now. "A map of Brussels. What was he trying to say?"

"Use your little gray cells," Gino Agnelli shouted, and Emmeline Paxton waved her copy of *The Siamese Twin Mystery* and said, "If only Ellery Queen was here!"

Phillida Marlowe stared at the paperback, mesmerized by its brightly colored cover. And then she walked down the aisle to row 11 and hoisted Nathaniel Steele's thick volume from seat 11D, where the dead man had left it.

"*Six Novels by E.F. Benson*," she read aloud. And then she opened the book to the table of contents and gasped.

"*Miss Mapp*," she said, reading out the title of one of the six novels.

The bus fell instantly silent, twenty-three pairs of eyes fixed on her intently, all but Lucia Caldwell, who never looked up from her knitting.

"Yes?" the inspector demanded. "And what comes after *Miss Mapp*?"

"I told him I thought we might make a lovely couple," Miss Caldwell said calmly, her steel needles never hesitating in their rhythmic clacking. "But he laughed at me, called me a silly old cow, said he wouldn't marry me if I was the last woman on Earth."

"*Mapp and Lucia*," Phillida Marlowe read aloud. "*Queen Lucia. Lucia in London. Lucia's Progress.*" She paused for a moment, and then read the final title: "*Lucia in Trouble*."

"He was such a disgusting little man," said Miss Caldwell, clucking in irritation at a dropped stitch. "And now I suppose I won't make it to the Basilica of the Holy Blood on time, after all."

Detective Inspector Van Laerhoven walked purposefully down the aisle to seat 7C and took the knitting from Lucia's hands.

"It would have been such a treat," she said.

THE BREAKER BOY

by Harriette Sackler

Destination: Pinewood, Pennsylvania
Life in a Pennsylvania coal-mining town is hard and bleak. The death of just another child working in the breaker doesn't seem to bother management. But it certainly bothers others.

When Franklin Dawes entered the town limits of Pinewood, Pennsylvania, he thought he'd arrived in the very bowels of hell. The lengthy rail trip from New York City, followed by a day's travel via rented horse and buggy, had taken him through scenic landscapes as yet untouched by the hands of men. But now, he found himself in a dark place. A haze of black dust blocked the sun, and everything about him bespoke of poverty and despair.

Franklin had made the trip to do what he did best. As an investigative reporter for the *New York Gazette*, his stories uncovered the plight of the working poor in industries that exploited those who were powerless. He had written about the sweatshops of the Lower East Side in his own city. He'd traveled to the South to learn about the exploitation of those who worked in the cotton mills. And now, he had come to learn about the working conditions in the coal mines of Pennsylvania. Even in this year of 1899, one year from the turn of the twentieth century, newly legislated labor laws were regularly ignored by those in pursuit of the almighty dollar.

As a newspaper reporter, Franklin knew that he didn't have a chance of being given permission to enter the mines, so a bit of deception would be required. He called the headquarters of the Liberty Coal Mining Company in Scranton, and explained that he was writing a textbook on the mining of anthracite coal in Pennsylvania and the surrounding states. By speaking with management, mine supervisors, and employees, he hoped to gather the information he needed to present a comprehensive book detailing the practices and procedures utilized industry-wide. His cover, which was close to the truth, was accepted.

After checking into the only boarding house in town and settling his horse in a nearby stable, Franklin decided to head to the colliery. It was mid-afternoon, several hours until the mine closed for the day. He'd been given directions to both the mine and the residences of management by the proprietor of the boarding house. Looking out the front door to the right, he could see quite spacious and well-tended homes terraced on a hill. To his left was a steep path leading to the workers' houses and, beyond them, the structures that comprised the Pinewood mine.

As he made his way toward the mine, Franklin passed through the company-owned shantytown that was the miners' village. The ramshackle dwellings were unpainted and looked as though a strong wind would reduce them to rubble. The streets were unpaved and muddy. They reeked of despair. Young children played outdoors, many barefoot, and most in clothing that was no better than rags.

What kind of place was this? Franklin had the uneasy feeling that his investigation would uncover more than he anticipated.

***

Franklin spent hours before the end of the work day with Liam Ryan, Pinewood's general manager. Short and stocky with a scowling face, the man's appearance resembled that of a bulldog. His booming voice and abrupt manner left Franklin with the impression that this was not a man to be trifled with: a man who ruled with an iron hand.

"My sole responsibility here at Pinewood is to make money for the management of the Liberty Coal Mining Company. The day I fail is the last day of my employment here. You can be damn sure of that. And the same goes for everyone who works here."

Obviously, Ryan pulled no punches and was acutely aware of the part each employee played in the scheme of things.

Franklin learned a good deal about coal mining over the next few hours. There was no doubt in his mind that work in a colliery, the mine itself, as well as in the surrounding buildings that processed the coal, was dirty and dangerous. In an area where the mine was the only source of employment, workers were a captive resource. They were forced to accept the wages and conditions set by the company. They truly were at the mercy of the mine owners.

At 6:00 p.m., an earsplitting whistle blast marked the end of the workday. Within minutes, workers blackened by coal dust began to make their way out of the mine's entrance. Franklin was shocked to see young boys descend from the breaker, the large building where coal was separated from impurities.

"Who are those children?" Franklin turned to Ryan with both shock and concern etched on his face.

"Those are the breaker boys."

"But they look too young to be working in the mines."

"The youngest is about eight years old. They work the breaker until they can move into mining the coal." Ryan was unperturbed by the idea of employment of children.

"Shouldn't they be at home? In school?"

"Not around here, Mr. Dawes. When there are mouths to feed, the young 'uns are sent out to work. Just the way things are."

Franklin now knew what the focus of his story would be.

***

Rather than leaving the grounds around the mine, men and boys gathered on the pathway leading from the breaker to the village road.

"Why aren't the workers leaving to return home?"

"One of the boys died in the breaker this morning. He fell into a coal chute and was smothered." Ryan spoke without any evidence of sadness.

"If the little fellow lost his life this morning, why wasn't he brought out earlier?" Franklin was having difficulty wrapping his mind around the information Ryan has just shared.

"The owners wouldn't take too kindly to the mine shutting down during work hours. Nothing we could do for the boy, anyhow."

All Franklin could do was shake his head in bewilderment. There were no words.

***

After all the workers had exited the mine and its adjacent buildings, forming two long rows to the road, a man emerged from the breaker with a filthy bundle in his arms. As he moved toward his fellow workers, Franklin realized that the bundle was the body of the dead boy. The man's face was expressionless, but tears created furrows on his coal-blackened skin. He walked slowly, shoulders slumped, feet dragging. Everyone stood silently with hats over hearts, mouths moving in silent prayer. Then the two rows of mine workers turned and followed the bereaved father toward the village. Franklin followed.

They slowly walked until they reached a house in the village that looked much like all the others. The bereaved miner went through the door while everyone else remained outside. There was silence for a moment, broken only by the coughing of men whose lungs were clogged with coal dust. Then came an otherworldly scream as a mother was told that her child was dead.

***

For the better part of a week, Franklin spent his days at Pinewood, observing. He traveled into the depths of the mine, thanking the powers that be that he didn't have to earn a living this way. The only light came from the lanterns workers wore on their hats. The suffocating air made it difficult to breathe. But the men and what appeared to be adolescent boys seemed to take it all in stride and worked with barely any respite for ten hours a day.

The breaker was the place that affected Franklin the most. It was a massive building with ear-splitting noise from machinery and the roar of coal traveling down chutes at breakneck speed. Young boys sat on rows of wooden benches, picking slate, rock, and other impurities from the oncoming coal. They controlled the flow with their feet, their bodies bent for hour upon hour, their fingers callused and numb. Breaker bosses walked among them, watching for slackers and boys who dozed from exhaustion. When such a boy was spotted, a rap from a heavy stick wielded by the boss was swiftly applied.

It was all difficult for Franklin to fathom. It was clear from his discussions with Mr. Ryan that the mine workers were barely paid a subsistence wage, and for families to survive, they had no choice but to send their young sons to work to supplement meager incomes. As a man who had come from a middle-class family, it was an anathema for him to see good people exploited this way. But, as a journalist, it was incumbent upon him to objectively report his observations and hope the stories that appeared in his newspaper would be a catalyst for change.

***

On the first Sunday after he'd arrived in Pinewood, Franklin sat in his room and worked on his investigative article. He intended to spend the next week interviewing residents and collecting any other information that would assist him in providing an accurate picture of life in a coal mining town. He was thoroughly immersed in his work until his empty stomach signaled that suppertime had arrived.

When he entered the boarding house's dining room, he quickly realized that something was awry. The other guests were chattering away about something that had happened during the early hours of the day. Franklin was shocked to discover that Liam Ryan, the mine's general manager, had met an unfortunate demise. It appeared that, while arising from his bed, Ryan had tripped and fallen, hitting his head against a heavy oak chest of drawers, thus splitting his skull. When he didn't appear for his breakfast before leaving for church services, his housekeeper went to check on him. She'd found him lying on his bedroom floor in a pool of blood and was able to determine that he was no longer breathing. She wasted no time in summoning the police who arrived shortly thereafter and declared the poor man expired. The room appeared intact and the only item missing was Ryan's pocket watch. But, since nothing else was amiss, it was decided that the watch could have been lost at the mine or in transit about town. It was determined an unfortunate accident, nothing more.

Having reported on a number of deaths for his newspaper, Mr. Ryan's didn't sit well with Franklin. Although it was possible that a terrible accident had caused his demise, it didn't seem probable. Ryan was a man who spent his days moving from one precarious location in the mine to another. His sense of balance provided him with the sure-footedness needed to avoid personal injury, and his unimpaired eyesight and sound judgment allowed him to make his way about in the darkness and haze of the underground chambers he supervised. It didn't feel right.

***

After supper, Franklin made his way to Ryan's home. When the housekeeper, eyes bloodshot and swollen, responded to his knock on the front door, Franklin introduced himself and explained his mission in Pinewood. He asked if he might visit the bedroom where Mr. Ryan lost his life, explaining he'd be better able to complete his book research if he had the full picture of what had happened to Mr. Ryan.

"Well, I suppose there's no harm in that," she concluded. "I'm Greta Caffrey, and I've worked right here in Mr. Ryan's home since the day he came to Pinewood. He was a good man and always treated me fairly and with kindness. Such a shame that the mineworkers never got to see that side of him. He had to be hard on them at the colliery, that's the way the owners wanted it. If there's anything you can find, go to it."

Mrs. Caffrey led him upstairs to a spacious bedroom that had yet to be put back in order since the police had visited the house. The heavy mahogany furniture and dark accessories spoke of the lack of a woman's touch. When he visited the mine, Franklin had learned from Ryan that he'd lost his wife in childbirth years before, and had never remarried.

"I have work to do downstairs, so I'll leave you to it." Mrs. Caffrey turned and left the room.

Franklin looked around him. A large splatter of blood had dried on the bare wood floor near a chest of drawers facing the bed. There were no obstructions between the two pieces of furniture. No rug that could cause a man to lose his footing. Franklin then checked the bed linens, but found no trace of blood there either. He knelt down to look under the bed, but, except for some dust, there was nothing to see. A chair on the other side of the room held the clothes Ryan had worn the day before.

Franklin moved to the window. Heavy draperies covered the open sash. He pulled them apart and looked out at an enclosed porch below that ran the length of the house. As he turned away from the window, something small and metallic on the window ledge caught his eye. He retrieved a tarnished button that must have fallen off a shirt or jacket. How had it gotten there? Maybe Ryan had lost it while opening the window before getting into bed. Franklin put the button in his pocket and left the room.

***

On Monday morning, Franklin arrived at the mine just as the workday began. Joshua Gridley, Pinewood's assistant manager, had already assumed Mr. Ryan's responsibilities to ensure there was no interruption in coal output and processing.

"Ah, good morning, Mr. Dawes. As you can surmise, we've already received word from Liberty's owners that I'm to assume the title of general manager here. Life goes on, and so does business."

"I was sorry to hear about Mr. Ryan's death. Such an unfortunate accident."

"Yes, it was unfortunate. We'd worked together over twenty years and enjoyed a friendly and cooperative relationship. You know, death is not a surprising occurrence in this industry. Coal mining is a dangerous business. But tripping and dying in your own bedroom? Hard to imagine." Gridley shook his head as he lit his pipe.

"Well," Franklin said, "on another subject, this will be my last day at the mine. I'll spend the next few days visiting with the families of both miners and supervisors and walking about the town. Then I'll be on my way back to New York."

"Feel free, Mr. Dawes. You got the OK from Liberty, so go at it. Stop by my house, why don't you. I'll tell Mrs. Gridley to expect you. I'm sure she'd be happy to have you to tea.

***

Franklin took Gridley up on his invitation and spent a very long hour with Eudora Gridley. A short, stout woman with auburn hair piled on her head and dark brown eyes, she was dressed as though she was on her way to a ball. She talked incessantly about her dislike of Pinewood and the lack of entertainment and shops in which she could purchase the finer things in life. She expressed disdain for the locals and described the miners and their families as uncultured, dirty, and, worst of all, poor. She felt no empathy for the mineworkers and their families and didn't seem to make the connection between their hard work and the privileged life she led.

"You know, Mr. Dawes, my husband and I were extremely distressed to learn of Mr. Ryan's death. When his dear departed wife, Bessie, was alive, we spent a great deal of time with them and enjoyed their company. How ironic that his unfortunate demise elevates my husband to the highest position at the mine."

"Yes," murmured Franklin. "I'm sure that bittersweet irony is deeply disturbing to you."

"Oh, it is, it surely is."

***

After leaving the Gridley's comfortable home, Franklin made his way to the company store which was located just outside the miners' village. It was quite a large establishment, filled with every kind of merchandise one would need, from fabric to food to hardware and mining supplies. He wanted to purchase some sweets for the village children and tins of coffee and loaves of bread for their parents. He found it surprising that, overall, the prices of goods were higher here in this depressed town than they were in New York City.

When Franklin collected the items he wished to purchase, he made his way to the counter where a clerk stood ready to assist him.

"Guess you don't get many miners shopping here. Your prices are very high," he observed.

"Well, there are a few other stores in Pinewood, but miners have to shop here."

"Why is that?" asked Franklin, thoroughly confused.

"Well," the clerk replied, "if the bosses find out the miners go to any other establishment, they lose their jobs on the spot."

Franklin realized this practice was just one more way to exploit the workers. He felt enormous disgust at the greediness and heartlessness of the company. Just another outrage to report in his story.

***

The following day, Franklin made his way to the miners' village along with a heavy sack filled with staples. He desperately wished to have the opportunity to speak with family members who could give him another perspective on life in Pinewood. He knocked on the door of the first dwelling he came to. A barefoot little girl in a worn dress responded, looking at him with suspicion.

"Hello to you," Franklin greeted her. "Is your mother at home?"

"Mama," she yelled to someone in the gloomy interior. "A man wants to see ya."

In a moment, a tired-looking woman came to the door. She was wiping her hands on a dirty rag and looked fearfully at Franklin.

"What ya want?" she asked.

He explained to her who he was and indicated that he just wanted to speak with her for a few moments about life in Pinewood. He pulled out some coffee and biscuits from the sack he carried.

"Please," Franklin said. "I'm not from the company and mean you no harm. I'll be leaving Pinewood tomorrow to return to my home in New York and wanted to speak to several families to learn about their lives in a mining town."

"Mister," she said, "this is a hard life. No matter how we try, we can barely keep food on the table for the young 'uns. Every day, I wonder if my husband and boys will be coming back from the mines. If my babies will live or die from the sickness that comes every winter. But, there ain't no choice."

Franklin heard similar words spoken at every home he visited. He was glad he was able to leave a tin of coffee, or some candy for the children, or a loaf of bread at each household. Lord knew, he wished he could do more. Hopefully, the story his newspaper would run would open the eyes of progressives who might make a difference.

***

The shrill whistle that marked the end of the workday sounded. Franklin knew it would only be a short time before the exhausted mineworkers would return to their homes, anxious for dinner and rest. But he had one more house to visit, the most difficult stop of all. When he arrived at the last decrepit dwelling in the village, he took a deep breath and knocked on the door. In a moment a woman heavy with child stood on the threshold and eyed him suspiciously. He noted that, at some point in her life, she must have been beautiful. Black hair now laced with grey hung limply around her face. Cornflower blue eyes were dulled with pain. Surprisingly, her skin looked soft and clear.

She looked at him quizzically, surely wondering why he could possibly be on her doorstep.

"Good day, Mrs. . . ." he said, realizing that he didn't even know her name.

"Annie. Annie McCoy," she responded.

"Mrs. McCoy, my name is Franklin Dawes. I come from New York City and have been in town for about ten days, gathering information about coal mining. I had just arrived the day your son suffered the terrible accident that ended his life. Before I left Pinewood, I wanted to pay my respects to you and your family."

Annie McCoy's shoulders slumped and she bowed her head. Franklin's kind and sincere manner seemed to break through her apparent reluctance to speak to him.

"Why, thank ya, Mr. Dawes. I'm beholdin' to ya for your nice words. I'm cookin' supper right now, but yer welcome to come inside and meet my husband and boys when they get here."

"I'd like that, Mrs. McCoy, if that wouldn't be troublesome."

"Naw, come on in and set for a while. Lucy, come on out and meet our visitor."

A young woman carrying a toddler came from a back room. She was a younger version of her mother, still possessing a brightness that hadn't yet been extinguished.

"Mr. Dawes, this here is Lucy, our oldest, and our little Johnny. Can I git you a cup of tea? Don't have much else."

"No, please don't bother. As a matter of fact, I've brought you some things from the company store I thought you might like to have. Just as a way to say hello."

"We don't abide by charity, Mr. Dawes. But I don't get the feelin' you meant to offer any. So, thank ya."

Just then, the door flew open and a man and two boys strode in. They were covered in coal dust from head to toe. Mrs. McCoy introduced Franklin to the rest of her family and explained why the visitor had come by.

"Pleased to meet ya," Andrew McCoy greeted him. "Won't shake yer hand till I clean up though. Same fer my boys."

Billy, the oldest, looked to be about fifteen, and Mikey, about twelve.

"Mr. Dawes, we don't usually take to strangers round here, but you seem to be a good fella. Why don't ya sit a spell and share supper with us?" Mr. McCoy looked at him expectantly.

Franklin knew how precious and scarce food was to the McCoys, but he appreciated the invite and didn't want to insult their generosity.

"I'd be honored to break bread with you. Thank you for your hospitality."

***

After a pleasant meal of a thin stew with the bread that he had brought for the family, Franklin rose to take his leave. He thanked them for both the supper and the enlightening conversation.

"Mikey," Mr. McCoy addressed his son. "You walk Mr. Dawes back to the boardin' house. Ain't safe for him to be goin' round alone after dark."

Mikey rose and reached up to the clothes hooks near the door to retrieve his jacket. As he did, it fell to the floor. Franklin, wanting to be helpful, reached to pick the jacket up. His back was to Mikey and the rest of the family, obscuring their view. Within a split second, Franklin's reporter's eye, so used to being observant, registered two things. First, he noted that a button on the jacket was missing. And, second, a gold watch had slipped from a pocket.

Without batting an eye, Franklin scooped up the watch and put it back in the pocket, then handed the jacket to Mikey.

"I'll welcome your company on the walk back to town."

***

Before he left Pinewood the following morning, Franklin visited the company store to pay in full the McCoy's outstanding bill. He also left funds to cover their purchases for the next month, explaining to the clerk that it was in memory of the son they lost at the breaker.

In his role as a reporter investigating coal mining and the life of the workers and their families who suffered so, just barely scratching out a living in the mines, he didn't feel it was his responsibility to do the work of the police. As far as he was concerned, Liam Ryan, the late mine manager, had died of an unfortunate accident.

DEATH ON THE BEACH

by Shawn Reilly Simmons

Destination: Ocean City, Maryland
Was the death of a young girl found half-buried on the beach an accident or something more sinister? Newlywed Ivy Derringer feels compelled to investigate.

"To the left a little more," the woman huffed from under her wide brimmed beach hat. Her cheeks glowed red even though the day was new and the sun still gaining its strength.

Fergal pulled the wooden umbrella post from the sand and hovered it a few inches over. "Here?"

"I don't know. What do you think?" The woman's little girl stood nearby, gaping at him with a thumb tucked between her lips. Her tiny Ocean City T-shirt was tie-dyed pink and orange.

"Umbrella rental is three dollars a day, or fifteen for the week," Fergal said.

"OK then," the woman said, rooting through the bottles of sunscreen and brightly colored towels for her wallet.

"Look, mommy, shells." The little girl pulled her thumb from her mouth and pointed at the ground.

"What's today's weather going to be like?" the woman asked as she handed Fergal three crumpled bills.

"The sun will be splitting the stones around midday." Fergal pocketed the bills and unfurled the umbrella, jabbing the wooden pole into the sand. A jolt went through his forearms and he pulled the pointed stake back out again.

"I'm sorry, splitting the what?" the woman asked.

Fergal jammed the pole into the ground again, coming up against the same resistance. "Splitting the stones. It's an expression back home in Ireland. Means it will be hot."

The woman watched Fergal stab at the ground again. "Is there a rock under there?"

"Not many large rocks on the Maryland shore," Fergal said with a grunt. "There, I've broken through. I'll just straighten her a bit." He pulled it out once again then suddenly dropped it at his feet and held his arms tight against his body.

The point on the stake was stained with blood.

"Oh my God!" the woman cried.

"Pretty shells," the little girl said, pointing.

Fergal looked down and saw four pink polished fingernails glinting in the sun. He turned and ran, legs pumping up the dunes to the Riviera Grande Beach Club.

***

"What's all that commotion down there, I wonder?" Ivy Derringer gazed from the balcony at the beach below as she sipped her coffee, her silky robe rippling around her feet.

"Hm?" her husband Bruce mumbled from behind his newspaper. He sat at the dining room table just inside, an untouched half of a grapefruit in front of him.

"I said, what do you think is happening on the beach?" Ivy asked over her shoulder. A crowd had gathered on the sand below their high-rise building, forming a loose circle around something she couldn't see. A beach patrol dune buggy puttered over and two police officers hopped off and joined the group.

"I don't know, dear," Bruce said. "You're the one enjoying the view."

Ivy turned and raised an eyebrow at him, which went unseen behind the morning news. "The police are here."

Bruce folded his paper and hoisted himself up, scraping his chair across the hardwood floor. He joined his wife on the terrace and stepped forward for a better look. "Maybe a dolphin has beached itself."

"And the police were called?" Ivy said, clicking her tongue.

"They might have been," Bruce shrugged. "Who would you call if you came upon a sick or injured dolphin?"

Ivy took another sip of coffee. "Maybe someone swam out too far last night and drowned."

Bruce looped his arm around his wife's slender waist and brushed a kiss against her neck. "Only a crazy person would swim in these waters at night. Look, it's nothing that concerns us. Come back inside." He tugged her gently toward the sliding glass door.

"It does concern us. They're right in front of our condo," Ivy said, sweeping her gaze across the sand. A group of workers from the beach club next door had gathered on the club's deck, shielding their eyes as they watched the police.

One of the officers went to the dune buggy and unlatched a shovel from the side just as an ambulance pulled up in the beach club's parking lot, its red lights circling silently. The officer with the shovel dug carefully as the paramedics made their way over, bouncing a stretcher across the dunes.

Ivy put a hand over her mouth and continued to watch. She couldn't quite see what they were uncovering, but she knew it wasn't a beached dolphin.

"Ivy," Bruce said. "Please come inside, my love."

Ivy reluctantly joined him at the table, eyeing his untouched grapefruit. "You should eat your breakfast."

"Breakfast," Bruce sighed. "Yes, wouldn't want it to get cold." He poked halfheartedly at it then popped a section into his mouth. He picked up his coffee cup and winced after taking a sip.

"Agnes!" he shouted at the swinging door leading to the kitchen. "Hot coffee, please!"

"Darling, must you shout that way? Why are you so grouchy?" Ivy said, her gaze drifting back toward the balcony.

"I'm sorry," Bruce mumbled. "The phone woke me up in the middle of the night and I couldn't get back to sleep right away." The sound of a pan clattering to the floor in the kitchen was muffled by the closed door. Bruce grimaced, then pulled open his newspaper again.

"I'll get the coffee," Ivy said, standing up and pushing her way into the kitchen.

Agnes was on her knees, a bread basket in her lap, plucking muffins from the floor. Ivy watched her put a few into the basket with shaking hands, then cleared her throat.

"Oh, sorry, Mrs. Derringer," Agnes said. She pulled herself up to standing, her hand heavy on the countertop. "I was just bringing the muffins."

"Are you OK?" Ivy said, eyeing one that had come to rest against the base of the refrigerator.

"Yes, I'm just a butterfingers this morning," Agnes said. Her faded red hair was intertwined with silver strands and piled in a loose bun on top of her head.

Ivy went to the coffee maker and grabbed the carafe, glancing quickly at the notepad next to the phone on the wall. A few numbers and letters, and a half-finished grocery list were jotted in Agnes's shaky hand, and a tall stack of unopened mail sat beneath it on the counter. When she turned back around, she saw Agnes was already out the door through to the dining room, her basket of dropped muffins in hand.

"Here you go, dear," Ivy said as she topped off her husband's mug in the dining room.

Agnes fussed around the table, straightening silverware and refolding the linen napkins. She swept a handful of crumbs from the tablecloth onto the floor.

Bruce crumpled his newspaper into his lap and sighed. "Agnes,

I know you weren't raised in a barn."

"Dear, let's just enjoy our—" Ivy began, stopping abruptly when her husband shot her a glance.

"Oops, I forgot the butter," Agnes asked.

"No butter," Ivy said quickly. "Mr. Derringer must mind his heart."

Bruce's bald head blushed pink and he bit his lower lip. "No thank you, Agnes. And please remember we don't throw crumbs on the floor."

"Oh," Agnes laughed, waving a weathered hand in the air. "I always vacuum after breakfast. It's how I do things."

Bruce rolled his eyes at Ivy, who shrugged in response as Agnes bustled her way back toward the kitchen.

***

From her chair on the deck of the Riviera Grande Beach Club, Ivy watched a man in a rumpled tweed jacket pace inside a circle of yellow police tape on the beach . Access to the beach was off limits, the police turning away families ladened down with coolers and umbrellas.

"Your Virgin Mary," Connie, the owner of the beach club, said, setting it down on the table next to Ivy. "With extra olives like you asked, Mrs. Derringer."

"Thanks, Connie," Ivy said. She pulled off her round white sunglasses and set them down on the table next to her drink. She crossed her long tan legs, smoothing out her linen shorts.

"Sure you don't want a splash of vodka in there?" Connie asked. "A day like today we all could use a stiff one." She gazed at the men on the beach with red-rimmed eyes, a troubled look on her face.

"No, thanks," Ivy said, sliding her hand down her flat belly. "It's not good for the baby."

"You're expecting, are you?" Connie said with surprise. "Couldn't tell from looking at you."

"Well, it's only been a couple of days, it's a honeymoon baby," Ivy said. "I feel as big as a house already." She pulled the plastic sword from the drink and slid an olive from it, popping it into her mouth.

"That's some happy news on a sad day. Congratulations to you and Mr. Derringer."

"Don't tell anyone yet," Ivy said.

"Oh, of course not," Connie said with a small chuckle. "It will be something to see, old Bruce with an infant on the beach next summer. Seems like yesterday we were just kids ourselves, but that's a long time ago now, before you were even a glimmer, I'm sure." Connie's cheeks reddened and she quickly added, "I know you'll make a beautiful family."

Ivy smiled and adjusted the strap of her bikini top.

"And where is Mr. Derringer today?" Connie asked.

"Golfing with a client. I was going to sit and read on the beach but . . ." Ivy's eyes flicked to the police as they began to fill in the hole. "Have you heard anything else about what happened?" She lifted her chin toward the ocean.

"The poor girl, Brianne," Connie said. She pulled a dishtowel from her apron string and wiped her hands. "The police said she must have gotten langered, then gone out for a moonlight walk. She fell in that hole, probably dug earlier in the day by a beachgoer who left without filling it back in. They reckon she fell asleep or passed out and the tide and wet sand did her in. Poor Fergal stabbed her with an umbrella pole to add insult to injury. He's still a wreck about it. It's a tragedy the whole way around."

"That's terrible," Ivy murmured. "Brianne was one of your employees? I don't remember seeing her here."

"She'd just started working for me last week," Connie said, nodding. "She was waitressing at The Salty Dog over on the bay side, but had a falling out with the owner, Don. He's the salty one, you ask me. Can get handsy after he's had a few from what I hear. Anyway, I hired her on. Felt bad for the girl being so far away from home without a job."

"How sad for her parents," Ivy said, slipping her sunglasses back on.

"Aye," Connie said. "It's just her mom back home, Brianne said. Poor woman. Summer's almost over, too. Brianne would've been back home in two weeks' time, then off to university."

"So you have kids come over to work here every summer?" Ivy asked.

"Yeah, for twenty years now. You've seen the photos, all along the back wall. Scores of kids have come through my beach club, so many apply every year I have a waiting list going. I give them work and a room during the last summer before they head off to school. It's a chance for them to see America, well, the Maryland shore at least, and pocket a few dollars in the meantime. I had a good group this year, no lazy ones, no fraternizing among the staff. No major problems, until now at least."

"Connie," someone shouted from inside. "Customer at the bar."

"That's me then," Connie said. "Let me know if I can get you anything else, Mrs. Derringer."

***

Ivy emerged from the beach club's ladies room a half hour later and paused for a moment, looking up at the pictures tacked to the back wall. She swept her eyes across the rows of photos, sun bleached and faded the farther back in time they went, eyeing the smiling fresh faces. She turned and walked to the bar slowly, then slid onto one of the stools and ordered a glass of wine.

"You sure, Mrs. Derringer?" Connie asked from behind the bar. "What about the baby?" she added in a whisper.

"Yes, I'm sure," Ivy sighed. "False alarm. And please call me Ivy."

Connie poured Ivy a generous portion of pale white wine and slid the glass over. "Sorry about that. There will be lots of children in your future, I'm sure."

Ivy bit the inside of her cheek and gazed up at a line of Polaroid photos over the liquor bottles behind the bar, the current crop of employees. Someone had written their names under each of their smiling faces.

"That's Brianne, then?" Ivy asked, pointing over Connie's head at the photos. Connie un-tacked it from the wood and looked it over.

"That's her," Connie said. "God rest her soul." She handed the photo to Ivy. Brianne had dark red ringlet curls and bright green eyes, almost the same color as Ivy's. Red freckles were splashed across her sun-kissed cheeks.

"She's beautiful," Ivy said.

"Aye," Connie said. "Beauty can be a curse, as you must know. But she bore it well."

Ivy handed back the photo and took a sip of her wine. Connie set it on the bar and studied Brianne's face as she began polishing a pint glass.

The front door opened and the detective Ivy had watched on the beach entered, making his way over to the bar. A silver badge was stuck on his worn leather belt and he held the bottom of his jacket away from it in what looked like a move he had practiced for many years.

"Mrs. Murphy?" the detective said wearily.

"Miss," Connie replied. "And Connie is fine."

"Detective Robbins. I have a few more questions about Brianne Kennedy. Is there someplace we can talk privately?"

Connie looked around the empty bar and through the open windows leading to the beach. "No place like here. We're closed to the public today, only the members allowed in. It's not like we're overrun at the moment."

The officer cleared his throat and glanced at Ivy, who got up and walked to the other side of the room, picked up a newspaper from the rack, and pretended to read it.

"We're still investigating, but our victim's death looks accidental," the detective muttered. "She was smothered when the tide came in and collapsed the wet sand on top of her. There doesn't appear to be any signs of violence. When did you see Brianne last?"

Connie pressed the damp towel to her chest. Ivy sat down in a club chair, keeping her eyes on the paper. "She closed up last night, left to go upstairs just after midnight."

"I'll need that contact information we spoke about earlier, we want to notify the family," he said in a low voice.

"But what was she doing out there?" Connie asked in disbelief. "The kids all know better than to be on the beach at night. Are you sure it was an accident? Maybe she was attacked, or robbed and left there."

"That doesn't look like what happened. She was holding a gold chain with a locket in her hand. Robbery is doubtful," he said. "About that contact information?"

"OK, I've a number for her mother in my files, and an emergency contact, too, I think," Connie said a bit shakily as she led him to the office.

***

The next morning Ivy sipped her coffee and watched Agnes serve Bruce scrambled eggs from a sauté pan. Her hands shook as she spooned them onto his plate, the blue veins showing through her papery skin.

"That's plenty, Agnes, thank you," Bruce said, distracted by his newspaper.

Ivy eyed the story above the fold. A picture of the smiling Brianne was next to the headline REGAL GRANDE CLUB WAITRESS FOUND DEAD. Her arms were crossed loosely at her waist, a pair of dark beaded bracelets dangled from her wrist, and a gold locket sparkled around her neck.

"What are you up to today, darling?" Bruce said distractedly.

"How about a day on the beach together? We could get lunch at the club," Ivy said.

Bruce shook his head. "I have an important client lunch today, and some meetings tomorrow, too. But this weekend, I'm all yours."

Ivy gave him a wan smile.

Bruce pulled out his wallet and plucked a few bills from inside, placing them next to her coffee. "Why don't you go shopping?"

"Maybe I'll explore the bay side today. Have lunch at The Salty Dog," Ivy said.

Bruce chuckled. "I don't think that's a good idea."

"Why not?" Ivy asked.

Bruce cleared his throat. "Let's just say, it's not the kind of place I'd want my wife hanging out in. It's always been a dive, I'm surprised it's survived this long."

***

Ivy slid onto a bar stool in the darkened restaurant. The vinyl on the seat was cracked, the stuffing poking through. She flipped the greasy menu over and pretended to ponder her choices. Three older couples sat around a table in the center of the room, but otherwise The Salty Dog Bar and Grill was empty.

"What'll it be?" the man standing behind the bar said.

"A Chef's Salad, and a glass of white wine, please," Ivy said, smiling.

Ivy took in her surroundings, eyeing the ship's wheels and anchors draped with nets and fake starfish, the heavy wooden interior making her feel like she was in the belly of a ship.

The man returned with a wine glass clutched in his fist, and placed it down in front of her.

"Thanks," Ivy said. "Nice place you have here. It's my first time inside."

"Wow," the man said, rubbing his round belly. He threw a glance at the elderly folks at a table who were sharing a couple of fried fish platters. "Thanks for coming in. We don't get a lot of ladies who lunch here, or trophy wives. You really class up the joint."

Ivy watched him lumber away, her cheeks reddening.

A few minutes later, a thin young man with long black hair wearing a stained apron emerged from the kitchen and set a plate of anemic looking lettuce garnished with two grey hardboiled eggs in front of her. His eyebrow was pierced with a gold hoop and the wooden beads of his bracelet knocked against the bar as he set her plate down. He shrugged and averted his eyes when Ivy thanked him, then loped back to the kitchen.

The bartender tossed a napkin wrapped around some utensils onto the bar.

"I'm Ivy Derringer," she said, feigning excitement at the salad.

"Bruce's girl," the man nodded. He craned his neck around to the TV to check the score of the game.

"Bruce's wife," Ivy said, flashing him her princess-cut diamond ring. "Are you Don?"

"The one and only," Don said with a sigh. "I heard old Bruce finally got hitched."

"It's my first summer here, I'm still getting to know everyone,"

Ivy said. She stabbed a watery tomato with her fork. "Are you the owner here?"

"Yeah, it's my place. Mine and the bank's."

"The girl who died yesterday on the beach," Ivy said, pretending like she'd just thought of it, "I read somewhere that she worked here."

Don's expression darkened and he studied her face. "Yeah, that's right. Some cop came through yesterday, asked a bunch of questions."

"It's sad what happened to her," Ivy said. "What was Brianne like?"

"I don't know. She was a waitress," Don said. "I don't get too attached to the summer help."

"You must have gotten to know her some," Ivy pressed. "She was very pretty."

"Yeah? I wouldn't know. I don't look at girls a third of my own age. No offence," Don added.

Ivy blushed and took another sip of wine. "You must have looked at her some."

Don shook his head. "Girls like that . . . That time for me has passed, if it ever existed in the first place. We don't all have a big bankroll to lure in the ladies."

Ivy chewed for a moment, then cleared her throat. "But what was she like?"

"She wasn't reliable," Dominick said flatly. "She was late for work a lot, missed a few shifts. More than once, I caught her using the phone back in the kitchen when she should have been on the floor. I fired her, good looking or not."

Ivy looked behind her at the nearly empty restaurant. "Do you have any other waitresses who might have been friends with her?"

"We're not exactly a culinary hotspot. This is a bar, for old timers and serious drinkers. I don't need a waitress most days. Sometimes a cute girl to run food brings in a few more guys. Brianne begged me to hire her, said she needed to spend the summer here."

"Why?" Ivy asked.

"Who knows," Don said. "Got the impression it was a love thing, chasing some boy probably. Who apparently didn't return her feelings. Look, things didn't work out. It happens. It's the end of season anyway. After school starts, things die around here until spring comes around again."

Ivy pondered his choice of words.

One of the customers shouted at Dominick from the dining room.

"Looks like the geezers are done with their lunch," Dominick said, shuffling out from behind the bar.

***

Ivy sat on her balcony the next morning overlooking the ocean and thought about Brianne Kennedy. Her eyes drifted to the spot in the sand where she was found, which was now surrounded by brightly colored beach blankets and umbrellas. It was just two days later and the world had moved on. The waves crashed and receded hypnotically, washing away the memories of the day before.

A loud knock on the door jarred Ivy back to the present. Agnes had gone out to the market, so Ivy hurried inside to answer it. Whoever it was knocked again, louder this time, pausing only when Ivy slid aside the deadbolt.

Detective Robbins was outside the door.

"Mrs. Derringer, I have a few questions if you don't mind."

"Questions?" Ivy stammered. "Um, sure, come in."

"Is your husband home?" he asked, stepping into the foyer.

"No, he had a breakfast meeting with a client," Ivy said, showing him into the living room and waving at the white settee.

"Did you happen to know the girl who died on the beach? Brianne Kennedy?" the detective asked.

Ivy paused and stared at him before sitting down carefully on the sofa. "No, I didn't. I've only been here a short time."

"How about your husband?" he asked.

"I'm sure he didn't. Why do you ask?"

Detective Robbins gazed at her with tired eyes.

"We checked the phone records from The Salty Dog, her place of employment. Someone from the restaurant called your residence numerous times over the several weeks. We think it was Brianne."

Ivy shook her head. "We've only just arrived at the beach. We've been honeymooning in Europe for a month."

"The last call was the night she died," the detective said. "At one in the morning."

A cold finger slid down Ivy's back as she remembered the ringing phone jarring them from their sleep. "But she'd already started working at the beach club downstairs by then," Ivy said, shaking her head. "It must have been someone else calling."

Detective Robbins nodded slightly as the front door opened. Agnes came inside, ladened down with shopping bags. She hurried into the kitchen, the swinging door closing behind her.

"Are you thinking what happened to Brianne wasn't an accident?"

The detective sighed. "We're still investigating. There's a new development."

"What do you mean?" Ivy asked hesitantly.

"This was found in her hand," the detective said. He pulled a plastic bag from his jacket and handed it to her. Inside was the heart-shaped locket Ivy had seen in the newspaper photo, opened to reveal two pictures, a recent one of Brianne taken in one of the photo booths on the boardwalk, the other an older faded photo. "That's your husband, isn't it? Odd for her to be carrying a picture of him outside of your home, don't you think?"

Ivy stared at the picture of Bruce as a feeling of dread washed over her. "You think she was trying to find Bruce? How would she know him, she's just a girl."

"That's why I'd like to speak to Mr. Derringer. The postmortem shows Brianne was pregnant."

Ivy's stomach dropped and the plastic bag slipped from her fingers onto the floor. "You can't think my husband would . . . No, she's just a girl," Ivy repeated.

"I'm sorry to have shocked you this way, Mrs. Derringer, but I need to ask the question," Detective Robbins said.

"Wait," Ivy said, holding up a hand. "Before you say anything else. Look at this." She bent over and picked up the bag, then held it out to him.

***

Ivy stood in her kitchen and tried to calm her shaking hands, hanging up with the concierge at the golf club after leaving a message for Bruce to call home right away, hoping to catch him before Detective Robbins arrived. She paced the floor, her bare feet warm against the cool tiles. She paused and placed her hand on the counter, staring at the silent phone on the wall. Her eyes drifted to the notepad next to the phone, the numbers and letters written there swimming before her eyes.

"Agnes," Ivy called. When Agnes entered the kitchen, she said, "You said you don't remember any phone calls, but what are these numbers? They're not written in a straight line."

Agnes looked at the notepad and then a relieved look came over her face. "I know, I kept dropping the pen. That's the number that kept hanging up. I asked the operator to look it up for me."

Ivy picked up the phone and dialed the number, hanging up after the familiar voice on the other end answered. She took a deep breath and glanced down at the stack of mail that had accumulated over the past several weeks. She began sorting through the envelopes, slowly at first then more rapidly, looking at the names through the plastic windows, all addressed to Bruce.

She stopped when she came to a personal letter, the address

written in faded blue pen in curlicued writing that leaned to the left. The letter was addressed to Mr. Bruce Derringer, with no return address, postmarked three weeks earlier from somewhere in Ocean City.

"What is that?" Agnes said, gazing at the envelope.

"Hopefully the answer to this madness," Ivy said. She hesitated a second, then tore open the envelope. The phone rang and Ivy snatched it up. "Bruce, thank goodness. You won't believe what's happened."

***

"Wait," Ivy said, as the skinny cook dropped another weak attempt at a Chef's Salad in front of her at the bar of The Salty Dog. "Samson, isn't it?"

The young man looked at her with a startled glance. Don eyed them cautiously, his thick arms crossed high on his chest. The rear door of the dark empty bar opened, the bright afternoon light dazzling the space around them. Detective Robbins stepped inside and headed for the bar.

"Mrs. Derringer," he began. "I encouraged you to let me handle—"

"I just stopped in for a drink and a bite to eat," Ivy said, staring at the cook.

Detective Robbins sighed and pulled a plastic bag from his pocket, placing it on the bar. It was Brianne's locket, with the pictures dislodged. The one of Brianne from the photo booth was folded open and Samson, the young cook stared from the picture with a faint smile.

Ivy removed the letter she'd found in her kitchen and placed it next to the locket. Detective Robbins cleared his throat.

Samson shifted on his feet, staring at the items on the bar.

"I recognized your bracelet when I was here the other day. Brianne wore a matching one. And this locket."

"Don't say anything, Samson," Don warned from behind the bar. "They're not on your side."

"And you are?" Samson spit defiantly. "This whole dumb thing was your idea, try and get money from the rich guy."

Don scoffed. "You're dreamin', kid. All I did was tell you Bruce was loaded. The two of you cooked up your stupid scheme all on your own."

"What scheme?" Detective Robbins asked. "Were you planning on extorting money from Mr. Derringer? On what grounds?"

Ivy pointed at the letter. "Brianne believed she was Bruce's daughter. That's what her mother told her. It's not true."

Samson laughed. "It's true, lady. Whether he wants to own up to it or not. And we were having his grandchild."

"It can't be true," Ivy said sadly. "Connie at the beach club confirmed Brianne's mother worked for her during the summer Bruce was away, volunteering for Habitat for Humanity down south."

"But her mom said . . ." Samson said, faltering.

"Her mom told her a story that wasn't true," Ivy said. "Why did you leave her out there on the beach all alone?"

Samson took a step back and showed her his palms. "No, wait. I said, let's just go over there and ask for the money. When the doorman wouldn't let us in or call up, she said she didn't want me involved anymore. She cried like crazy, and then she dumped me. Again. She asked me to leave her alone."

Detective Robbins cleared his throat and said, "Brianne died of accidental suffocation on the beach. It happens sometimes when people fall asleep, forget where they are."

"Brianne died of a broken heart," Ivy said quietly. She picked up the locket and stared at the pictures of two happy young people unaware of what life was bringing.

RIDGELINE

by Peter W. J. Hayes

Destination: Nicaragua
A dark horror from the past brings Jeff and his wife to Nicaragua. Jeff had a driving need to respond to a message from an old compatriot, but will what lies ahead of him help to quell his inner demons or create new ones?

"Tell me about Duvan."

Emily wondered if she'd pronounced Duvan's name correctly. From Jeff's terse explanations, she understood that he was from Jeff's past, the years before they were married—or had even met, for that matter.

"We need to talk about this." She was angry and a bit scared. A single letter from Duvan and Jeff called off work and booked a flight to Nicaragua, as if that country was his bedrock, as if the twenty-six years of their marriage were an afterthought.

"Duvan," he repeated. The SUV's engine strained, pulling them higher into the thin air of the Cordillera Isabelia mountains.

"Yes."

She waited while he negotiated a switchback. In the distance Lake Managua looked as inert as a fragment of blue tile. "You have to understand the time," he said finally. "Nicaragua in the 80s." She heard the distraction in his voice, as if he was unpacking long-forgotten items from a storage box. "The Somoza family ruled for decades. They controlled the wealth. Duvan's family was connected to them, until the Sandinistas overthrew the Somozas. Afterwards the Contras challenged the Sandinistas. Duvan was a Contra."

"And that's when you met?"

"Yeah." Jeff's eyes didn't move from the road. "Duvan's family owned mines. He trained as a geologist. His father placed one of his brothers with the Sandinistas, Duvan with the Contras, and sent the youngest brother to Miami."

"Do people actually do that stuff?"

A rare smile played over his lips. "I guess so. His father wanted the family's power back. He put money into the Contras. The same way the U.S. did."

"Part of which was you." She drew in a breath, trying to relax, because it wasn't only the letter. Even before their wedding, Jeff's aloof, wary silences and bursts of anger worried her. For a time, thanks to the buffer and diversion of their growing sons, she thought it was behind them. But the arrival of Duvan's letter brought it all back, as if a hard-bitten dog had slipped its leash and was gnashing inside him.

"And Duvan is so important that when he writes a letter, you fly down here. As quick as you can. We never talk about your time in the army. We avoid it." She struggled to put aside her anger, because she knew that avoidance was rotting the center of their marriage. It was why she had insisted on coming with him. They needed to face it.

After a moment he said carefully, "I know."

She stared at him, relieved. "How many years has it been since you were in Nicaragua?"

A slow breath slipped between his lips. "Too many to count."

She touched his arm, the muscle still lean and hard from twenty years of leading work crews for the local electric company. She wanted him to know she needed an answer.

"Thirty-one," he said finally. "I was army for six years."

"I don't understood why you won't tell me more."

"I was two years regular army. Then I tested into special forces."

Emily heard the caution in his voice. It sounded as if he was gauging his own reaction to the words he spoke. She decided to meet him halfway. "I guess I know that. The first year we were married I looked in your trunk, the one you keep locked in the basement? I saw your certifications. The green beret."

"It's called a foot locker," he answered.

Unsure what to do, she pressed the button and cracked her window. The air conditioner strained, as if it was distrustful of the new air.

"I was in several places," he said suddenly, his voice raw. "Brazil and Argentina for a time. I trained government special forces units."

She nodded, encouraging him.

"I was bored most of the time and focused on leading my training sessions. I studied Spanish and Portuguese in the evenings. Drank beer. Mostly it felt like a waste of time. Until I got to Nicaragua."

"But Nicaragua was different."

"Nicaragua was different." He checked the mirror, as if he was worried that something from behind might be trying to catch up. He picked his words carefully. "In Nicaragua, we went on missions with the Contras. I was an advisor to Duvan's platoon. I liked him. He was funny when he could be, and we got along. We understood each other. For a time."

"There was fighting," she said, through a tightness in her throat. "And something happened in this village Duvan mentioned in the letter? That's why he wants you to come?"

"Yes." His hands flexed on the steering wheel. "I'm not trying to be difficult. I just need to get back to the village. I need to figure it out."

That last phrase was how he signaled he was finished with a subject. She hesitated, worried that stopping the conversation now might end it forever. But she knew this was hard for him and she needed to respect that. She closed her eyes and made her choice.

"And then you will tell me about it?"

"Yes."

"OK," she said quietly. But she had taught junior high school for more than twenty years and knew every nuance of the word yes. And to her ear, it sounded as if he had dismissed her question, not affirmed it.

***

A day later, Jeff lowered his binoculars and wiped the sweat from his upper lip with his shirt cuff. On a narrow plateau below him, a row of army ATVs sat next to a faded blue trading post. Soldiers lounged along the post's front porch like dark green piglets suckling a sow. He recognized their bored and indifferent movements. They were waiting for orders. With a quick shrug he settled his backpack on his shoulders and angled downhill, plotting a detour around them before he rejoined the path to Duvan's village.

As he walked, he worried about Emily's questions. He knew she was right. On their wedding day she had dedicated her life to him. She'd proven that over the years, while he spent his days keeping the most important part of himself from her. He simply didn't want her to see the anger he felt, to hear the ways he had failed when it mattered most. But she deserved more from him, and he knew from her dry and perfunctory goodbye kiss at the trailhead that she believed it as well. She would be back in Managua by now, waiting for him, and he knew that when they met again, he would need to tell her.

A sharp smell sliced the air and he dropped instinctively to one knee and glanced around, angry at how his mind had wandered. He guessed he was seventy yards downhill from the soldiers, and was surrounded by scrub brush. Sniffing carefully, he recognized the odor. He had learned it thirty-one years ago in these very mountains.

The shattered body, when he found it, was of a middle-aged man, broken at the bottom of a steep section of cliff that rose vertically to the plateau. He waved at the cloud of flies and saw how the man's torso had burst open from the fall. But he also saw the rope marks on his wrists and the cigarette burns around his eyes and across his neck. His clothes belonged to neither a soldier nor a peasant. On his tanned wrist was a band of pale skin where a large square watch was once strapped.

He breathed through his mouth, tasting the salt of his sweat, listening to the buzz of the flies. Recognition slithered inside him, something about the man's long jawline and deep set eyes. He hefted his pack and angled along the hillside, searching for the trail to Duvan's village.

When he rejoined the path, he hiked west, past tree ferns and matapalo trees and over ridges that rose before him like wave caps. Three hours later he crested a ridge higher than the rest and heard the distant murmur of a stream. He stopped, staring at the way the path angled over the ridge and down into the forest. He shuddered as a train of memories passed through him: crossing this same ridge at dawn, the rustle of the forest floor underfoot, birdsong, the sweet smell of wood smoke.

The horror to come.

But the valley was different now. Muntingia shrubs and nogal trees stood where houses once sat. Carefully, he crossed the ridge and walked crab-legged downhill, his hands aching to hold a weapon. When the ground flattened, he kneeled again, straining to hear the echo of someone chopping wood or calling to a child, but all that came to him was the rustle and heave of the wind. Glancing about, he saw a six-inch square column of grey stone sticking a foot out of the ground. He stared at it, knowing it was out of place, understanding that it was too precisely square to be natural. Someone had roughly cut the stone and buried it upright. He shuffled nearer. Chiseled onto the flat top was the number thirty-six.

He spotted another stone a yard away and saw that it was numbered thirty-seven. Looking back, he saw another on the far side of the first stone, one more beyond that, their placement circumscribing a gentle curve. He followed them, past stone thirty-four until he reached number twelve, which sat among the fin-like roots of a kapok tree. He stepped around the root flare and with a jolt recognized the center of the village. Only the scorched foundation stones of the buildings remained, scattered across a broad clearing. The tree canopy gave the space the soaring emptiness of a church. Long shafts of sunlight fell from above, trapping insects and dust motes. Five yards away, a small girl perched on one of the stones, watching him. Their eyes met. She cocked her head, interested and unafraid, her brown eyes bright. He guessed that she was about ten. Her formless white shift was smudged with dirt and ended just below her knees. A thatch of curly brown hair hung midway down her back. She was barefoot, and even at that distance he saw how her small brown toes pinched over the edge of the carved stone.

"*Hola*," he called, trying to sound kind, and dropped to one knee to make himself smaller. The girl smiled, spun, and skipped onto the stone behind her, the movement pure and graceful, and he knew instantly that she frequently played on these stones. She turned back to him, a smile on her face, a small hand held over her eyes to protect them from a beam of sunlight. It was as if she was saluting him.

"*Hola*," he called again, hoping she would respond, but she pivoted and hopped from stone to stone, moving away from him fluidly, her hair bouncing. As she skipped between some bushes he heard her laugh. The sound reminded him of a chime in the wind, and he wondered if she thought they had started a game.

He started after her, checking each stone as he passed. When he reached the bushes he stopped, his eyes drawn back to the stones. The nearest was numbered one, the stone next to it one hundred and twelve. He realized those two stones completed a circle that enclosed the clearing. He had reached the beginning, and the end.

"Very few people visit this place," called someone from his left, in English. He turned carefully. Several yards away a man gazed at him, a .45 held against his thigh, the black of the gun's metal a smudge against his pale canvas pants. Repeated washings had driven the blue from the seams and pocket flaps of his chambray shirt. His hair was long, stringy and white, but Jeff recognized the long jaw and deep set brown eyes.

"Duvan," he said. The girl emerged from behind him. She studied Jeff intently with eyes that he decided were beautiful. Stray strands of her thick hair floated upward in the breeze.

Duvan was motionless. "I am glad you are the first. I thought some of my countrymen would be first."

"I don't know anything about that."

Duvan nodded, his eyes thoughtful, then pointed the .45 away to his right, so Jeff could see him thumb the safety lever into place. "Perhaps you would like something to eat," he called.

"I would."

Duvan turned up a narrow path. The girl smiled at him, her entire face alight, before she darted forward and around Duvan, taking the lead.

Jeff followed them to a small structure with a stone foundation and plank walls that he guessed were salvaged from the village's buildings. To the left, a long table sat underneath a tarp, its top littered with rocks, chisels and different-sized mallets. Duvan gestured to a nearby smaller table and four chairs.

"Sit down," he called, and disappeared inside the house.

At the table, Jeff lowered his backpack to the ground, the air cold against the sweat-soaked shirt on his back. The girl edged toward him on tiptoe, tentative, her eyes wide and curious.

"*Hola*," he said again.

She stopped, unsure.

"Say hello to this man," called Duvan from the doorway. "He was my friend many years ago."

"*Hola*," said the girl softly. Then she raised her eyes and said in passable English, "I have never met a friend of Papa's before."

"First we will eat," called Duvan, "And then my friend will tell me everything he has been doing for these many years, and everything he has seen on his way here."

***

As they shared plates of beans and rice, Jeff learned that the girl's name was Odili, and that she was Duvan's granddaughter. When the darkness settled around them in varying shades of blue, black and grey, Duvan retrieved a kerosene lamp and a bottle of guaro from the house. The lamp he placed on the workbench under the tarp, the bottle between them after pouring each a glass. Odili watched them, her eyes bright.

Jeff sipped the sweet liquor. "When we got here you said I needed to tell you everything I have seen. What did you mean?"

"I am afraid, my friend, that you will have to answer some questions first."

So, as the evening air cooled, Jeff explained his disgust with the military after Nicaragua, his job running work crews for a utility company, his marriage and how his sons had both attended college and were now married.

"And what brings you back here?" Duvan asked finally, emptying his glass.

"Your letter. But you know I had to."

He nodded, and somewhere in the distance an animal crashed through the brush as if it had lost its way. "Tell me about the stones," Jeff asked. "Did you carve them?"

Duvan's head ducked in the semi-darkness. "Yes."

"And the numbers on the stones?"

"A number for every person who was in the village."

The air changed as if a large bird had flown overhead. Jeff's chest tightened, his mind locked on the precision of it, the exact number of the dead so carefully numbered and remembered. "How long did that take?"

"I don't know. Years. I couldn't live in Managua. I left my wife and son and came here. I did not pay attention to the time."

"That night," Jeff said, but Duvan held up a large hand ridged with muscles and calluses. Just then the crashing in the brush grew closer, and a black dog separated from the shadows and limped toward them. In the dim lantern light Jeff saw a mutt with a chunk of one ear missing and a clouded eye. That blindness was the reason he made so much noise in the woods, he decided. A long scar ran from his chest to his front leg, explaining the limp. Duvan rubbed the top of the dog's head and the dog circled, preparing to lie down. As he did Jeff saw that his scrotum was scarred and he was missing a testicle. The care in Duvan's eyes as he watched the dog was unmistakable.

"What do you call him?"

Duvan smiled. "Of course, I call him Lucky."

Jeff laughed, he couldn't help myself, and saw a large smile on Odili's face.

When they stopped laughing, Duvan asked Odili to go to bed. She left her chair without complaint, but Jeff could see that his arrival had excited her and she didn't want to go. She kissed Duvan on the cheek then lifted the dog's snout in one hand and rubbed his ears before disappearing into the building.

They sat in silence for a time, listening to the wind in the trees. Then Jeff turned to Duvan.

"The night before it happened, why did you order me to stay at the trading post? You had to know what your men planned to do. I could have helped you stop it. I blame myself that I wasn't here to stop it. I think of it every day."

Duvan nodded, as if he had expected the question. "There was no stopping it. My men wanted revenge. Blood for the men we'd lost the week before. The village headman here was Sandinista. My men would have killed us both to have their blood."

"But I saw it all the next morning."

"I had no reason to hide it."

"I saw everything," Jeff said. "How the women were tied on their backs on tables. The babies at the bottom of the well."

Duvan stayed silent and Jeff couldn't stop himself. "I close my eyes and I see it. Everything. I smell it. The way your men were gorged with it. I should have crossed the ridgeline with you. Been here to stop it. I cannot forget that." He struggled to regain his breath.

Duvan shook his head. "Do you think my men really listened to me? I was the son of a wealthy man, dropped among them to help my family regain power. Do you think they didn't understand that? They felt no loyalty to me. If I tried to stop them they would have shot me. They would have shot you. But you're American. I was under orders to protect you. We needed American money and arms. You had to stay alive."

As his heartbeat slowed, Jeff noticed a soft, unworried tone to Duvan's voice. It wasn't quite that Duvan had made peace with it, he decided, but rather that he had reviewed all the arguments and found them useless, leaving only the fact of what happened.

"So I came back here afterwards," Duvan said. "Like you, I could not forget. That was impossible. I had failed the people here. But, unlike you, I chose to remember it. All of it. So I found the stone. And I began."

They were silent for a time. Insects buzzed past Jeff's face, searching for blood. "And that helped?"

"No," Duvan said gently. "But each day I had something to do about it."

"And so you survived."

"If you want to call it that."

Jeff looked about, the years rising in him like bile. "It's never gone for me. Every memory is always there, just waiting. They're like the shadows under tables and chairs. The cancer that runs in your family. They never leave you, even when you're not thinking about them."

"And they come out at night."

"Oh yeah. They come out at night. And it's put a goddamned black door in the middle of my marriage that I'm scared to open. I don't know what Emily'll think of me if I do. Do you know what's worse? The things I saw, those are one memory, and that's bad enough. But the other is how I lied about it. I reported everything to my commander and he said it never happened. Ordered me to write my after-action report that way. As if it never occurred. And I did. I fucking did."

"I know. I wrote a detailed report. How many dead. Men, women, children. The ringleaders in my platoon. But my commander said the American report made no mention of it. So he burned it. In front of me."

The wind dropped and Lucky let out a deep sigh.

"It is the way of governments," said Duvan. "And people like you and me are the ones who live with it."

"But it's worse." Jeff drank off the last of his guaro. "My wife loves art. Paintings. Going to museums. I didn't care about art before I came down here. But afterwards, after I saw all this death, it was different. Those paintings, the colors, the way artists catch a moment, show the spirit of a person. I see now how they celebrate life. Defy death. I finally understood what makes something beautiful. But it was exactly because of what I saw here. The murders gave me that gift, and I hate myself for it."

"No," said Duvan. "Take that gift. It is from the people who died here. It is so some good can come from all this." He twisted the watch on his wrist.

Jeff saw the motion and something moved in his mind. He focused on Duvan's watch, the size of it, the unusual square face. Lucky stirred and raised his head. Jeff said slowly, "There were soldiers at the trading post. Six ATV two-seaters, twelve soldiers. They tortured and executed a civilian."

Duvan's eyes settled on him in question.

"He was wearing a white shirt and black pants. He'd worn a large square watch." He pointed at Duvan's wrist. "Like that."

A look crossed Duvan's face as if he had lost his way. He scrubbed at his cheek with a knuckle. "These soldiers, they will come here next." His voice was hoarse.

"How do you know?"

He looked at the sky. "For Christmas, many years ago, my wife gave my son and me the same watch. Odili's father. Two weeks ago my son went to Managua to talk to the government. I told him it was a mistake, but he is a lawyer by training. He feels the need to do things in a certain way."

Jeff felt things slipping away from him. "They killed him? Why?"

"Why do governments kill? I've found something of value. They want it."

Jeff watched him rise and cross to the doorway of the building. He called Odili's name several times and then spoke to her. As he walked back to the table, he scooped up something from the work bench.

"What's going on?"

Duvan placed a black, egg-shaped stone on the table in front of him. "This."

"What is it?"

"While searching for granite to make the columns, I discovered this. Tantalite. A mineral needed to make electronics. It is the largest deposit in the country. Whoever mines it will be rich. Rich beyond anything."

"Of course you'd discover something to mine. I should have guessed."

"So you begin, so you end. My son thought it a way to make the government appreciate our family again. Reestablish us. We argued about it. I was sure our government would kill us and steal the deposit. And then I saw how the promise of wealth was already tearing my son and me apart, the way it did my country all those years ago."

"So what are you going to do?"

"It is more what you are going to do."

"What do you mean?"

"I want you to take Odili. Follow her to the next village. There is a building there, Odili knows which one, and my car is inside. I want you to take Odili to America."

He thought of Emily, and what she would say. "Even if I did, how do I cross borders with her?"

"Her mother was sent to stay with my brother in Miami while pregnant. She gave birth there. Odili has an American passport."

"Shouldn't she be with her mother?"

"My friend. I am counting on you for this. If my son is dead, Odili's mother has been arrested. I sent you the letter in case this happened."

"I'd rather stay here. Fight with you. The way I should have. I won't miss it again." He looked at the darkness of the treetops and was sure of it.

"My friend, I know why you came. I know what you are prepared to do. But you cannot ever really make amends. You cannot forget. I have learned this and have done what I can to remember the dead. It isn't enough. Like your art, make something good come from this. So I ask you. Take my only grandchild to safety. Let Odili be that good."

Jeff hesitated, torn inside. "But why would they kill you? Don't they need you?"

"My son had a map showing the location of the deposit. If they killed him, they've found it, and they are coming for me. If you can destroy a village by burning a report, killing an old man is simple."

Odili appeared in the doorway to the house, lugging a large pink Hello Kitty backpack.

Duvan smiled at her. "See? I said this man is my friend. You will go with him, Odili. Show him where I keep my car. Can you do that?"

Odili nodded, then turned shy eyes to Jeff. Slowly, his mind blank, Jeff rose. Duvan was right. He couldn't leave Odili here. When he shouldered his backpack, Duvan pressed a plastic bag and the egg-sized stone into his hands.

"Odili's passport and a map. The true map. The one I gave my son was false, although I didn't tell him that. When everything is finished tomorrow, the government will send geologists, but they will find nothing. It took me ten years to discover the deposit. You decide what to do with it. Keep it, give it to my brother, I don't care. I just want Odili safe. I trust you in this."

Duvan wrapped his large, horned hand around the back of Jeff's neck for a moment, gave him a slight tug, then dropped to his knees and hugged Odili for almost a minute. She seemed confused, but afterwards led Jeff downhill. Lucky followed them for a time, then fell back, as if he wanted them to go on without him. Jeff watched Odili's hair bouncing in his flashlight beam and saw how lightly she moved on her feet. He thought about how innocent she was, how she was unaware of her father's death and what was coming for her grandfather. He carried the weight of knowing, and one day he would have to tell her. He didn't mind that, he decided. He minded the black egg that had already turned father against son, jailed Odili's mother, and if left to hatch, would feed on every family it could find.

***

It was mid-morning when they reached Managua. Odili was asleep, stretched across the back seat. The wind through the windows moved strands of hair across her cheek and lips. Jeff glanced at her repeatedly, as if he needed to imprint her plump cheeks and dark eyelashes in his memory. He called Emily from his cell phone and told her to meet him at the museum by Lake Managua, the one that displayed the preserved footprints made by people two thousand years earlier.

"Just come back to the hotel," she said.

"No. At the museum, as quickly as you can get there. Check out. Bring everything. We have to leave, I'll explain when you get here."

He waited outside the car until he saw Emily approaching. By then his mind was made up, and he overhanded the black egg far into the listless lake. He jammed the map well down inside a garbage bin.

He quickly explained about Odili, and despite Emily's concerns, soon they were driving south along Route 1 in the rental car, headed to Costa Rica. Emily sat in the back seat with Odili. They were talking, and he recognized a tone in Emily's voice he hadn't heard in years. In time Odili fell asleep and the car was quiet.

"So you found Duvan," said Emily. Jeff glanced in the mirror and saw the top of Odili's head on Emily's chest.

"Yes." He checked the road. "Look. I need to explain this. All of it. Starting at the beginning. When we get into Costa Rica, OK?"

Emily felt Odili's body warm against her, and that warmth suddenly spread throughout her body. A tear streaked down her cheek. Jeff saw the tear in the mirror, and also a gradual smile, but then her brow furrowed.

"Can we really do this?"

"I don't know. First Costa Rica. Then we talk to the American Embassy. She's a U.S. citizen and a political refugee. Maybe."

Emily nodded, and in the mirror he saw the way she looked at Odili, the unabashed happiness in her eyes. He realized his obsession with memories had led him to miss something. Emily gave birth to their sons. Raised them. But she'd never had a daughter. Watching her now, he realized that Emily had her own black door, and that it was finally ajar.

"Perhaps we could sponsor her somehow," he added.

Emily raised her eyes to him. "I would like that."

He slowed for a turn then accelerated, feeling the shiver of the rental car through the wheel in his hand. Unknown to him, Emily's eyes were drawn to his hands. She remembered how, years earlier, on their first date, she had noticed them. Their strength, how the knuckles were large and purposeful, their confidence and how he didn't hide them in his pockets. Afterwards, sitting in the half darkness of her parents' kitchen, a spoonful of vanilla ice cream melting on her tongue, she had suddenly imagined those hands touching her body. She had warmed from head to toe, a body blush, stunned she could have such a directly sexual thought about a man. She had known in that instant that she would marry him, if he would have her. How did that happen, she wondered. In all the world, what instinct reached through the darkness to touch her, so she would know the right thing to do?

HO'OPONOPONO

by Robin Templeton

Destination: Kaua'i, Hawai'i
Makaio has taken on a special charter to show a developer around the island. Awaiting them is an ancient sea cave which may be the hidden entrance to Hawai'i's royal valley or a gateway to either revenge or forgiveness.

Makaio Kamaka was ready to meet his biological father. It couldn't be called a reunion—he had no memory of the man. But over the last nine years, Makaio had amassed an impressive dossier on the drive-by mystery man he had never called his makua, his father. The gift of true fathering had come to him from teachers, coaches, and from the many uncles of Kaua'i.

Makaio—or Mack, as his friends called him—had gotten up hours before dawn and quietly prepared a small backpack for his solo voyage. He didn't want to disturb his wife. Kika was eight months pregnant and still teaching classes at a yoga studio in Kapa'a. She needed every second of rest.

He silently opened his bureau drawer and pawed through his socks and underwear. When he felt the reassuring solidity of his Glock 19, he wrapped a T-shirt around it and placed it in the bottom of his backpack. His pacifist wife would completely freak out if she ever found a gun in their house.

Mack had been careless. He'd intended to return the newly purchased firearm to the safe in his office right after yesterday's shooting practice. Stuffing an extra T-shirt and pair of shorts on top of the gun, he zipped his pack and closed the bureau drawer.

His wife shifted onto her back and snored gently. When Kika's belly got too big for her favorite turquoise yoga pants, she'd started referring to herself as a beached humpback. But Mack thought she'd never looked more beautiful. He leaned over and kissed her forehead. "Sleep soundly, my beloved, Iekika." Then he patted her swollen belly with a feather touch. "You as well, Kaimi. My son."

Mack felt the gun shift in his backpack. He wasn't sure whether he was praying to a Judeo-Christian god or a Hawaiian god when he got to his knees and whispered, "Help me, please. For the sake of my family, for the sake of my unborn son, I beg for justice and resolution. Amama."

***

Mack had just hidden the Glock in his safe when he heard someone jiggling a key in the back door. Damn. He'd hoped to have the office to himself for at least another half hour. A bead of perspiration slid from his forehead to his nose. He slammed and locked the closet, wiped his face with his forearm, and fell into his oversized luxury desk chair. By the time Paz ʻAkamu walked in, Mack had covered his desktop with client forms and files.

Paz straddled the straight-back chair to the right side of Mack's desk. Nobody stood on formality at Captain Mack's Guided Boat Tours and Dives—least of all Paz. He was one of Mack's second cousins, and, more importantly, his childhood friend and business partner. Paz was also a top-ranked diver and a premier guide. Mack was grateful his buddy had stayed with him through all the lean years. Both of them had survived to earn a good living at a business they loved.

His partner gestured toward the files on the desk. "Anything exciting? Any celebrities? It sure was jumping around here before Kareem sold his place. That man brought us a ton of business!"

Mack smiled. "Well, maybe the Obamas will island hop now that they have a little more time on their hands. Our job is to keep our reputation solid, no matter who hires us."

They sorted through paperwork and discussed crew assignments until the intoxicating scent of Kona coffee wafted into the room. Mack inhaled deeply and Paz laughed. "Oh, yeah. Lisa drove in with me today. She brought in some of that great Portuguese fry bread, too."

Both men headed for the kitchenette. Lisa was already pouring thick rich coffee into three of their signature Captain Mack mugs. The pretty blond handed each of them a steaming cup. A plate of egg-shaped malasadas sat next to the coffee pot and Mack helped himself to two. After brushing sugar and crumbs off his T-shirt and taking a gulp of Lisa's always-perfect coffee, Mack said, "Can you two handle the launches over the next couple of days? We don't have any dive trips until Friday and I'll be back by then."

Lisa studied her boss. "Where are you going? Is Kika OK? How about the baby?"

For the locals, it wasn't just that Hanalei was a small town. It was all of Kauaʻi. Everybody knew everybody else's business.

Mack wasn't used to keeping secrets from Paz and Lisa. "Kika's fine, the baby's fine. I'm not going out of town, but I have errands today and I'm making a run with a private client tomorrow.

I've already scheduled the *Iolana*. You won't need her until Friday. OK?"

Paz frowned. "I haven't had a chance to put the Iolana through her paces. Are you sure she's seaworthy?" The Zodiac boat was also a recent acquisition—just like the Glock.

"Have her fully inflated and ready to launch by two and I'll take her out myself. Jimmy T. swore by her condition and I'd trust Jimmy with my life."

Paz shrugged and held his thumb and smallest finger out, in the Hawaiian shaka gesture of good will. "Will do. You're the boss, Cap'n Mack."

***

Mack pushed his personal kayak into a secluded section of Hanalei Bay. It would take him a while to work his way to his destination on the Nā Pali Coast, but he didn't care. He needed to plan. He needed to feel the sea and the ancestors giving him guidance and strength for tomorrow's mission.

Fast and sure, each side of his paddle sliced the surf. The bow of the kayak leapt forward. Already Makaio Kamaka could feel the ancestors spurring him on. His thoughts were like the pounding waves of the Pacific or the mesmerizing rhythms of the ceremonial pahu drums. Driving syllables pulsated in his brain: Hoʻoponopono. Hoʻoponopono. Over and over and over.

It was March fourteenth and although the sun rose in Hanalei around 6:45, the Nā Pali Coast was still in shadow and pleasantly chilly. Mack had made good time. The currents were with him as he worked his way counterclockwise around the north shore.

The great lava cliffs rose from the sea and went on for miles. On the windward side, the rainy side, the mountain foliage was plentiful and the awe-inspiring waterfalls seemed to come out of nowhere. Shafts of light beamed over the mountains, igniting the morning mist and electrifying the lush green of the foliage.

The water was gentle this morning. Mack stopped paddling. Closing his eyes, he felt the waves rock his kayak. Hoʻoponopono. Hoʻoponopono. Surely his mother had rocked his cradle just as Kai, the sea, rocked his kayak and his soul. Hoʻoponopono. Hoʻoponopono. It was the only thing his mother had asked for on her deathbed. Could he grant her dying wish? For her? For the ancestors? For his son? For him?

Rushing water. Mack opened his eyes. He had drifted near a mountain waterfall. The sun sparkled through the cascading water, creating dancing rainbows in the air and on the surf. Magic. Was it a sign? He knew he was nearing his destination.

It was one of the many cliff caves along the Nā Pali Coast. A number of them were large enough for a catamaran or a Zodiac, and it gave the tourists a thrill to float under the waterfalls and into the mystical spaces. No matter how many times he'd experienced it, Mack was always thrilled, too.

It could be risky. If the waves crashed too high, a craft could be trapped inside the cave. Even the strongest swimmers would have trouble battling the rising Pacific along the Nā Pali Coast. If you knew what you were doing, you could dive deep below the water and come out on the other side of the waves, but it was disorienting and dangerous. You could get caught on the rocks or pulled into one of the many riptides along the coast. Ho'oponopono. Ho'oponopono. He had to focus on his mission, not his fear, or he'd lose his nerve.

This morning it was hard to imagine Kai being so deadly. Mack trailed his hand along the side of his kayak. Kai was deep, deep blue and playful—at least while he drifted with her current.

Nai'a! Two spinner dolphins leaped from the water as if to greet him. And then he saw his landmark. Was it another sign?

On a kayaking trip the previous summer, Mack had found the right cave. He'd measured the entrance in October and again, just two weeks earlier. It was perfect for his plan and he'd marked the spot with a rock formation.

Paddling swiftly, Mack's kayak easily entered the cave. He knew he didn't need to measure the mouth again.

He checked his watch. It was noon, but the waters would be higher by two. The winds would be stronger, too. The afternoon was always rougher along the coast, and Mack had already heard the next day's weather report. The morning would be fine. The afternoon? Just the right amount of challenge.

Some say you can't con a con man, but that wasn't true. With the right bait, con men could be the most easily conned of all. It's because they believe they're smarter than everyone else. And, with the right bait, blind greed strips them of any protective caution and judgment.

Mack contemplated the cave's interior. The water within created an opalescent turquoise lagoon and the cave walls had ledges like seats in a sauna. It wasn't far from the Honopū Valley—the Kaua'i version of a valley of the kings. Royals might have used this very space for private baths or trysts. His eyes wandered upward. There was no ceiling egress in here. If the Pacific entrance was blocked, if the waters rose . . . What if he died in here? What if they both died? Tentatively he called out, and the walls echoed his voice back to him, "Ho'oponopono. Ho'oponopono."

Mack exited the cave, quickly paddling to a deep crevice to hide his kayak. It was almost one o'clock. He'd told Jimmy to pick him up at one. Usually, going by island time, Jimmy might not arrive until three. But he had impressed upon Jimmy the importance of the mission. Only Jimmy knew what he was up to, and Mack was certain the old man would take his secret to the grave.

Sure enough, he saw Jimmy's Zodiac boat crashing through the waves. Mack waved at his friend and jumped into the water so Jimmy wouldn't have to risk puncturing his inflatable boat on the sharp rocks. Diving in the cool clear water felt good. Cleansing.

"All set?" Jimmy asked.

"All set. Take me back to the dock. I'm going to test drive the *Iolana*."

"She's the right boat for the job."

Mack looked deeply into the old man's eyes. "She's the only boat for the job."

***

Mack woke with a start five minutes before the alarm sounded. It was March fifteenth. The Ides of March. Could there be a more fitting day? A day associated with judgment, betrayal, and death. Tourists might think the islands were all about the Aloha spirit, and, to some extent, that was true. But deep beneath that spirit was an undercurrent of royal warring and treachery—just like the deadly riptides beneath the sparkling blue surface of Kai.

Kika was awake. Breakfast was on the table and two white boxes sat on the kitchen counter. Mack wrapped his arms around his wife and buried his nose in the coconut-scented waves of her shining black hair.

"This omelet looks great," he pronounced, taking his seat at the kitchen table. On cue, the neighborhood roosters crowed. They both laughed. In 1992, when Mack was only seven years old, Hurricane Iniki ripped across Kaua'i, destroying farms and chicken coops. Most locals agreed that's when the population of free range chickens exploded.

Kika sprinkled sea salt on her eggs. "Shall we get a mongoose for a pet?" she teased. "Or should we see if our son discovers a better solution to control all the chickens? He's going to be brilliant, you know."

Mack watched his wife as she lifted the eggs to her lips. Would he ever see her again?

Kika stared back at her husband. "Are you OK? Is there a ghost in the room?"

He smiled. *Yes, my darling. Many ghosts. And I'm going to try to exorcise them this afternoon. For you. For my son.* Aloud he said, "I have a full schedule today. I might be late for dinner. A mainland real estate developer wants a complete tour of our coast."

Kika frowned. "Since when do you like showing developers your island? What are you planning to do? Drown him?"

Damn. Being married to Kika was like having a lie detector strapped to his chest. "I like showing developers my island when they pay me six thousand dollars for my navigational skills and expert advice."

"Six thousand?" Kika's deep brown eyes got huge.

"He wanted the best, so he got the best. But I don't come cheap."

She grinned. "You're a bargain at any price. Try not to be too late. If you call before leaving the office, I'll reheat your dinner for you." She pointed to the boxes on the counter. "And there are the special lunches you ordered, plus Hawaiian beer, spring water, and Pellegrino in the cooler. Now I know why you wanted to go all out. Maybe I should have included caviar."

"If your roasted chicken with fresh pineapple and ginger doesn't make him swoon, the man has no taste buds. Thank you, Kika. I am one lucky man. And I love you with all my heart. You and our son."

She flushed with pleasure and rewarded him with a kiss and a hug. "I love you, too, Makaio. Don't forget to come home to us."

***

Kenneth W. Salisbury was waiting on the dock when Mack arrived. The man looked older than he did in most of the dozens of pictures Mack had collected. The once dark brown hair was white, and his shoulders stooped a bit. He wore khaki shorts, a navy T-shirt with a club insignia, and a loose, long-sleeved white shirt—presumably to protect him from the sun. Expensive tan leather walking sandals completed the ensemble.

Mack extended his hand. The man looked Mack up and down before inflicting his haole version of a perfect handshake, not too limp, but not too firm. Is this jerk's blood really running through my veins? But his mother's diaries had been quite explicit. And when he asked his grandmother about the entries, the venom in her answers told Mack that every word was true.

Salisbury offered his black Centurion American Express card to Mack. "You can put the balance on that."

Tempting. But what would prime beach acreage in Hanalei be worth today? Six million? Seven? Ten? Instead, Mack just charged the three thousand dollar balance due him for the tour.

After getting the gear into waterproof bags and loading the

Zodiac, Mack helped Salisbury aboard. His passenger's eyes looked at the boat's name patched next to the manufacturer's insignia. "*Iolana*. I knew somebody by that name once. What does it mean?"

It means Jimmy named his boat after my mother, you cesspool of a human being. "Oh, the Hawaiian language is pretty fluid. Some say 'she who soars.' Some say 'she who knows.' I think it's a beautiful name."

Fortunately Mack didn't have to chit-chat once they were out to sea. Between the outboard motor and the crashing ocean, normal conversation was impossible. As he slowly circled the island, Mack obediently cruised into harbors and coves wherever Salisbury requested. The man used an iPad to take pictures and scribble notes.

At noon, Mack glided into a shaded cove, stopped the motor, and pulled out the cooler. "Hungry?"

Salisbury nodded. He took a can of Maui-brewed craft beer out of Mack's hand and said, "Our mutual friend, Jimmy, said you knew where some special antiquities might be hidden. Don't get me wrong, this tour has already been invaluable. I spotted a number of potential investments. But I asked for you personally based on Jimmy's recommendation. I'll make it worth your while. On top of your fee."

Mack chewed a bite of chicken as if considering his answer. "Oh, we islanders always talk about hidden treasure. That's all most of it is. Just talk."

Salisbury took another swig of beer. "Jimmy said you and he got to drinking and talking. And you said you'd uncovered another entrance to the royal valley. Through a cave."

Mack looked Salisbury in the eye. "So what if I did? That's sacred land. You don't disturb the ancestor bones. It's bad luck and worse karma."

"What if I do the disturbing? And I double your fee?"

Hook, line, and sinker, thought Mack as he restarted the *Iolana*'s motor. Ho'oponopono. Ho'oponopono.

***

"It's getting rough out here!" Kenneth Salisbury's face looked more green than tan as he shouted to Mack.

Mack continued to slam the Zodiac into every possible wave he could. "Yeah, this is a rough part of the coast at this time of day. Get down in the bottom of the boat and I'll strap you in. Don't want any accidents out here."

Captain Mack stopped the motor, and the craft rolled up and down the ocean. Between the Maui beer and the movement of the waves, Salisbury looked like he might lose Kika's excellent lunch. Mack pointed over the side of the boat to the roiling Pacific. "Feel free to puke—it's just fish food out there."

The man was too sick to notice or care what Mack was doing with the harness. Jimmy had installed it to help the tourist fishermen who weren't used to the sharp yank of an ocean fish on their lines. Mack had added something additional for his special passenger—a hook and a keyed padlock. When he locked Salisbury into the harness, he felt a gun holster strapped to the man's side. Oh. So the shirt hadn't just been for sun protection. Should he take Salisbury's gun now? He pretended to tighten the harness strap while he felt the holster. It had a flap. Mack decided not to touch the man's gun. But if the confrontation did turn into the Wild West, Mack knew he could outdraw Salisbury.

"All set!" Mack chirped cheerfully. He started the outboard while Salisbury hung his head over the side of the boat.

By the time they got to the cave, Mack's passenger had hurled into the Pacific twice, and then fallen asleep. Held upright by the harness, his head drooped over his shoulder and it was debatable as to what was noisiest—the surf, the outboard, or the man's snoring. "Pathetic," said Mack out loud. But Salisbury's drunkenness served his purposes perfectly.

While Salisbury slept, Mack surveyed the exterior of the cave. He didn't want to damage the boat or the motor if he could help it. But he wanted to make sure the craft was good and stuck through the entrance. Mack aimed the Zodiac for the mouth of the cave and, with a prayer and a shout, gunned the motor.

The boat screeched like a banshee as it wedged tightly inside the cave, but seemingly sustained no damage. Mack quickly cut the motor.

"What the fu . . . Where the hell are we?" Even with the limited light spilling into the cave, Mack could see Salisbury's eyes rolling frantically as he tried to free himself from the harness and orient himself.

The *Iolana* half-filled the tiny cavern, blocking all but a small triangular space at the top of the cave entrance. It was from there that the light filtered into the space. Mack's voice, calm and sure, answered his passenger's question. "Not hell, Kenneth Salisbury. Not yet. Maybe it's purgatory. We need to have a conversation. Do you know what name is on my birth certificate?"

Salisbury looked confused. "It's not Makaio Kamaka? That's the name on your license. I saw it in your office."

"That's my name now. Kamaka is an ancestral name. After you left, my mother called me Makaio. It means 'gift of god.' I put the two together and had my name changed."

Salisbury was starting to sober up and he looked scared. "What was your original name?" he whispered.

Mack looked into Salisbury's face. Was that what he'd look like in another thirty-five years? He hoped his face would show his mother's kindness and his grandfather's strength instead of the face of this thief and coward. "I think you've figured it out. My mother named me after you. Before I changed it, my name was Kenneth W. Salisbury, Jr."

Salisbury watched the water rise against the cave walls. It finally seemed to register in his brain that he was trapped inside. A wave pushed the Zodiac deeper into the cave, sloshing water into the bottom of the boat. Salisbury's shorts were soaked. When he tried to get out of the harness, he saw the padlock.

Anger replaced fear on Salisbury's face. He started to reach for his gun when Mack said, "I wouldn't do that if I were you. I just put a ten-round clip in my Glock and I don't think I'll miss at this range. Keep your gun in your holster and we both might get out of here alive."

Salisbury stared at the gun pointed right at his heart. "You wouldn't shoot me, would you? Your own father?"

After all the years of pent up rage, the words ripped out of Mack's soul. " Father? Ha! You deserted us, you son of a bitch. As soon as you got her to sign over her property to you, you left for the mainland and never looked back. When she was served the divorce papers, she was too frail and hurt to fight you. And she still loved you, you bastard. She'd been engaged to Jimmy before you seduced her. Did you know that? He adored her. Even after she got breast cancer, he wanted to marry her. He could have gotten her to doctors to save her life but she wanted to die. She died of a broken heart and shame over losing the land that had been given to our ancestors by King Kamehameha. In her diary she said she wanted to forgive you and make things right, but she couldn't. She tried to contact you but you never answered her letters. That's what finally killed her. On her deathbed that's all she wanted—Ho'oponopono. You haoles came to our islands and took our women and our land, but do you understand anything of our culture? Our soul? Do you even know what Ho'oponopono means?"

The sea had continued to rise and another wave crashed over the boat. There was almost no light left except for a strange iridescent green glowing from the walls of the cave. With the next wave, Mack and Salisbury's heads bumped against the cave's ceiling. The odors of the confined space had changed, too—into an unpleasant melding of mineral deposits, dead fish, and fear.

Salisbury struggled to get free. "Kid, you're crazy. Let's have this conversation someplace else. You said there was a back exit to the royal valley. Let's get out of here before we both die."

Mack's voice echoed eerily in the cave. "There's no back exit. I lied. I needed you to know what you've done."

Mack heard Salisbury unsnap the holster of his gun and he said softly, "I can shoot in the dark, Father. You won't live to get the safety off."

Salisbury left the gun holstered. "Look, Mack, I've made a lot of mistakes. I don't want you to make even bigger ones than me. I'm an old man. But I'm a rich man. Do you want to be reimbursed for your mother's land? I could do that. I can't return it—I built on it and sold it. But the property can be assessed and I can compensate you for it. I am your father. That's been established. I believe your story."

The disgust in Mack's voice reverberated off the water and cave walls. "You believe my story? That's a laugh. I've looked into your history. I had lots of reasons to change my name but I'm not even sure where your name came from. Your birth records are pretty sketchy, Mr. Zillionaire. Compensate me? That's a big fucking laugh!"

For a few moments, the only sounds in the cave were of the two men breathing and the surf crashing over the ledges of the cave walls. Finally, slowly and quietly, Salisbury spoke. "I didn't know my name, son. I was put in foster care when I was a kid. My mother was a heroin addict and a whore and she didn't know who my father was. So I made up a new past for myself. I guess I've been doing that all my life. Believe it or not, I loved your mother. I was going to come back for her and for you but . . ."

Mack wasn't buying it. "But what?"

Salisbury sighed. "But nothing. I got greedy. I got scared. I got full of myself."

Mack's heart started to soften, but then he remembered the anguish in the girlish scrawl of his mother's diaries. His voice stayed hard when he said, "Hoʻoponopono used to happen when the family came together to make things right. Deep forgiveness that would wipe the slate clean, wipe our souls clean. It's all Iolana wanted from you, but you couldn't give it to her, or to her parents.

"There's no family left except my wife and my unborn son and I'm going to go to them now. The modern healers believe we can bring about Hoʻoponopono at any time by saying these words. I say them now, even if you can't. I'm sorry. Please forgive me. Thank you. I love you. Each addresses a stage of healing in the heart, as well as atonement to God, to our families, to the ancestors, and to ourselves. I don't believe it's something you're capable of understanding, Father."

In the dark, Mack put the Glock in a waterproof bag and into his backpack. He threw the key to the harness on the floor of the boat. Then he pushed himself off the back of the Zodiac and gripped the opening of the cave.

Salisbury screamed, "You can't leave me! I'll die. You'll have murdered me. You can't sue my estate. We can settle this."

His words echoed back at both of them from the cave walls.

Before Mack squeezed through the exit into the pounding sea he said, "Do you really think this had anything to do with money or your fucking estate? I've left you with two means to save yourself. Good luck."

Waves crashed Mack against the cliff as soon as he exited. He felt weak from the ordeal with his father, but he had to stay strong. Damn! Killer surf. When he bobbed to the surface, he saw the twilight and believed he'd be OK. However, the cave was filling quickly. Salisbury had only minutes to free himself or die.

Mack's fingers clutched the slick cliff face as he made his way to the kayak he'd hidden near the cave. He flinched when he heard two sharp reports echoing from inside the cave walls. Had Salisbury shot himself or the *Iolana*? Had he realized that with the boat slightly deflated he'd be able to push it out of the cave? Mack had even left a patching kit and a flashlight in the gear pack. Perhaps the old man had thought of one of the ways to save himself.

Then, just barely, Mack heard shouted, desperate words emanating from the cave entrance: "I'm sorry. Please forgive me. Thank you. I love you."

Mack heard the words three times and, with the third time, Salisbury added, "I love you, son." Could he believe Salisbury? Had his mother's final wish been granted? This man, his blood makua—should he try to save him or would they both die? A lot depended on the condition of the boat and how much water was now in the cave. Makua. Father. He also thought of his mother, his wife, and his soon-to-be-born son.

Makaio Kamaka dove into the churning ocean. But the waves swallowed him. No matter how hard he fought, the current wouldn't let him swim back to the cave. There wasn't time to get the kayak and attempt a rescue. Mack came up for air, then plunged into the Pacific again. But the warrior waves of Kai threw his body against the rocks.

It was too late. He couldn't help. Kai had decided.

He dragged himself from the water and started sobbing.

Through his tears, he shouted to the wind, to the sea, and to the cave, “I’m sorry. Please forgive me. Thank you. I love you.”

Ho‘oponopono.

AUTHOR BIOGRAPHIES

AUTHORS

JOHN GREGORY BETANCOURT is a best-selling science fiction and mystery author (though he now has little time for writing due to his work as publisher of Wildside Press). He won the first Black Orchid Novella Award from *Alfred Hitchcock's Mystery Magazine* and the Nero Wolfe society, The Wolfe Pack.

Although Edward D. Hoch Memorial Golden Derringer Award recipient **MICHAEL BRACKEN** has written several books, including the private eye novel *All White Girls,* he is better known as the author of more than 1,200 short stories published in *Alfred Hitchcock's Mystery Magazine, Black Cat Mystery Magazine, Crime Square, Ellery Queen's Mystery Magazine, Espionage Magazine, Fifty Shades of Grey Fedora, Flesh & Blood: Guilty as Sin, Mike Shayne Mystery Magazine, Noir at the Salad Bar, Snowbound,* and in many other anthologies and periodicals. He has received two Derringer Awards, was nominated for a third, and has earned several awards for advertising copywriting. He lives and writes in Texas.

SUSAN BREEN is the author of the Maggie Dove mystery series, published by the Alibi imprint of Random House. Her short stories have been published by *Alfred Hitchcock's Mystery Magazine, Ellery Queen's Mystery Magazine*, and *Best American Non-Required Reading*, among other places. She is also the author of the novel, *The Fiction Class*. Susan teaches at Gotham Writers in NYC. She lives in a small village in the Hudson Valley with her husband and two little dogs. She's never been to Tahiti, but her daughter and new son-in-law recently went on their honeymoon to Bali, which set Susan's mind to churning over the murderous potential of tropical islands.

CARLA COUPE's short stories have appeared in several of the *Chesapeake Crimes* series, as well as Malice Domestic's *Mystery Most Geographical* and *Mystery Most Historical*. Two of her short stories were nominated for Agatha Awards. She has also written many Sherlock Holmes pastiches which have appeared in *Sherlock Holmes Mystery Magazine; Sherlock's Home: The Empty House*; *The MX Book of New Sherlock Holmes Stories, Part VI*, and *Irene's Cabinet*. Her story, "The Book of Tobit," was included in *The Best American Mystery Stories of 2012*.

SUSAN DALY has found her niche in the world of short crime fiction, where she enjoys restoring the balance of good over evil. Her stories pop up in a number of anthologies: *The Whole She-Bang 2 & 3*, The Guppies' *Fish Out of Water,* and the Malice Domestic anthology for 2017. Her historical mystery, "A Death at the Parsonage," won the 2017 Arthur Ellis Award for best short story from the Crime Writers of Canada. She lives in Toronto a comfortable distance from her grandkids, and can be found at www.susandaly.com.

PETER DiCHELLIS concocts sinister tales for anthologies, ezines, and magazines. His mystery/crime writing ranges from humorous whodunits to dark suspense stories. Peter is a member of the Short Mystery Fiction Society and an Active (published author) member of the Mystery Writers of America, Private Eye Writers of America, and International Thriller Writers. For more information about Peter's stories, visit his site, Murder and Fries, or his Amazon author page. Additionally, Peter's light essay about short mysteries ("Five Reasons to Love Reading Short Mystery Stories") is available on the Short Mystery Fiction Society blog.

JUDITH GREEN is the sixth generation of her family to live on her hillside in rural western Maine, and the seventh and eighth generations live just down the road. She served as the Adult Education Director for her 11-town school district, and wrote 25 high-interest/low-level books for adult students. Her mystery stories have been chosen for thirteen of the *Anthologies of New England Crime* published by Level Best Books. "A Good, Safe Place," published in 2010 in *Thin Ice*, was nominated for an Edgar®. She is currently working on a novel set in North Whitby, ME, which looks suspiciously like her own village.

KERRY HAMMOND is a recovering attorney who now works for a nonprofit in her adopted hometown of Denver, CO. She has been a mystery fan all her life and has written for Criminal Element and the Mystery Playground blog. "To Protect the Guilty" is her first published short story. She spends all her free time writing, traveling with her husband, and leading the Crime & Beyond mystery book club, which is so hardcore they have a yearly Murder Mystery Costume party and a Wiki page.

PETER W. J. HAYES is a former marketing executive turned mystery writer. The first novel of his Pittsburgh Trilogy, *The Things That Aren't There*, will be published in July 2018. His short stories have appeared in various anthologies, magazines, and online publications, including Malice Domestic's *Mystery Most Historical* (#12) and *Mystery Most Geographical* (#13), *Black Cat Mystery Magazine, Mystery Weekly, Mysterical-E, The Literary Hatchet, Shotgun Honey,* and *Yellow Mama*. He has also won the Pennwriter's short story contest and was shortlisted (and Highly Commended) for the Crime Writers' Association's Debut Dagger Award. You can find him at www.peterwjhayes.com or on Facebook.

KATHRYN JOHNSON, author of over 40 novels with major U.S./foreign publishers, writes under her own name and as Mary Hart Perry. She has been nominated for the prestigious Agatha Award, and won the Heart of Excellence and Bookseller's Best Awards. Kathryn's novels include historical fiction with mystery elements: *The Gentleman Poet: A Novel of Love, Danger, and Shakespeare's "The Tempest"*, and a trilogy of Victorian thrillers inspired by the lives of Queen Victoria's daughters. In 2008, Kathryn founded *WriteByYou.com,* a writer's mentoring service to aid authors in reaching their publication goals. She teaches locally for The Smithsonian and The Writer's Center. Her popular course, *The Extreme Novelist*, inspired the book by the same name, now available everywhere. Kathryn can be reached at:
Kathryn@WriteByYou.com.

ELEANOR CAWOOD JONES is author of A Baker's Dozen: 13 Tales of Murder and More and Death is Coming to Town: Four Murderous Holiday Tales. She began writing in elementary school, using a #2 pencil to craft crime stories starring her stuffed animals. Recent stories include "Killing Kippers" in *Malice Domestic 11: Murder Most Conventional* and "Salad Days, Halloween Nights" in *Midnight Mysteries*. "A Snowball's Chance" in *Chesapeake Crimes: Fur, Feathers, & Felonies* debuts in Spring 2018. "Keep Calm and Love Moai" marks her twentieth published short story. A former newspaper reporter and reformed marketing director turned bookstore employee, Eleanor lives in Northern Virginia. She plots constantly, travels frequently, and drinks coffee unapologetically. One day she'll finish that novel, too.

KRISTIN KISSKA used to be a finance geek, complete with MBA and Wall Street pedigree, but now Kristin is a self-proclaimed *fictionista*. Kristin contributed short stories of mystery and suspense to the Anthony Award-winning anthology, *Murder Under the Oaks* (2015), *Virginia Is for Mysteries—Volume II*

(2016), *Fifty Shades of Cabernet* (2017), and *Day of the Dark* (2017). When not writing, she can be found blogging on her website, posting on Facebook, and Tweeting. Kristin lives in Virginia with her husband and three children.
KristinKisska.com
KristinKisskaAuthor
@KKMHOO

G. M. MALLIET's first St. Just mystery won the 2008 Agatha Award for Best First Novel and was chosen by *Kirkus Reviews* as a best book of the year. It was nominated for many prizes including the Anthony, the Macavity, and a Left Coast Crime award for best police procedural. Her subsequent mysteries and short stories have been nominated for nearly every major crime-writing honor. Writes *Cleveland.com*: She "may be the best mystery author writing in English at the moment (along with Tana French). She's certainly the most entertaining. . . ." She and her husband live on the East Coast and travel often to the UK, the setting for all her books. Her 7th Max Tudor book, *In Prior's Wood* (Minotaur), will be published in April 2018.

CHERYL MARCEAU's mystery short stories have appeared in several anthologies including in Level Best Books' *Thin Ice*, and in the Guppy anthology, *Fish or Cut Bait*. Her subjects range from historical mystery to what some consider verging on paranormal. This short story in *Murder Most Geographical*, "Payback With Interest," is her first set outside New England. When she is not writing, Cheryl is happiest traveling, whether roaming the back roads of New England in search of interesting new-to-her places or visiting archaeology sites here and abroad. The American Southwest is a favorite travel destination. Cheryl and her husband live in the Boston area.

Agatha- and Macavity-nominated author **EDITH MAXWELL** writes the Quaker Midwife Mysteries, the Local Foods Mysteries, and award-winning short crime fiction. As Maddie Day, she writes the popular Country Store Mysteries and the new Cozy Capers Book Group Mysteries. *Called to Justice*, Maxwell's second Quaker Midwife mystery, is nominated for an Agatha Award for Best Historical Novel. She is president of Sisters in Crime–New England and lives north of Boston with her beau, two elderly cats, and an impressive array of garden statuary. She blogs at WickedCozyAuthors.com, at KillerCharacters.com, and at midnightwriters.blogspot.com. Read about all her personalities and her work at edithmaxwell.com.

A four-time Derringer finalist, **WILLIAM BURTON McCORMICK**'s fiction appears in *Ellery Queen's Mystery Magazine, Alfred Hitchcock's Mystery Magazine, The Saturday Evening Post, Sherlock Holmes Mystery Magazine, Over My Dead Body!, The CWA Anthology of Short Stories: Mystery Tour,* and elsewhere. A Brown University alumnus, William earned his MA in Novel Writing from the University of Manchester, studied Russian language and history at Lomonosov Moscow State University, and was elected a Hawthornden Writing Fellow in Scotland in 2013. His historical novel of the Baltic States, *Lenin's Harem*, was published in English and Latvian. A native of Nevada, William has lived in seven countries including Russia, Estonia, Latvia, and Ukraine for writing purposes. He is presently co-authoring a thriller, *KGB Banker,* with real-life financial whistleblower, John Christmas.

LAURA OLES is a photo industry journalist who spent twenty years covering tech and trends before turning to crime fiction. She served as a columnist for numerous photography magazines and publications. Laura's short stories have appeared in several anthologies, including *Murder on Wheels*, which won the Silver Falchion Award in 2016. Her debut mystery, *Daughters of Bad Men*, is a Claymore Award Finalist and an Agatha nominee for Best First Novel. She is also a Writers' League of Texas Award Finalist. Laura is a member of Austin Mystery Writers, Sisters in Crime, and Writers' League of Texas. Laura lives on the edge of the Texas Hill Country with her husband, daughter, and twin sons. Visit her online at lauraoles.com.

ALAN ORLOFF's debut mystery, *Diamonds for the Dead*, was an Agatha Award finalist, and his most recent novels are the thrillers *Running from the Past* and *Pray for the Innocent*. His short fiction has appeared in numerous publications, including *Jewish Noir, Alfred Hitchcock's Mystery Magazine, Chesapeake Crimes: Storm Warning, Mystery Weekly, Noir at the Salad Bar, Black Cat Mystery Magazine, Snowbound: Best New England Crime Stories 2017, The Night of the Flood*, and *Mystery Most Geographical*. His story, "Rule Number One" (*Snowbound*, Level Best Books), was selected for the 2018 edition of *The Best American Mystery Stories* anthology, edited by Louise Penny. Alan lives in Northern Virginia and teaches fiction-writing at The Writer's Center (Bethesda, MD). He loves cake and arugula, but not together. www.alanorloff.com

JOSH PACHTER (1951-) is a writer, editor, and translator. Almost a hundred of his short crime stories have appeared in *Ellery Queen's Mystery Magazine, Alfred Hitchcock's Mystery Magazine, Black Cat Mystery Magazine, Shotgun Honey*, and many other periodicals, anthologies, and year's-best collections. *The Tree of Life* (Wildside Press, 2015) collected all ten of his Mahboob Chaudri stories. He collaborated with Belgian author Bavo Dhooge on the zombie-cop novel *Styx* (Simon & Schuster, 2015). He co-edited *Amsterdam Noir* (Akashic Books, 2018) with Dutch writer René Appel, and *The Misadventures of Ellery Queen* (Wildside Press, 2018) with Dale C. Andrews, and edited *The Man Who Read Mr. Strang: The Short Fiction of William Brittain* (Crippen & Landru, 2018). His translations of short stories by Dutch and Belgian authors appear regularly in *Ellery Queen's Mystery Magazine*'s "Passport to Crime" department.

ANITA PAGE's short stories have appeared in the Murder New York Style series of anthologies, most recently *Where Crime Never Sleeps*. The series includes *Family Matters*, the MNYS anthology which she edited. Other publications include *The Prosecution Rests* (Little, Brown), *Windward* (Level Best Books), *The Paterson Literary Review*, and a number of webzines. Her short story, "'Twas the Night," published in *The Gift of Murder*, received a Derringer Award from the Short Mystery Fiction Society in 2010. Anita Page's crime novel, *Damned If You Don't* (Glenmere Press), is set in the Catskills where she worked as a freelance feature writer for a regional newspaper. She currently reviews classic crime films for the webzine, *Mysterical-E*.

At Malice Domestic conventions, **NANCY PICKARD** has been Toastmistress, Guest of Honor, and Lifetime Achievement honoree. She has won several Malice Domestic Agatha Awards for her books and short stories. She is the author of *The Virgin of Small Plains, The Scent of Rain and Lightning,* ten books in the Jenny Cain series, three in the Marie Lightfoot series, and three in the Eugenia Potter series. She is a four-time Edgar® Award finalist, and the winner of multiple other awards from the mystery world. She lives in Prairie Village, KS, where she is writing her 19th novel.

KEENAN POWELL'S first publications were illustrations in Dungeons and Dragons, when still in high school. Art was an impractical pursuit (not an heiress, didn't have disposition to marry well, hated teaching), so she went to law school instead. Right after graduation, she moved to Alaska. Earlier in her career, she defended criminal cases, including murder, for several years. She still practices law in Anchorage, AK. In 2009, there was a string of homeless deaths which the Medical Examiner had ruled were the result of "natural causes." While attending a seminar, she learned of a little-known law that permits the ME to rule natural causes without autopsy. These deaths and this loophole were the inspiration of her debut, *Deadly Solution*, published by Level Best Books in 2018.

MICHAEL ROBERTSON writes The Baker Street Letters series, published by St. Martin's Press/Minotaur. For *The Brothers of Baker Street*, *Booklist* said, "The last third of the novel, with its murder-and-chase scene, is one of the finest, scariest sequences in current crime fiction. For anglophiles, crime-o-philes, and all fans of wonderful writing." For the most recent book in the series, *The Baker Street Jurors*, *Kirkus Reviews* said, "Robertson outdoes himself in the most effervescent of his five Baker Street cocktails to date." The sixth book in the series, *A Baker Street Wedding*, will be available in December 2018. Mr. Robertson lives in San Clemente, CA, where in his spare time he surfs, clumsily.

VERENA ROSE's story, "Death at the Congressional Cemetery," is the second story featuring Constable Hezekiah Wallace set during the year 1860 in Washington City. Tensions are high regarding the issue of slavery and the Civil War is on the horizon. An avid reader of history, Verena loves researching the pre-Civil War period. She continues to work on an idea for a novel featuring her characters: "Zeke" Wallace, Horace Kingsley, and Noah Hackett. Verena also works fulltime as a tax accountant, and is the long-time Chair of Malice Domestic, an Editor of the Malice Anthologies, and an Editor and Co-publisher at Level Best Books. She lives in the Maryland suburbs with her four cats and loves spending time with her teenaged grandchildren, whenever possible.

HARRIETTE SACKLER has served as Grants Chair of the Malice Domestic Board of Directors as long as she can remember. Assisting unpublished writers along the road to success brings her a great deal of satisfaction. In addition, she adores the Malice Domestic convention and her fellow Board members. Harriette is a multi-published, Agatha Award-nominated short story writer who focuses on social issues in her stories. As a principal of Dames of Detection, Harriette is a co-publisher and editor at Level Best Books. Harriette lives with her husband and their two Yorkies in the DC suburbs. She is an animal advocate and works with several rescue organizations. First and foremost, Harriette is mom to two fabulous daughters and Nana to four magnificent grandkids. www.harriettesackler.com

SHAWN REILLY SIMMONS is the author of the Red Carpet Catering Mysteries featuring Penelope Sutherland, a behind-the-scenes movie chef The series is inspired by Shawn's own experiences cooking for the rich and famous. Her fifth book, *Murder on the Rocks*, was released in February 2018. Shawn is a member of Sisters in Crime, Mystery Writers of America, the Crime Writers' Association in the UK, and the International Thriller Writers. Shawn is also an editor at Level Best Books, publishers of award-winning mystery anthologies. When she's not writing, editing, or planning for Malice, Shawn is in the kitchen testing out new recipes, reading, drinking wine, practicing yoga, or running. She lives in Frederick, MD, with her husband, seven-year-old son, and English bulldog.

TRISS STEIN returned to her roots on the New York-Canada border for this story. Usually she writes mysteries set in Brooklyn, her adopted home for most of her adult life. Her current book is *Brooklyn Wars*, where her heroine, Erica Donato, witnesses a murder at the historic Brooklyn Navy Yard and is drawn deeply into old and bitter conflicts.

ROBIN TEMPLETON is a Virginia-based writer who loves to travel. Robin's story, "Hoʻoponopono," invites the reader on a wild ride along the Nā Pali Coast of Kauai, and she was thrilled when it was chosen for *Malice Domestic 13: Murder Most Geographical*. Robin also has a story in the new anthology, *Chesapeake Crimes: Furs, Feathers, and Felonies*. In "Hunter's Moon," Robin tracks the nature of man and beast through the Virginia Highlands. In addition to her short stories, Robin's experiences as a professional photographer and private investigator form the basis of her work-in-progress, *Double Exposure*, for which she was awarded the William F. Deeck-Malice Domestic Grant for Unpublished Writers. You can find out more about Robin's writing and photography adventures at www.robintempleton.com.

SUSAN THIBADEAU grew up on Long Island and now lives in Pittsburgh, PA. Although she loves her current home, she has fond memories of growing up in Ronkonkoma and swimming in the lake that's featured in "Marigold in the Lake." Her short story, "Lucky on the Charm," appeared in *Lucky Charms: 12 Crime Tales*, an anthology from the Pittsburgh chapter of Sisters in Crime. Her short story, "The Vanishing Vacation," appeared in *Alfred Hitchcock's Mystery Magazine,* and her novella, "The Discarded Spouse," also appeared in *Alfred Hitchcock's Mystery Magazine* and was awarded the Black Orchid Novella Award given in conjunction with The Nero Wolfe Society. A fan of Wodehouse and Kingsley Amis, she works to bring a touch of humor to her mystery tales.

SYLVIA MAULTASH WARSH was born in Germany to Holocaust survivors who emigrated to Canada. She is the author of the Dr. Rebecca Temple series: *To Die in Spring* was nominated for an Arthur, *Find Me Again* won an Edgar® award, and *Season of Iron* was shortlisted for a ReLit Award. Project Bookmark Canada chose *The Queen of Unforgetting*, an historical novel, for a plaque. Her novella, *Best Girl*, came out in 2012. "The Emerald Skull," published in *Thirteen*, was nominated for an Arthur for Best Story (2014). Her story, "The Ranchero's Daughter," appeared in *13 Claws* (2017). Sylvia has recently finished writing an historical coming-of-age novel set in 1840s America. She lives in Toronto with her husband and recently became a grandmother. She also teaches writing to seniors.

An award-winning author of American history books and biographies, **LESLIE WHEELER** has written three living-history mysteries: *Murder at Plimoth Plantation, Murder at Gettysburg*, and *Murder at Spouters Point*. Her new book, *Rattlesnake Hill,* is the first in a new series of Berkshire Hilltown Mysteries. Leslie's short stories have appeared in such anthologies as *Day of the Dark, Stories of Eclipse*, and Level Best Books' *New England Crime Stories* series, where she was formerly an editor. A member of Mystery Writers of America and Sisters in Crime, she is Speakers Bureau Coordinator for the New England Chapter. Leslie divides her time between Cambridge, MA, and the Berkshires, where she writes in a house overlooking a pond.

CPSIA information can be obtained
at www.ICGtesting.com
Printed in the USA
LVOW03s0531040418
572204LV00004B/7/P